MRS. O'LEARY'S COW

A novel by Ryan Patrick Sullivan

with Tom English

Order this book online at www.trafford.com
or email orders@trafford.com

Most Trafford titles are also available at major online book retailers.

Printed in the United States of America.

ISBN: 978-1-4907-2096-8 (sc)
ISBN: 978-1-4907-2098-2 (hc)
ISBN: 978-1-4907-2097-5 (e)

Library of Congress Control Number: 2013922441

Trafford rev. 02/07/2014

 www.trafford.com

North America & international
toll-free: 1 888 232 4444 (USA & Canada)
fax: 812 355 4082

This book is dedicated to the memory
of my Grandma, Billie Sullivan, the first
person to teach me how to read and the
most loving and kindest soul I've ever
known.

And to my late Mother, Rita Sullivan, I'm
filling the pages you couldn't and trying to
gracefully embrace the gifts you've left me.

For Shea and Nicole, Mom and Dad, and
my big, wonderful family. For the beautiful
souls I'm blessed to call friends. For my
fellow Imgurians on the Internet, who
always make me laugh. And for the brilliant
people who call the greatest city on the
planet — Chicago — home.

"But, they're goldfish, and a goldfish's memory erases itself every three seconds. This is how this generation swims through life: 'What's this? Hey look — I'm an entitled American!' Three seconds later — 'What's this? Hey look — I'm an entitled American!' Three seconds later ..."

SIDE 1 TRACK LISTING:

1. Plumber's Craic

2. An Unexpected Explosion

3. Doggy Style

4. Gold Locket

5. The Baader-Meinhof Phenomenon

6. "Our day starts when your day ends"

7. Sun Sneezing

8. When I Wake Up in My Makeup

9. "There are no cherries left in the world, only the boxes they came in."

10. Super Bowl Commercials that won't be Shown on Television

11. A Barfly on the Wall of the Pub Crawl

12. Hobo Spider

13. Peeling Pink Lotus Petals

14. The Legend of Chetan "Hawk" Littlejohn: Cheating the Baseball Game of Life

15. Pig Tales

1. Plumber's Craic.

"Tell me what's wrong with youth these days," inquired Raymond McMahon. He was an erect Komodo dragon wearing a green flannel button-up and enough Old Spice to singe every hair in your nose.

"Tell me why they're in such a damn hurry."

As Raymond spoke, the daytime bartender at Mrs. O'Leary's Cow and moonlighting drummer of the freshly signed The Farrow Moans, 24-year-old Tommy Shannahan looked at the grizzled man before him. As Raymond sipped his Guinness — sucking the promise out of the sunny, quiet Sunday that Tommy hoped for — Tommy pondered:

- Why is this man so angry? He has an extra manic twinkle in his eye today.
- Why does he always have to be the first person here when I open?
- How amazing would it be to be sleeping right now?
- Carmen Swisher's legs.
- Did I forget the snare at the gig? I think I put it in the van next to the hi-hat.
- Carmen Swisher's denim skirt and panty shot she gave while accidentally*1 rocking back on the bar stool and laughing at Cal's terrible joke. Was she humoring him? Does she really like corny-ass puns?
- The lack of youthful and cool people that come into The Cow during the day.
- Maybe we should change our set list. Maybe we should lead off with "Shattered Halo." Mental note: Run that past Cal.
- I can drum as good as Patrick Carney*2. Right?
- Carmen Swisher's silver, silky thong. Why do the hot chicks gravitate toward the lead singers? "Oooh, I'm so ironic. I'm a lead singer. Check me out. Run your fingers through my gorgeous, sun-blessed hair." I bet Cal banged Carmen Swisher last night.
- Why is this dickhead staring at me? Didn't he ask a rhetorical question?
- I'm gonna need an energy drink to get through this — two of them actually.
- He's going to wait all day for an answer isn't he?

"Do you think it's because of all this technology?" Raymond interjected in his thick, Chicago accent before Tommy had a chance to answer. "Has the brain adapted and evolved to understand all this computer mumbo-jumbo and how to satisfy itself with instant information and gratification, but in doing so — in the process of that — did it dumb-down and deteriorate other aspects? Things like common sense? Things like logic? Things like courtesy?"

Before Tommy could answer, Raymond continued, "Are they so overcaffeinated — I mean, c'mon, there's a coffee shop at every corner — it's unbelievable! Breakfast, lunch, dinner, dessert — it doesn't matter, they're drinking it all damn day. I remember when you'd have a cup or two to get things going in the morning and that was about it. Go to any Starbucks, at any time of the day, and you'll find dozens of teens in there sipping away. Shit, I didn't start drinking coffee until I was 25 years old."

Raymond, pressing the brim of the glass to his lips, gathered his thoughts with a 1,000-mile stare. He lowered the beer without taking a sip and then carried on.

"Or, now hear me out for a second," he said. "Are they are too overhydrated? Think about it now. Doesn't it seem like everyone's got a fucking bottle of water sewed into their faces — that is to say, when they're not drinking coffee? So, maybe they're so overhydrated, their brains turn into putty. Is that what's going on? Bunch of 10-pound waterheads roaming the streets? What the fuck did people do in the '20s, for fuck's sake? I don't see historic film of people carrying around rusty tin cans and guzzling down water every time they walked up a flight of stairs. Christ Almighty. Maybe all the water they're drinking is battling it out with all the caffeine they're drinking? An entire generation of mush brains, walking around and banging into each other like Boxelder bugs in the fading autumn. Maybe it's a combo of both, you know?

"Or, here's another idea … is it something they're putting in the water that's watering down brainwaves? I don't want to sound like a conspiracy theorist*3, but it's starting to make me wonder. No one drinks the fluoride-loaded tapwater from yesteryear anymore. Why do they put fluoride in our tap water anyway? Do you know how terrible that stuff is for your insides? Maybe the FDA — those trustworthy souls — maybe they're in cahoots with some of the bottled water companies and putting only God-knows-what in it. You ever think about that? How do you know where your water comes from? Do you visit the company when it is being bottled? The label says it's from the Fiji Islands — you could say — but how do you know?"

Tommy grabbed a handful of his curly, chestnut hair and gave it a squeeze as if he was about to turn it into a ponytail or stuff it underneath the baseball cap he was wearing. He considered the old man's lament and felt Raymond made some valid arguments, but he wasn't about to humor him.

"OK, how about this one," Raymond said, "Are they so oversexed — check that, probably more like overmasturbated — that it screws with their logic? I mean, they can watch a porno anytime they want. Get it delivered right to the palm of their non-jerking hand in less than a minute, the way these phones with those Internets work. Do they walk around not giving a shit because they're only a few moments of privacy away from releasing a huge dopamine dump? Do they stay home all day, cranking away on their self, and then, when they actually wander into civilization, do they not know how to handle the reality? Don't even get me started on chivalry. It's an endangered species. Men these days wouldn't know the first thing about courting a lady. Maybe they don't feel they need to, because it's easier to rub one out as opposed to having to work for the real thing."

Tommy pulled his phone from his pocket and took satisfaction in knowing he wasn't going to have to put too much effort into the conversation. Raymond was going to continue with or without any interjections, per usual, and all he would have to do was nod or utter "yep" every so often.

He started typing Cal a text message.

"Let's say, for whatever reason, God time-traveled you from 1901 to the present," Raymond said. "Or maybe a bottle washed ashore and you rubbed that son of a bitch and a genie popped out, granting you a wish. And your wish in 1901 was to visit right now. And once you get here, the first person you meet is some asshole. And this asshole tells you that in his pocket, he holds a device where, with a couple (pretending to dial a phone number) beep-beep-beep button pushes, he could call any country in the world and talk to another human with hardly a second of delay. And then, with a couple more button pushes, he could answer virtually any question you had — on virtually any topic, about any fucking thing you ever wanted to know, and he could give you the answers in nanoseconds — you'd be blown away! But after a while, once you got to know this asshole with the magic device, you would come to find out that all he really uses it for is to watch people fucking so he can rub one out. Or so he can send his buddies a funny video of a monkey sticking a finger up its ass and then giving it a sniff. Or, even better, he gets on the Internets so he can argue with complete strangers about his shitty opinions of religion, same-sex marriages, gun control and presidential elections. Then you'd be baffled. You'd say, "gimme that fucking thing!" and you'd try your damnedest to find out how to grow better crops, raise healthier animals, build better machines for farming, or how to make medicine for your family — you know, the shit that really matters in life."

Raymond had a sip as a gauche Tommy put his phone back in his pocket.

"What about this one — give this one some thought," Raymond said after a few moments of silence. "Are these kids so overmedicated — check that — depressed, because their big ol' American life sucks so much — because mommy and daddy didn't buy them a brand new Hummer for their 16th birthday, that their tiny brains just completely give out in crucial moments like say, when they're backing out of a fucking parking spot and aren't paying any attention to my pickup truck behind them — my fire hydrant-red, giant fucking pickup truck!?"

Tommy tried not to laugh and pinched his glabella with his finger and thumb like he ate ice cream too fast.

"Here's the kicker," Raymond said, "the motherfucker writes a note to me and sticks it under my windshield wiper. The note says, 'I accidentally hit your truck and I'm writing you this so it looks like I'm doing the right thing because there are people who are watching me right now. Sorry. Shit happens. Like when I can't afford insurance.' And that was it. Can you believe that?"

Tommy couldn't help but wonder if the karma police finally caught up to oldfangled Raymond McMahon and stuffed his lousy attitude into the back of a cruiser.

"Twenty-two thousand, one-hundred sixteen miles was all she got to roll before someone dinged her up." Raymond said. "Lady flagged me down as I was having a meltdown — throwing punches at the air and kicking the hell out of the tires. She said I barely missed the kid. Said he just sped out of the lot. And she didn't get his plate number either. She thought he was doing the right thing in writing that note. They're always in such a big fucking hurry until you get stuck behind one of them in aisle of a grocery store and they've got their nose buried into their phone like it's a stripper's bleached balloon knot."

As Ray continued blabbering, Tommy ran a comb of fingers through his hair and delved back into the conversation he was having with himself:

• Did I grab the amp? Being your own roadie sucks.
• Will my ears permanently ring for the rest of my life? How many years do I have left until I'm completely deaf? Twenty? Twenty-five, tops?
• Sleep. I'd lie on this cherry wood bar and use that smelly bar rag as a pillow if I could. It would feel great. Just five minutes. That's all I need.
• What time does sweet Blue come in to relieve me today — 4 or 5 p.m.? I can't remember what she said. I've got to check the schedule.
• I wish I was in my bed. Why do I always agree to work Sunday mornings — especially after a gig? Junior could miss Mass every now and again, and Jesus wouldn't fire lightning bolts up his ass. We need to hire another daytime bartender.
• My hair is driving me nuts and this hat is beginning to stink. Should I shave it all off? Or does Carmen Swisher like long hair? Cal's got such good, long hair. Lead singers ... lucky assholes.

"They're goldfish," Raymond said, but his words fell on Tommy's deaf ears. "You want to grab them and shake the shit out of them and say, 'You're not the only fish swimming in the bowl! Wake up! Look around, man.' But, they're goldfish, and a goldfish's memory erases itself every three seconds*4. This is how this generation swims through life: 'What's this? Hey look — I'm an entitled American!' Three seconds later — what's this? Hey look — I'm an entitled American!' Three seconds later ...'"

Mrs. O'Leary's Cow, or "The Cow" as it was known by regulars, is a traditional Irish-themed pub located in the 2700 block of North Halsted Street, priding the legacy of Irish-Americans in Chicago. There are framed newspaper articles on the walls near the front doors telling the story and theories of the Great Chicago Fire of 1871. Legend has it, Mrs. O'Leary, a perfect scapegoat for the blaze because of her Irish-Catholic immigrant roots (an unpopular ethnicity to be in those days), owned a cow that kicked over a lantern and ignited her barn, which then engulfed the city*5.

Tommy had been a fixture in the bar since the day he was born. Actually, his parents conceived him in the back office after a New Year's Eve party sneakaway, so he's been a part of the pub's history before he was born. Tommy never knew that. His uncle, Michael Jr., inherited the bar from his father, Michael Sr., and The Cow had been a landmark in the neighborhood for almost a half-century. Tommy's first job, when he was 11, was as an errand boy who did odd jobs around the bar. He'd run out for supplies when things got low. He'd fill ice coolers. He'd stock liquor in the cellar. He'd help roll kegs into place. He'd get regulars cigarettes. He'd pass love notes for shy patrons drunk in infatuation, when they finally got tipsy enough to work up the courage to spill. He'd run bets for his eldest bookmaking-bartender brother, Kevin. Hell, he even delivered the details to an alderman about a mob meeting.

He, along with the entire family, was well-liked and well-known in the neighborhood. Tommy followed in Kevin's footsteps as a bartender the day he turned 21. He was the pulse of the place, and people came to him for more than just drinks. The Cow was more of a home to Tommy than his apartment.

Another aspect of The Cow that makes it different from other bars — no TVs. The main reason was to encourage conversation, and so local musicians can play whenever the spirit caught them. "House" instruments littered the walls, and anyone was more than welcome to play. At times, this philosophy was a double-edged sword for Michael Jr., drawing more artistic and methodical thinkers, but losing sports fans — and most importantly, the Sunday football drinking crowd.

The change came when Michael Jr. took a holiday to Ireland and was fascinated with the absence of TV in the country's pubs and the presence of so much "craic" (pronounced /KRAK/ or "crack", an Irish slang term for news, gossip, fun, entertainment and enjoyable conversation) amongst drinkers. He loved that publicans would learn so much by simply exchanging their thoughts, ideas or anecdotes from their daily lives, instead of looking up at the TV like a transfixed zombie.

Upon his return, Michael Jr. removed every TV that The Cow owned, swapping them for guitars, flutes, whistles, drums, a piano, and even a crwth. He installed stunning wood shelving that was shipped from Ireland to create and house a library of books for his customers to use and share under the pretext of the honor system. He also began placing copies of the Chicago Tribune along the lengthy bar. And his final change was removing a massive second bar and lounging area in the back room (which was called "the emerald isle" because the walls, floor and ceiling were painted with glow-in-the-dark green paint and the room was lit by black lights), only to erect a stage to showcase live music, which wasn't restricted to traditional Irish music. Since Tommy was a member of an up-and-coming band, Michael Jr. left most of the music-related responsibilities to his nephew, and The Cow was known for booking local, talented musicians.

"Did you hear a 12-year-old girl got shot by a stray bullet yesterday?" Raymond said, flipping through a newspaper.

Tommy, mindlessly drying pint glasses, didn't reply.

"Goddamned drive-by in broad fucking daylight. What a bunch of pussies." Raymond balled up his fist and shook it like he was about to throw dice. "It used to take balls to walk up to someone you had a problem with and loosen their teeth for 'em. Times have changed. Now, these cowards throw lead anytime they get angry."

There was a long pause while Raymond drank. Tommy used his index fingers as drums and lightly tapped a beat from a Moans' song on the glassware while he waited.

"It's all about instant gratification these days — everyone needs it for just about everything they do," Raymond said. "How rich is the revenge, when something as fast as a trigger pull can satisfy it? Wouldn't you rather punch someone in the face and feel the connection? Wouldn't you want the intimacy? Wouldn't you want to stand over him after you leveled him, soaking in the triumph, before picking the bastard up off the floor, dusting him off and ending the beef? Wouldn't you want to be the bigger man and let him think about the shame and embarrassment of catching a beatin' for the rest of his life, instead of taking it — his life — away from him with a bullet in a matter of seconds? What happened to the good old days? Did the sue-happy society we live in cause this? They'd rather you shoot someone and run away rather than punch someone and scoop 'em up?"

Raymond had another sip, and his words started adhering to Tommy's mind.

"I remember one time," Raymond said, "I think it was in '77. I was working a job on the south side — local plumbing outfit — Irish outfit, you see. I had about three guys I was supervising that day. It was hot. Hotter than a freshly fucked fox in a forest fire — I can tell you that much, buster. It was July. The humidity was awful and there was no relief coming off the Lake. So we were doing this job — I was on the first floor, soldering some quarter-inch copper with a torch, and my crew was doing an underground."

Tommy humored his guest with an inquisitive raised brow.

"An underground is digging trenches, you see. We give 'em a diagram and they go down a couple feet of code, where the cast iron is laid to supply water into and throughout the house ... and then another pipe carries shit and piss away ... eventually it all ties into the sewer system. That's Plumbing 101 for you. Anyways, I'm keeping track of these three gophers, you know, laborers. I called 'em gophers. You know, ditch diggers. Whatever you want to call them, they were earning some cash during the summer break from college, you see. They were good kids — hard workers. Kind of like you. Bustin' your hump and trying to make it as a musician, right? You work your ass off, I know, I see it. You're a dying breed. Your old man probably taught you about ethic — a good work ethic — did he teach you it?"

Tommy was taken aback. Raymond truly sounded complimentary, and he was unaware that Raymond knew his father. The compliment tuned Tommy's ear.

11

"Actually, he was rather strict growing up," Tommy said. "He's blue collar himself. He drives a truck for Jewels*6. He was on the road a lot when I was a kid, but he always made sure we worked hard. He isn't too crazy about me wanting to play music for a career, or the bar business, but he knows school isn't for me."

"School isn't for everyone," Raymond said, nodding approvingly. "Probably because they're teaching the wrong things in schools, I digress — but it shows ... your hard work shows. I've been coming in here for years. Your family — your uncle Mike now — he keeps this place as ... as pristine as a bar can be, I suppose. It must be in your family's blood — that ethic. Your grandpa kept this pub afloat for a long time. I never met a man that worked as much as him. I always wondered if he ever slept. He passed it on to them and now you got it, and it shows. I've only seen your Dad up here twice. Both times I was too shitfaced to recall what we were talking about, but I'm pretty sure it was fun in nature."

"Yeah, he doesn't come around here much anymore," Tommy said. "Him and my uncle had a falling out."*7

"That's a shame," Raymond said. "Brothers are like that sometimes. They'll get over it one day. Anyway, the point I was making is — you have to be hard on kids — even if they already got their nose to the grindstone. You can't let up. Back then, we didn't pat 'em on the back too often or it would go to their heads. Last thing you wanted to do was try telling a bunch of prima donnas to do something labor intensive. That's why the kids these days are so soft. They think they're so fucking entitled to everything. Somewhere down the road, this society allowed that shit to happen. They coddled 'em. Probably the same guy who says, 'I want my kid to have it better than I did growing up.' What an idiot. What does that even mean? You've heard parents say this, right?"

"I've heard it," Tommy said.

"Don't you want to slap them?" Raymond said. "How do you further your kid — how do you better them if you give them everything without them earning any of it? What's that say about you, the parent? How bad did you have it growing up, to be in the spot you're currently in — to be able to give your kid everything? You're forgetting how you got there. You're not your kid's rich friend — spoiling your kid to death just because he's your fuck trophy! Your friend — your buddy, he's a guy you go have beers with and talk about the girls you wished you could've fucked in high school. That's your friend — that guy. Your kid craves discipline and structure and praise. Parenting isn't about handing those things out like Halloween candy, it's about them learning how to earn it. Your kid should never be your friend. And you shouldn't bullshit kids either. You don't like to be lied to as an adult, so why do parents kick off their kid's formative years lying to them? 'That's a great drawing, Billy,' parents and teachers say, even though it looks like a piece of shit. Or it's, 'YAY! No one loses in a tie! Let's go get some ice cream, kids!' says the soccer coach. What does that teach a kid? Why are you rewarding them? Life isn't about ties. You can't move forward and achieve your goals if your soul's stuck in neutral. Take education for example: You either get in the college you applied to because you put forth the effort and it's recognized by the university and they're proud to accept you or ... or you don't. There's no tying there. You can't graduate from some dinky, crapshoot junior college and then submit your resume to NASA with an asterisk next to your shitty alma mater that says, 'But I'm really a MIT man at heart,' and expect to be taken seriously. It doesn't work that way."

Tommy agreed with a nod and picked at some calloused skin on his left palm.

12

"Anyway," Raymond said. "I'm wandering off the reservation here. What was I talking about — oh, yes, now I remember … its July '77. I'm in charge of a couple gophers. It was hot. Super-hot. It was hell, deep-fried and served on a sizzling fajita plate. Sweat's dripping off my head and landing on the sawdust near my boots. Have you ever noticed what sweat dripped into sawdust looks like?"

"I can't say that I have," Tommy's said as he stopped drying the glassware.

"It's the strangest of things," Raymond said. "Each drop beads in the dust and they end up looking like little pennies. They really look like they're pliable. Like you can grab 'em, you know? My sweat would've been worth about a hundred bucks if you added up all the change that day.

"But anyways, one of them yells up to me. The gopher says … he says, 'Ray?' I shout down through a cut out hole in the plywood I'm standing on. I says, 'Yeah?' And he yells up to me, 'We can't do this, Ray. It smells awful. We're gagging like sick dogs down here.' And I said to them … I said, 'Suck it up! This city was founded on a rotting onion patch*8. Your great-great-great-grandfathers dug the canals and railroads of this fine city. There's an Irishman buried under every tie. You should be so lucky that you have anything in your stomachs to puke up. They didn't! Now get used to it.' Or some halftime-locker-room-speech and they went back to work, you see."

Raymond cut off his story by shaking his empty glass.

"Can I have another bowl of loud mouth soup?"

Tommy was too enthralled in the yarn to notice Raymond's Guinness dried up. He hurriedly grabbed a pint glass, tilted it at a 45-degree angle, pulled the tap down and listened to Raymond continue while the dark liquid flowed.

"So, about 10 minutes later, the kid yells back up the hole, 'Ray? We can't do it. I'm sorry. It's just horrible down here. Sean's over here dry-heaving. I got my shirt wrapped around my face. We just can't do it, man.' So I have a peek back down the hole and sure as shit, the little fucker's wearing his shirt over his face like a Middle-Eastern rock thrower. The three of them down there were fanning the air and making a big spectacle. So now I'm all fired up — calling them names and threatening them with things like, 'If I have to come down there, I'm thumping you all in the head with a shovel,' — stuff like that. I'm thinking the whole time they're full of shit because they don't want to be in that sweltering basement a second longer — can't say I blamed them neither. But hey, tough titty, that's what you gotta do if you want that milk — however the saying goes. So, I go down there …"

As Raymond sustained, Tommy released the tap handle when the glass was three-quarters full. He set the glass down, allowing the Guinness to settle, put a boot up on an ice chest and gave Raymond his undivided attention.

"… and these guys weren't joking. It smelled like shitty diapers. It smelled like riding the red line on a Saturday morning at 3 a.m. It was so pungent, it watered your eyes and barrel rolled your stomach. Just awful, you know. To this day, if I close my eyes, I can still smell it. Lord, help me if I ever go blind."

Tommy pushed the tap forward until a creamy head rested proud above the rim and then he delivered it to Raymond.

"So anyways, I can tell right away that this wasn't coming from stagnant water or a sewer break or, you know, a dead rat buried under the gravel. It was none of those things. I could tell right away that it ... it was shit! Literally, human fucking shit! Do you believe that? There was a stinking pile laying around somewhere down there and we had to find it and find it fast. So I asked the boys where it seemed to be coming from and they pointed me to a corner. And I grab one of their shovels and I start scraping over some rocks and sure as shit, there it is — shit. A huge helping of this mushy, but not quite diarrhea shit. What kind of asshole would do that type of thing, you know — no pun intended. And then I started to think about it and the only other crew working on that house with us that day was the Pollock bricklayers. One of them had to do it. It was that fresh. And the thing about that one was there was a goddamn port 'o potty right out in the front — right by their trucks — right where they were working. Whatever animal did it, did it to intentionally piss us off. It was 90-something-fucking degrees and moister than a mermaid, and this jerkwater thought it would be funny to bury a turd right where we'd be working."

Once the Guinness finished cascading, Raymond had himself a quenching sip and left a frothy beer mustache on his upper lip. A smile slowly emerged around the corners of Tommy's mouth.

"So, I'm mad as hellfire and hotter than the devil's asshole after judging a chili contest and I scoop up this sick bastard's steaming dookie and I tell my boys to get out of my way and I start marching up the stairs, holding this shovel out in front of me like a pole-vaulter. I get outside, have a look around, and these dumb Pols are up on their scaffolding, working their ass off and talking in a language I don't understand.

"So I says to them ... I says, 'Which one of you sick bastards took a shit down there?' And these imbeciles play the old, 'I don't understand English game,' hardly even acknowledging me. So I repeated myself. I says, 'I'll try this again: Which one of you sick bastard comedians took a shit down in that basement!?' And again, none of them budge. By this time, my crew is standing behind me grabbing as much fresh air as they can. So, since none of the Polskis wanted to fess up to their little funny games, I marched that shit shovel right over to their mortar mixing machine and I hovered it over the open hole — where they throw in the dry cement and the water. And then all of the sudden, they all know English. Fucking miracle, right? They're screaming, 'No! No! No! Please don't! Stop!' and crawling down the walls like fucking Spider-Man!"

Raymond had another swallow as Tommy refrained from bursting into guffaw.

"See, the thing with bricklayers," Raymond said, trying to bury a burp, "they have to use their bare hands with that stuff. So, I waited for them all to come down, and as they scrambled toward me like lunatics, I dumped that hot load right into the machine. Wanna know why? Because fuck them — that's why."

Tommy laughed hysterically.

"What happened next?"

"Well, I didn't really think that one through," Raymond said. "Those Pollocks are brutes. Their arms are just as chiseled as the walls they build. Think about how strong bricklayers' hands must be. You wouldn't want them ringing your neck. So, I told my boys to get ready and we put up our dukes. It was heathenism at its finest — the will to fight your fellow man over a pile of shit!

"As they approached, I realized how outnumbered and undersized we were. It put my heart crossways and pounding. But then I thought, 'Fuck it — we're Irish.' And just as they start to surround us, the foreman of the job site rolls up in his truck. He's got the 'what the fuck' look on his face. He ended up getting between us and stopped it. He threatened to yank both our rackets off the job without pay. I explained to him what happened and he ended up kicking the Pols off the site for the rest of the day. One unfortunate prick, the fucknut who I assume did the shitting, had the daunting task of ridding the cement mix — scrubbing and hosing it out. It served him right. But the point of the story, Tommy … the next day, everyone returned to the job and no one gave a shit and no one brought a gun."

Raymond raised his beer boastfully.

Tommy was in stitches. The tale made him do a complete turnaround on how he previously felt about the man in front of him. He unlocked the deadbolt, opened the door and finally allowed Raymond McMahon to stow some belongings in his attic.

"Great. Fucking. Story!" Tommy said in between gasps of laughter and a soft to heavy, slow-rolling, crescendo clap. "Your next pint is on me!"

SIDE 1. TRACK 1. LINER NOTES:

1. Carmen Swisher deliberately flaunted the view between her thighs to frontman Calvin "Cal" Slankard, the poster child for any aspiring rock star and Tommy's bandmate in The Farrow Moans. Tommy didn't want to believe it, but it was true. However, Cal didn't actually notice the incident. He was too busy snickering at his own joke. Carmen and Tommy didn't know Cal missed the legs-spread-apart sight, because it should have been blatantly obvious. Tommy had been thinking of the moment, the view, all morning. He lusted for Carmen Swisher since the first time he met her at a gig at the Double Door, which was almost a year ago, but he never shared his feelings because he thought he didn't stand a chance at dating her, especially with the way she ogled Cal.

2. Patrick Carney is the drummer for The Black Keys. And, no, Tommy is not as talented as him.

3. Raymond wasn't a conspiracy theorist in the traditional stereotypical sense. The terms "crackpot" or "nutjob" didn't describe him. He didn't wear aluminum foil on his head while listening for voices from aliens. He didn't network or co-conspire on the Internet in secret groups trying to expose the Government's "master plan." In fact, he didn't even own a computer. He simply read and conversed with people a lot. His brain wasn't filled with lunacy or paranoia either.

However, he did often wonder why scientists never cured diseases with medicine any more, but rather only treated symptoms, which often led to side effects, which then required people to take more, expensive medicine to combat the side effects caused by the original medicine, which then led to even more side effects and so on and so forth. He thought the entire process was a vicious cycle which made a lot of wealthy people wealthier than they made sick people healthier.

There was only one conspiracy theory he stood 100 percent behind and constantly defended whenever the subject was brought up: World Trade Center Tower 7 was additionally and deliberately destroyed on 9/11. Long before the group, Rethink911, was gaining notoriety, Raymond felt there were ruses to the truths on that dreadful day. He felt Tower 7's free-fall collapse and the news reports of it crumpling before it actually did, proved some entity of power, quite possibly the U.S. Government —

or certain members of it — had knowledge that the attacks were planned, or they, themselves, did the planning.

When he thought about the motive of the U.S. Government allowing or masterminding the 9/11 attacks, he came to this conclusion: That "enemies" attacking the U.S. on its soil would rally the people to stand behind the idea of starting another war — a war for crude oil and the adaption of the USA Patriot Act of 2001. The fact Tower 7 housed CIA offices and documents concerning the Enron scandal when it imploded, was the cherry on top. If the Government wanted to get rid of anything they were hiding in those offices, what would be a better way to do so than blowing it up?

His theory wasn't that a group of CIA agents snuck into the building like ninjas and taped dynamite to the walls while the Twin Towers were crumbling. But, he did hear testimony from a painter who was hired to coat certain interior walls of the building weeks before 9/11 with a type of paint the man had never seen before. The way science and technology evolves, Raymond was convinced there was an accelerant mixed into the paint and something as simple as a placed cellphone call detonated the charges.

He also watched video documentation from firefighters at Ground Zero who said the support beams had been heated to such an extreme temperature, they turned to molten steel, or lava, and the liquid metal was running down the channels. Raymond wasn't a rocket scientist, but he didn't have to be to know an office fire —which was what Government officials originally classified Tower 7's demise as — couldn't generate enough heat to melt steel. Their explanation contradicted the laws of physics.

Raymond, alike everyone else, was glued to the TV on 9/11 and he remembered watching CNN report Tower 7 had collapsed an hour before it did. The BBC also informed of its fall while the building was still standing in the background behind the reporter. And legendary anchorman Dan Rather said on live TV that the building was intentionally destroyed by dynamite — the only time it was ever stated. Raymond thought Tower 7's collapse was designed to look like it buckled from the heat of the Twin Towers, but to him, the explosions were too flawless, like staged pyrotechnics — blasting outward in perfectly timed charges.

4. Raymond was completely inaccurate about the longevity of a goldfish's memory. Research proved goldfish can retain recollections for months at a time and in certain experiments, using music to coincide with feedings, they were documented recalling memories for at least a year.

5. There was great debate as to what ignited the Great Chicago Fire of 1871, which caused more than 300 casualties, burned roughly 34 city blocks to the tune of $220 million (nearly a third of the city's worth) and left more than 100,000 people homeless. The early speculating suggested that Mrs. Catherine O'Leary's cow kicked a lantern in the small barn bordering the alley behind 137 DeKoven St. at about 9 p.m. Oct. 8. Chicago Republic reporter Michael Ahern, who covered the story, later retracted the "cow-and-lantern" yarn, admitting it was fabricated.

Another idea within the O'Leary tale was the cow released a flatulent near the open flame of the lantern, combusting the gas and causing the hay in the bar to catch on fire. The fart hypothesis was later debunked by scientists. There was also the notion the fire started when Daniel "Pegleg" Sullivan, who first reported the fire, ignited hay in the barn while trying to steal milk. "Pegleg," who was a drunk, could've blacked out in the hay with a lit tobacco pipe or cigarette. Over the years, there's been other theories, including everything from a meteor shower to an unruly craps game headed by a man named

Louis M. Cohn, but there's still no conclusive evidence as to who or what truly happened.

6. "Jewels" is Chicago slang for the regional grocery store chain, Jewel-Osco. The jargon is more commonly said and heard on the city's South Side, and depending on who you asked, adding the unnecessary "s" at the end of Jewel is sometimes found to be commonplace, humorous or irritable.

7. Tommy's father, Seamus, and Seamus' only brother, Michael Jr., did have a major falling out. The siblings hadn't been on speaking terms for nearly three years. The incident started on Christmas Day at The Cow, when Seamus proudly delivered a gift to his big brother.

The gift was a life-sized, flame-retardant fiberglass cow which was once a featured piece in the Cows on Parade art exhibit. The cow, which weighed 125 pounds, was reinforced with steel rebar and mounted to a cement base that weighed 400 pounds. The exhibit included hundreds of creatively painted, randomly themed and realistic-looking cows which were placed at various locations throughout the city in the summer of 1999.

Seamus got a good deal on an "Irish Cow" he just so happened to see out of the corner of his eye while driving past an estate sale. He thought it would look great in the pub. It was a standard-looking dairy cow — painted white and black and it had a large Kelly green shamrock on its left hindquarter. To get the cow into The Cow, it required Seamus and Tommy to temporarily remove the front doors, and then solicit the manpower of four additional men.

After Michael Jr. was beckoned to open his gift, he walked the few blocks from his home to the bar. He took one look and didn't share in Seamus' excitement. In fact, he loathed it. Seamus was crushed. Michael Jr. insisted it be taken away and even arrogantly punned it "cheesy," which then instigated a fistfight — a good and bloody brawl that Tommy and the four helpers had to break up. The fiberglass cow was removed and has been taking up a car's worth of space in Seamus' garage ever since. The scuffle was the 27th and last time the two brothers fought. Seamus will tell anyone that he has a 20-7 record against his older brother. Michael Jr. claims to be 25-2 against Seamus, with his only losses coming by way of a pool cue and a 4x4 piece of wood, both which were cheaply blasted across his head. Much of their fighting happened before they were adults, but an intense rivalry surfaced the day that Michael Jr. inherited Mrs. O'Leary's Cow from their father, who intentionally left Seamus out of the family business. As a result of shunning and sour grapes, Seamus hasn't returned to the watering hole nor spoke to his brother since.

8. Chicago wasn't built on rotting onion fields at all. The word "Chicago" is a French version of the Native American word "shikaakwa," which means "stinky onion" because of the wild flowers that grew along the Chicago River. Somewhere in time, Raymond botched the information, but continued to tell people his version.

2. An Unexpected Explosion

Click.

"Today is December 23rd. My name is Alex Hedlund. If you're listening to this, it means I'm dead. And if I'm dead, it's imperative that you learn the intricate details of my murder and become my messenger. My children deserve to know the truth as to why I've left. Or, why someone has taken me away. You must do this for me. I beg you. It is my last wish. When my children are old enough, please tell them my story, and how I loved them so very much … and that they were worth dying for.

"Where do I start? Let's see … this entire crazy situation kicks off with me walking in on my junky-wife getting fucked *1 by her drug lord boyfriend on my couch, while our two sons were locked in my music room down the hall — Frisbee-flinging my CD collection*2 against the walls. Who knows how long they were locked in there. Ice addicts tell time worse than the blind. But I can tell you this … my littlest guy had a full days' worth of shit oozing out of his diaper when I finally broke the lock and smashed through the door. When I found them, those poor boys were hiding in the corner — arms wrapped around each other and trembling. Don't believe me? Ask their therapists in about 15 years. So strap yourself in, because everything I'm about to tell you will be as straight as the bullet I'm going to put in between the eyes of Cody 'The Mongoose' Grantland!

Click.

"Since you're hearing this, it likely means you've found this device in my abandoned car, which will most likely be in Byron, where the shit has gone down … and where I currently am at the moment, driving back to Chicago. You, dear listener, are most likely a cop, so I assume you already know more than enough, but probably not the full story … and on the odd chance you're not a cop, you're in for a real doozy of a tale …

"… Byron, Illinois. What's to say about it? I feel sorry for you if you live here. It's a lame town surrounded by boring farm fields and these two gargantuan, nuclear reactors looming off in the distance and they give me the creeps, man. Those smokestacks produce these abnormal, cartoonish-looking clouds. Like the ones you see in The Simpson's intro. The steam coming out of them casts curious shadows onto the cornfields below. I wouldn't eat anything grown over there if I were you. And if those reactors reacted, you'd see the end of your world coming and you'd have about two minutes to say goodbye. And in that time frame, in those two minutes, you could say goodbye to everyone in town. But saying goodbye in a place like Byron is unnecessary. What are you saying goodbye to? Everyone knows everything about each other. Everyone despises one another too, but they don't tell each other, because deep down they want to keep on being nosy. Everyone has an agenda here and it's usually about worrying what everyone else's agenda is. If those stacks erupted, everyone would continue the town's gossip in Heaven, so there wouldn't be any real umph in the parting. Unless you are an outsider trying to find out where a drug dealer — who's harboring your wife and kids — lives, then all of the sudden, no one knows shit about what you're even talking about! I hate this fucking place, man. Don't ever become a stranger in this shithole. If you've been holding your piss for an hour, don't even pull over to piss in Byron. You'd rather the whites of your eyes turn yellow. Fuck them — fuck Byron! I'm coming unglued here — hold on …"

Click.

"I'm sort. I haven't slept in days. I hope talking into this thing will keep me from falling asleep at the wheel and killing myself before I get the chance to kill 'The Mongoose' and get my kids back."

Click.

"I've just rewound my mind to about three weeks ago and now I'm hitting play: Desiree, my junky wife, took my kids away from me and shacked up with her meth dealing boyfriend — despite my best efforts to stop her. A falsified domestic battery charge landed me in an orange jumpsuit at the Cook County Department of Corrections. The boys in blue and Social Services were of little help to me preventing a mother from taking her two children far away from a "vicious," wife-beater husband. Look man, I'm 5-foot-nothing and 130 pounds sopping wet. How big of a monster can I be?

"I was stuffed into the back of a squad car in front of a group of my neighbors. What a feeling. They gave me finger points and disapproving stares, and cast curses upon me. One even shook her head at me as the cruiser backed out of the drive. As the copper slowly rolled us down the street — parading me in front of the gawkers like some circus freak show — the group huddled and immediately started collaborating, putting their twist on a story they knew nothing about. I knew right then and there they would no longer view me as that nice guy who was always seen blissfully tossing his children in the air on the front lawn after giggles entered their open windows on warm summer nights. I was no longer the nice guy that used to help them lug their groceries up the steps or wrangle their loose dogs. Nor would I be remembered as the nice guy who coordinated the yearly neighborhood BBQ. I was now just a wifebeater they were stuck living next to, man. I'm sure there was one loudmouth in the bunch who told everyone that they always knew I was a violent asshole and that they tried to tell everyone back in the day, but no one would listen to them.

"But I didn't give a fuck about the neighbors. It was when I saw my two boys waving goodbye and their whore mother giving me the double middle finger as the cop drove off — that hurt me the most, man. I can't un-see the sadness in my kids' eyes as the flashing lights were reflecting in them.

"I was taken to the local precinct, where I was booked. I got fingerprinted, got a mug shot and was shot with ridiculed glances from fat-assed cops loitering around the station and listening to the windy, reporting officer talk about how I mangled that poor woman's face. I thought the $150 in my pocket would've been enough for bail, but that's not how domestic battery charges work in the State of Illinois. My next stop in the criminal justice tour was being shipped off to the Cook County Department of Corrections to stand before a judge. Fucking awesome, man. Get your binoculars out, folks. We're going to the zoo.

"My accusations of self-defense — protecting my child from potential bodily harm and of the wife's drug habit, were jollied by the judge at my bond hearing the way a fat man laughs at his long, squeaky farts when no one is around. Hell, I imagine the court recorder typed, '(inaudible) Judge Thompson chuckles' on the transcript. So, I was kept there for three days, virgin butt intact, but worried about, and led like a lamb to the slaughter.

"After doing the mandatory 72-hour hold inside the jailhouse — monkey cages for feces-throwing sick fucks — I was finally sprung. 72 hours locked up with these ... these super-parasites, ones that live and feast inside host parasites that are living and feasting inside the bowels of a sick dog I-capitol-E, society, man — the lowest of the low: Child molesters, pimps, crackheads, TRUE wifebeaters, murderers, trannys, perverts, gang bangers, losers, the clinically insane, drunks, rapists, more fucking losers man, arsonists who like to light kittens on fire ... you name it, they live there like a reality show shot in Hades. A three-day dream vacation for yours truly. A cellmate even said to me at one point in my stay — with his thumb buried deep into my throat, "When you go to sleep tonight, I'm going to use your mouth to jerk myself off — but I ain't no flaming fag — you fucking faggot!" and then slammed me against the wall. Sounds fun, right? I didn't sleep one minute that I was in there. All of this, because the cop basically goaded my 4-year-old into agreeing with his mothers' testimony that daddy hit mommy.

"Sure, my elbow did rearrange her nose into a banana bend, man. If she flung her hair out of her eyes, she probably could hurl a booger like a Jai alai ball, but that was from her own doing, man. I'm willing to bet that every scumbag wifebeater tries professing their innocence to any "I've-heard-this-story-a-hundred-times-before" cop before getting the cuffs slapped on them. But, I'm NOT a wife-beating asshole. Make no mistakes about it, even though it would've been justifiable in most rational people's pupils — if you saw the state my wife was in at that moment and how violent and irrational and high SHE was in front of our children. I mean, c'mon, man!

"I returned to our 4-flat apartment and it looked ransacked. Clothes were spewed about like an unsettling lunch. The kids' toys — some still left on, but battery-drained, flickered with electronic light blips and pops. My recording equipment and instruments were knocked over and damaged. Garbage, trash and random papers added to the mess. And I think I already told you about my CD collection being busted into bits and laying around my music room like shrewd shrapnel.

"There was a strange voice coming from my sons' shared bedroom down the back hall. I picked up the first blunt object that I saw — a toppled over mic stand, and tip-toed down the hall with it. I tried to avoid random items scattered about the living room. Things like ... like ... 'what the fuck is the toaster oven doing here?' I slithered my way down the hall toward the kids bedroom, I thought for certain that my heart would give me away to any plundering intruder — someone in the house looking for my wife's stash — with its 'pow-pow-powing' against my chest like an alleyway gun fight.

"Ten feet away from the room, I slowly backed against the wall, wishing I could meld into it, man. I listened intently while a single trickle of sweat dripped down my forehead to the tip of my nose and stalled there momentarily, the way water dangles from an icicle in sunlight before it finally takes the plunge.

"The sound continued, but then it became clear to me that it the sound wasn't from an intruder. You can't possible know the feeling of relief, thinking you're about to be ambushed by a lunatic that is out of his gourd on mind-altering chemicals and rooting around your bedroom looking for any hidden drugs, only to find out there's no fiend there. But then, the relief is only momentary and isn't worth a piss because, what if, and even worse, what if you potentially might be finding your unforgettable children, forgotten ... and what if they're possibly hanging on to life because their mother abandoned them and anything close to resembling a little thing called "responsibility" in her drug-addicted life? And then when you walk into the room, you come to discover your children aren't there, and there's more relief — almost joy. But then that relief — that slight joy, it quickly becomes washed away and turns into more nervous worry, because the scenario you just thought of, that you just walked in on and hoped not to discover and the one that didn't come true where you currently stand, could possibly be going on in some other room of some other house in some other place — a place you have no idea to where it exists. And you're helpless and worried and sick and angry.

"I discovered the sound. It was a toy robot creepily repeating droned verbiage while stuck face-first on a floor made of laundry.

"After an hour of being on the verge of hyperventilation, I calmed down enough to allow my mind to think. And all I thought about was those two sweet boys of mine. My boys: Marcus, 4, and little Chandler, only 2. Their Daddy should have seen this all coming, man. What asshole father lets his kids' mother pedal crystal methamphetamine — no matter how good the money and risk? Yours fucking truly, that's who, man.

"But, I couldn't allow myself to self-wallow. I can't. I have to fix things and pronto. That's why I'm going to visit my friend, Tommy. I need a gun. Tommy's a man that can get anything and get it fast. I'm going to get my boys back for Christmas and I will mow down any motherfucker who gets in my way to do so. Mark my fucking words! They're not spending Christmas morning in a meth house — absolutely not! It isn't going to happen!"

Click.

"During my first trip to Byron, I created this elaborate scheme to rescue my kids. A two-hour trip with nothing to see but tiresome fields will do that to a guy. I had pepper spray and a butcher knife ready to put to use. I was planning on sneaking up to the house, entering through a window and slicing Cody's throat while he was blinded by the spray. But his Adam's apple would never land on my black Chuck Taylor All Stars the way I had seen it happen a thousand times while carving up the idea.

"For now, I'll spare you all of the details of how I found where my wife and my boys are, but let me tell you man, I had to sift through a lot of rotting decay and human garbage before I finally found the one tweaked-out friend of the wife, who would finally spill the beans. The 411 cost me $50 and a future tetanus shot, but it was worth it. Be advised, there are some gutters in Chicago that you can stand in where you think you're standing in hell itself, man. And just when you can't possibly think anything in the world could be any worse, you realize that the gutters and all the waist-deep shit in them, they all roll downhill, man, and to someplace in this vast city where it all collects. Well, I found that one pool and there are no lifeguards. And you can't even imagine what the people swimming in it are like, man.

"So with my newly purchased info, I drove to the Rockford area — to Byron, and after hours and hours of searching and talking to all these pieces of white-trash shit, I finally figured out which farm my family was holed up at. I drove up to it, and there was no way I was going to be able to just waltz my way up to the house with the pepper spray and knife I was telling you about. Razor-wired fencing surrounded the home and as far as I could tell, at least three pit bulls patrolled the grounds. I really should've thought things through more thoroughly. This Cody 'The Mongoose' is a huge drug lord supplying Chicago with meth. I knew that, and why I thought I'd find him as some small-time cook in a trailer home, was a complete lapse in my judgment. Maybe I watched too much 'Breaking Bad' on TV. Or maybe all the stress was imploding my brain, man. Getting my children back wasn't going to be the simple task that I heroically envisioned. I'd get shot or chewed to shreds and then shot, if I rushed into things. It has taken me weeks of planning to take back what is mine. But, I guess if you're hearing this, it must've been a lousy plan."

Click.

"I've been commuting back and forth from Chicago in my little Civic after running surveillance. I even looked for any reasonably priced apartment or a room to rent so I could be as close to my boys as possible, but none of these slack-jawed hillbillies in Byron were willing to rent a city slicker anything affordable, man. They didn't want me. So, I had to continue driving — and it isn't cheap using those empty fields as a blank page to plot the kidnapping of my own kids. Even for a Honda, I burn up almost a half of a tank of gas doing the loop. And that's not good on the wallet of an unsigned guitar player in an indie-rock band whose family breadwinner quit sharing the dough and our happy little family unit with me altogether.

"There. I said it. Yes, I'm still living out a pipe dream. I bet you rolled your eyes just like my Dad does when you heard that. I bet every time he thinks of me he rolls his eyes. It's OK, man. People like to say that adversity fuels the creative fire, or some shit like that. Maybe it does. Hey, some people are put on the planet to cut some sorry sap open, pull his guts out, dump them onto a frigid and sterile metal table, tinker around a bit inside the rotting cavity while he and his cohorts crack jokes about the size of the patient's cock or a funny-looking birthmark on the incapacitated man's right butt cheek or maybe even a discussion on what color paint the doc's wife used on the walls leading down to their personal wine cellar — I bet you it was a "desert caravan taupe." I'm not one of those people. But, my fingers on guitar strings have been known to drop women's panties the same way a surgeon can with his financial portfolio. And that fuels my creative fire. Or, at least it did, until Desiree DeRosa — that's my wife's name — came carousing around after The Zoloft Superheros gig at Schubas Tavern one June night, swarming me: Buzz, buzz, buzzed. She buzzed me like a honey bee to the honeycomb and eventually wet the wick, snuffing my rock star lifestyle out the second she missed her period.

"I should've listened to Tommy, the man who I'm about to pay a visit and ask a favor of, back in the day when he was checking us out one night and trying to steal our bass player. He came up to me after Desiree went to powder*3 her nose and Sharpie "I love Alex" on a bathroom stall door inside the ladies' room — something she showed me later on that night while blowing me in the stall. Tommy put his hand on my shoulder and said, 'That Italian bird wants a peck at your salami. Be careful, though. She'll ruin The Zoloft Superheros. She has a history of that. She fucked up Willy C's head for about a year once things went south between them, man. Why do you think the Urgency of Now broke up, Alex?' or something like that.

"But at the time, who the fuck cared what Tommy said. He was a drummer for a band heading nowhere. They might as well been called, "Who the fuck cares?" Or … or so I thought. That was before they got their lead singer — the one with the hair, and that unbelievably talented guitarist. Where in world did they find that guy? Anyway, Tommy did have a valid point, man. One that wasn't revealed to me as being so sharp until it was far too stuck."

Click.

"I had seen her around the scene a couple times but never had the stones to approach her; partially because you could never quite tell who she was with at any given moment. I completely forgot that she had been Willy C's squeeze until Tommy brought it up. I thought she was the lead singer from Pocket Rocket Feline Control — what was her name? Melissa? Michelle? Yeah, Michelle. Michelle Figler — that's it. I thought she was Figler's girlfriend. Hey, I don't judge. Bisexuality is common place in our circuit."

Click.

"Desiree is a gorgeous girl — she was — until the meth punched her teeth out and stomped on her face with golf cleats. She is 5-foot-nothing too and she had the body of a college football cheerleader, man. A slight booty-jiggle was always the last thing to come to rest after she entered a room — always reverbing, 'Hello, boys.' Now she's just walking bones wrapped in a sack of itchy

22

skin. Her raven hair, once a bed of curls that attracted and snagged metal rings and wrist watches like the way pickpocketing monkeys rob tourists in those third-world countries. Now it's just stringy and I find more of it clumped on the floor than on her head. Her extra virgin olive oil skin once made her emerald eyes transfixing, like when you can't stop watching waves roll in from the Atlantic. Eyes that make you look past her self-described "schnoz." She would shamefully say things such as, "But, you only see it when you look at me. I see it every time I look at anything." But nowadays, her olive oil skin is dried out and scratched off and her eyes are dull. Dead. Unless she's running out of ice, then they're wild."

Click.

"You don't need to mention what I just said to my kids, even if it's true, man. I don't want them to know all the bad things about her and us and our choices. You can leave that shit out. You can tell them how beautiful she was if you want — you should ... her eyes ... her hair. Assuming she's dead when you hear this ... which she may be if she tries stopping me."

Click.

"Look, I've never stuck up for myself my entire life. I've never had moxie. I'm not some tough guy. I was born this short, skinny dork, that happens to be good at playing the guitar and writing songs ... and that's about it. I was born the opposite of a meat-headed, hyper heterosexual high school stud athlete ... like our father wanted me to be. I didn't inherit his souped-up testosterone, man. I never knew it to be in my DNA and he blamed me instead of my mother for it. I should've gone to Julliard, but the old man thought Julliard was for Nancy boys. It was what it was — until I found out I did share a touch of his mongrel blood, when someone took away the two things I love more than music — more than anything! — and I found out that I'm not afraid of anything anymore, even if it means dying for what I love ... those two beautiful boys.

"FUCK! GET OUT OF THE WAY, ASSHOLE!"

(Loud honking is heard)

"I have to put this down. I'm in the city right now ..."

Click.

Raymond McMahon was half in the bag when Alex walked into Mrs. O'Leary's Cow. Tommy had been feeding him Guinness after Guinness, letting him ramble on and on about how much he misunderstood the lazy, entitled youth of today.

At first, Tommy couldn't make out who Alex was, the way the sunlight followed him through the door and draped him in an angelic haze. But as the door shut behind him, Tommy's eyes lit up at the sight of the huge mess of hair atop his old friend's head.

"Alex Motherfucking Hedlund!" Tommy boasted. "What on God's green Earth are you doing here? Aren't you supposed to melt when exposed to light?"

Alex marched up to the bar with a slight smile on his face.

"I could," Alex said. "You know me — I only come out at night."

The two men exchanged a hearty handshake and if the bar didn't divide them, Tommy would've given Alex a hug.

"I haven't seen you in forever. Are you still playing the guitar?" Tommy asked, checking him over.

"I'm always playing," Alex said. "But as far as The Zoloft Superheroes go … we're taking a break."

"I see," Tommy said.

"I snuck into a Moans' gig a couple weeks back," Alex said. "You guys … you guys have a really good thing going on. You're gonna hit the big time."

"Why didn't you come backstage and say hello?"

Alex shrugged.

Tommy looked down at Alex's plain white T-shirt and noticed the digital voice recorder nestled in the sagging fabric of the pocket. He thought:

- He's going to make me listen to a couple of guitar riffs.
- Shit! He's going to want to join the band, isn't he? This was always his MO in the past*4.
- He is a hell of a guitar player, but it doesn't jive with our sound.
- Man, this guy doesn't look so good.

"You OK, man?" Tommy said. "How's the wife? How are the boys?"

"Things are not good," Alex said. "Not good at all. That's why I am here, Tom. I was wondering if you could do me a solid, bro."

"Anything," Tommy said. "Just name it."

Alex suggested they take their conversation down the bar and out of the ears of McMahon.

"You still drinking Sloe Gin Fizzes? The girl scout shit."

Alex laughed off Tommy's tease and nodded a reply.

"Cool, because I just got this new toy I've been dying to play with."

"What is it?"

"This super-duper carbonation maker," Tommy said. "This thing fuckin' rocks."

Tommy started making the drink. He added a scoop full of ice, 1 ounce of Sloe Gin, 1 ounce of Tanqueray gin, the juice of a half of a fresh squeezed lemon, and 1 ounce of a simple syrup*5 into the

24

Perlini cocktail carbonator. This was the first time he used the new professional mixologist device, but he was briefed on how to do so by co-bartender Blue Trillium the day before and felt he had a handle on how to execute the new shaker.

Alex moseyed down to the end of the bar and took a seat. He rested his elbows on the bar, slouching his posture. His flimsy breast pocket could barely hold the weight of the voice recorder, so he removed it and attempted to stuff it into the front left pocket of his jeans. But his act was lazy, and the recorder haphazardly rested half in and out of the pocket.

Tommy walked toward Alex screwing the top to the carbonator. He added a CO_2 cartridge to the filled shaker and pressurized it. In his free hand, he grabbed a cocktail napkin from a fanned-out stack and set it down in front of Alex. He placed a rocks glass on the napkin and gave the Perlini several shakes.

"So, what can I help you with?" Tommy said.

Alex hung his head for a moment and then sadly looked up.

"I need you to get me a gun," Alex replied.

Tommy paused the shaking to give Alex an inquisitive look.

Then he set the shaker on the bar top, and as he did so, the unsecured top to the Perlini cocktail carbonator busted away from its clear cylinder and exploded directly in Alex's face.

Alex shot up from his stool in shock, and as he did so, the voice recorder to fell to the floor, bounced and then came to a halt, hidden underneath the foot rest.

SIDE 1. TRACK 2. LINER NOTES:

1. When Alex opened his front door and caught his wife cheating on him, he almost raced to her defense. At first glance, he thought she was being raped. Cody 'The Mongoose' Grantland was aggressively jamming away on her and he appeared to be strangling her with his left hand.

But once he heard her caterwauling cries of ecstasy — sounds he hadn't heard her make in quite some time — but grunts he could never forget, he understood she was enjoying the conjugating and the infidel act knocked the wind out of him. He stood unnoticed in the archway of the front door for more than 30 seconds, watching Cody gyrate on her like a dolphin on a tourist.

Finally, the man atop his wife turned to the doorway and locked eyes with him. He mean-mugged Alex, then stuck out his tongue, and perversely flicked it rapidly while giving Desiree several extra pumps. He only dismounted because Desiree pushed him off and squirmed out from beneath him. It was the first time Alex had learned about any infidelity in the relationship and once the coitus ceased, Alex allowed the much larger man to exit without any physical confrontation.

2. Alex had a vast CD collection that mostly consisted of 1970s Punk rock and 1990s Alternative genres. He was a huge Nirvana fan and he had one of the most extensive collections of imports, bootlegs and other rarities. As the music world went away from CDs and toward digital audio

and about-faced with vinyl, Alex was too invested to his CD collection to change with the times.

By the time his children, and then later, his wife, finished destroying 70 percent of his assemblage, there was little left of value. The collection he started when he was 12 was reduced to rubble in a matter of hours, and he couldn't decipher what hurt more — his wife cheating on him or his CDs being demolished.

3. By "powder her nose," Alex meant that Desiree snorted cocaine in the bathroom. Cocaine was her gateway drug into crystal meth, which, believe it or not, derived from an accidental snort of methamphetamines.

4. When Alex's band, The Zoloft Superheros, was struggling to get gigs or having creative differences, he'd often run to Tommy with demos of his guitar work on the audio recorder and try to convince Tommy to make him a part of The Farrow Moans. He thought he could help the band become a surging success, but his advances were always rejected.

5. Tommy made the simple syrup two days ago. It is his trademark recipe at The Cow. His secret was substituting wildflower honey for sugar and adding a few sprigs of fresh mint into the water and honey mixture when it reached a soft boil. He got the notion before attending the 136th running of the Kentucky Derby when he ordered a mint julep at a dive bar near Churchill Downs called Magnolia Bar & Grill.

The drink was made by a bartender named Amber who added an eye wink and her phone number for garnish. He called her after winning $180 on the Derby — $10 to win on the 4 — and the two walked hand-in-hand through the rain-soaked streets of downtown Louisville. Amber became his personal tour guide as they traded bartending war stories and recipes, and Tommy windily told her all about the wonderful city of Chicago and his band. They ended up having a one-night stand and Tommy eventually wrote a song about her.

3. Doggy Style

After a pitiless fight with dysania, Bill Doddano awoke and looked at the sunshine probing his naked torso through the frunchroom window as if it were an alien. If the near-empty bottle of bourbon wasn't still cradled in his arm like a football, he could have dismissed the vague, foggy memories of yesternight as pieces of dreams.

He set the whiskey bottle on the coffee table next to him and gave it a slight "get away from me" shove. It slid a few inches along the wood, hit a sticky patch, rocked forward, almost tipped over and then balanced itself out. He tried focusing to check the time on a cat-shaped clock on the wall, but it was easier said than done. He slept in his contact lenses, again, and his eyes felt like they had been drenched in jet fuel. He licked the tips of his pinky fingers and wet his lenses. When the contacts finally became unglued, his vision adjusted, and he realized he was running late.

He shouted, "Fuck!" but instantly regretted doing so, because it pulsated in his brain.

His head was as hot as a three-cord fire. He must have taken his T-shirt off in the middle of the night. Perhaps it was from a bad dream. Perhaps it was from a detoxing sweat. Either way, as he sat up to retrieve the shirt, his tacky back peeled free from the leather couch like the separation of two pieces of Velcro. He grabbed the shirt off the floor and put it on. He stood up, still wearing a pair of wrinkly jeans from the night before and the night before that, and looked like an un-made bed.

He hovered over the coffee table and stared down at the bottle. He could smell the sourness in the hooch as it fluttered up his nose and it made him squeamish, or "Beamish," as he called it. Or maybe it was his own stench, oozing from his pores that made him nauseated. Maybe it was a combo of both.

One way or another, it was moments like these, where advertisements and commercials showcasing handsome gentlemen having the times of their lives as they toast-drank the marketed brand with dazzling women clinging to their free arms, where the creative brain trusts failed to mention what their product does to that "lucky" bastard the next day. He knew getting drunk wasn't any way to grieve, but he knew no other way.

The orange cat rubbed against his leg and bellowed a cry. It was obviously hungry, but he didn't know how much to feed it. He didn't know why he didn't pay attention to that before. He didn't know why he never cared, but now, he really wished he would have. He walked to the kitchen, reached in a cupboard, found a can of tuna, opened it with a can opener and placed it on the tiled floor. The cat purred and immediately started feasting. For the first time since he could remember, he actually bent over to give the cat a bona fide pet. He had come a long way since the days when he used to yell at the wife when she'd be in another room, "I took the trash out" after booting the cat out the door for some fresh air when the mere sight of it would elevate his blood pressure.

Opening the closet door in the foyer to retrieve a jacket dropped him to his knees. The scent on her winter coat slugged him in the nose like it was the heavyweight champion of the perfume world. It was floral and summery and he smelled a ghost.

After sobbing for several minutes, he uncurled himself off the floor. He reached back in the closet, snagged a blue fleece vest off a hanger and, just as he noticed her purple cashmere scarf on the shelf, it took him back to the top of a Ferris wheel ride on a fall day at Navy Pier. This time, the tears actually hurt as they poured out.

He stood near the front door looking at his reflection in a wall-mounted mirror. Behind him was a larger mirror propped up against the wall, reflecting the mirror in front of him, and providing a strong sense of being ubiquitous. This was her doing — so she could see all of herself before she left in the morning. As he stood there — 35 going on 55 — the image of all of him to see was a mystifying paradox, because he didn't feel alive. He put on a Bulls cap and walked out the front door, wondering how he was going to get through the day. Even though it was yet another Groundhog Day, like every day had been for him during the last three months*1, the loss still wasn't getting any easier.

An hour later, he, Bill Dodanno, caught one of his employees sneaking a pickle off of the serving line when his cellphone rang.

"I'm docking you nine cents from your paycheck," he told the overweight teen in mid-crunchy bite.

"If those were a cent apiece," Bill barked, "I wouldn't give a fuck. But, those fuckers are the Cadillac of pickles and you fuckers will bleed me dry if I let you snack on them all day. Don't forget (points toward a security camera), I see everything you guys do."

There was enough sincerity in his tone to make the kid slightly cower. Bill walked away from the young man and the grill area, and into the tiny back office of the hot dog stand, slamming the door shut behind him. He ignored the ringing phone in his fleece vest pocket, flopped down into a creaky chair, rested his elbows on the cluttered desk and epigrammatically put his head in his hands.

After the moment was up and the phone's ring just about put him over the edge, he reached under the desk, opened a small mini-fridge and produced a can of gelid Budweiser. He set the Bud on the desk next to a stack of mounting bills and cracked it open. When he tried to lift the beer to his lips, the hoarfrost can slipped from his shaky, greasy fingers, tipping over and spilling brew all over the paperwork and his Sports Illustrated swimsuit desk calendar. He loudly cursed "fuck" and righted the can, placing it in between Kate Upton's cleavage.

He looked at the three boxes of Doggy Style T-shirts that were stacked in the corner and swiftly grabbed one free. He hurriedly cleaned up the mess before the sweet liquid ruined all of the documents. The phone stopped ringing as he wiped and he vaguely chuckled at the wadded T-shirt in his hands. He was amused at the idea that he was holding his creation in his hands — factually and figuratively — and he found the moment quite complex because there he was cleaning one mess, with another.

His drinking was getting as bad as his business. With this ironic thought racing through his mind, his laughing turned into full-fledged hysterics when he looked at the sexually subliminal logo he created for the business a couple years ago when pushing a cart turned into pushing a broom in a real storefront. Embroidered on the shirt was a cartoonish image of a hot dog wedged into a voluptuous bun, where the hot dog ejaculated mustard into the air that spelled out the words of the restaurant's name.

Bill believed in the old saying that sex sells, but that was only true if the wieners weren't flaccid. And his were. One horrific Yelp review annihilated Doggy Style Chicago Style Hot Dogs Inc. The food reviewer indicated that he found a bloody Band-Aid*2 in one of his hot dogs, and when he approached the manager on the matter, the owner propelled the situation by creating a drunken debacle. The authorities were called by another customer and only resolved the matter after locking Bill up with a disorderly conduct charge. The Yelp review*3 eventually caught the media's attention, which then caught the attention of the health department, which caught the attention of the general public*4. As a result, Bill's business became grilled to a char.

As he continued to absorb the beer with the bundled cloth, he flipped the T-shirt over. On the back of it he read the mustard-spewed-slogan aloud: "We cram our huge wieners inside your steamy buns." His flabby belly was jiggling from laughter when the phone started to ring again. He pulled the phone free from his vest pocket, checked the caller ID and answered it in stitches.

"Hey, pal!" he said. "Did I walk out on my tab again?"

(Male voice, inaudible)

"Yeah, sure," Bill said, with his voice becoming more cautious. "I'm still in the ... uh ... catering business."

(Male voice, inaudible)

Bill lifted his hat, ruffled his salt and pepper hair, and paused.

"How soon do you need all this ... food?" Bill said.

(Male voice, inaudible)

"What's he looking to spend on this package?" he asked.

(Male voice, inaudible)

"Of course my hot dogs are hot!" Bill said, looking around the desk. "His meal will be hotter than a Kate Upton bikini shoot."

(Male voice, inaudible)

"$500. Times are tough —— with the economy and all this gun-control hoopla."

(Male voice, inaudible)

"Give me an hour to put his order together," Bill said, ending the phone call.

He momentarily sat in the chair and looked up at the ceiling for answers. He then had a hearty swallow of beer, finishing what remained. He shoved off and the chair wheeled back a couple feet. He looked down toward his feet where there was a Chicago Bulls rug covering a section of wooden floorboards.

He bent over, grabbed a corner of the rug, and folded it over like he was turning a page in a book. He opened a drawer in the desk and produced a flathead screwdriver. He began to pry up a board with the screwdriver and pulled out four more rows of hardwood. As the boards were removed, a shiny silver face to a cylinder-shaped safe became exposed.

29

He turned the knob on the padlock dial to the right three rotations, landing on 26. He then turned the knob to the left a revolution, pausing on 34. He gave the knob one last turn, right again, until it landed on 9 and popped open. He lifted the lid off the cylinder and reached down the whole. Elbow deep, he fondled around the safe until he retrieved what appeared to be a burlap sack.

He put the sack on his lap and removed its contents in a desultory fashion. He produced a shiny, silver 9mm Glock handgun and looked it over, ever so slightly. He inspected the segment where the serial numbers should have been engraved along the barrel. He ran his finger across the rough surface and was content with only feeling a course, sandpaper grade texture.

He sat there holding the gun. He doused the Edison's and leaned his head back into the chair. A minute went by and then the next. Then, without any indication he was planning on moving any time soon, he opened his eyes, swiftly crammed the gun into his mouth and squeezed the trigger. Nothing happened. He squeezed several more times in rapid concession, but the results were the same. He slowly removed the gun from his bite and placed it on the burlap sack resting on his lap. He swashed the metallic saliva around in his mouth before giving a spit on the floor. He took a deep breath.

He removed the clip from the gun and couldn't believe it was empty. He set the clip on the desk. He stood up, dug his hand into the burlap satchel once more, retrieved another magazine, checked to see if it was loaded, which it was, put the clip into the gun, and then sat back down on the chair.

He grabbed another beer from the fridge, cracked it open, and then began to slowly pour it into a Doggy Style embroidered paper cup he found on the desk.

He curved the cup with a squeeze of his hand, forming a U-shaped semi-funnel — a trick he picked up while watching a man win a beer-chugging contest inside a beer garden outside of Wrigley Field. He brought the cup up to his unlocked jaw, opened his throat, and guzzled the beer in less than four seconds.

He sat there for several minutes, belching and letting the alcohol absorb into his bloodstream. He reclined in his seat and closed his eyes once more. He rubbed them with bawled-up fists and the pressing caused phosphine, where a kaleidoscope of iridescent colors was seen against the black backdrop of his eyelids. Then, again without warning, he jammed the gun back into his mouth. After looking at the framed picture of his wife as she appeared in front of him on the desk, he closed his eyes.

SIDE 1. TRACK 3. LINER NOTES:

1. Most days he would actually shower, shave, brush his teeth and put on clean clothes. Today, because of obvious time constraints, he didn't do any of those things.

2. During the ruckus, the bloody Band-Aid that spawned the entire disaster was never found. Bill did knock the cardboard container housing the hot dog and alleged Band-Aid out of the hands of the man who claimed it was there. Even after he sobered up, while sitting in a holding cell, Bill couldn't recall if even saw the Band-Aid.

3. Here is the original Yelp review*A that caused the ruckus:

Justin H. — 1 OUT OF 5 STARS: DOGGY STYLE HOT DOGS

DO NOT EAT HERE! I repeat: DO NOT EAT HERE! The worst dining nightmare imaginable occurred at this miserable excuse of a hot dog stand when I ordered a dog with everything on it, oh, and I got everything on it. "Everything" included a BLOODY BAND AID for a condiment!!! Three bites into my dog, I noticed something that seemed out of place lurking underneath a pickle spear and there it was: A blood-soaked appendage stuffed neatly between bun and tubed meat. I gagged, choked and turned green. I immediately took up a complainant with the sweaty, obese slob working on the food line who then backpedalled his way into an office, only to retrieve and steady the drunken, pathetic excuse of an owner as he clumsily approached me at the counter. Even with a couple feet of separation, I could smell his boozy stench billowing off him as he called me a "liar" and accused me of trying to embezzle him out of money for a future civil lawsuit. When I denied his allegations and told him I was merely concerned about my health and the health of other patrons, he chased me around the stand with a hot poker. I ended up calling 911 and pressing charges on him for assault. He was arrested on the spot and I will have to appear in court. I promise you I will be there the day of the hearings and it won't be for money or damage repercussions. I'm doing it to serve as a martyr for public safety! Please avoid this place at all costs! Ps. After being checked out at the ER, I was given a clean bill of health and never became ill as a result of eating the hot dog. THANK GOD!

A) The Yelp review was removed from the website within 48 hours after Justin H. contacted the Channel 4 Action News, who then aired a segment about the incident during their newscast.

Bill, freshly sprung from jail after posting $100 bail for disorderly conduct and public intoxication, caught wind of the story and contacted his attorney, Thaddeus Supernaw, who ultimately threatened to sue the website if it wasn't immediately removed — which the site subsequently obliged.

4. After the health department was contacted by the police department, they did an emergency inspection and the restaurant was closed for the day. The neighborhood responded by not eating there. Those who knew about the Band-Aid debacle from the news report chose not to dine there. Those who didn't see the news saw the health department vehicles camped out in front of the restaurant and subliminally thought Doggy Style must've been dirty or shoddy or had an insect infestation.

4. Gold Locket

This Sunday morning started out like almost every Sunday morning for Jackson S. Schmidt. He rose within the fourth hour of Amplitude Modulation like clockwork, but without needing an alarm clock. He got out of bed, had some toast with a coffee, read a newspaper, took a shower, put on a suit, had a glass of orange juice and drove to church. He enjoyed going to Mass and spent most of his day there, even after spending most of his week there as their employed handyman. Sometimes the kneeling, standing, sitting, kneeling, standing, sitting and so on nagged his bones and gave him a bit of vertigo, but aside from the minor discomforts, he truly took great pleasure in listening to a priest's homily, praying to God and being surrounded by people alike.

Jackson S. Schmidt wasn't much of a sinner. Aside from accidentally cussing here and there and complaining about the Government, he was a very decent man. And, for the most part, he lived his entire life as such. He was one of the few people who was always honest. In fact, the last time Schmidt told a lie, any kind of lie — white ones included — was when he was 17. That was 59 years ago. He was dating a 16-year-old girl, who would become his wife two years later, when it happened. And the only reason Jackson lied that day was because a friend asked him if he was still a virgin. Instead of saying "no" and lying to look cool, like most boys would do, he lied and said he was still a virgin, because having sex before one was married was severely frowned upon in his religion. In those days, it was better to lie and deal with the consequences of God, than having that information recited to a scorning priest.

Aside from his extreme honesty and the rarity that it was, he was also a faithful and wonderful husband. He was a man who lived within his means. He was a man who never took shortcuts. He was a man who was always pleasant, even when dealt with adversities. He was genuine. He wasn't prejudiced. He wasn't sarcastic. He was a loyal friend. And he was a good neighbor.

Jackson S. Schmidt was a model citizen and a modern goddamned saint.

Like most people his age, and the ones he conversed with, he entered the I-better-get-my-shit-straight-with-God-and-my-faith-and-hopefully-I-will-get-into-Heaven-if-I-come-clean-and-beg-for-forgiveness-of-anything-horrible-I-may-have-done-in-the-past stage of his life. But he didn't have much to worry about. He was a devout Catholic since his earliest memory*1, one that took place in Catholic Mass, actually. If Jackson S. Schmidt wasn't getting into Heaven, then there's a good chance no such place exits.

Besides an elderly female getting her shoe snagged on a pew and taking a spill, the 11 a.m. Mass went without a hitch. Jackson stood around talking to dozens of people when it was over. He even had a half-hour discussion with Father Paul about some of his favorite passages in the bible and how Jackson was planning on spending the upcoming holidays.

"Don't forget the flowers," Father Paul said.

"Poinsettias," Jackson confirmed. "She loved them."

"And use those directions if you need them," Father Paul said.

"I won't. I've been living in this city since I was a small boy. I know where to go."

Jackson tried to hand the piece of paper he was clutching back to the priest.

"Hold on to them just in case," Father Paul said.

Jackson obliged and happily walked through the parking lot of Saint Rita of the Angels, found his old, midnight blue gunboat Lincoln, and fired it up.

He drove east on West Cortland, crossed the Chicago River, went north on North Racine, then east on West Armitage and north on North Sheffield, all while thinking about Father Paul's sermon. He was headed to a florist on North Halsted to pick out the flower arrangement for a gravestone. It was an unfortunate Christmas tradition for Jackson S. Schmidt — but one he cherished.

Father Paul was Jackson's favorite priest at Saint Rita of the Angels. Today, his sermon was on looking for the little signs that God gives. It was encouraged that if you kept an open mind and allowed God into your heart, you would see his doings just about everywhere you looked.

As Jackson started to put today's message to good use, he thought about a locket he saw hanging from the neck of a woman outside the church. It was a simple heart-shaped locket, open to the glittery grin of a little girl, husband, mother, sister, brother, niece — it was anyone's guess. It dangled there, turning ever so slowly, sparkling in the sun. Whoever it was from, they must have meant the world to her the way she held it and showed it off. It reminded him of a locket*2 he had once seen before, but couldn't put his finger on as to when or where.

You see, Jackson S. Schmidt's life was quite an anomaly. The goodness that was constantly inside of him, like the memory of the gold locket, was always being sucked away as if it swam in a perpetual vortex. For example, imagine working for a company for more than 23 years and then getting terminated less than 17 months before you could collect a pension. Jackson couldn't believe it either, but that's what happened. However, you never would've known it ever bothered him the way he continued to go about his life the way he always had: constantly chummy. During that period, he never was late, never used more than seven sick days and was always a model worker. His title at Hammerhill Transit was Linguistic Supervisor. His responsibilities included ensuring the tool and dye companies' products were put on distribution trucks in a timely, precise manner.

The products were handcrafted, aluminum car part molds for Ford Motors. He was well respected by the men under him, as well as the bosses. But being liked wasn't job security. So, as manufacturing and the automotive industry turned to technology — replacing men with robots — he and others were no longer much use for Hammerhill. They gave him a six-month severance check, removed him from their insurance and health care, and didn't even pat his back as he walked out.

About a month later, Jackson lost his wife in a horrific accident. This was 17 years ago. Cheyenne Schmidt was a petite, mousy woman with a lump-of-sugar-sweet demeanor. It wasn't until the couple's eighth year of marriage before they were informed Cheyenne would never be able to conceive a child. She was heartbroken she would become nullipara. It was also around that same time she developed a rare condition of dizzy spells and vertigo. Some days, the spells would debilitate her for hours. Other days, they would come and go as fast as one could smile then frown. She had seen every specialist in the region, but none of them could find a reason. She was always told to drink more water or there was always some alternative medicine*3 she could try.

One fall morning, Cheyenne was seen holding her head and staggering on the platform at the Clybourn Metra station. She dizzily shuffled forward, then to the side, then she wobbled backward and stumbled forward again. She eventually fell directly off the ledge, exactly as the inbound train was lulling to a stop, wedging herself in between the slowing train and the platform. When the train stopped, Cheyenne was pinned upright and smothered in shock. One eyewitness described the situation as "watching a drunken pirate walking off a plank and right into an airborne whale."

With the train halted, she was immobilized and affixed in the space — her arms extending out on the platform with palms down as if she was holding onto a ledge atop a cliff. She had no idea her legs were a twisted mess below her.

The first responders evaluated the circumstance, a bleak one. Cheyenne, named after a grandmother she never met, and a mother she would never become, was suspended in disbelief when they looked her over. She couldn't comprehend why they didn't simply move the train and let her carry on with her day.

The emergency crew analyzed the situation and determined that as the train was approaching and when Cheyenne fell into the gap between the moving railroad cars and the concrete wall that separates the tracks from the platform, the force behind the train suspended her in air and began to spin her lower extremities violently as the inertia proceeded, the way apples in a plastic grocery bag would coil the handle area after being spun to tie. It happened so fast, Cheyenne most likely didn't feel any pain.

The rescue crew instantaneously understood what would happen to her innards the second the train moved away and her legs were allowed to un-spin themselves. It wouldn't take long for the blood in her body to rupture every vein and artery. This spot that she was in — a rock and a hard place, if you will — would be her deathbed.

In the gasping crowd, a woman named Suzanne Shaw stepped forward and advised police officers she knew the victim, as they were rolling out yellow CAUTION tape. She was a co-worker of Cheyenne's at Fast Snail Catering, where they both worked on an assembly line, packaging foods. They rode the same trains from Clybourn to downtown's Ogilvie Station every work day, but they never sat near each other*4. Informed of the information, the officers rushed Suzanne to Cheyenne.

Police asked Cheyenne if she had a husband or any family, and she gave them Jackson's name and their number. A witness actually had a brick-sized cellular phone, and he lent it to officers so they could call Jackson. When they didn't reach him at home, they tracked him down at Saint Rita, where he had recently started working, and they gingerly informed him of the dreadful news.

The sergeant in command had his district's dispatch center contact a priest, and he was summoned for last rites. With calm, soft voices, the paramedics and a plainclothes doctor, who happened to be on the scene, tried to inform her that she was going to die. They tried to clarify the magnitude of her injuries, even though she pleaded that she felt fine and demanded they move the damn train. They gave her a brief tutorial on centrifugal force and what will happen to her extremities and blood supply during the seconds after the train moved. But she didn't assimilate any of it. She simply repeated "I'm fine" over and over in a subtle mantra.

Suzanne held Cheyenne's hand as she stared blankly ahead. Cheyenne was eye-level to the designer shoes that some of her fellow travelers wore in the distance and her face was so close to

34

platform that she could smell dirt, a cigarette butt and a discarded potato chip that a few ants where nibbling on. She wasn't in pain, but completely terrified. And to make matters worse, she hated Suzanne Shaw.

The Chicago-to-Harvard Metra line was delayed for almost 45 minutes while they waited for Jackson. Time was as critical as her condition. He raced through the morning rush-hour traffic like he was driving in the Indy 500, but it wasn't enough. Because of the major stoppage and backups, the powers that be pressured Metra to move the train. Jackson was eight minutes and 36 seconds late to witnessing her die an inevitable death. As he ran to the platform, he was held up by policemen and a female Metra paralegal, who was summoned for damage control. Upon hearing the catastrophic news, he collapsed, and was rushed to a local hospital.

When he awoke in a hospital room, the story of why he was there was relayed to him again, and he lost consciousness once more. It wasn't until they conveyed the info for the third time — and under much sedation — before he was able to grasp the enormity of his loss.

As time mended, Jackson never once blamed his Savior for taking her away. He purely continued to live the life he was given, honoring Cheyenne throughout its duration, and he couldn't wait to join her in Heaven.

This morning, Jackson wasn't thinking about her death. He wasn't thinking about much of anything. He was just trying to remember how to get somewhere he had to be and had been circling the neighborhood for 20 minutes. He became increasingly frustrated as each moment went by. He grabbed the directions on the passenger seat, giving in.

He eventually found West Diversey like the directions suggested and stopped for a red light to go southbound on North Halsted. As he waited, he skimmed his surroundings. Everything looked unfamiliar, but his inner compass told him he was in the right spot. The traffic light turned green. He turned down North Halsted and scanned several buildings, but he didn't locate the flower shop. He looked down at the directions. He looked up at addresses. He looked back down at the directions and back up at buildings. And as he did so, he blew past his target destination of Angel Gardens Florist for the sixth time in the last half-hour.

He continued south on North Hasted, shaking with aggravation. He drove past the Hidden Shamrock and Mrs. O'Leary's Cow on his left, looked down at the directions once more, and then shot a glance at a platinum blonde girl as she walked along the sidewalk. And as he straightened his line of vision is when it all happened.

SIDE 1. TRACK 4. LINER NOTES:

1. Jackson's earliest memory was indeed in a Catholic church. It was shortly after his family became citizens, having moved to Chicago from Germany. His younger brother, Frederick, was accidentally dropped into a baptism fountain after bucking away from a priest whose hands were wet and slippery from Holy anointing oil. The child was fished out, unscathed. However, the then 4-year-old Jackson became nervous and started bawling uncontrollably at the sight of potentially losing his brother. Jackson was reassured Frederick was going to be fine after his parents allowed him to put his hands on his brother's heaving chest.

2. Jackson worked 68 hours of overtime and saved every penny to purchase the 24-carat gold locket. Always the quixotic, he gave it to her on their first wedding anniversary and Cheyenne cherished it. It was her favorite piece of jewelry. Inside the locket was a picture of the couple on their wedding night. The original picture was never replaced, nor was it ever even taken out of the locket since the day he gave it to her. It was one of the last things he looked at when he closed her casket. It should be noted Cheyenne was supposed to be buried with the locket, but unbeknownst to Jackson, or to anyone other than a gravedigger named Jeremy Ledbetter, it was stolen from her cadaver.

3. Cheyenne spent several years trying alternative medicines for her vertigo. One doctor, Dr. Roberts, convinced her that various allergies and depression were the culprits and prescribed her a plethora of Phenegran (antihistamine), Benzodiazepines, Meclizine Hydrochloride and tricyclic antidepressants to combat the sadness. She hated the effects more than being dizzy. But Dr. Roberts upped her dosage and the worst stages of the pill-popping occurred less than a year before she died, when she would start her mornings out with taking a mixture of seven different medications. Dr. Roberts was positive the smorgasbord were curbing her dizziness. She changed doctors after a peculiar incident took place. She was sitting alone in her and Jackson's shared bedroom, stoned on their bed and staring at her reflection in the mirror. She sat there perplexed, because she couldn't figure who the lady in the room was. Jackson heard chatter from the living room and stormed in. He found her carrying on a lengthy, disjointed discussion with herself in the mirror and rushed her to the hospital.

4. Cheyenne and Suzanne Shaw couldn't stand each other. They refused to talk to one another at work, even though they stood less than 20 feet apart for eight hours a day. Their hatred for one another stemmed from an incident where Cheyenne's lunch was continuously being stolen out of the communal refrigerator. She eventually caught Suzanne, barging into a bathroom stall while she was wolfing down Cheyenne's meatball sandwich. Instead of reporting her to a supervisor, Cheyenne created fliers of Suzanne's picture with the words, 'MEATBALL SANDWICH THIEF' and taped them to just about every free space at Fast Snail Catering.

5. The Baader-Meinhof Phenomenon

Alex Hedlund, with his left eye no longer stinging from alcohol, was working on his third Sloe Gin Fizz. Tommy redeemed himself and successfully made three excellent drinks with the Perlini Cocktail Carbonator. The drinks, coupled with Alex's all-night stakeout*1, made him weary. He was starting to nod off when the sirens pulled away from the fire station directly across the street, snapped him out of his fuzzy mentality and back into his miserable life.

"What do I owe you, Tommy?" Alex asked. "I can't wait around all day. I'm spent, man. Working on an all-nighter here. I need to grab me a nap."

"I understand." Tommy replied. "He should've been here by now. I just left him another voicemail. You don't owe me nothing for them drinks. But your tab*2 is up to $600. I can call you when I get your order in if you want?"

Alex reached into his right jean pocket and pulled out his billfold. He removed six $100 bills from a stack of nine.

"I know you're protecting yourself from something that isn't my business," Tommy said, taking the cash. "And you know that what happens here stays here. I hope it's the same from you on your end, Alex."

"Of course," Alex said convincingly.

"Hey, with that being said," Tommy continued, "The Farrow Moans are throwing together a little show, right here, tomorrow night around 9. Perfect time to jam and forget about Aunt so-and-so's cooking and Uncle so-and-so's sales pitch from the family Christmas party. Why don't you come by, bring a guitar or two, and plug in with us?"

"Thanks for the offer," Alex stated hesitantly. "It sounds like a great time. It really does, but I don't know how that would go over with my guys in The Zoloft Superheroes. When I pick up that item, I'll get back to you on that. I'd love to play. I've been working on some good stuff."

"Yeah, no problem," Tommy said. "The offer's on the table."

Alex stood up, put his wallet back into his pocket and briefly patted at various spots on his torso like he was forgetting something. Tommy extended his arm for a handshake, interrupting Alex's train of thought. Alex reached his hand across the bar and shook.

"I'll be in touch," said Tommy.

"Thanks again, Tom. I really appreciate it."

Alex gave Tommy a grateful smile and walked out in the opposite direction of where sirens were now wailing.

Tommy removed Alex's glass and wiped up his area. He was summoned by Raymond McMahon.

"Hey, tenderfoot," Raymond said. "You mind pouring me one more glass of breakup brew? One for the road is all I'm good for. The old lady doesn't like me too stinky when I come home."

"Coming right up."

As Tommy poured Raymond's draft, the pretzel-bender struck up another conversation.

"You ever heard of the Baader-Meinhof Phenomenon?" Raymond asked.

"I can't say I have." Tommy said, putting a foamy head atop the glass.

"Let me blow your mind for a moment," Raymond said. "It goes like this … you know how you'll be going about your business and then all of the sudden, you'll hear a word or see a picture of something, or maybe you read about something you never knew or heard about before, and then ..."

Tommy delivers the beer to Raymond.

"… Thank you. And then, all of the sudden, that thing — whatever it is that you didn't know about before … now it's everywhere. POW! Right in the kisser. I mean, the thing isn't an obvious one. The thing is completely random, like say a … a … a puffer fish. Now I don't know shit about puffer fish. I mean, I obviously do if I'm using it as an example — and why I chose puffer fish, I dunno. But for the sake of this conversation and for the sake of this phenomenon, let's say I didn't even know what a puffer fish was until you brought it up to me, say, like two minutes ago. OK? You do know what a puffer fish is, right?"

"Yup," Tommy said. "It's a poisonous fish."

"Exactly," Raymond said. "So, let's pretend I didn't. What would happen next is: I'd leave here, go home, and then I would come across a special about puffer fish on the boob tube while flipping through the channels. Or maybe I'd open up this paper (arbitrarily turning a page from the newspaper in front of him) and there would be a story on how the Shedd aquarium built a new exhibit for puffer fish. Or maybe five minutes after you told me about puffer fish, some guy would walk in here, take a seat next to me, and tell you to hit him with something strong, because he just found out his black-widow-of-a-wife tried poisoning him with puffer fish venom. It's fucking amazing. It then becomes everywhere. Then you start to wonder how much shit you really miss in the world. Think about that. I'm 63. How much have I seen and not realized I had?

"So, the other day I started thinking about it and it was driving me mad. I needed to know what this thing is called. I mean, there has to be a name for it, right? I can't be the only fella in the world this weird thing happens to. So, I go to the library. I start walking around looking for signs of it in these big psychology books, and then it dawns on me … there's no way I'm going to find this thing — a thing I don't even know what to call it — I'm not going to find it in big books with fancy words, or even in a card catalog. I find a librarian and get her to show me how to use a computer, because I don't do technology, and I started poking these bear claws (pretends to type on a keyboard) on the buttons and I Google it. Guess what — it does exist — and I'm not crazy! Well, maybe I am crazy, but this thing does exist. It's called the Baader-Meinhof Phenomenon. And I think to myself, 'that's a pretty neat name. It sounds like what this thing should be called.' Then you know what happened?"

"No clue," Tommy said.

38

"That very same day, I'm riding the 'L' home from the library, and I overheard this one guy ask his buddy if he's ever heard of the Baader-Meinhof Phenomenon! Do you believe that shit?"

Tommy laughed as Raymond hung his nose over his draft.

"You ever have it happen to you ... are you picking up what I'm putting down here, Tommy?"

"Yeah, actually I know exactly what you're saying!" Tommy said. "This is nuts. I didn't know this thing had a name either, but it recently happened to me. Some guy was in here joking around about how he was drugged with tryptophan at Thanksgiving dinner and he woke up pregnant with a food baby growing inside of him. I asked him what the hell tryptophan was because I had never heard it before ..."

"Me neither. What is it?"

"I think it's a chemical*3," Tommy said. "It's the stuff in turkey that makes you tired after you pig out."

"Oh, that's what it's called, huh?"

"Yup," Tommy said.

Raymond chuckled.

"Like I said, that was around Thanksgiving, and then, like you say, this bad mind cough thing — I started hearing the word tryptophan all the time after that."

"Baader-Meinhof," Raymond politely corrected. "It's the Baader-Meinhof Phenomenon."

"Yep, that thing," Tommy said. "It is pretty interesting. I mean, how many times do you think I've missed hearing tryptophan? Hundreds? Everybody talks about how tired they are after eating Thanksgiving turkey, so I've had to have heard it before."

"See, you get it! I'm telling you, now that you know about it, the next time the Baader-Meinhof happens — and it doesn't happen every day — sometimes months will go by before the next time it does, but when it does, it gives you a really weird feeling."

"Exactly. It's kind of like how déjà vu makes you dizzy."

"'Tis," Raymond concurred, raising a toast. "To ... to ... tryptophan: A thing I'll be hearing about all the time now."

They both laughed and then Raymond took a long sip, prepping for a certain story behind why he brought up the Baader-Meinhof Phenomenon. As soon as he lowered the glass, in through the door rushed an oak tree of woman who appeared to be in her 40s, and the pending story dissolved to naught.

She blew past Raymond like a linebacker shedding a block. The zaftig woman's breasts bounced rambunctiously while clodhopping across the floor. During her stampede, her long hair breezed and her arms flailed while her hands played an invisible harp. She picked out a spot in the middle of the bar, took her oversized red purse off her shoulder, and plopped it down.

"Holy shit," she said in a Latino accent. "I need booze!"

Quick to appease, Tommy was already walking toward her when she ordered. He quickly observed:

- This woman has crazy written all over her.
- She moves fast for a biggin'.

"Is everything all right?" Tommy asked.

"I just saw a dead body," she said. "Dios mío! I saw a dead man! A block up (she pointed behind Tommy's head)."

Tommy and Raymond both swiveled their heads in the direction of the large front windows of The Cow.

"What — what happened?" Tommy said to the woman, still looking outside.

Raymond got off his stool and tipsily marched to the front door.

"If he checked out from tryptophan ..." Raymond began to say, but trailed off.

"I walk out the alley," she said, flipping her hair out of her eyes with the back of her hand. "I turn the corner and I see man with a pistola — a gun!"

"Are you serious?" Tommy said.

"Can I get a fucking drink?" she said.

"Yes — absolutely — sorry," Tommy said, returning his focus to her. "What can I get you?"

"Jose Cuervo," she said, holding up two fingers. "Dos."

Raymond disappeared for a moment, then poked his head through the door and shouted, "She isn't fucking kidding, man!"

Tommy shot a quick glance to Raymond, then retrieved a bottle of tequila and a shot glass, and delivered them to the woman.

"Lime?"

"Of course," Tommy said.

He set the glass down in front of her, reached into a cocktail caddy, produced a lime wedge, set it down and filled up the glass.

Her nervous hands spilled a little of the tequila, but quickly righted the glass and slammed the drink with authority. Once swallowed, she whacked the glass down on the bar top and Tommy filled it right up. She instantly pounded the next shooter, sucked the lime and let out a long "ahhh."

"Gracias — thank you," she said. "I'm sorry to be rude. It's been a long time since I saw a dead hombre. Can I have a bottle of Miller Lite?"

"No problem." Tommy said.

He set the bottle of Jose Cuervo on a shelf, took a Miller Lite out of an ice trough, cranked off the cap, slid it to her and made his way out from behind the bar.

Tommy walked out the front door and returned a short time later with Raymond. They both looked out the window as squad cars and police officers were blocking off the intersection of Halsted and Diversey.

The full-figured woman, Maria Rivera, chugged her beer. Upon competition, she shook her head from side to side, pushing the warm tequila deep into her stomach. As she tried to come to grips with what she just witnessed, she put a quivering hand to her mouth and looked for answers.

It was then she saw it — somewhat hidden underneath the foot rest of the bar. Maria saw twinkles of silver faster than a raccoon during dawn's first sign of light. There it was again, rearing its ugly head. "The Feeling" was back and it took over. It had been two years since she last stole anything, but whatever it was laying there, it was begging her to take it.

She couldn't figure out why there was the urge to steal again. She remembered hearing somewhere that seeing and hearing fireworks caused flashbacks with war veterans. She began to contemplate if seeing the dead guy and then being grilled by a cop on what she saw triggered the idea of lifting something again. But her deliberating didn't last long. She was going to get her mitts on the shiny thing.

With Tommy and Raymond's backs turned to her, rubber-necking the scene out the window, Maria looked over her surroundings. In one fluid motion, she bent down, scooped up the glittering object and stuffed it into her purse without skipping a beat.

She made her way into the restroom, found a stall, had a seat and examined her find. To her discovery, she was holding a digital voice recorder*4. She put it back in her purse without turning it on, exited the stall, ran some hot water in the sink and washed her hands. She gave herself a long look in the mirror.

This was how it always started. A small item she never needed would be all she needed. She wasn't addicted to drugs or alcohol, so she wasn't supporting a habit. It was the rush she was addicted to. Almost all of the things that she stole*5 were either thrown away or hid in secret places she rarely returned to. Some people skydive for a thrill, Maria stole.

As she stood in the bathroom looking in the mirror, she knew what would happen if she kept the voice recorder. It would be her gateway to more stealing. Nothing would be safe from her grasp. She would lose family members again — especially her triplet sisters — siblings she spent the last two years attempting to regain their trust. She would lose her new friends as they began to lose their possessions. There would be no one left to bail her out. She would lose another job. She would again become kummerspeck and gain more weight.

Maria looked down at the voice recorder in her open purse. She snapped the two folds shut, gave the red bag a little spank and walked out of the restroom.

Tommy and Raymond were still standing, gawking out the window when she retook her seat. They still hadn't noticed she was evanescent.

"Barman!" Maria yelled, trying to get Tommy's attention.

He turned to her.

"Tequila!"

"On my way," Tommy replied, jogging back behind the bar.

He brought the Cuervo and stood in front of her.

"If you don't want to talk about what you saw," he began to say, "I completely understand. But, do you know what happened over there — this one is on me, by the way."

He finished filling the shot and slid it to her. She took it down.

"Like I told the pigs," Maria said. "I go out of the alley and boom! — there was a dead guy on the sidewalk! A big car is on him! And there's a gun. This one guy … the old man driving — he was standing there in his suit and he was shaking. There were a lot of people running up to see. The fuzz shows up and everyone runs away. They grab me and ask me questions and … I had to go, man!"

Tommy nervously fidgeted with the gold label on the bottle.

"That's crazy," he said. "How old — what did he look like?"

"He looked like a dead gringo, homes."

"I'm sorry."

"It's OK," she said. "Today's been crazy! I just want to chill, dude."

"I understand," Tommy said, smiled and walked away.

Although she just experienced a jolt to the system, it was thinking of the series of crime scenes she was soon going to be a part of that made her push Tommy away. She could feel the excitement building in her loins. All she could think about was stealing anything she could get her hands on. It was an obsession. She again considered if it was the flashing blue and red lights that triggered the feeling. Or maybe it was being interviewed by a cop. She couldn't be certain. Either way, she felt strangely alive.

Tommy reached the front window and briefly stood next to Raymond before stepping out the door to smoke a quick cigarette while he looked over at the commotion a couple hundred of feet away.

As he did so, Maria opened her purse, picked up the shot glass and stuffed it in. She felt fantastic about it, like itching an itch raw, and the beer tasted even better than before.

Looking for more items to steal jogged her memory back to a time when she was in an orange Department of Corrections jumpsuit. She moved into 2700 S. California Ave. on a seven-month stint for retail theft and probation violation. She considered it easy, because she stood five feet, 11 inches tall, weighed close to 260 pounds and was as rugged as twisted metal — prison life still wasn't any fun.

Only two weeks into her sentence, she shaved the flowing, brown curls from her head — the same ones that took her three years to grow back — because she couldn't stand how quickly her hair would stink after using the awful shampoo the facility provided. It was minute luxuries like shampoo she missed the most about the outside world. There were also the major things too, like not being told what to do all the time or wondering if she was going to get jumped in the shower or missing what the outside world was like. But, she forgot about those things today, and she added the stainless steel shot tumbler that was left on the bar rail into her purse.

Business at The Cow started picking up as a result of the death investigation less than a block away. Near the front window, a group of men who had just finished playing basketball at a rec center were occupying four seats there.

There was also a couple in their mid-30s, working on Bloody Marys and staring out the window as well. They, alike the men, only stopped in after stumbling upon the crime scene on their way home from a gym and wanted to gawk.

A young woman hurriedly strayed in and took a seat in between the Bloody Mary couple and Maria.

Maria instantly recognized the woman, Kaylee Fearn, from the scene. Even if Maria was straight*6, Kaylee wasn't easily forgotten. Her heavy application of makeup, the pink yoga pants glued to her ample body, the shiny eyebrow piercing, a designer white gold watch and her platinum hair accompanied by the overwhelming scent of freshly cut apples. As much as she wanted to, Maria refrained from bothering the 23-year-old while she nervously ordered a Captain Morgan and Sprite.

Kaylee took a quick sip, took her cellphone out of her brown Prada purse and began tapping buttons. She fired up the Facebook app on the phone and updated her status: OMG!! Just saw a man get murdered! For reals! I even got interviewed by the cops! I need a drink!! Who's down? I'm at Mrs. O'Leary's Cow!!! Meet me!!

The notifications began to blow up immediately and Kaylee rapidly responded to her post.

A few minutes went by and Maria's mind finally wandered away from items she couldn't wait to steal. After all, they both just witnessed something that doesn't happen every day. She delicately struck up a conversation with the bubbly girl.

"You see him too, girlie?" Maria quizzed.

Taken aback, Kaylee slowed her busy fingers, took her nose out of her phone and gave Maria a shocked glance.

"The dead man?" Kaylee posed. "Were you there?"

"I saw him. Crazy shit, huh?"

Kaylee agreed with a nod.

A now edgy Tommy eavesdropped on their conversation, trying not to look suspicious. The pieces were falling into place. He was now convinced the dead man was Bill, his "hot dog guy," but he needed more evidence. He was going to have to pry that information from the ditsy blonde, since the big one wasn't forking anything over. The last thing Tommy wanted was to be involved in a murder investigation. He knew the cops would find his number on Bill's phone and he knew it was only a matter of time before they were going to be calling. The ideas spun around his head:

- I'll tell the cops he was a regular and I was planning on using his business to cater one of our bands' shows.
- I'll tell them that I would have no clue why he would be carrying a gun. "Maybe it's because there's already over 500 homicides in the city this year, officer."

- "No, I don't know why someone wanted him dead. It wasn't because his hot dogs sucked, I can tell you that much. That's why I wanted his food catered for the gig."

"What did you see?" Kaylee asked Maria, cracking Tommy from his muse.

"I walk out the alley," Maria said. "I came from my job. I left to go to my car, and I'm walking around the corner and … I see the dead dude. And the big car. Holy shit! What did you see?"

"I was walking on the sidewalk," Kaylee said. "I heard the car's engine rev. I turned and looked. It was aiming right for the guy. The guy froze. Then he pulled his hands out of his pockets and he was holding a gun*7. He started to get out of the way, but it was too late. It was so crazy!"

Tommy took mental notes while his head was hidden behind a row of beer taps.

"No shit," Maria interjected. "I'm sorry we saw that."

Kaylee erratically started fanning her face, gesticulating she was about to cry.

"It … was … horrible. His head … it sounded like a smashing pumpkin." Kaylee said, bursting into tears.

Maria got off her stool to counsel Kaylee.

Raymond piped up from his post near the window, "The scumbags are here. Looks like NBC and ... I think Channel 7 too."

Tommy met Raymond to have another gander.

Maria put a big, jiggle-jelly arm around Kaylee's shoulder, leaned her bosom into the girl and gave her a warm squeeze. Kaylee somewhat shyly, but graciously, patted Maria's arm in return. As Maria hugged her tighter, she looked around the bar, snuck her hand inside Kaylee's purse and latched on to the first item she felt.

"It's OK," Maria whispered.

As she held Kaylee, she fleetly removed the item from the purse and held it behind her back in an undetected swipe. Maria broke away from the girl and took a quick glance of the tube of lip gloss in her hand before stuffing it into her back pocket.

"Thank you," Kaylee said.

Maria took her seat.

"No problem, girlie," she replied.

SIDE 1. TRACKS 5. LINER NOTES:

1. Alex had been awake for exactly 38 hours and 12 minutes when he started to doze off. The night before, he alternated sitting in his Honda Civic for warmth and military crawling as close to Cody 'The Mongoose's' farmhouse as he could, chronicling any and all activity. He saw his son, Chandler, in an upstairs window for all of eight seconds. It made him bawl.

It was also there, laying belly-down on the frozen ground in the early morning hours at around 5, where Alex decided the best way to get his children back was to assassinate Cody from point-blank range with a handgun. His mental notes reflected that every Sunday and Thursday, the driver of a white box truck picked up several packages that Cody personally exited the house with to hand-deliver. He was going to have to sneak under the porch without the detection of the dogs if he wanted to pull it off.

2. Alex's "tab" was obviously the prearranged price that Tommy had made with Bill for the handgun, plus an additional $100 for Tommy's cut in the deal.

3. Tryptophan is not a manmade chemical or preservative added to turkey. It's a natural amino acid found in the fowl that can make a consumer drowsy.

4. The Sony digital voice recorder obviously belonged to Alex. Consumed with fatigue, he completely forgot about it when he exited the bar, although he knew he was forgetting something but couldn't put his finger on it at the time.

5. In Maria's most honest recollection, she was certain she probably had stolen more than 3,000 times in her 44 years. The most expensive thing she ever stole was a new 1999 Chevy Tahoe, which she drove for six minutes. The least expensive thing she stole was a cancer charity change jar from a gas station that contained 83 cents.

6. Maria was bisexual. Sometimes, she'd claim to be a lesbian. Other times, she claimed to be bisexual. Today, if someone would have asked, she would answer she was a lesbian.

7. At times, when traumatic situations occur, the mind often sees what it wants to see. Kaylee thought she saw the deceased man removing a gun from his vest pocket and aiming it at the driver before being struck. In actuality, and from her vantage point on the sidewalk, it was almost impossible to be 100 percent certain he actually had a grip on the gun.

6. "Our day starts when your day ends"

Carter Woodbine hung up the phone and looked through a large series of square windows in the office and gazed out at the afternoon's ephemeral light climbing on naked tree limbs along the 800 block of West Addison. It was only a week ago when autumn was clinging to a warm womb with wearied talons. Fall surpassed Mother Nature's due date longer than anyone expected, but today, winter was a hungry newborn.

The looming sun gave the promise of yet another unseasonably warm day, but as a frosty draft from an open window crept into the office, he knew the sunshine was likely subterfuge. It was Chicago after all — a place that could get all four seasons in one day.

He was airing out, wearing a white, pit-stained Chicago PD Homicide Division T-shirt where blue lettering announced, "Our day starts when your day ends" when he decided to shove away from the desk. He grabbed his navy pinstriped oxford off the backrest of the vacant chair at the cubicle next to his. He was the only one in the office, so there wasn't a concern about professionalism. He stood up and feebly reached into each sleeve hole like he was feeling around an ocean floor for a lost wedding band. Once his hands emerged from the cuffs, he fastened each button at the pace of a masturbating sloth. His stomach launched a series of hungover hiccup-burps as he buttoned. Then, he ring-tossed a previously tied, but loosely held together, canary yellow tie over his head and slid the knot up to his neck. He stuffed the shirt's lower hem and side gussets into his blue trousers and loosened any tautness flaunting his flabby gut.

Once dressed, he walked to the door and hesitated. He deliberated whether or not to grab his navy peacoat hanging from a brass hook a few feet behind him. He stood there, considering the coat while holding the doorknob like strangers holding hands during a long church sermon. Finally, he decided to take the coat. "Fuck it." He swathed it over his shoulder, picked up his black, square duty bag off the carpet and walked out.

While strolling down the hallway, his indecisiveness over retrieving the jacket was questioned again. His withdrawing nervous system sent a hot flash through his body. Drinking was the hamartia in his personal life. He hung out at the corner of bad drunk and good goddamn cop. At home, his drinking was open and pervasive. At work, he hid his problem better than the best.

To hide it, he started his day off with a shave and a blistering hot shower to sweat out toxins. He'd stay under the heat until it was unbearable, then spinning the knob to a frigid temperature, allowing the icy water to tighten his pores. He'd get out only after his testicles shot up to his bleary head like a hammer strike. Then, he'd dry off and excessively douse Brut splash-on aftershave into his hands like Tobasco sauce on a taco before lathering it into his cheeks like oil to a baseball glove. The next steps were a sousing of Brut cologne, a teeth brushing, followed by a gargle of hydrogen peroxide — which hopefully killed any alchytosis — and then he'd get dressed.

Once he arrived at work, he'd alternate smoke breaks with a coffee regimen. Sip, sip, sip, dump and refill. Sip, sip, sip, dump and refill. The smoking and java routine would go on all day — an excuse to move and not get cornered by a close-talking co-worker or interviewee.

Even with his precautionary measures, everyone in the office knew he was a drinker. And no one blamed him for coming in groggier than most, based on what they knew about his wife's mental state. But he did hide it so well — they never guessed how ruthless his dependency had become.

46

While walking in the corridor, a second flush of heat waved through his insides, causing him to break out in another sweat. The blazes were becoming reminiscent to a menopausal woman and he felt inadequate being an oft-sweaty detective. He stopped again in deliberation over the coat. This time, he reflected in front of a motivational picture of a snow-covered mountain range saying, "ATTITUDE: What happens to a man is less significant than what happens within him."

He elected to bring the jacket, stepped into the elevator and hoped the crisp air would help. He reached ground level and walked to the lobby of the police station. The room always had a changing smell to it. Some mornings, it smelled like cologne from an officer who entered the building minutes before him. Some mornings, it would stink like booze or vomit or piss or shit — or all of the above — drifting off an arrestee waiting for a ride after being bailed out.

But today, Carter couldn't smell anything but burnt coffee. The source was a near-empty pot left on a hot plate in the adjoining room behind the lobby's bulletproof reception window.

Carter couldn't stand Community Service Officer Mark Adams, the redheaded man that was supposed to be, but currently wasn't, manning the front desk. Carter assumed he was probably tending to the burning coffee and it pleased him knowing he wouldn't have to make small talk on his way out.

The dislike for Mark stemmed from a variety of reasons. For starters, Carter made the mistake early on to tell the young baseball nut that he played minor league ball and was once a highly sought-after prospect. To which Mark would often ask endless amounts of questions about his career. Another reason for the dislike of Adams was because Carter hated the Chicago Cubs and their fans in general, and Mark was a fanatic. Carter found Mark to be like a majority of Cub fans — ultracrepidarians who didn't know jack about baseball, but talked like they did, and mainly went to Wrigley Field for its nostalgic ambience.

Carter's two favorite teams were the Chicago White Sox and whoever was playing the Cubs*1. He understood Mark's chatter was just a way of being friendly because they shared the same passion for America's pastime, but it wasn't enough, and Carter still couldn't stand him.

Another reason he disliked Adams was because Carter didn't respect a man who didn't have the guts to become a sworn officer. Mark would always talk a big game about becoming a cop, but whenever it was time to test for the position, he'd routinely manage to come up with a lame excuse to not go through with it.

Carter continued through the empty lobby toward the front door, fanning his shirt and craving a chilly breeze to smack him across his face the way his wife did the night before during another drunken and overly-medicated debacle. He reached the doors and loosened his tie with an agonizing tug. Beads of sweat littered his forehead like a Slurpee cup left on a dashboard in the hot sun. He wiped his brow with his sleeve and the cottony fabric soaked up the perspiration the way a paper towel erased spills.

He opened the doors, stepped outside and a breezy zephyr refreshed his flushed face. But the relief was short-lived, because as he stood in the sunshine, apricity began to cover him like a wool sweater. He hid in the shadows of the metal DISTRICT 23 sign and became cognizant of the fact he'd forgotten his coffee. He hadn't the time to retrieve it, nor was he willing to chance being confronted by Adams, so he looked toward the sky, trumped by his forgetfulness.

With his vision in the air, he felt a sneeze coming on. He sneezed three times in a row and when the fit subsided, he checked for his car keys with a pat of his left pant pocket. A bony protrusion and a muffled jingle confirmed they were where they were supposed to be. He checked his right pocket and only found his billfold.

He squinted, thinking harder about what he thought he was forgetting, and then he solved the mystery. He dug his hand into his duty bag and corralled a pack of Red Apple cigarettes and a lighter. As he did so, a silver necklace that supported a shiny silver badge with a royal blue No. 41 engraved in it fell out.

He scooped up the necklace and badge and put it over his head. He ran his tongue from left to right over his top six teeth, and they were still smooth from his morning brush. He short-tossed the Red Apple at his wet lips and the cigarette stuck to them long enough for him to light it. He had a long drag and enjoyed the breeze. In a few short minutes, he was going to see a dead body, and it didn't even faze him anymore.

After finishing the cigarette, he put out the butt with a brown dress shoe the way he used to dig into the batter's box. Carter took a right on the sidewalk at North Fremont and walked to the secluded spot in the rear of the police department where he parked the squad car.

His black, unmarked take-home 2008 Ford Crown Vic sat next to a fence line and under a depleted mulberry tree. It was a spot no one ever wanted to park under in the summer, when the tree's fruit was plentiful and the robins emptied their bellies, rifling bird shit on hoods like they were targets in a game of paintball.

He set his duty bag down next to the front passenger door, dug his left hand in his pocket for the keys, opened the door, hung the peacoat on the headrest and tossed the bag on the front seat. He shut the door, adjusted his holster and 9mm handgun near his right hip, attuning the cellphone secured to his belt, walked around to the driver's side door and sat down in a limboesque-dance-squat. He shut the door and fired up the car. He looked at his reflection in the rear view mirror — and didn't like what he saw.

The once proud and chiseled face was now covered in a flabby mask he couldn't remember putting on. His glacier blue eyes, which formerly reflected shimmering glares, were now clouded like an overcast day. In high school, he drew comparisons from his classmates to a younger, follicle-challenged version of Magnum P.I. He hated the comments, even if some were compliments from giddy girls, because he always thought Tom Selleck looked old enough to be his father. Today, if he unexpectedly grew a butt crack on his convex chin and (spitefully) threw a Detroit Tigers' hat on his head, he could win an overweight Magnum P.I. look-a-like contest. After all, he sported the token cop mustache and it boomeranged around the corners of his lips.

With the Crown Vic idling, he lowered the window, anticipating another cool gust. He tilted his head forward and to the sides, observing the two patches of gray hair around his temples in the mirror. They seemed to be taking over the dark brown shag. He never imagined himself as the salt-and-pepper type, even back in the day when he used to razz his father for coloring his hair when it started corroding. But this was him now — suddenly old like he remembered his father. He wondered what happened to his boyhood looks.

He took a deep breath, and as he exhaled, steam briefly appeared and then dissipated through the cracked window. He couldn't pinpoint where the fog went into the atmosphere, just like his youth. He looked himself over in the mirror one last time. He thought that if he shaved off the mustache maybe he wouldn't appear so ripened. But then he remembered the last time he shaved — for a high school reunion — he didn't like the way the skin over his upper lip drooped, so he abandoned the thought.

He checked the dashboard, examining the gas gauge, and his eyes fixated on the small piece of paper. It was a note*2 in his wife's handwriting, unexpectedly left there after last night's blowout. For, he had taken an alcoholiday and was having a difficult time recalling anything from the previous diurnal. He hadn't even noticed the note on his way to work at 0800 hours, when he was still sobering up. It read, "Don't forget to curse me when you leave."

He ran his fingertips over her words like he was reading Braille. He couldn't help but to admire her penmanship when each letter emerged from beneath his prints. He found the ink flowed flawlessly like it was written with unicorn tears. He couldn't believe that a nerve-wracked, highly medicated person such as herself could've created it. Then, as instructed, he cursed her under his breath. If he could trade in his old heart for a new liver, he would, so he could drink more and care less.

Carter was the only detective in his squadron working today. His partners, Detectives Espinosa Mendoza and Kimberley Hess, and their supervisor, Lieutenant Harrison Fenton, all were on vacation for the holidays. If the call actually was a valid homicide, he was going to be working it alone. Carter wished it that way. He believed in his own gravitas and he hoped Fenton believed in it too when it was time for a recommendation to the promotion of Sergeant of Investigations — a vacant position in his scope and one he was earmarked for.

Carter was briefed on the situation near North Halsted and West Diversey via cellphone by the on-scene beat sergeant, Dennis Bowers. The initial report Carter received was that patrol was investigating a possible vehicular manslaughter or homicide, and the deceased victim, a male white — possibly in his 40s — was seen aiming a gun at the driver. The driver was a male white in his 70s and the owner of an older model Lincoln that ran the victim over — blasting him onto a sidewalk where the vehicle came to a stop on him. They were still working on all the particulars, but since there was a gun near the body, Bowers requested someone from homicide take a look.

As he drove to the location, Carter assumed the elderly driver mistook the gas pedal for the brake and accidentally ran the guy over, as he had witnessed happening many times. But, hearing about the gun being aimed at the car did adjust the odds of it being a homicide to 50-50 — just as he felt everything in life was.

It was 1354 hours when Carter pulled up to the taped-off intersection. He flashed his badge at a beat cop securing the perimeter and the young officer lifted the yellow caution tape over his head, giving Carter barely enough room to drive underneath it. He parked about 300 feet north of the accident scene.

After turning the engine off, he grabbed his bulky duty bag and stepped out. There was a slight wobble in his stance as he shut the door and tried to swing the strap of the bag around his shoulder. But the balancing of the weight wasn't attributed to the 20 pounds worth of miscellaneous gear inside the satchel. It was because he was trying to steady his sea legs from the rocky ship that kept taking on firewater last night. Even though it had been 11 hours since his last sip, alcohol had a funny way of waving him the next day.

As he walked toward the crash, a Roman candle was launching sparks inside his head. He begged for the cacophonous, belling jow and the hazy heat to go away. He would've said a quick orison; promising God that he would never drink again if he could make the pounding stop, but he was long past making promises and he was long past keeping promises, let alone to a man he had a hard time believing existed.

A bald officer in his late 40s with a shiny gold badge started walking toward him from the scene. A warm smile came into Carter's sight when the men locked eyes. The officer was Sgt. Dennis Bowers, a 24-year-veteran of the force and an old partner. Behind Bowers, Carter could see that a 6-foot-tall white plastic partition was erected, surrounding the victim in a semi-circle near the front of the car and where it was being guarded by two patrol officers. Bowers greeted Carter about 20 feet away from the partition. The men shook hands. They exchanged some small talk in regards to the last time they had seen each other*3 and Bowers continued to talk shop.

"It's been one of those days already, Carter." Bowers said, chuckling. "Listen to this one. Right out of the gate — the first 911 of the shift — dispatch puts out a disturbance call at a residence. Neighbors report they hear yelling — something about someone bleeding and they think there's a fight going on in the home. We show up. The house is pitch-black. We don't hear jack at first. We're knocking on the door and shouting, 'Police! Police!' I got my flashlight out (mimics shining a light) looking in every window I can find, and I can't see anything. Then the rookie over there (points to an officer at the crash scene behind him) goes, 'You hear that, Sarge?' And we start hearing this banging — BOOM ... BOOM ... BOOM — coming from upstairs. I mean the fucking windows rattle every time we hear the hullabaloo. We yell again, and nobody answers. So (imitates kicking a door) we bash the thing down — guns drawn, and this woman flies down the stairs — she's wearing this latex, Catwoman-suit thing. It's got zippers and trap doors and all sorts of bells and whistles. She's short and thick, and she's got one titty flopping out of this latex contraption — a complete a train wreck."

Bowers covered his mouth with a fist in an attempt hide his laughter and maintain integrity because of the many bystanders present. Carter followed suit with a cupped hand.

"So, I'm trying not to stare at this big ol', mamma jamma booby that's out on display for the world to see," Bowers continued. "We ask her what's going on and she won't spill the beans, because she is pissed off that we knocked her door down. We barge past her and make our way upstairs to this bathroom. There's this guy sitting on the toilet — his face is covered in blood, and he's just rocking on the toilet. BOOM ... BOOOM ... BOOM. The tank part on the crapper is crashing into the wall every time he rocks. I ask him if he's all right, because I can only see one side of his face and I'm thinking there's gotta be a butcher knife stuck in the other side or something. He doesn't respond. So I shine my light in his face and tell him to look at me and he eventually does. The blood is pouring out of his nose like a fucking sieve, but there's nothing I can see that's caused it. So, we call a rig for him. I ask him what his name is and he keeps telling me, 'I'm fine. I'm fine.' I ask him what happened and he just keeps repeating, 'I'm fine.' The ambulance finally shows up and they're asking him questions like, 'Do you know your ABC's?' and he's saying stuff like, 'Q, A, O, L' completely wacked-out. They ask him his name and he answers, 'Ambulance.' What a trip. I mean, I haven't even had a sip of fucking coffee yet and I'm dealing with this shit."

Carter did his best to hold in hysterical laughter.

"So, they scoop him up and get him the hell out of there." Bowers said. "After some pressing, Catwoman — who we finally got to put on a robe — tells us they're married, and they're into some kinky shit. She goes on to enlighten us that they're into this ... I had a Spanish speaker write it down for the report (reads from a small notepad that was in his pocket) 'Surra de Bunda' or in English, get this, 'butt-beating.'"

"What the hell is ... do I even want to know?"

"Oh, you do," Bowers explained with a crooked smile. "Catwoman kneels in front of him with the trap door on the suit wide open and facing his face — her legs are up on the guy's shoulders — locking her ankles tightly around each other. Then she pulls his head forward and rams his face into her ass and goo canoe with the rhythm of the music."

"I'm at a loss for words."

"Un-fucking-believable, right?" Bowers declared. "Somewhere in the nastiness, she climbed up on the headboard and gave him a dumbo drop, most likely breaking his nose and giving him a concussion. I'm telling you Carter, you can't make this shit up."

"No," Carter said. "No you can't."

"Don't you miss it?" Bowers asked. "Banging the beats — when are you coming back to patrol? You and I ... we ran this city. You like being caged in the office?"

"Some days," Carter said, "I do miss it. But, I'm getting too old to be kicking in doors."

After the reminiscing of the good old days concluded, Bowers turned and looked at the crime scene behind him.

"All right," Bowers said. "I know you have a job to do. Here's what we got ..."

Bowers brought him up to speed with where the investigation was at since the last time they spoke over the phone:

● The suspect/driver, a Mr. Jackson S. Schmidt, was sitting in the back of a squad being detained and awaiting transportation to the District 23 Precinct for additional statements and questioning. There was no indication that the driver was intoxicated and he was never placed under arrest.
● Patrol officers were gathering testimonials from witnesses and (if any at all) video footage from their cellphones. Once completed, any and all compiled information would be turned over to Carter.
● The Cook County Medical Examiner's Office had been notified and an official would be viewing the deceased as soon as Carter turned the scene over to their custody.
● The Accident Investigator had started gather preliminary mathematical data.
● An Evidence Technician was on scene, waiting for Carter to examine evidence before he would collect any.
● Two patrol officers were canvassing the area for any and or all security cameras from local businesses that may have captured the incident. The results were, so far, inconclusive.
● There was no identification on the deceased's person. Patrol officers were probing into the matter. Since the victim was on foot and wearing light clothing, a K-9 and its handler were requested to the scene for a scent track. It was supposed the victim hadn't traveled far. The K-9's estimated time of

arrival was an hour.
- Paramedics of the Chicago Fire Department, who first examined the deceased's medical condition at the scene, would be emailing their reports to the reporting officer.
- The on-call lawyer from the District Attorney's Office was briefed via cellphone.
- The first responder was still on scene and would be Carter's complete subservience, if need be. His name: Officer Matt Lyons.
- A tow truck was on standby to take the Lincoln to District 23's evidence lot.
- The dispatch center advised that the media had already inquired about the accident, probably from monitoring police scanners, and that they were likely due at any moment. Officers would contain them as best as possible.
- If there was anything that Carter needed, Bowers and his crew would help in any way they could.

Carter thanked him, apologized that his district was understaffed and stressed his gratitude that he could use Bowers' men as he needed, to which Bowers replied, "My rookie — Lyons, is good. Damn good."

Carter and Bowers shook hands again and Carter proceeded toward the victim and car. As he approached, he spotted the Accident Investigator, a Detective Stuart Grimsen, while he was pushing a Keson "Roadrunner" distance measuring device alongside a fresh set of skid marks left on the roadway.

Grimsen was a pock-faced leptosome fellow, whose straw-colored hair was always shaved close to the scalp except for the small, circular patch growing directly above his forehead. The haircut drove Carter bonkers. The two men met several times — usually under these circumstances — and Carter had a difficult time looking at him because of the hair. Carter bee-lined toward Grimsen and waited to speak to him until the A.I. was finished jotting numbers down. Carter set his duty bag down near the car, took out his gray Moleskine notebook and pen, and surveyed the scene.

After taking a mental panoramic picture, Carter squatted down and began to put on a pair of latex gloves when Grimsen walked over to him.

"How's it going, Woodbine?"

Their conversation was brief — Grimsen was a taciturn man. Per usual, they didn't delve into personal affairs nor was there much chitchat. Grimsen still had a lot of mathematical evidence to collect before he would begin to apply the numbers and findings. Carter didn't take much of value from Grimsen's information, anyway.

Having gathered as much insight as he was going to get from his cohort, it was time for Carter to get his hands dirty. He put the pen in his breast pocket and stuffed the notebook in between his pants and tucked-in shirt, where it rested against his lower back.

He approached the midnight blue, 1979 Lincoln Continental and had a peek inside. It was immaculate. A Bible, which was on the floorboard of the passenger seat, was the only thing out of place. There wasn't even a smudgy fingerprint on any part of the posh interior, as far as he could tell.

He stood back and had a gander at the crumpled hood of the car. As he studied the damage, he noticed a baby-faced patrol officer nearby watching his every move. Carter peered at the kid's nametag on his chest and it read "LYONS." He gave the youngster a whistle and motioned for him to join him with a wave. Lyons trotted over to Carter.

"What's your name, rook?"

"Matt Lyons, sir."

They shook hands — Carter's hand was left throbbing from the kid's excited squeeze.

"All right, Lyons," Carter said. "You're officially my errand boy. First things first, I need a fresh cup of coffee."

Lyons sprinted off and Carter continued to work his vision along the sleek hood like he was watching an invisible stripper slide down a pole. He briefly took note of the gun resting on the hood and advanced his eyesight down to the giant grill. The bumper was no longer intact and pieces of the metal grill were scattered about the street and sidewalk from the rear of the car to the front. Carter's eyes crept along the driver's side front quarter panel and there wasn't a scratch. It appeared all of the damage occurred at the front of the car.

The fluffer for this nasty bang was seeing the victim's right leg flipped around like a contorted pretzel near the front left tire. The wreckage became clearer with each inch he stepped closer to the face of the fiend.

Carter reached down next to the man's right jean pocket and found a cellphone that the Evidence Technician removed searching for the dead man's ID. He looked through the phone for any owner information and couldn't find any. He then checked the call history. The last time it was used was when the owner of the phone answered a call from "Tommy The Cow." There were also two missed calls from that same number. Carter removed his notebook and dialed the number.

A male voice answered on the sixth ring.

"Hello, I'm Detective Woodbine with the Chicago Police Department," he said. "May I ask whom I'm speaking with?"

(male voice)

"Tommy was it?" Carter asked, while removing the ballpoint pen*4 and scribbling in his notebook.

(Tommy's voice, inaudible)

"Tommy, could you help me out here," Carter said. "We've got a situation and I need to know whose phone I'm calling you on. Do you know whose number this is?"

(Tommy's voice, inaudible)

"Bill the hot dog guy — but you don't know his last name?" he asked.

(Tommy's voice, inaudible)

"He owns a hot dog restaurant?" he asked, jotting down the info.
(Tommy's voice, inaudible)

"Doggy Style," Carter repeated. "Got it."

(Tommy's voice, inaudible)

"He was, was he?" Carter said.

(Tommy's voice, inaudible)

"And where was he supposed meet you at?" Cater asked.

(Tommy's voice, inaudible)

"Mrs. O'Leary's Cow," Carter repeated, looking around the street until he located the bar about a half block south of where he was standing. "Can you walk over here and meet with me — I'm less than a block away?"

(Tommy's voice, inaudible)

"No one can watch the bar for you, huh?" Carter said. "What time do you work until?"

(Tommy's voice, inaudible)

As Tommy spoke, Carter, who was still looking down the street at The Cow, noticed a platinum-blonde girl in her early 20s exiting the pub. She was being consoled by a man about her same age as they walked along the sidewalk, toward the scene. The young lady seemed to be shaken up while reaching as far as the caution tape would allow her to go and pointing at the accident, but that wasn't the reason she caught Carter's attention. She looked extremely familiar to him, but he couldn't put his finger on it*5.

"Well, unfortunately I can't get into specifics with you over the phone at this time," Carter said. "But I would like to talk to you later and then I can fill you in. Is it OK if I call you or stop by a little bit later?"

(Tommy's voice, inaudible)

"Thanks for the help, Tommy," he said. "I'll be in touch."

Carter hung up and wrote "Tommy the Cow's" number down in his notepad before continuing to search through the victim's phone for any information.

He typed the names "Jackson," "Jack" and "Schmidt" into the search and his results yielded nothing. He then started typing the words "Home," "Wife," "Mom," "Dad," "Old Lady," "Honey," "Sweetheart," "Aunt," "Uncle" and "Grandma," but the results came back with nothing. He then typed in the word "Work" and got a match. He dialed the number. On the third ring, a young man answered.

"Can I speak to Bill?" Carter asked, while sardonically looking down at Bill's head as his brains were trickling out of it.

As the young man answered Carter's question, Lyons returned with the coffee while he was jotting down the word "errands." Carter thanked Lyons with a nod and gave him a "one second" finger. Lyons stayed put.

"My name is Detective Carter Woodbine with the Chicago PD," Carter said. "We have a situation down here and I was wondering if you can give me Bill's last name?"

Carter wrote: "D-A-D-A-N-O" as he listened to the kid talk.

"Can you spell it, please?"

Carter corrected his note: D-O-D-A-N-N-O.

"I'm sorry. I can't really get into all the details at this time," Carter said. "Do you know if Mr. Dodanno is married or has a girlfriend or ..."

The young man interrupted Carter and he tapped his pen on the pad while he listened. A moment later he scribbled "cancer" on the paper.

"That's a shame," Carter said. "Can I get your name, buddy?"

Carter carved "Dee" down on the pad.

"DeVon — Dee, what I'm going to do is send an officer over to talk to you, OK?"

Carter listened to the man and then said, "Thanks again, Dee" before hanging up.

"Lyons, I need a uniform to go over to Doggy Style Hot Dogs," Carter said. "I think it's about three blocks east of here. We need to notify next of kin (points down toward the body), he runs that business. Our victim here is Bill Dodanno. D-O-D-A-N-N-O. Can you get someone over there for me?"

Lyons nodded, keyed-up on the portable radio attached to his shirt and started talking in a bass-heavy voice.

Carter then waved over the evidence technician, Officer Theodore Lapp, who was mere feet away, kneeling down and organizing his ET kit. Carter introduced himself to the 16-year veteran and took note of the brillo pad of silver hair atop his head as they shook hands.

"OK, Lapp, bag up that cellphone."

Lapp removed a plastic bag from the toolbox he was previously organizing and put the phone it.

Carter then picked up the handgun for inspection. It was silver, Glock 34 GEN 4 9mm with the serial numbers deliberately filed off. Its clip was left intentionally separated from the gun when Lyons arrived on the scene and secured the area. It appeared that not a single bullet was missing from the magazine and one was still in the chamber.

Carter spent the next hour inspecting evidence and scrawling notes. He had Lyons drive Jackson S. Schmidt to the station, asking him to monitor his demeanor and note anything he said.

After Bill was tagged and bagged by personnel of the Medical Examiner's Office for an autopsy and a toxicology screening, Carter left the scene. Before he got into his squad car, he was greeted by a small group of reporters who were shouting questions at him. He fielded a few requests behind the yellow caution tape and ended the session with a vague and scripted summary of the incident: "All we know is we have an unidentified white male in his 40s who was found deceased on arrival of our first responders. We want to thank the boys from Engine Company 55*6 for racing — literally running over here, to provide medical attention and trying their best to save the man's life. Our victim appears to have been fatally struck by the vehicle and we're still investigating if this is an accident or intentional. As further information is obtained, the Chicago PD will keep you informed and send you a press release. That is all I have at this time."

SIDE 1. TRACK 6. LINER NOTES:

1. Carter became a Chicago White Sox fan at an early age. Although he grew up on the north side of the city, closer to the friendly confines that is Wrigley Field than that of the White Sox south side home, Comiskey Park, he found a love for the Sox. Although his father and the majority of his family and friends were Cubs fans, and although he was encouraged thousands of times to be a Cubs fan, Carter didn't share any of their enthusiasm. Ultimately, it was the White Sox's 1976 uniforms that captivated the youngster. The garb consisted of a navy blue and white, pull-over-pajama-style-V-neck-collared jersey with a bold CHICAGO embroidered on the front.

2. When Carter saw the note, he realized the drunken argument he had with his wife the previous night (but could hardly recall in the morning) must've been cutthroat. By her walking out to the driveway where his squad was parked, meant he surely got her blood boiling. For, she hadn't left the interior of their home in months, not even to step out onto the porch to retrieve a newspaper.

3. The last time Carter and Bowers had actually seen each other was when Bowers assisted Carter in the apprehension of a murder suspect from the Two-Six street gang. They shared a laugh, while violating department standard operating procedure, when they opened the rear passenger squad door where the suspect was sitting and handcuffed, and allowed several members of the rival Gangster Disciples gang to "holla" unpleasantries and generally let the suspect know how dreadful his and his family's future was going to be while he was incarcerated.

4. Carter received a $931 Montblanc Meisterstruck Solitaire ballpoint pen — the Rolls Royce of pens — as a gift from a wealthy man named Vito Randazzo. Although Carter never researched how expensive and iconic the Montblanc pen was, he still valued it as one of his most favorite possessions.

5. Kaylee Fearn was the platinum-blonde girl Carter recognized, but couldn't initially remember how he knew her, while scanning over the crime scene. She was an exotic dancer at the Admiral Theater and she went by the stage name "Champagne."

Carter received a lap dance from her on three separate occasions when he used to frequent the strip club about a year ago. He had since quit going to the Admiral after a dancer named Porsche threatened to call the police on him for fondling one night when Carter was on a toot. Though the police were never called, Carter decided it was in his best interests to take his hobby elsewhere.

Kaylee was also quite the Internet sensation on various pornographic websites. She made underground porn — sky rise porn — mostly filming her escapades in a posh loft apartment where the city's skyline was visibly showcased as the backdrop. The Gold Coast apartment belonged to a local business mogul named Win Vedder. Mr. Vedder was a sugar daddy to Kaylee's co-worker and fellow dancer, Ginger (aka Brin Flannery). Vedder was responsible for the filming of Kaylee. And Brin, who sometimes joined Kaylee as her partner, was responsible for the dissemination of the videos. As an amateur porn actress, Kaylee's niche was wearing a pink mask, akin to one a professional wrestler would wear to conceal identity. She went by the name of "Pink Lotus" and her licentious ways netted her an additional $100,000 a year.

Not one member of her family or any of her old friends from back home knew she was an exotic dancer and did porn. Her parents, who lived in the northwest suburb of Wauconda, thought she had a lucrative career in marketing — creating advertisements for Ogilvy & Mather. Most of her old friends nattered over whether or not she was a gold digger because of her good looks and physique, the pictures she posted on social media of her expensive wardrobe and endless supply of valuable accessories, her elusiveness of information provided within her Facebook profile, and because she rarely revisited her old stomping grounds or kept in contact with them.

While dancing, she was always cautious and scanning the faces in the crowd. She prayed she would never be recognized by an old classmate or friend who might potentially leak the news of her occupation back home, which would eventually find its way to her conservative parents.

6. Carter's "thanks" to the Chicago Fire Department Engine Company 55 was partially a preventative maintenance maneuver and partially a sarcastic, backhanded compliment. By thanking them, Carter hoped in mentioning them being heroic in front of the cameras, they might see it on the TV or read it in print and hopefully follow the codes of ethic by not leaking any information (in particular that the victim was carrying a gun) the media might try prying from any limelight-seeking firefighter who couldn't help themselves.

The second half of the "praise" was a cynical undertone only his fellow police officers would detect — a "fuck-you-very-much" for clodhopping over to the victim and doing very little to preserve the crime scene, which was something police officer believed firefighters and EMD's did.

7. Sun Sneezing

It was 1450 hours when Carter returned to the station. Officer Matt Lyons was waiting for him in the hallway between the homicide division office and interview room No. 2, where Jackson S. Schmidt had been sitting in solitude for the last hour.

Lyons gave Carter a manila folder filled with information pertaining to the case. Lyons then brought Carter up to speed with any statements Jackson made and what his demeanor was like on the drive to the station and since he's been waiting.

He, along with the help of a desk sergeant Mark Mayfield, had interview room No. 2 prepped for video and audio recording, and Jackson was being monitored by Mayfield in the panic room*1. Carter thanked Lyons and requested a favor — to fetch him another coffee and Jackson a bottle of water.

Carter walked into the office and dropped his duty bag next to his desk and the folder on it. He took a seat, leaned back and searched the brown, water-damaged ceiling tiles. He felt a sneeze coming on and strained his eyes toward a flickering florescent light and swiftly sucked air through his nostrils in choppy snorts until the light and the oxygen jarred the sneeze loose. After another sneeze, he remained reclined and racked his brain.

Carter interrogated hundreds — maybe thousands — of individuals over his career. He'd seen and heard so much testimony, deciphering whether or not someone was lying was sometimes easier than choosing toppings for a pizza.

He loved the power of interrogation. It was a game of cat-and-mouse, and Carter wasn't a pussy about it. He liked to open the interview with several moments of awkward silence — often staring at the suspect for a minute or two. One time, a 23-year-old man even confessed*2 to a homicide without Carter saying a thing.

His jettatura was better than any question he ever could ask and he would use the stone-cold staring as his approach to Jackson. He was hoping to work a confession out of the old-timer, but if Jackson muttered the word "lawyer" right away, expressing his legal right to terminate the interview, Carter would slap a charge of homicide on the guy — letting the D.A. figure it out, and then go get blasted at a tavern.

He sat at his desk reviewing the documents in the folder, thinking about the questions he was going to ask, until Lyons returned with the coffee and water. He thanked him and struck up a brief conversation.

"Dennis tells me you're a helluva cop," Carter said. "Say's you're the best he's seen in a long time."

"Sgt. Bowers said that? Wow. That's only because he trained me."

"Dennis isn't the type of guy to give you an atta boy, but after seeing you working out there and (points to the stack of paperwork) looking through some of this, it looks like you know what you're doing. And I appreciate your hard work."

"Thank you, Sir." Lyons said.

Carter lolloped and then looked the young man over.

"Say, you want to watch me interview that crusty old bastard?"

"Really?"

"Absolutely. Go in there and pull up a seat. You can write your report afterwards. And if Mayfield gives you any shit, tell that fat fuck I gave you permission. And if he has a problem with that, come and get me. I'll give him another set of problems."

"Cool! Thank you, Sir."

Lyons happily exited the room as Carter raised the Styrofoam cup to his mouth with a shaky hand. The reason it shook wasn't because he was nervous. The first sip of coffee burned his lips. The bit of pain, coupled with the fact that this case could make him late for beer-thirty, made him as bitter as the coffee. He then read Jackson's written statement twice, sipping his coffee.

Before entering the interview room, Carter poked his head in the panic room and spotted Lyons sitting next to a pudgy Mayfield. He was leaned back with his hands placed comfortably on his fat stomach like it was a pillow, observing several small TV monitors that captured surveillance of the entire building. Carter told them he was going in and wanted to make sure the camera and audio were functioning properly, which they were.

At 1523 hours, Carter walked into the diminutive bricked-box room with his notebook under an arm and the coffee and water bottle in his hands. He briefly hovered over Jackson like a lamp in a dark basement. Carter looked up at the humming florescent light hovering over him and had a fierce sneeze.

"Gesundheit," Jackson said.

Carter didn't thank him, opting to force out another sneeze — spilling a little coffee on the floor as he did so.

"Gesundheit." Jackson said once more.

Thanking Jackson wouldn't coincide with his premeditated interview approach, so he didn't. Jackson appeared to be insulted by a lack of acknowledgement, but he wasn't in any position to be defensive.

Carter set the drinks and his notebook on the metal table and grabbed the unoccupied chair that was positioned across from Jackson. He took a long, deliberate seat and then shone his eyes on Jackson's face like a spotlight. Time was about to tell whether or not his plan to get Jackson to chirp first would work.

The energy in the room was intense. Several minutes went by without either man making a peep and when the old man wouldn't crumble under the silent treatment, it angered Carter. He reverted back to another strategy to get Jackson to budge and he abrasively introduced himself.

"Hello, Mr. Schmidt," he said. "I'm Detective Carter Woodbine, Chicago Homicide."

Jackson's gaze was afar, barely making eye contact with Carter as the detective protracted his hand for Jackson to shake it. Jackson was obviously distraught and fatigued, and his hand was as sweaty as his glossy forehead. He appeared to melt in front of Carter's very eyes like a popsicle at a picnic.

Carter decided to switch to a neuro-linguistic programming technique and began to make small talk in an attempt to coax Jackson into opening up. Carter talked about his wife and daughter and what he was getting them for Christmas*3 and Jackson eventually came around, warmly smiling at Carter's Christmas anecdote. They both knew the interview was about to start and Schmidt took a deep breath.

"It was self-defense, Sir," Jackson stated.

"We know what happened has happened," Carter said. "We can't change the past. We can't take it back. But, we can move forward. We must. It's the laws of physics. I know this isn't an easy thing. But, if you're completely honest with me — completely honest with yourself — it'll help this process and help what you're going through and help things move as smoothly as possible. I know you already made a written statement for Officer Lyons. I have not read that statement yet, because I want you to tell me what happened in your own words. It's hard to explain things when you're trying to write something as important as this down, especially with some rookie cop breathing down your neck. Am I right? I imagine things were very hectic back there. Now that you've had some time to reflect on what happened, I want you to tell me everything. OK?"

Jackson broke down. He stared at the floor for a solid minute, but if you were to ask him what color the tile was, he wouldn't have been able to recall. He eventually raised his head and began to speak. He told Carter his entire accord without any interruption. Jackson reiterated he was innocent and that everything that happened did so in self-defense. Carter took notes the entire time Jackson spoke and very rarely took his eyes off the man while he scribbled on yellow legal pad.

Once Jackson finished his story, Carter sat back in his chair, interlocked his fingers and rested his hands on top of his head. His eyes darted back and forth from the ceiling to the old man as he gathered his thoughts. A minute or two escaped without either man speaking. Then, Carter slid the bottle of water over to Jackson. He broke the silence and continued with the cognitive interview process.

"Start from the beginning again," he said. "Let's hear that one more time."

Jackson did as he was told. He advised Carter that he was traveling south to a florist shop to buy flowers for his late wife's headstone.

"Which flower shop?"

Jackson told him it was called Angel Gardens Florist and that they did a lot of arrangements for his church over the years. They even did a nice spread for his wife's funeral and he had been a regular customer the four or five times a year he needed flowers.

"What church do you belong to?"

Jackson told him he was a member of Saint Rita of the Angels.

"Continue with what happened, please."

Jackson picked up where he left off by saying he was driving north on Halsted when he noticed a man running across the street armed with a gun.

"What was the man wearing? Paint me a picture, Mrs. Schmidt."

Jackson: A red hat, blue vest, jeans I think.

Carter: Did you know him?

Jackson: No.

Carter: So the name Bill Dodanno doesn't ring a bell, huh?

Jackson: Is that his name?

Carter: It was. You don't recognize that name at all?

Jackson: No. I've never ever seen him in my life before. Was he married? Do you know if he has kids?

Carter: We'll get to that later. Let's concentrate on what happened first, all right? Which way was the man running?

Jackson: East.

Carter: East, from the west side sidewalk, going to West Schubert, correct?

Jackson: Yes.

Carter: Would you say he was jogging or sprinting or walking fast?

Jackson: Sprinting.

Carter: What happened next?

Jackson: Well, um, let me think ... So he comes sprinting across the street ...

Carter: How far away were you at that time?

Jackson: Maybe 100 feet.

Carter: Does he see you coming?

Jackson: He might have looked in my direction.

Carter: But you're not sure?

Jackson: No.

Carter: What was he looking at?

Jackson: There was a girl walking alone on the sidewalk.

Carter: Which way was she walking?

Jackson: South — the same direction as me, but on the other side of the street.

Carter: Can you describe her?

Jackson: Pink pants. She had blond hair.

Carter: Was she white, black …?

Jackson: White.

Carter: How old would you say she was?

Jackson: 20s.

Carter: So, the male white in his mid to late 40s is running east across Halsted with a silver handgun toward a female white, in her early 20s with blonde-hair and wearing pink pants, who is walking south — the same direction as your vehicle is traveling and you're about 100 feet away, right?

Jackson: Yes, sir.

Carter: How fast are you traveling at this exact time?

Jackson: Maybe 20 miles an hour … 25, tops.

Carter: Which hand was the gun in?

Jackson: His right.

Carter: Is he aiming it at anyone?

Jackson: No. I believe it was at his side.

Carter: So, his right hand would be most south on his body, correct?

Jackson: Yes. I believe so.

Carter: Well it would have to be, right? If I'm holding my gun in my right arm and facing east, my right shoulder is going to be south of my left one (pretends he's holding a gun just as he's describing the events). Right? Would you say that is a correct assumption?

Jackson: Yes. It makes sense.

Carter: So it is safe to say that the gun would be slightly obstructed by his torso if he was sprinting across the street — seeing as the arms usually pump when they run?

Jackson: That's true.

Carter: To verify, he isn't running with his right arm extended outward while holding the gun. The right arm is flaccid, but moving like an arm normally would while running, perhaps pumping with every stride. Is that accurate?

Jackson: I would say yes.

Carter: OK, so what happens next?

Jackson: I'm kind of slowing down because I don't understand what I'm seeing. I take my foot off the gas. And as I get closer, coasting, I can clearly tell he has a gun.

Carter: How many feet are you away at this point — where you are completely certain he is holding a gun?

Jackson: Maybe 50.

Carter: Were you wearing your corrective lenses at the time.

Jackson: Corrective lenses?

Carter: Those very glasses you're wearing on your face right now? Your driver's license states you're restricted to corrective lenses, Mr. Schmidt. Did you have them on?

Jackson: Oh — yes. Yes, I was wearing these glasses.

Carter: All right. Go ahead. Continue with your story.

Jackson: So I look over to the left and I see the blonde walking by herself and I see him running toward her with the gun and I'm thinking he's going to shoot her or mug her or …

Carter: … Why? What makes you think that?

Jackson: The way he was running toward her and there was no one else around.

Carter: When you say "there was no one else around" are you referring to the blonde? That there was no one else on the sidewalk near her and or aside from her?

Jackson: Yes. At that moment … yes.

Carter: All right. What happens next?

Jackson: I start to speed up. I feel I need to do something. I'm an old man. But I need to do something. I'm compelled to. So, I think that maybe the Lincoln has the engine to cut him off before he gets to her. I floor it and as I'm getting closer, he sees me and he slows down his run and turns to me …

63

Carter: ... So now his shoulders are squared to you — facing north?

Jackson: Yes.

Carter: Does he take aim at you?

Jackson: Yes.

Carter: The gun comes up and is pointed at you, correct?

Jackson: Yes sir.

Carter: And when you answered "yes" to my last question, is he aiming at your head or the car — the tires or the engine block? Can you specify where he's pointing the gun at?

Jackson: I think my head. It was definitely at me.

Carter: So at this point, where is he in the roadway? Is he near the sidewalk? Is he smack-dab in the middle of the intersection?

Jackson: He's in middle of the opposite lane. Kind of in front of — I think there's a bar there.

Carter: Are you still in the southbound lane of North Halsted?

Jackson: At that time ... yes. But I was about to turn toward him.

Carter: Why do you think he stopped to aim at you? You said you were still in your lane going south and he cleared that lane going east. Why would he turn his attention to you?

Jackson: Maybe he heard me punch the gas. That old Lincoln isn't quiet. That's what I think.

Carter: Is there any chance, and based on your statement that you have never met or know anything about him — Mr. Bill Dodanno — that he knew who you were and recognized your car?

Jackson: I doubt it.

Carter: All right, what happens next?

Jackson: I crank the wheel and honk.

Carter: You crank the wheel left, aiming for him, and you cross the center lane and then enter the northbound lane of North Halsted — Is that correct?

Jackson: Yes.

Carter: When you honk, what does he do?

Jackson: He scoots toward the sidewalk.

Carter: That would be to his right at this point, still going eastbound on Schubert, correct?

Jackson: Yes.

Carter: Is he still aiming at you as he "scoots?"

Jackson: Yes. It appeared so.

Carter: Is it correct to say that you have abandoned the idea of wedging your car between the gunman and the girl whose well-being you were worried about at this point?

Jackson: Yes.

Carter: You are certain you're traveling more than 25 miles per hour, but not faster than ... what?

Jackson: 50.

Carter: Go on.

Jackson: I'm aiming at him and now he stops aiming at me and is trying to move before I hit him.

Carter: How far away are you at this point?

Jackson: Maybe 15 feet.

Carter: Do you have time to stop?

Jackson: I tried. I locked up the breaks.

Carter: Are you sure about that?

Jackson: 100 percent positive.

Carter: Why? Why would you now try to stop? Wasn't it your intention to strike him with your vehicle?

Jackson: Because I knew I was going to hit him. There's no way he could get out of the way at that moment. I didn't want to plow through him and then into the blonde or the buildings over there — the bar.

Carter: Then what happened?

Jackson: I ... I ... I hit him.

Carter: Was he still pointing the gun in your direction at that time?

Jackson: Yes.

Carter: Did he fire a shot?

Jackson: No.

Carter: You're positive you didn't hear a gun shot?

Jackson: Yes.

Carter: And at the moment you struck the gunman, is it your understanding that the girl could attest that the gunman was, in fact, aiming at you?

Jackson: Yes.

Carter: In your best recollection, is there anyone else in the area when you struck the gunman with your car that could verify your statement that the man was aiming at you?

Jackson: Maybe. There was a woman who walked out of an alley right before it happened. After I saw that I didn't hit the girl with my car, that woman was the next person I remember seeing. I know for a fact, because I thought I was going to plow directly into her too.

Carter: How come you didn't mention this woman before?

Jackson: I didn't?

Carter: No.

Jackson: Huh. Well she was there.

Carter: Can you describe her?

Jackson: She was a big lady … Tall … Kind of fat. Maybe fat is the wrong word. She was broad in the shoulders. Her shoulders were really wide. I thought she was a man at first, until I saw she was carrying a purse.

Carter: Was she white, black, Asian, or Hispanic?

Jackson: White. I think. She had dark hair and dark skin. I think she was white, though.

Carter: How old do you think she is?

Jackson: I don't know, Sir. There was so much happening.

Carter: Do you remember what she was wearing at least?

Jackson: She had a big red purse. That's about all I can remember. All sorts of people started coming out of the woodwork. So, I could be confusing myself. My noggin got dizzy.

Carter: I have to level here with you, Mr. Schmidt … I'm finding some inconsistencies in your version of events. Let me remind you, any and all details that you can remember might help out your situation immensely. If your testimony matches up with the witnesses statements, it only helps your cause. I don't know if you realize this or not, but you're sitting in an interview room of the homicide division in a Chicago Police Department. Homicide means murder, Mr. Schmidt. We take this kind of thing very seriously around here.

Jackson: I know. I'm sorry. It's been a very strange day. I'm tired. My head is racing. It hurts. I'm trying to do the best I can. This isn't easy. I can't remember everything. I'm just so tired. I'm in big trouble. Father Paul is going to be so angry with me.

Carter: I imagine it is quite a jolt to the system. Do you know, Mr. Schmidt, there's statistical evidence indicating that the mind doesn't recall the intricate details of a memory only five minutes after experiencing a traumatic event?

Jackson: No.

Carter: You should see how much the brain doesn't recall after six hours has gone by. Time is of the essence in situations such as these. That being said, shall we move on now?

Jackson: OK.

Carter: So, you strike him with your car. What happened next?

Jackson: I get out. The girl starts screaming. I see the gun. I see the man.

Carter: Was he still alive?

Jackson: I don't think so. His head ...

Carter: I know it's hard. Take your time.

Jackson: His head was in real bad shape. It wasn't holding anything in it anymore.

Carter: Did you try to help him?

Jackson: There was nothing that could fix it. God himself couldn't help the shape he was in.

Carter: Do you think he's dead at that point of the incident?

Jackson: Yes.

Carter: What happens next?

Jackson: I don't really remember. Maybe someone was talking to 911. I think someone said they were calling the police. I need to call Father Paul. Can I call Father Paul now?

Carter: In a little bit. We're almost finished ... Is there anything else that you want to tell me about what happened? Is there anything — and I mean now is the time to do so — is there anything else you want to tell me about what happened out there?

Jackson: I don't think so.

They studied each other's faces and a minute went by.

"Can I ask you a question now?" Jackson said.

"You just did," Carter said. "But feel free to ask another one."

"Am I being charged with anything?" Jackson asked.

Carter stared the man down for a few beats before answering him.

"Not at the moment," he said. "That could change, though. I have to be honest with you, Mr. Schmidt; this isn't a good spot to be in. There are discrepancies in your statements. You should anticipate the worst-case scenario. I'm not saying you will be charged with homicide or vehicular manslaughter or anything criminal, but I'm not saying you won't either. I'll gather everyone's testimony, all the evidence, and turn our case over to the District Attorney. We'll make a recommendation of a charge, if any at all, and they'll make a recommendation on your fate. But for right now, at this exact moment, you're free to walk out of here."

"What about my car?"

"It's in our evidence impound," Carter said. "We'll let you know when you can take possession of it — which could be a long, long time from now. Let me get one of our uniforms to give you a lift home."

"Thank you anyway. Like you said, I'll walk."

Jackson stood up, extended his hand to Carter. Carter, mulling over Jackson's last sentence, stood up and shook Jackson's hand. He then moved the chair out of the way and handed the old man a business card.

"If you think of anything else, feel free to call me," Carter said, and then added a deceitful "We'll be in touch."

The old man briefly looked at Carter's card and then slowly walked toward the door. Before he could turn the handle, Carter stopped him with another question.

"There's one more thing I forgot to ask, Mr. Schmidt," he said.

Jackson turned to him, "Yes?"

"Were you wearing your seatbelt?" Carter asked.

SIDE 1. TRACK 7. LINER NOTES:

1. The "panic room" of the District 23 headquarters was nothing more than a small room where three LCD flat-screen televisions were positioned on the wall under a computer terminal.

2. Jason Temple was the 26-year-old man that Carter made confess to the fatal stabbing of Dino Randazzo outside of Spybar nightclub. Carter sat down in the chair opposite of Jason in interview room

No. 2 and stared at the young man for just shy of 14 agonizing minutes. Unbeknownst to Carter, Jason Temple found Carter's eyes to bear a striking resemblance to his then, recently deceased father, and he was so guilt-stricken while looking at them, he came clean and admitted killing Randazzo. There has been plenty of speculating to whether or not Dino's father, Vito Randazzo, was behind a murder-for-hire-revenge-hit. The case was Carter's easiest homicide he ever solved. A parking garage security camera caught the entire incident on video and with Temple's confession, Carter spent less than seven hours on the case.

3. Carter fed Jackson a heaping scoop of blarney when he discussed his Christmas gift to his wife and daughter. He told Jackson he purchased a weekend spa treatment getaway package at the Grand Traverse Resort and Spa in Traverse City, Mich. The truth was Carter hadn't even begun shopping.

8. When I Wake Up in My Makeup

Jenna "Blue" Trillium*1 sat completely naked in front of a full-length mirror while applying makeup to her angelic face. She mouthed Nora Jones' smoky voice as it quietly filled the air in her apartment bedroom from meager laptop speakers. When she leaned in closer, peering at her reflected lavender-blue eyes*2 and steadying her charcoal-gray-eyeliner, she stopped singing along and couldn't help but become engrossed with the four-inch crescent-shaped scar*3 that began at her left jaw line and curved up high on her cheek bone.

There was an uncertainty whether or not the scar, one that she believed prevented her from landing modeling jobs when she was a late teen, was also responsible for her recent surge in tips as a bartender at Mrs. O'Leary's Cow.

It had only been two weeks since she became comfortable enough to not cake on makeup in an attempt to cloak the trauma reminder. She went through the laborious routine of covering it up — sometimes up to four times or more a day — for almost exactly six years. She often kicked herself for not going to Hollywood and getting a job as a special effects makeup artist. After all, one firm, revealing swipe over the scar with an alcohol-soaked cotton ball would've sealed the deal in any job interview.

Since she stripped herself down to facial nakedness, tips became more bountiful. She was proud to be making more money and even prouder with her bravura to expose the infandous scar.

She slid on a sexy purple thong, boosted her ample breasts under her left forearm — making sure to cover her gumdrop nipples. She seductively emblazoned her profile and her black Kokopelli tattoo seemed to dance on her hip. She grabbed her camera phone, pursed her lips and snapped a libidinous picture of her reflection in the mirror. She checked the photo, found the scar and her naked flesh to be beautiful, and was pleased enough to download the image to her laptop. She logged in to one of her favorite websites, theCHIVERY, and sent the picture to the site: "First time Chiver — Keep Calm and Chive On, "Blue" from Chicago. The weight of the world seemed to lift off her shoulders as she clicked the submit button.

She was basking in her newfound confidence, when her phone began vibrating atop her five-drawer mirrored dresser. It was Tommy. He wanted to give her a heads up and advised her there was a possible murder investigation going on close to the bar, but there was nothing to worry about and he didn't want her to freak out on her walk into work. She appreciated his thoughtfulness and told him she would come in earlier than scheduled to help out if need be, to which he gratefully agreed.

An hour later and now fully dressed, Blue, with her long-legged strides, walked the eight blocks from her apartment to North Halsted. By the time she got close, most of the news crews and cops were already gone. As was the body, the car and most onlookers.

She sauntered her lissome frame into the bar with a God-given gait that belonged on a catwalk. She took off her black winter coat, pulled down the bunched-up long sleeves on her green Mrs. O'Leary's Cow shirt*4, tugged her tight-fitting jeans up by two belt loops while doing a come-hither butt wiggle and started greeting familiar faces with her contagious smile.

There was no scientific proof behind Tommy's theory that by simply taking one glance at Blue's smile, it made the viewer gorgonized and left them in a state of ataraxia. But it was always true for him.

Today, when she funneled behind the bar, Tommy couldn't have been happier to see her.

"So what the heck happened?" Blue said.

"The sewing circle says someone ran a guy over with a car because he was going to shoot someone. But who knows?"

"Anyone know who anyone is?" she said.

"I think I know the dead guy. But I'm not a hundo on it."

"Whoa, that's crazy," Blue said. "Have I ever met him?"

Tommy scrunched his face, squinted and shook his head. Blue believed Tommy with a nod.

Tommy printed out his customers tabs while Blue left, en route to the back office to retrieve a cash register.

Tommy worked his way down the bar advising his guests that his shift was ending and asking them if they would like to close their tabs.

Raymond McMahon was already gone. He was forced into taking a shot of Jeppson's Malört, paid his $18.50 bill in cash, and gave Tommy a $50 tip. He told Tommy, "This is for you. Merry fucking Christmas, kid. See you soon" and then he staggered out of The Cow. Tommy was shocked and grateful and thanked him repeatedly. The same man that only tipped a few bucks here and there in the past not only left Tommy with a lot of actual currency, but he gave him an enormous amount of mental wealth too.

When Tommy stood in front of Maria Rivera, she was good and buzzed, and working on a fresh beer he just got her. He asked her if she would like to close out with him or if he should transfer her bill.

"How much I owe?"

"$32.75," he said.

She retrieved two $20 bills and told him to keep the change. He did and he thanked her.

Blue returned to behind the bar when Tommy was done collecting.

"I'm really sorry about your friend," she said. "That's nuts."

"If it's even him — I think it is — he didn't answer my calls. He was more like an acquaintance. But thanks, Blue. And thanks again for coming in early for me."

"No worries, Tom." Blue said, while chucking a bottle cap toward a trash can that missed horribly. Tommy gave her accuracy an unapproved, yet friendly glare.

"I was actually trying to kill a spider," she said, winking.

He covered his mouth with his free hand, smiled and brought her up to speed on with all of the customers. He told her that everyone was paid up and that the bar was hers. He also advised her everything was fully stocked with booze, beer and supplies. He also enlightened her on the gig The Farrow Moans were going to be playing the next night and encouraged her to spread the word.

"I heard — Cal told me," she said with a meddling smile.

Tommy looked at her smile and thought:

- Cal? Why's he calling her? Please tell me she isn't in love with him too.
- Her teeth are so white, I bet they can't dance.
- Damn is she tall. She looks taller than normal today.

"Get on out of here — I think I can handle this," Blue said, sarcastically gazing over the deserted bar.

"Awesome. I'm exhausted. Last night's show kicked my ass. And it's been a long, goofy day."

"Sounds like it," she said, amiably touching his face. "Are you OK, Tom? You look … green."

"I'm fine," he said. "Just need some rest."

"If I can do anything for you …" she started.

"… Oh, I forgot," he butted in. "Junior will be here soon. Said he's got a surprise for us. Said something about it being hot off the press — whatever that means."

"Sweet," she said. "Good deal."

Tommy's stomach was a clenched fist and his forehead a sweaty palm. His mind was racing with frightened suspense. He nervously ran a shift summary on the cash register, took out his till and walked into the office woolgathering:

- I've got to call Alex and let him know what's going on.
- I need to talk to Dad. I won't tell him everything and he's probably going to be pissed, but I need his advice before Junior finds out.

A minute or two later, he emerged from the office, closed the door behind him, shouted "goodbye" to Blue and sped through the back door.

Blue waved to Tommy, finished tidying up the bar, walked up to Maria Rivera and greeted her with a smile.

"How's it going?"

"It's getting better." Maria replied, hoisting her beer. "I saw a dead body."

"You saw him? What happened?"

Before Maria got into specifics of the crash, she started to unravel. Perhaps it was from the alcohol. Or, perhaps it was because she had an instant crush on Blue the second she walked in and shook her ass while adjusting her pants. She suddenly was overwhelmed by everything and everything was breaking down.

Maria gave a long-winded, sob story of how terrible her life was and how she was a kleptomaniac and how seeing the dead man jolted something in her. She emptied items from her purse that she'd stolen inside the bar. She said she didn't want to go back to jail. She said she wanted to be a good person and she wanted to live a life that someone valued and how she was looking for love and that she was single, if Blue was interested.

Although she was completely blown away by Maria's mental collapse, Blue didn't judge or verbally reprimand her. In fact, she thanked her for the honesty, sympathetically apologized for the lousy day she was having, told her she was flattered by being hit on — but conveyed she was straight, and then offered to buy Maria her next drink. Maria politely rejected the drink offer.

She stood up, looked at the items spread before her and placed her hand on the digital recording device. She thought about picking it up and running out the door with it, but she didn't. She slowly raised her hand off of it, gave Blue a smile, and then wobbled out of the bar singing "Been Caught Stealing" by Jane's Addiction.

Blue scratched her head as the woman walked away and took an inventory of everything on the bar top — the shot glass, the stainless steel tumbler, a metal bottle opener*5 and the digital voice recorder. She placed the bar utensils back in their places. Then, she held the voice recorder in her hands and was confused to whom it may have belonged to. With the bar now empty, she hit the back arrow button on the recorder to the beginning and pressed play. Alex's voice slowly filled the area:

"Today is December 23rd. My name is Alex Hedlund. If you're listening to this, it means I'm dead."

She immediately hit stop and her eyes bulged out. She grabbed her cellphone and called Tommy. When he didn't answer, she left him an urgent voicemail for him to call back as soon as possible.

SIDE 1. TRACK 8. LINER NOTES:

1. "Blue" was a nickname Jenna Trillium's father, David, gave her within minutes of birth. The first time she ever opened her eyes, David said, "Her eyes are so blue! Beautiful and blue! They're like … they're like Blue Jay feathers. Baby Jenna and her Blue eyes. My little Blue Jay!" The nickname stuck, where it was eventually shortened to "Blue."

2. In an ironic twist of fate, Blue inherited "Heterochromia Iridum," which changed the intricacy to the colors of her eyes and made them quite recherché. She had "central heterochromia" which left her right eye with an orange to lavender-blue coloring transfer in her iris and she also had "complete heterochromia" in her left eye, which turned from lavender-blue to green/hazel by the time she was 2.

3. Blue received the scar on her face when she was 4. It was a result of a freak accident when

the family dog, a big, black Labrador retriever named McTavish, playfully chased her around and she accidentally tripped on a roller skate — crashing into an iron poker resting inside a tool set next to a brick fireplace. The sharp point on the iron poker gnashed into her flesh as she fell forward, producing a large amount of blood.

As she lay on the floor, face-first and screaming in agony, the frolicsome McTavish misinterpreted her cries of pain as squeals of joy and he began to sweetly lick at the back of the poor girls neck. When her father heard the crash and screams from the kitchen, he raced in. When he arrived, he saw the dog on top of her and the blood pooling around Blue's head. A terrible, dogmatic reaction transpired, and David started beating the ever-living hell out of the dog.

After the dog was pulled off of her, Blue rolled over and watched her dad punching her beloved pet with everything he had. When McTavish fled, she watched her dad chase after him holding the very poker that carved her face. Watching the violence hurt worse than the pain throbbing from her face. She tried to tell her dad to stop, but she couldn't get it out through her gasping sobs.

It was only after McTavish hid under a bed and when Blue explained what happened, that David was able to fully comprehend what an unfortunate set of circumstances the entire thing was. McTavish and the family's relationship with him was never the same after that. And the poor dog would cower anytime anyone made any sudden movement. Hundreds of stitches and three plastic surgeries later, the scar reminded her of that feeble dog every time she looked in the mirror — and she missed him.

4. The Kelly green Mrs. O'Leary's Cow long-sleeved T-shirt that Blue wore was always for sale at $15 apiece. The logo, which was embroidered on the back, was an abstract and drunken-looking cow standing next to a large glass of beer in front of The Cow with the Chicago skyline reflecting on the windows. It was Blue's personal creation. She drew it up for last year's St. Patrick's Day and it was a big hit.

It's worth noting that Blue worked at The Cow in an attempt to save enough money to one day go to graphic design school.

5. Maria stole the metal bottle opener from the rail of the bar where Tommy had left it, when he and Blue had their backs turned to her and while Tommy and Blue discussed the dead man. For a large woman, she went incredibly unnoticed.

9. "There are no cherries left in the world, only the boxes they came in."

At 1719 hours, Carter entered the revolving doors of the deserted Doggy Style Hot Dogs and went to the counter. He was surprised the restaurant was still open after its owner had just died, but he thought maybe the staff forgot to hang the "Closed" sign.

He stood there, tapping his notepad on the countertop, waiting for someone to greet him. The scent of freshly cut onions tried to water his eyes, but he combated it with a long, tight blink.

He looked around and found the place to be the typical hot dog joint — a red, white and blue color-scheme littered the chairs, tables and décor. Black-and-white framed photos of 1950's rock 'n' roll musicians covered the walls and an old jukebox with original 45s behind the glass of the machine begged to be played. Booths with plastic-puffy seating were scattered about the quaint dining area and metal stools resembling mushrooms were planted in front of a nook attached to the looming storefront windows. A chalkboard behind the counter showcased the hand-written menu — which consisted of hot dogs, brats, Polish sausage and French fries. Next to the menu was a red sign with white lettering which read: "IF YOU CHOKE TO DEATH ON A HOT DOG, THAT IS NATURAL SELECTION. MANAGEMENT IS NOT RESPONSIBLE. THANKS." Carter smiled. For the most part, the restaurant was clean and he couldn't figure out why it was empty, if it actually was open. But he wasn't there to salvage a dying business, what he was looking for was security cameras to hopefully see the owner leaving the restaurant.

Another minute went by before Carter barked "hello!" A toilet flushed in the distance and then a couple moments later, a young man finally emerged.

Carter introduced himself with a flash of the badge. The kid turned out to be Dee, the lone employee working at the moment, and the young man Carter called from Bill's phone at the scene of the accident.

DeVon "Dee" Whitaker was an obese late-teen whose pair of red-framed glasses constantly slid down his oily nose just as fast as his stretched T-shirt constantly climbed up his big belly. Dee was visibly nervous, and he kept tugging the shirt down and pushing the glasses up in a never-ending cycle. Carter couldn't believe the kid could be fat, with the way he perpetually moved. Carter apologized for Dee's loss and then he began to ask him several questions:

Carter: Did Bill have a business partner?

Dee: I don't think so.

Carter: Does he own this building or is there a landlord?

Dee: Umm ... I don't know.

Carter: Does Bill have any family that you know of?

Dee: I ain't never seen anyone come here or never heard him talk 'bout anyone other than his wife. Know what I'm saying?

Carter: How long have you worked here?

Dee: Almost a year.

Carter: How many other people work here?

Dee: Three ... and a cleaning crew's sometimes in here.

Carter: Is there any security cameras?

Dee: We got one (points behind him, near the food-prep area) he got it pointed at us.

Carter: (looking) Where?

Dee: (points again) There.

Carter: Oh — I see it now.

Dee: That shit don't work, though.

Carter: There isn't any more that you're aware of?

Dee: Nope. And if there is, ain't nobody watching 'em.

Carter: Was Bill in any trouble that you were aware of?

Dee: Just with paying the bills. Dude was broke as a joke. Two weeks ago, we didn't get our checks. But a couple days later, he paid us in cash. Even gave us a little extra because he felt bad.

Carter: Does he have any enemies that you know of?

Dee: Like I told the other cops before you got here ... no. I don't think so.

Carter: Did he ever talk about owing money to anyone or anything like that?

Dee: I don't know ... No. He don't talk much ... When he wasn't yelling about this place, he didn't really say boo about boo. Know what I'm saying?

Carter: Is there anything that you can think of, that you think I should know?

Dee: He's a drunk. Well, he was a drunk — I can't believe he got faded. This is crazy. He got really bad after his wife died.

Carter: How long ago was that?

Dee: A couple months ago.

Carter: You never heard him talking to his or her family, or anything like that when she was sick?

Dee: Nope. As far as I knew, he'd take her to treatments, we'd run the place for him, and then when she was done, he'd come here and work until close.

Carter: What about her — did she have any family that you know of?

Dee: You're asking the wrong guy. I ain't never met her.

Carter: What about friends? Did Bill have any friends?

Dee: I'm sure he had some at the bars. One time, some cat walked him back here when he was messed up. Know what I'm saying?

Carter: But, you didn't see anyone ever come up here and meet with him on a regular basis?

Dee: I'm trying to tell you, man — when the guy was here, I did as I was told and that was about it. He could get mean as a junkyard dog.

Carter: Why'd you put up with that — why didn't you quit?

Dee: It's a job, dude. There ain't a lot of jobs out there for a guy like me. I'm in high school — black as midnight — trying to save up some money for college, or for a tech school. My family — we're not rich folk. I come here to work and to get out of the hood. I ain't no banger, Detective. His attitude, I can put up with. A bullet, I can't.

Carter let the kid's words mule kick him in the head. He felt he deserved it.

Carter: I wasn't trying to sound like a dick. You seem like a smart kid — that's why I was wondering why a smart kid like you would put up with that kind of a boss. That's all. I'm sorry if it came across abrasive — as rude.

Dee didn't respond, but felt vindicated.

"Do you mind showing me his office?"

"All good."

Carter walked behind the counter and Dee led him past the food line. Carter stopped and had a look at the camera. He reached up, got on his tippy-toes and felt around the camera like a blind man in an orgy. He grabbed a hold of a greasy electronic cord and slowly pulled on it until it fell free. The end of the cord was completely frayed like a rat used it as chew toy.

"Told you that thing don't work, slick." Dee said.

They continued walking to Bill's office. Before entering the office, Carter paused to look at a hot dog cart left abandoned in a storage area down a hallway.

"That's the mothership right thur," Dee stated, trying to enlighten Carter. "That's how Billy got to where he got. He told me one time he pushed that buggy for 15 years to get in this place. Now, he gone. All that work for nothing."

Carter gave a compassionate exhale.

They stood there looking at the lifeless stand before Dee escorted Carter into the confined office and flipped on a light switch. He made room for Carter to enter by sucking in his stomach like he was at a beach with his shirt off and a beautiful girl walked by. Carter squeezed through the tight quarters of Dee's large frame and the desk, just as a small group of voices were heard entering the in the dining area.

"You haven't closed this place down for the day?"

"I don't know what else to do," Dee said.

"I see," Carter said, crinkling his nose and looking up at the florescent lights.

Dee was waved off by Carter to go assist the customers while he was trying to push along a thunderous sneeze — one that eventually ended with a loogie launching into the unknown. With Dee gone, Carter closed the door. He took a seat behind the desk and started snooping. He sat there in disbelief, contemplating how a guy, who owned a business, didn't have a computer.

He opened the top desk drawer and there were pens and pencils and paperclips and, besides a framed picture of a woman he assumed to be Bill's late wife and the beer-stained picture of Kate Upton in a bikini, there was nothing of interest. He looked over the calendar. It mainly had delivery schedules and mindless doodles. Carter pulled out his cellphone and snapped a few pictures. Then he rifled through the stack of papers, gathered them up and placed them in the back of his notepad.

There was a small fridge on the floor next to the desk. He opened it and saw it contained several cans of beer. Carter scratched his head and flung the door closed, resisting the urge. On the other side of the desk was a cardboard box filled with T-shirts. He took one out and gave the shirt a glance. He saw the logo and laughed. He balled up a large, and stuffed it in his peacoat.

Sitting in the chair, he thought he was missing something important in his hungover head. A minute or two elapsed before he grabbed his phone and made a call to Sgt. Bowers (who was conducting a search at Bill's house with Officer Lyons and a couple of other uniformed officers).

(Sgt. Bowers, inaudible)

"Hey, Dennis," Carter said. "You got anything for me?"

(Bowers, inaudible)

"A couple of cats — that's it, huh?"

(Bowers, inaudible)

"Did you find a computer?"

(Bowers, inaudible)

"No? This is a goddamn Easter egg hunt."

(Bowers, inaudible)

"I'm in his office right now," he said. "Not much here. Not even a computer."

(Bowers, inaudible)

"No cousins or an old dying aunt or … anyone?"

(Bowers, inaudible)

"What," Carter began, "did they meet at an orphanage*1 or something?"

(Bowers, inaudible)

"I can't remember the last time I had one of these and the dead guy didn't have any family. What about the dead wife … she got any family?"

(Bowers, inaudible)

"He has a clear criminal history, right?"

(Bowers, inaudible)

"As far as I can tell, no," Carter said. "This place looks clean, but maybe it's a front for something else."

(Bowers, inaudible)

"I don't buy that for a second, Dennis." Carter said. "There's no way this guy's cleaner than a virgin's honey pot."

(Bowers, inaudible)

Carter chuckled while listening to Sgt. Bowers talking.

"Say that one more time, Dennis." Carter replied. "I'm going to write that one down."

(Bowers, inaudible)

"There are no cherries left in the world, only the boxes they came in," Carter repeated aloud while snickering and jotting words down in his notebook. "How true. That's great. I'm going to have to steal that one from you."

(Bowers, inaudible)

"Well, keep me posted on that, Dennis," he said. "There's a lot of red tape and leg-work and hoops we'll have to jump through if there isn't any family. No one's got time for that shit."

(Bowers, inaudible)

"OK," Carter said. "I appreciate it, Dennis."

Carter ended the call, looked back at the fridge and bit his lower lip. Then his phone began to ring. He looked at the caller ID and it was his wife. He stared at it while it rang and then gave the "jerk-off" gesture. Finally, on the seventh ring he answered it.

"Hello," he said.

(Shelby Woodbine, inaudible)

"Look Shelby, I'm working a possible vehicular homicide right now. I'm the only one in the office today — everyone else got the holidays off. I need this from you right now like I need a fucking hole in the head!"

(Shelby, inaudible)

"Shelby, I can't get into this right now!" Carter said. "When you said 'I do,' you did know exactly what I chose for a career. Wherever you forgot that, you might want to retrace your steps, find it and then put it in your pocket. This is what I do, babe."

(Shelby, inaudible)

"I don't know when I'll be home."

(Shelby, inaudible)

"You can't put a time table on these things," he said. "This is someone's life we're talking about. I can't just say to my boss, 'Sorry, Lieutenant Fenton. My wife needed me to come home so I could hold her hand through life just like I've been doing for 10 years now, because she doesn't like needles, has her spells*2 and can't leave the house or be a productive member of society. I'll get back to that dead guy tomorrow ... maybe.' How many times do I have to explain this aspect of the job to you?"

(Shelby, inaudible)

"I know we've got a lot to talk about, Shell," Carter said.

(Shelby, inaudible)

"There isn't much difference being married to my job and being married to you," he barked.

(Shelby, inaudible)

"No. That's not the difference, Shelby. The only difference between the dead people I investigate and you is that you still have a pulse."

(Shelby, inaudible)

"No! No, I'm not at a bar drinking right now!" he said. "Turn on the god damned news if you don't believe me. Halsted and Diversey. Dead Guy."

(Shelby, inaudible)

"I may be the poster boy for lush assholes," Carter conceded. "And you're a clinically proven insane nut. But hey, I can always sober up, nevertheless, you're proof there's no fixing crazy!"

(Shelby, inaudible)

"You're clouded out right now — like always, and this is a pointless conversation you won't even remember in three hours."

(Shelby, inaudible)

The arguing had met a stalemate. They both remained silent and after a few moments of quiet, he began to focus on the fridge. He no longer could resist. He put the phone down on the desk and set the speaker option on. As he did so, her crackling voice slowly filled the air.

Shelby: You do realize your daughter never came home last night?

"No, she did," he said. "Her car was in the driveway when I left this morning. I had to wheel around it — someone needs to teach that girl how to park."

He swiveled the chair, bent over with his head in between his thighs, put his hand on the handle of the fridge. He was about to pull the door open when he noticed something out of the corner of his eye. It was the Chicago Bulls floormat. There was a slight protrusion to it, like a mouse pitched a tent.

Shelby: Well, she's not here now. Where do you think she is, Car?

"She's probably at one of her girlfriends," he said, getting a closer inspection of the rug. "She usually goes over to her friend … what's her name … Annessa. She's usually over at her house."

Shelby: She won't answer my calls or texts.

"Did you check her Facebook yet? She's always on it."

Shelby: No.

He grabbed a corner of the red mat and gave it a toss like a matador waves his cape in a bull fight — which was ironic, seeing the logo. He inched his sight forward and noticed one wooden floorboard was out of place and slightly sticking out like a newborn's belly button.

"Check her Facebook and I'll give her a call in a little bit."

Shelby: But I'm worried about her, Carter.

He tugged a few more floorboards out of their grooves and there it was — the safe.

"Well, no shit, that's why you're bugging me," he said. "Like I just said, I'll give her a call in a little while. She's a good kid, Shell. I'm sure she's fine."

He grabbed the handle on the safe and said a quick mental prayer.

Shelby: Do you think she left because she heard us fighting?*3

He pulled up on the handle while she spoke, but it wouldn't budge. He cussed under his breath.

"I imagine she did, Shell! Who would want to listen to us screaming at each other every night? I'm tired of it, so I can only imagine how she feels!"

Shelby: Isn't there any way that you can track her phone on a GPS thingy and find out where she is? Don't you have that kind of stuff at your work?

He tried tugging the safe open and again it didn't open.

"FUCK! Shelby, I don't have time for this."

Shelby: This is just like you, Carter! Putting your job before this family …

He sat up while she spoke and reached for the phone.

Shelby: … she's 17 …

"She's fine! You're not. You obviously need a fix. Shoot yourself up! Leave the poor girl out of your addiction!"

Shelby: Go to hell, Carter!

"I'm already there — in the sodomy section. I'm hanging up now."

He kept his word and hung up with a push of the button while she was in mid-sentence. He quickly returned to the safe. As he dropped to his knees, getting closer to potential treasure, his phone started to ring again. He ignored it, because he knew who it was.

He played with the combination, hoping that if he slightly turned it backward, it would revert to finding the last number and pop open, but it was of no use. And he cussed again.

He remembered seeing a screwdriver in the desk drawer and snagged it just as his phone stopped ringing. He tried to pry the top of the safe open with the screwdriver, but it wouldn't budge.

He sat back up just as there was a knock on the door.

"Enter," he said.

Dee opened the door with hot dogs and fries in his hands and a confounded look on his face.

"How's it going, buddy?" Carter asked.

Dee dropped the hot dogs off on the desk.

"Detective Woodbine," Dee said. "I'm going to be out of a job, ain't I?"

"I dunno," Carter said. "But it's not looking good, kid."

"What am I going to do?"

Carter thought long and hard.

"You're going to keep this place open today and then we'll figure something out."

Dee humbly smiled.

"Hey," Carter said, pointing down at the safe. "Did you know about this?"

Dee walked a few feet over and looked at what Carter was pointing at.

"Nope. I ain't allowed to spend no time back here. Know what I'm saying?"

Dee started to leave, but he paused.

"I wish I was more help."

Carter smiled. Dee shut the door behind him as he left.

Carter leaned back in the chair and looked up at the ceiling. He brooded for a few minutes and then redialed Bowers.

(Sgt. Bowers, inaudible)

"Do you know how to crack a safe?" Carter asked while taking a snappy bite of a hot dog*4.

SIDE 1. TRACK 9. LINER NOTES:

1. Unbeknownst to Carter, Bill Dodanno and his wife did meet at an orphanage. Years had expired since their last encounter — a teary-eyed departure with one another at the orphanage on the day of her 18th birthday. They reunited by happenstance, when she saw Bill pushing a small hot dog cart at the intersection of West Addison and North Sheffield. He treated her to one of his hot dogs and they brought each other up to speed on their lives. It didn't take long before they started dating and were subsequently married in less than a year.

2. Shelby Woodbine had an acute panic attack disorder. Soon after the 9/11 tragedies, and while her and Carter's marriage was still idyllic, the Woodbines decided to take a family vacation to Disneyland. For some bizarre reason, at O'Hare International Airport, Shelby's panic attacks first began.

The family was standing in line and waiting to go through security, when Shelby felt her heart race, her fingertips start to tingle and she began to sweat profusely. She thought she was having a heart attack. Carter summoned the help of nearby staff and they whisked her away in an ambulance. After some tests were performed in an emergency room, she was informed by a doctor that her heart appeared to be in great shape and that an upset stomach, or even gas, may have been the culprit of the discomfort she was feeling. She was released a few hours later and Carter elected to take his family home to let Shelby rest instead of trying to board a later flight. They tried to fly out again two days later, but it was there, while standing in line waiting to pass through security for the second time, when the same exact thing happened. They decided to cancel the trip altogether and get a second opinion.

Two additional doctor visits and several referrals later, she was diagnosed with having an acute anxiety attack disorder. It didn't take long before her minor attacks turned into total manic paranoia. For nearly a decade after she was first diagnosed, she participated in hundreds of consultations with psychologists and other mental behavioral health experts to rid her aliment, but it was to no avail.

During said time-frame, she had also undergone an overabundance of treatments and medications, but all the medication seemed to do was keep her locks lopless — a newfound acersecomic, and a highly irrational and depressed woman — that is to say when she was coherent and not incapacitated by a potent cocktail of Valium III, Xanax, Zoloft and Valrelease. As time went on, she was also reliant on various forms of tranylcypromine sulfate, sertraline hydrochloride, generic serotonin-reuptake-inhibitor's, Lexapro, Effexor, Celexa, placeboes and then a variety of powerfully sedating sleeping pills.

Doctors came and went, and they tripled and then quadrupled her medical dosage to combat her extreme phobias. She spent her days in a never-ending cycle of being paranoid about having an attack until she worked her mindset into having one. The only way to combat her anxiety was by ingesting enough medication to kill a baby hippopotamus. But, after all the medication she was consuming failed to aid her with any progress, she was misdiagnosed with having a fast-acting liver — one which was alleged to break down her medication before the receptors in her brain could receive their benefit. Even though she was deathly afraid of needles, her despair had developed into such interpersonal disarray, she volunteered to take part in an alternative approach and medical study for treating depression with injections of the drug ketamine.

When she first started taking the drug, she relied on Carter (who, at the time, was gung-ho with hope that this new approach would become the miracle medicine and his wife would return back to the woman he fell in love with) to shoot her up. But as the cure from the new drug became nihility, he opted out of injecting her altogether, and she would coerce Chloe into sticking her with the needle and pressing down on the plunger. She would say, "Feed me," while anticipating the needle entering her veins and she would squeeze her eyes shut while biting down on the green stress ball she toted around all the time. It didn't take long for them to see she would most likely never return to some sublevel of normalcy.

Before 9/11 and before Shelby's panic attacks, Carter was a social drinker. Shelby's illness and dependency on narcotics, coupled with his promotion into the homicide division and his work, elevated his social drinking into full-blown alcoholism in only a few short years.

3. Carter and Shelby's fighting was close to reaching a boiling point. If (a big if) he came home at a reasonable hour without hitting his regular rounds at local taverns and strip clubs, he would avoid his wife at all costs. He usually would escape to the basement, his man cave. It was there, most often, where Shelby would confront him and become combative. There was a heating vent in the basement

that carried his cigarette smoke, their voices and their syllogisms into their daughter's bedroom. Chloe would lay in bed, listening to her parents scream and disrespect each other.

The word "divorce" was ubiquitous in the household, but unbelievably, neither party consulted an attorney to get the proceedings started — even after years of sexual abstinence took place between them. Secretly, Carter was holding on to hope that Shelby would overdose or kill herself before she could take him and his pension to the cleaners. Shelby, believe it or not, was still in love with Carter and knew there wasn't any other person in the world that could put up with her. During rare moments she was clearheaded, she would have sobbing fits, wishing they both could change their ways and restore their relationship.

4. Dee gave Carter two Chicago style hot dogs. Carter found them delicious and couldn't figure out why Dodanno's business was failing if every dog he sold was as good as these.

10. Super Bowl Commercials that won't be Shown on Television

Tommy Shannahan turned down the radio and parked his noisy cargo van in front of parents' home, his childhood home. He got out, ended his third unanswered call to Alex Hedlund and walked up the driveway. He noticed how tall an oak tree he planted in fifth grade had grown in the front yard — something, for whatever the reason, he hadn't paid any attention to until now.

His father, Seamus, emerged from the side door of the detached, two-car garage with a beer in his hand. Tommy noted:

- Mom must've told him I was coming over.
- He's out in the garage again — oh shit! This isn't good.
- Is that The Stones I hear?

"Hey, Pops," Tommy said, approaching the garage. "Mom said you'd be in here. She also said she's making meatloaf and mashed potatoes for dinner."

Seamus gave Tommy an inquisitive look and told Tommy to follow him. He disappeared behind the shadows of the garage. The Rolling Stones' "Brown Sugar" slightly rattled the metal garage door.

He then heard the familiar crackle and pop of an aluminum can being opened as he opened the small entry door that led into the darkness of the warm, smoke-filled garage — where the glow of a cigarette and the lights from an old stereo outlined his father sitting on a canvas chair.

Seamus leaned forward in his chair and drove his right hand into the open cooler he was using as a makeshift ottoman. As his thick fingers crashed in, it made a sound reminiscent of a cheap chandelier crashing onto an even cheaper laminate floor. He fished out a can of Budweiser and launched it at Tommy like a grenade. It struck him in the chest and fell into his hands like a perfectly planned trick that neither man could see because the room was so dark. Seamus shoved the cooler a couple feet away with a leathery boot and when he did, the lid slammed shut with an inertia-ending poof. He reached over once again and rapidly patted the top for Tommy to sit.

"Thanks," Tommy said, cracking open the beer and taking a seat.

A minute or two went by with only Mick Jagger and a chorus of black women saying anything in the blackness.

"Can I turn on a light or something?"

"There's a flood light plugged in somewhere," Seamus said, pointing to a direction Tommy couldn't see, but lent enough vocal steer to narrow a search. "But leave off the overheads."

Tommy stumbled across several small tools strewn on the concrete in no particular order, looking for the flood light.

"What are you?" Seamus mumbled. "An elephant?"

Tommy found the plastic cord plugged into a socket along the back wall. He followed the cord to the ground with his right hand and coated his palm in a layer of dust. He eventually reeled in the light from a few feet away like a fish. He flipped up the metal cage around the bulb and pushed a button that turned the light on in a popping noise he wish he could've recorded for percussion to a song he was working on.

"I'm surprised you're not watching the Bears game," Tommy said while aiming the lamp randomly about the garage. "They're on right now. I was listening to it on the drive over here …"

"… Don't say a word!" Seamus interjected. "I'm recording it. Your Mother hates when I yell at the TV. 'Don't be silly, darling. You're screaming at an inanimate object,' she says in that snide tone. She doesn't get it. She doesn't understand superstition or how wearing your favorite jersey magically helps them. But, I try to make her happy. So, when they're on, I come out here and play the music loud so I don't hear the neighbors — I can gauge the score by their groans or cheers. I don't answer the phone or watch the news or do much of anything until after she leaves for work the next day. Then I plop down in my leather chair, crack a brewski and press play. I can rip ass and yell and scare the dog all I want to without bothering her."

"How does cheering for them tomorrow help them win today?" Tommy quipped while walking the light toward his father.

"Button it, Thomas …"

"… Does it roll over to next week like a lottery jackpot?"

"Button that lip tight or I'll fatten it for you."

With the lamp illuminating, Tommy observed more of the cluttered garage. Tools, cardboard boxes filled with scrap metal, boxes upon boxes of fireworks, cardboard boxes filled with aluminum cans, small engine parts, a humongous model train table, train sets and other whatchamacallits or thingamabobs were scattered everywhere.

"What are you doing, starting your own firework emporium?" Tommy said while hanging the hook of the lamp on an overhead joist and aiming at several boxes of fireworks.

"Every time I used to drive through Indiana or Wisconsin I had to stop," he said. "They're dirt cheap in those states and you can't get them here."

"Yeah, Pops. Everyone knows that. You probably shouldn't have them in here with the space heater … that blow torch over there … and with the way you smoke, you're gonna blow yourself up."

"Far out. It'll be my grand finale. You can take a box or 10 when you leave, if you want."

Tommy walked back to his father and took notice of the large fiberglass cow taking up a good portion of space. And with the history behind the cow, Tommy wasn't going touch bringing it up with a 10-foot pole.

His phone began to vibrate in his pocket. He took it out, saw it was Blue, ignored it and jammed it back in his pocket. He lit a cigarette and sat down on the cooler.

"The meatloaf will be dry and the potatoes … even she can't mess those up — God bless her."

Seamus said. "Too bad your brother isn't home from his World Tour. He could give her some pointers."

"Have you talked to Kevin lately? I haven't."

"He belled a week or so ago," Seamus said. "He's in the south of France, I believe. Met up with some man who took him in — like an internship. He's learning how to make cheese native to the region or some fancy shit like that."

"That's pretty cool," Tommy said. "I can't wait to see him."

"Well, he can only fool around over there for so long," Seamus said. "His visa's almost up. He needs to get his ass home, find some work — hopefully at a nice restaurant downtown, and start paying off his student loans. Kendall College wasn't cheap and I'm a man without a job*1."

"What are you going to do about that? Mom says you're holed up out here for hours and hours every day. Says you don't even have your phone turned on anymore and she's bringing it to you like she's your butler."

"Well, that's because I'm thinking about my options, Son." he said. "I'm figuring out my next play and I don't like to be interrupted."

"What are you thinking about — what are your options? You're an over the road truck driver. That business is always hiring. That is your option, Pops."

"I've being driving truck since I was your age," he said. "I want to do something fun too. Like you and your band and your brother with the culinary arts."

"What are you talking about?"

"I dunno," he said. "Something different. A change of scenery."

"That's what driving truck is," Tommy said. "That's the beauty of it. You're always seeing new things. Member all the stories you used to tell us about life on the road? You gotta get back in the business. You're good at it — it's all you know, and Mom said you're gonna lose the house if you don't get the show back on the road. You can't sit out here all night, night after night — having a pity party. You got fired — big fucking deal! Move on ... keep trucking on."

"I'm off the whiskey," Seamus said.

"Thank God," Tommy said. "You got to get out of this rut, Pop. They got medicine for depression these days. Go see a doctor. He'll fix you right up."

"I haven't seen a doctor in 15 years — and that was only because I was pissing kidney stones like shark teeth!"

"Dad, you have to go back to work," Tommy said.

"No I don't, Son," Seamus said. "It's being grieved. Litigation takes time. If I'm lumped into the 10 percent of people out of work in this city, so be it. I'll proudly pick up my check. I'm far less worse of a person, than … than the animals that are collecting the dole because they profit from shitting out a kid every nine months and having our tax dollars raise 'em."

"Whatever — I'm not going down that road," Tommy said. "What are you going to do?"

"I've got some tricks up my sleeve."

"Like what?"

"I've been tinkering with writing commercials," Seamus proudly replied.

"What are you talking about?"

"I'm an inventreprenuer. I've got a big brain, Son. I have my own creative side*2. Where do you boys think you get it from? Not Mrs. Meatloaf — God bless her sweet heart — I can tell you that much."

"What kind of commercials?" Tommy asked with a cynical chuckle.

"Who knows football and beer better than me?" Seamus said. "Here's my latest one ... for the Super Bowl. It's a Budweiser ad — speaking of which, are you ready for another?"

"Nah, I'm good," Tommy said, lifting off the cooler and opening the lid.

"Suit yourself," Seamus said, reaching in the cooler and cracking another beer.

Tommy closed the lid and sat back down.

"So, it starts off with these two polar bears — not real ones, but computer-made ones like in the movies, and they're sitting on a globally-warmed glacier, disgusted with how hot the colas in their hands are. You remember the Coke polar bears — just like those. It's a ribbing on Coca-Cola, see?"

Tommy nodded.

"The sun is pouring down on them. They're sweating. They got the sad eyes going. Cut to a super-smoking-hot skinny supermodel in a bikini, carrying a silver briefcase. She's brunette and her hair is blowing in the wind. If you closed your eyes, you could smell her hair. Anyways, along the way, she comes across a broken-down locomotive, right? And as she gets to the front, she sees a set of twin blond bombshells with big jugs. They're wearing daisy dukes and are in their bras as they're working on the engine with big metal wrenches or some shit like that. They've got grease and grime all over their naked flesh. Boom! It hits the audience — they're the Coors Light twins — member those commercials?"

"And twins!" Tommy humored, singing part of the Coors Light jingle.

"You got it!" Seamus said. "So, the brunette gives them a look. She can see how hot and sweaty they are and they need a cool down. Big time. She opens up that mystery briefcase coolly and there's an extreme close up — CLICK, CLICK — the latches come undone. Maybe the code is 6-6-6. The brunette removes two ice cold Budweisers and tosses them to the twins."

"Jesus Christ, Pops," Tommy chimed in. "Is this your mid-life crisis, old-guy-fantasy …"

"… Let me finish," Seamus re-interrupted after a rough swallow. "It gets better. It's this kind of shit that sells beer to football fans."

"OK," Tommy said, shaking his head. "Let's have us the rest of it then."

"So, now the twins have abandoned the train — a subliminal F U to Coors …"

"… Who else are you going to piss off?" Tommy interrupted again. "Coke, Coors, the global-warming people, feminists, animal rights activists …"

"… And they are now following the brunette as they walk on," Seamus continued without giving into his son's queries. "Great time for some slow-mo action there, by the way. Bouncy. Real bouncy. And then, all of the sudden, they come across those computer animated polar bears from before. And they all kind of have a stare down, like a Mexican standoff with eyes instead of guns. They're all looking at each other's drinks and the polar bears are licking their lips. So then, our hero, the brunette, she's fast on her feet and she sees that she and the twins could be in some serious danger here, so she tosses the briefcase in front of the bears feet. One of the bears nudges his friend to open it and the second bear does so with his big claws. The camera cuts to the brunettes face; where a smirk immerges. She even sexily squints. Bingo! Out of the case jumps a wild man wearing caveman type clothes and waving a huge knobby bat like BamBam. The Wildman is like Nick Nolte or Gary Busey or someone like that — computers can make him appear out of the case …"

"… I thought Busey and Nolte were the same guy," Tommy interjected.

"Then Budweiser shouldn't have a hard time casting one of them," Seamus said. "So, Nolte pops out of the briefcase and starts clubbing the shit out of the polar bears …"

"… Parents are going to love this," Tommy said, cutting his father off.

"Stop interrupting me, Thomas. It's about selling beers, not Barbies. And don't get me started about violence. You see the shit these kids play on the Innuendos?"

"Nintendo," Tommy corrected.

"Whatever. Look at football … that's a damn violent sport, Son. Human missiles crashing into each other and trying to rip each other's heads off and we cheer, so spare me. Anyways, Nolte is clobbering these polar bears with the bat. The girls are jumping up and down and cheering on their hero — another good time for some slow-mo there — if you get my drift. Cut to later in the evening. There's a campfire roaring and hunks of polar bear meat are hung over the open flames on a spit. The three gorgeous ladies are dangling from Nolte's shoulders as he tears apart a chunk of the meat and washes it down with a humongous swallow of Budweiser. He lets out a wail. Cut to a real cute baby seal as it's scooting across the frozen ground toward the campfire and making happy seal sounds. The girls gush from his cuteness. Nolte can't even help but smile as the seal approaches adding a, 'Hey little, guy.' He offers the seal a sip of his beer and then … all of the sudden … plot twist! Will Ferrell, dressed in a Navy SEAL uniform — 'Merica! — unsheathes himself from the seal carcass with a knife in his hand and slices Nick Nolte's Achilles tendon — dropping him instantly, and then he beheads him — holding Nolte's head up and out by that wild hair of his. He uses Nolte's big, white teeth as a bottle opener, popping the cap off and enjoying a refreshing sip of Beachwood aged, Budweiser. Then he says something like, 'Man it was so hot in that carcass' the way only Will Ferrell can deliver a line. The girls rush to his side all bubbly-like, with beers in hand. He then explains to them Nick Nolte was a Russian spy, trying to get the secret recipe to making ice cold Budweiser ... or something like that ... I haven't ironed out his last line yet."

Tommy couldn't help but laugh. It had been a long time since he they had shared any significant time together. He was soaking it in.

"They could cast Bill Fucking Murray for Ferrell if they want," Seamus said. "Murray's the greatest of all time. He'd nail the role."

Tommy couldn't stop laughing.

"So what do you think?"

It took a minute for the laughter to subside.

"I think ..."

"Go on." said Seamus.

"I think it would be hilarious to see," Tommy said. "I really do, Pops. But I think you should probably stick with driving truck."

"What are you talking about? It hits their demographic right in the cocksucker. It's got the four Bs — Boobs, Beer, Blood and Barbecue!"

"Well, let me know how that works out for you," Tommy said.

"I got more ideas," Seamus said, feeling around at the ground behind his chair. "Hold on a second."

"Really, Pops — I'm good," Tommy said holding his hand out in a stopping motion.

Seamus ignored Tommy, retrieved a leather suitcase and brought it to his lap.

"Oh, Jesus Christ," Tommy said. "You're still lugging that thing around with you like its Linus' blanket?"

"Son, you never know when you'll lose it all," Seamus said, opening the case.

He peeled back the top and it was loaded to the brim with items. A notebook sat on top and Seamus removed it.

"I don't think it's healthy for a grown man ..."

"In case there's a fire, Thomas," Seamus chimed in. "In case they come to get me — do you see how crazy the people around here are these days? All they do is rob and kill each other. Sometimes just for your Air Jordans. I've got my gun. I've got my phone — who knows if it works anymore, but it's in there. I've got old family photo albums, home videos of you kids growing up, the deed to our mortgage, addresses and telephone numbers, Mom's doctor's number and maps. There's my original pressed "White" album on vinyl. I've got (searching in the suitcase) my knife in here, ponchos, and bunji cords, and survival shit. And I got sweatshirts and socks and gym shoes and a flashlight and matches. I even got my personally autographed football from Dick Butkus. You should smell this thing ..."

Seamus digs around, finds the ball and has a whiff.

"My goodness," he said. "This brings me right back to my childhood — hundreds and hundreds of memories, Son. There's magic in this pigskin."

He holds the ball up to the limited light and reads the signature.

"To: Seamus," he began, "Tackle life to the ground, Dick Butkus."

He smelled the football again before tossing it to Tommy.

"There," he said. "Get some of that. That's what the winter of 1967 smelled like, buddy."

Tommy brought the ball to his nose and the cowhide, mud and grass played inside his nostrils.

"He was the greatest linebacker to ever play the game — you can keep that Brian Urlacher," Seamus said.

"I dunno, Pops," Tommy interrupted. "Them are fightin' words."

"And I was just a knobby-kneed boy, standing there next to my hero while he signed the ball and asked me how I spelled my name. That ball ... that ball preserves the memory, Son."

Tommy read the autograph and let his father carry on.

"You never know, Thomas," he said. "You never know when you got to get out of somewhere and you'll be fucked if you're not prepared. Everything else is replaceable, but some of the stuff in here ... it's priceless to me."

Tommy handed the ball back to his father. Seamus gave the football one last closed-eye whiff, before putting it back in its case.

"You seriously tote that thing in here from the house?"

"Well, yeah," Seamus said. "If I know I'm going to be out here for a while ... yeah."

"You're a strange bird," Tommy said with a smile. "You can't control life, Pops. You can only manage your response to it."

"Let me pitch you another ad," Seamus said, pulling the notepad free.

"I don't want to hear about your Super Bowl commercials," Tommy said. "I came here to talk to you about something."

Seamus put the notepad down.

"What's going on?" he asked in a concerned tone. "Is it your shithead uncle — what's he up to now?"

"No — it's not about Junior. Why does it always have to be about him with you?"

"He's an asshole, Thomas," Seamus said. "We're sitting here flat-broke and that jackleg is living the high life. He hasn't once thought about flipping us a bone. I know he was behind the old man leaving me out of the will. Half that bar should be mine, Tommy!"

"Jesus," Tommy said. "You need to get off it. It's the same old song and dance with you. I bet you if you asked …"

"… Screw that and screw him! I shouldn't have to ask for his charity. He should want to help his brother out. He should come to me."

There were several moments of quiet tension between the father and son. They sipped.

"What did you want to talk about, Son?"

"Pops … if this album takes off like we think it might … You know I'll do whatever I can to help you and Mom."

"You're a good boy, Thomas," Seamus said. "You always have been. I'm proud of you. I hope you guys strike it rich with your music. But, your Mom and me … we'll manage. We always do — enough about us. Tell me what's going on? How can I help you?"

There was a tender moment of silence. It was the first time Tommy remembered his father praising him about being a musician. Then the idea of disappointing him set in and Tommy took a long time choosing the right words.

"You just did," Tommy said softly, not willing to ruin the moment.

Tommy stood up and chugged the last of his beer.

"Grab your blanket, Linus," Tommy said, gesturing to the suitcase in his father's lap. "Let's go see Mom and have a bite of that meatloaf."

"Trust me," his father began. "It'll do the biting."

SIDE 1. TRACK 10. LINER NOTES:

1. Seamus lost his job with Jewel-Osco, where he drove a truck for more than 20 years. His firing happened after a road rage incident. He had gotten the semi turned around, making a delivery

drop-off, and while he was trying to back his trailer from a frontage road, an impatient cabbie failed to reverse his taxi out of his way, which would've been simple to do. Instead, he honked his horn for two minutes.

Seamus lost his cool. He got out of the truck with a tire iron in his hand, smashed the (finally reversing) cabbie's side window out, dropped the weapon, pulled the man from the window, and proceeded to beat the man with his fists until onlookers pulled him off.

2. Seamus's "creative side" was fueled by unemployment, whiskey, resentment toward his father and brother, resentment of both of his sons for working for his brother in his father's pub, and because of general self-pity. He had always been a man who worked best with his hands and he was never creative with finance and proprietorship or knives and culinary arts or an instrument and music. He felt not being imaginative was partially a result of the rut he was in. He planned on writing "The Truck Drivers Bible" (a guidebook to food, bars, lodging and sights), but mostly spent his time in the garage fiddling with tools, small motors and his train set.

11. A Barfly on the Wall of the Pub Crawl

Carter drove south on North Halsted, following Jackson S. Schmidt's exact route. He hoped to visualize what Jackson claimed to see while mimicking the speeds the Lincoln was allegedly traveling.

He intentionally stopped at the intersection of North Halsted and West Diversey, even though the light was green. The car behind him honked and Carter waved him around. The driver gave him a dirty look as he went by, but his face turned apologetic after Carter stuffed his badge out the window.

He waited at the green light until it changed to yellow, then to red, and then to green again. He continued southbound on North Halsted, passing Mrs. O'Leary's Cow on the left, and went up about a block. He checked his speed and imitated Jackson's testimony. He didn't swerve into on-coming traffic, because there was traffic, choosing to continue through the scene, before doing a U-turn about a block north. Now driving north on Halsted, through West Schubert, he found a parking spot a few hundred yards away from Mrs. O'Leary's Cow and pulled in. He thought about the trial run and felt that Jackson's statements of the speeds he was traveling were credible.

Carter entered The Cow at 1804 hours and brushed past Michael Jr. who was on his way out after dropping off a stack of newspapers to Blue Trillium. Carter's plan was not to announce his himself until only after he got a feel for the place, if at all. He wanted to try to understand why Bill would leave the busy lunch hour of his business to meet Tommy. He hoped on an odd chance he'd also get a better understanding of what kind of a person Tommy was by asking some casual questions. But he truly hoped the eavesdropping would produce a windy gossiper who was talking about the crash.

He kept his peacoat on and buttoned, continuing to conceal his gun and badge around his neck, as he took a seat at the front of bar. Carter, no rookie to taverns, glanced around the establishment and found it to be very clean. He could get used to this place. He also took note of a brightly glowing neon shamrock mounted to the wall behind the bar and sneezed. Then he sneezed again. The sneezing caught the attention of the beautiful bartender at the end of the bar. She was reading an open newspaper when she shot Carter a squint. She walked over to him, and as she approached, Carter noticed several patrons bellied-up were reading the same newspaper.

"I didn't see you sneak in," Blue said. "I'm sorry about that. What can I get you?"

It was torture for an alcoholic to be in a bar and not be able to drink. It pained Carter to still be on the clock.

"No need to apologize," he said with a beaming smile. "For the time being, could I get a large glass of tonic with two limes in it?"

"Not a problem."

Blue turned to get his drink and Carter's eyes followed her tight jeans from ankle to firm bottom. Her body was the most satisfying thing his eyes had seen all day, but if he had to make a choice, he would've chose a gin and tonic over a sip from the tall drink of water she was.

Blue returned with his tonic and set it down in front of him. He locked eyes with her and noticed her scar. And if it wasn't for the marking, he could've sworn she was a time-traveled doppelganger of a girl he knew 20 years ago when he was playing ball in the Pioneer League, but couldn't recall her name. As he deliberated over the oddity, he noticed she had noticed him looking at the scar on her face. He avoided staring at it any longer, even though he actually thought it added distinctiveness to an already gorgeous face, and he wanted to tell her as such. But, considerately, he didn't say anything.

"So, what's the good word?"

"Not too much," Blue said. "Well, that's not entirely true. A guy died out on the street earlier today, so everyone around here's kind of freaking out."

"What — really?" Carter said, pretending to be enthralled.

"Yup," Blue said. "I guess some maniac mowed him down with his car."

"Is that right?"

"That's what people are saying," she said, wiping the bar with a rag — a bartenders Adderall.

"Wow," Carter said. "This is a great neighborhood, too."

Blue nodded and fidgeted with some bar napkins.

"Well, I'll leave you be for a bit," she said apologetically. "I'm kind of in the middle of something. But, I'll keep an eye on you or just holler if you need anything."

"Oh, I'm sorry to keep you," he said.

"Not at all," she said. "You're not keeping me at all."

"OK, good," he said. "I hate to be a burden. Real quick — you don't mind me asking ..." Carter looks around the bar, visually pointing out the patrons reading the thin newspaper and continued with his question "... What's everyone reading in here that's so fascinating? Did they find out who really killed Kennedy or something?"

Blue gave an ersatz chuckle.

"Have you ever heard of TheSkinny?"

"I don't know," he said. "I don't think so. Is it a comic or something?"

"No, it's a free newspaper," she said. "You see it around the city — mostly at bars and coffee shops and places like that. You can get them in those red newsstand boxes on almost every street corner. The mag covers the city's nightlife pretty well."

"Now that you mention it, I have seen it around."

"Well," she began, "one of our bartenders here, Tommy — who's also a one heck of a drummer — they wrote up a nice article about him and his band."

"Is that right? I know Tommy! That's why I'm here. I thought he would be, too."

"Bummer. He went home a little early. You didn't miss him by much."

"That sucks," he said. "Hey, is there any chance I could borrow the article when you're done?"

"I'll do you one better," Blue said. "I've got one you can keep. We got a ton of them to pass out — we're really proud of him. I'll be right back with it."

"Thank you," he said, adding another smile.

Blue headed for a stack of the newspapers. She grabbed a copy and brought it to Carter.

"Here you go."

"Thanks," he said. "You know, I didn't catch your name."

"I'm sorry," she said. "I'm Blue."

"Blue? That's an interesting name."

"As in the color ... not the feeling. I think the article starts on Page 9," she advised, walking away.

"Blue, huh?" Carter whispered while watching her saunter.

He had a sip of tonic and hated it. He opened the paper. Blue was correct — the article was on Page 9. Above the article, there was a picture of Tommy smiling at the camera with a pint of Guinness in his hand. The caption under his picture read, "Tommy Shannahan, drummer of The Farrow Moans, enjoys a draught while catching up with TheSkinny."

The article read as follows:

Here at TheSkinny, we like to feature stories about the pulse of Chicago and from the people who pump its heart. In this issue's installment, we caught up with Tommy Shannahan, head bartender at Mrs. O'Leary's Cow and drummer of the up-and-coming and recently signed band, The Farrow Moans. Cheers!

– Crystal Loch

Crystal: So, what's new with The Farrow Moans?

Tommy: A lot, Crystal. Great things! We were recently signed by Fat Tire Records and we just finished up recording our first full-length studio album.

Crystal: That's very exciting!

Tommy: Yes, we're really proud of the album. We're hoping this one puts us on the map*1. We changed some things up — we found the most amazing guitar player in the world, this cat named

Mookie Brownstone*2, and we really feel we're on the cusp of doing some great things.

Crystal: Good for you guys! I haven't seen Mr. Brownstone play yet, but and I heard he can light it up!

Tommy: You have to see the magician live — he's really something? He pulled a future for us out of his hat, I can tell you that much.

Crystal: Of course. All of us at TheSkinny have had you guys in our sights for a while now and we hope Mookie's a wonderful addition.

Tommy: TheSkinny has been a tremendous benefit keeping fellow Chicagoan's informed about our shows and bragging us up. You're good liars.

Crystal: No lying here, Tommy. We give credit where credit is due. So tell us, how was the recording and what's the album called — can you take us through that a bit and when is it due out?

Tommy: The album is called, "Once We Got to the Edge …" and it's set for release in early March … March 4th, I believe. It was an amazing time recording it. We did most of it here, in Chicago, at Windy City Records.

Crystal: That's fantastic, Tommy! Great place.

Tommy: I have to thank our lead singer Cal Slankard*3 for that. He's a man who knows a guy who knows a guy type of guy. I mean, Cal knows everyone! He got us in. The first day we get there, I walked in and was blown away — just completely blown away. Some big names have recorded there. We wanted to keep our album as true to the city as possible, so why not do it here?

Crystal: Very cool. So, what's the vibe of "Once We Got to the Edge …"?

Tommy: Well, it's real bluesy. There's some alt-rock spittle drooling from it, but its electric blues all the way. We didn't stray too far away from the stuff we're playing at our live shows. I mean, our city is known for the blues. Why should two guys from Akron, Ohio, get all the credit for it? And that's not a slap in the face to The Black Keys either — I love their stuff. So, yeah, there's some dirty-water rhythm to it — we shunted some Delta cargo up the Mississippi and unloaded it here. We tried to reincarnate some of the old-time, '50s and '60s, urban-synergy-stuff the guys in the south-side ghetto dive bars were playing. But, you know, we incorporated some alt-rock into it too — our spin on evolving the blues. We think it's pretty rocking and we hope you do too.

Crystal: We can't wait to find out! So, does the upcoming album release mean you get to quit your day job? Are you officially a professional musician now?

Tommy: I can't crash my Ferrari just yet, Crystal! We're trying to get there. We even have a tour in the works. We're hoping to be a part of Bonaroo, SXSW and of course, hopefully Chicago's own Lollapalooza!

Crystal: How awesome would that be?

Tommy: We can dream! But, until all the details are hammered out, I'm still slinging the sauce a couple days a week at Mrs. O'Leary's Cow. I need some walking-around money too, you know.

Crystal: How is Mrs. O'Leary's Cow? I haven't been there in a while.

Tommy: Great times as always, Crystal. You should stop by sometime. Your first Guinness is on me, as always. We have the best Guinness in the town at The Cow. I can promise you that. If the fine people reading this don't believe me, you'll have to give it a try and try to prove me wrong.

Crystal: Sounds like a challenge!

Tommy: And as you know, we're always featuring live music at The Cow. Me and my mates from The Moans even practice there on occasion. Free music, guys! Stop in, anytime.

Crystal: It is a great place to hear music. Thanks for taking the time to catch up with us, Tommy. We wish you the best on the new album.

Tommy: Thank you, Crystal. As always, thank you for all that you and the wonderful staff at TheSkinny have done for The Farrow Moans and for giving Chicago an excellent newspaper. Brilliant stuff — it really is.

When Carter finished the article, he was cognizant there was a burnished smile on his face the entire time he was reading. He forced it shut like he was rubbing in lip balm and he got back into character.

He rapidly finished the last of his tonic water in a noisy slurp and then flagged Blue down for a refill.

"This is a great piece," he said, pointing at the newspaper.

"I know, right?" she replied with a smile.

"It really captures Tommy nicely," he said.

"Sure does. How long have you known him?"

"Funny you ask that," he said. "I've actually never met him."

"But, I thought you said …" she trailed her words off with a perplexed look on her face.

"… I know of him," Carter interjected. "I was hoping to meet him here."

Carter unfastened the top two buttons of his peacoat and flashed Blue his badge. Her jaw slightly dropped from his skullduggery.

"Do you know why I'm interested in talking to him?" he asked.

"It probably has something to do with Alex," she said. "Tommy said he knew him."

"Who's Alex?" he asked inquisitively.

"The guy — the dead guy," she said, but quickly wished she didn't.

Carter's mind raced and he tried to hang her up in her statement.

"I wasn't aware that anyone's names were made public yet." Carter said.

"I don't know what's going on." She said, backtracking.

"Well, what do you know?" he asked in a genuine tone.

"All I know is that Tommy asked me to come in early because some guy died outside of the bar," she said. "When I got here, he was acting really weird. He said that he thought he knew the dead guy. He zoomed out of here and then this crazy woman — a kleptomaniac lunatic — told me she saw the guy die and hands me a tape recorder thing and all sorts of other crap that she's stolen from my bar and runs out of here. So, I listened to the recorder and there's this guy named Alex talking about how he knows he's going to die …"

"… Whoa, whoa, whoa," Carter stopped her. "What are you talking about? What crazy woman at the accident? And what tape recorder?"

"Hold on a second," she said, retrieving the recorder from behind the bar.

"This," she said. "A huge, crazy Hispanic lady stole it and for whatever the reason, dropped it off with me and took off out of the front door."

Carter usurped the voice recorder from Blue.

"How long ago was this?" he said while looking it over.

"I'd say … about an hour ago."

Carter searched the bar and found a few patrons were watching the situation unfold. They quickly turned away the second he gave them the high beams.

"Do you have a back room or an office I can use?"

"It's back there," she said, pointing to the rear of the bar.

He got up with the audio recorder in his hand and walked toward the back. Blue met him at the end of the bar and led him to the office.

SIDE 1. TRACK 11. LINER NOTES:

1. The Farrow Moans had previously recorded a seven song EP titled "Firecracker." The track listing went: 1. Escape Hatch. 2. Louisville Lovers. 3. Slumpbuster. 4. Group Flogging. 5. Snow Day. 6. Love Blister. 7. Shattered Halo.

The band sold the CD for $10 at live shows and it was received with limited acclaim. They also had T-shirts for sale with three different styles of prints on the front and the band's logo on the back. The concert T's were spawned from Blue's original drawings, as well was the band's logo: A litter of piglets surrounding a naked mythical siren in a semi-circle as she stands seductively with her legs spread apart, her head tilted back and her arms out to the side in an inviting pose. At the time, when Tommy commissioned Blue to draw the logo, she was recently hired as a bartender at The Cow and didn't know anything about Tommy's "new" band. Through small talk, while Tommy was training her behind the bar, she informed him that she was an aspiring graphic design artist trying to save money for school. Tommy jumped at the bit, offering Blue the opportunity to create an insignia and the reason was twofold. 1) He quickly became infatuated with the new girl and 2) the band was desperately in need of a logo and album art.

In a strange turn of events, when he told her the band's name, she misheard and misinterpreted it. Their original title was intended to be "The Feral Moans" — a play-on-words for a wild cat in heat and a way to create "pheromones" within two words. Blue wasn't aware of the correct meaning, for Tommy didn't deliver its connotation with enough gusto (offering "think of at it as lustful — like a siren calling in the night" and "it's open to interpretation" and "create anything you wish") and later on that night, when she was brainstorming ideas, she remembered the play-on-words to create the word "pheromones" within the two words, but she misconstrued the word "Feral" and interpreted it as "Farrow." After researching its definition, she learned the word "farrow" meant "a litter of pigs" and she fancied it ironic.

When she finished the drawing and brought it to Tommy (who then showed it to the rest of the band) for approval, they were extremely delighted with the image and completely taken aback with Blue's interpretation. In fact, they were so fascinated with her elucidation — pigs (metaphorically men) yearning for a nymph — they officially kept it as the name of their band.

2. After "Firecracker" didn't generate the notoriety or revenue they hoped it would, The Farrow Moans changed their lineup of musicians. They ousted guitarist, Pedro "Chido" Rodriguez and then his replacement, a 23-year-old topline wannabe named AJ Arient less than a month later. Mookie Brownstone was brought in as lead guitarist and the well-traveled bluesman was the difference maker in the band's success. Slankard got the band studio time and within months, their "Once We Got to the Edge …" album reached Fat Tire Records executives, who quickly signed the band to a two-album deal, polished up their recordings and were currently in the process of packaging the group's future.

3. Cal slept with a musical talent scout and producer named Sophia Mankiewicz. Cal wasn't interested in a relationship with the 46-year-old woman, but he did know her connections within the music industry and he used her as a trump card while the cougar used him for sex.

12. Hobo Spider

Maria Rivera was still drunk when she reached the police station by way of a taxi at 2103 hours. Carter gave her his archetypal silent treatment when she first sat down in interview room No. 2.

He tracked her down with the phone number she provided in her statement to Officer Lyons. It was a good thing Carter called when he did, because if another five minutes had passed, she would've passed out. After some resistance, he finally negotiated her to come down to the station.

Carter reached down next to the table and removed a thick manila folder from a cardboard box. As he tossed the folder on the table, it bounced like smoked brisket on a cutting board and made a sharp slapping sound. Maria looked at the folder and saw the word "klepto" handwritten in permanent marker on its cover. Even though it was upside-down to her vision, it didn't take long for her to comprehend the folder contained her extensive criminal history.

Carter opened the file, riffled through some papers and broke the silence.

"Ms. Rivera," he began, "this is your life."

Maria looked at Carter and then back down at the folder as he flipped through papers. She saw various mug shots of herself, taken at different times from her past.

"Let's see what's in here," Carter said. "We've got some glossies of you (holding up a mug shot of her when she was 15). What else we got (he shows her another photo)? Here are some of your tats. (He briefly showed her another photo) Is that a black widow on your wrist? (He put the picture back in the stack) You're pretty inked up, huh?"

Maria pulled the sweater sleeve on her right arm up and exposed a tattoo of a brown spider perched below a horizontal web.

"It's a hobo spider."

"That's nice, honey," Carter said, never lifting his nose out of her file and retrieving his Montblanc pen from his pocket. He constantly clicked the pen while scanning the paperwork.

She tugged her sleeve back down and found him abominable.

"We've got your fingerprints in here and, whoa, what is this thick stack of oh-my-goodness? This is your rap sheet."

From pinky to thumb, Maria repeatedly tapped her fingers like a pianist.

"October 21, 1994, theft under $300," Carter said making a small checkmark next to the charge with his pen. "August 12, 1995, theft under. August 14, 1995, theft — shit, that's not even three days apart. September 13, 1996, motor vehicle theft — damn, there's 30-something pages in this file."

"Chinga tu madre," she said, breaking her silence. Then she yawned.

"Ms. Rivera," he said, drumming the folder with the pen, "you've got some sticky fingers, huh?

I'm surprised I got my hand back when we shook."

Maria remained silent and her demeanor became more atrabilious.

"Did some time for it too, huh?" he said, squinting at the documents.

"Why does my past have anything to do with why I'm sitting here tonight?"

"A tiger doesn't change its stripes, Ms. Rivera," Carter interjected.

He felt her giving him a wicked glare so he raised his eyes from the folder.

"Being a thief means being a liar," he said. "Instead of using your mouth, you use your hands. But it's the same thing. You're lying to yourself when you steal, because you think it's easier to take something for free rather than earning it through hard work."

"Look, I don't need a lecture on what I did in my past. I've kicked my own ass long and hard for my choices. But I've moved on. I saw a crime today and I helped you pigs out. That's it. I shouldn't have to sit here and be treated like a criminal!"

Carter shut the folder.

"That round of speed dating is over," he said. "I know a lot about you now and I want you to get to know me. As I stated over the phone and when we met one another, I'm Detective Woodbine, and I'm in charge of a death investigation. The very death you had a tremendous vantage point of seeing. I read the statements you made with our officers at the scene and here's the thing — right now, I'm not necessarily interested in hearing you tell me what you saw. The reason why you are sitting here before me is simply because — I need your help. After revisiting your past, I have to be frank with you Ms. Rivera. I wonder if you're capable of giving anything away — like the help I'm requesting. You strike me as more of the taker. But, I'm willing to give you the benefit of the doubt. By you coming down here, it leads me to believe you're willing to help and I appreciate it. That being said, in order for me to believe anything you tell me, I'm going to need to be able to trust you. So, you see this (he picks up the folder and tosses it into a garbage can located a few feet away from the table) it's all gone. It's history. When I look at you now, I'm looking at a clean slate."

She was baffled, but humored him with a semi-smile.

"Let's cut the shit and get right to the heart of matters. I'm going to give you a couple of names and I want you to tell me how you know these people. M'kay?"

Maria confusingly nodded.

"Cody 'The Mongoose' Grantland?"

"Who?" she asked with a muddled face.

"Alex Hedlund?"

"Never heard of him."

"What about his wife, Desiree DeRosa-Hedlund?"

"Nope. Who are these people ...?"

"... Are you fencing with me, Ms. Rivera?" he interrupted.

"Fencing?"

"Are you playing with me?"

"I don't understand."

"What about Tommy Shannahan?"

"Who's Tommy?"

"Oh, come on," Carter said. "Do you think I was born yesterday? You think this is my first rodeo, honey? What's happening to our trust, Ms. Rivera?"

"I have no idea of who any of those people are."

"Let's line it up straight," he said. "I've read your statements. I talked to a few other witnesses and here's what I got — you were walking down the street when a dead man lands practically on you. After that, you to talk my officers and give a statement, and then you just so happen to stroll into a bar and fork over an audio recorder to a bartender. And on that recorder, there's the voice of a man plotting a murder. And now, when I ask for your help, when I ask you to enlighten me with what you know — you play dumb — acting like you're the victim and you expect me to believe that you're being honest with me?"

"I swear, homes. I've never heard of these people!"

"Bullshit!"

Carter hung his head momentarily. The silence in the room was deafening.

"Then how do you explain the tape recorder, Ms. Rivera?" Carter continued. "I've got a bartender, on record, stating that you gave it to her — the same recorder (points down toward the cardboard evidence box) we lifted your prints off of and that's sitting in that very box. If I show it to you, would it stir some memories?"

"Yes, it's true," Maria began, "I did have the recorder. But, I don't know what's on it! I never listened to it! I found it on the floor of the bar after I ordered a drink and then I gave it to the bartender so she could give it to whoever lost it."

"You expect me to believe that too?" Carter said, holding in a laugh.

"It's the truth!" Maria cried.

"You're a liar, Ms. Rivera," he said, jettisoning her yelps of truth. "A big, fat, liar. And you always have been."

Carter dropped the pen on the table and hung his head in his hands. As he did so, Maria quickly lifted her right arm off the table, tucked a lock of hair behind her right ear, scrunched up the sweater on her right arm with her left hand and purposely exposed her tattoo once again.

"You know why I got this tattoo, Detective?" Maria asked as if she was about to show him an ace up her sleeve.

Carter only answered with eye contact.

"The hobo spider is symbol of honesty," she said. "When I first got this ink, I didn't know it. Look, as you know, my shit didn't always smell like roses. But, it was only until a few seconds ago that I realized what (points to the tattoo) this stands for."

Carter sat up and gave her his attention, but stayed suspect to any potential mythomania she might purge.

"Maybe you caught me at a good time, because I coming down from being fucked up," Maria said. "Maybe you caught me as I'm shedding some skin. Maybe I saw the dead guy and it did something to my head. Maybe I don't want my money wasted on the cab ride down here, only to be not believed in. Or, maybe Detective, it's time to finally be honest for the first time in my life. However you got me, you got me — I'm yours, and I'm here, about to tell you things that I've never told anyone — because I don't want to go back to jail and because it sounds like you're not fucking around."

"I'm all ears," Carter said with a skeptical, he's-heard-this-before tone.

"When I was a little girl, we didn't have nice things. We didn't have any money. My mama and papa kept jobs, but the money wasn't enough to put much more than rice or beans on me and my sister's plates. One time, mama took me to work with her. She used to clean rich gringo's houses. I was 8 the first time she took me with her to help clean. She pulled up the driveway to this beautiful mansion! I'd never see anything like it before! Maybe it wasn't really a mansion, but back then, anything bigger than the two-bedroom apartment the six of us lived in was a mansion. We walk in and she tells me not to touch anything. And I didn't even want to. It was so clean and incredible. I remember thinking, 'Why do we even need to clean this place?' It was spotless to begin with. Mama put me on dusting detail and as I was walking around, I see all these TVs. There's a TV in every room! Can you believe it? We only had a little black and white TV with those (she puts her two index fingers atop her head) what are they call …"

"… Rabbit ears?" Carter said.

"Yes! That's all we …"

"… Ms. Rivera," Carter barged in, "I'm sure your sob story has some sort of point — possibly even a spiritual revelation, but unless it ends with you telling me what you know about those names I previously mentioned, then I'm sorry, but I don't care. Time's a-tick-tick-ticking."

Maria closed her eyes, took a deep breath and continued on with her narration as if she never was interrupted. Carter had no choice but to listen.

"Later, she took me to another house and it's the same —— another huge mansion! This time, she had me sweeping the kitchen floors. As I'm sweeping, I come across this door and I open it. I look inside and I can't believe it! It was stocked from floor to ceiling with food! Cookies and sweets and chips and snacks and all these yummy things I've never seen before! It was the first time I ever realized that if you were rich, and you got hungry, all you had to do was walk over to it and eat whatever you wanted. We never had that luxury growing up. The more I helped my mom, the more I saw what people had —— the more I saw what rich people threw away. I did the garbage too when I helped —— I saw a lot of food, winter coats —— they threw away so much perfectly good stuff ..."

"... Ms. Rivera," Carter said, trying to butt in again.

"One time, at this one house, I was dusting in this little girl's room. She had a picture of herself on her dresser and she and I appeared to be about the same age. Mama told me in every house that I helped clean not to touch anything, but this time, I couldn't help myself. This girl had this gold jewelry box on the dresser and I had to open it. I had to know what was in it. I closed my eyes and slowly unlatch the box. As I opened my eyes, the anticipation made my heart race. Inside, there were sparkling necklaces and shiny rings and all of this beautiful jewelry! This little girl —— who was the same as me —— got to have all of this wonderful stuff! And, why? Because she was born better than me? Because she wasn't a freakin' Rican like me? It didn't seem fair. As I looked at those beautiful things, I thought about taking a necklace —— surely she wouldn't even notice, right? But, I remember my mother's words about not touching anything and I closed the box. I wanted something —— anything, from in there so badly, I hurt inside. I helped my mom clean for a couple years, and each day this pain inside of me grew into something much bigger. And that's when it started, Detective. I was like 12 and I couldn't control it anymore. It —— this feeling —— was pushing me to steal like a strange gravity. And one day, I couldn't resist any longer. Do you want to know what the first thing I boosted was?"

"Sure," Carter said, warming up to Maria.

"A Twinkie —— no joke —— a fucking Twinkie! It was the first time I ever tried one. And the feeling was incredible! It tickled my spine and I felt high."

Carter hid a smile under his mustache while Maria continued.

"I kept things small at first —— a few cookies or some crackers. Stuff from kitchens —— food rich people probably didn't even realize they had. Stealing things —— even a cookie —— fed my appetite. And I'm not talking about literally being hungry. It's hard to explain. Stealing filled holes inside of me."

"I bet they were the most delicious cookies in the world," Carter said.

"That's the thing —— you think I would've snuck off to a different room and jammed them down my throat when mama wasn't looking, but that's not how this thing worked. She would've killed me, or even worse, she wouldn't take me back to those beautiful houses if she found out I was stealing. Sure, during the cold months, I hid what I boosted in my coat. But when it was warm out, I couldn't hide cookies in my pockets —— the crumbs would end up all over the floor and when your mom vacuums for a living, lord knows she'd notice that shit. So, I came up with this crazy way to hide stuff."

"How's that?" Carter asked.

"I hide them where no one would think a little girl would hide stuff. A spot, where not even you

106

mama would think to check — I crotched them. I put them in my underwear. Hey, if stuff goes missing, you could check my pockets, but I knew no one would check my 'pocket.'"

Maria smiled slyly and Carter gave her some teeth of his own.

"It sounds crazy," she said, laughing and making a circle with her index finger near her head. "But I didn't fucking care. I was 12. I was poor, sad and hungry. Cookies were as good as things got in my life."

"I can imagine," Carter said, slowly seeing verisimilitude in her character.

"Not long after, I went from lifting food to boosting necklaces or rings or anything shiny — even men's watches. And like the cookies, I had to keep these things close to me — I would jam them down there! Feeling the jewelry rub against my lady parts as I mopped floors along with the fear of getting pinched — what a rush! The feeling would last until I got home and when I could lock myself in our bathroom to finally get some privacy to inspect my steal. And you know what was so silly?"

"What's that?"

"How cheap those gringos are."

"How so?" he asked.

"Say I crotched a piece — and you know how those rich men like to tell their women the jewelry they bought is gold or platinum or sterling silver. Well, sometimes they weren't. And I didn't have to go to a jeweler to tell me so either. You know how sometimes people get an allergic reaction — you know how cheap jewelry can turn your skin green? It's because they didn't get their old ladies any of those precious metals they said they did. What they really got them was copper (Maria starts chuckling). I know this, because sometimes those men bought me a green coochie!"

Maria finally cracked Carter and they both enjoyed a hearty laugh. Eventually, Maria returned to a solemn state.

"It didn't matter, though. I started craving it more and more."

"It became an addiction," Carter said.

"Yes. And it didn't take long before these homeowners noticed their things were disappearing and they start accusing mama of being a thief. She begs and begs — say's she didn't steal anything, but no one believes her, and the company fires her. One time, I looked her straight in the eyes when she asked me if I was doing the stealing. And I said, "No," and pretended to be insulted — I even stripped down to my bra and panties in front of her to prove it."

"What did you do with all the jewelry?" Carter asked.

"That's what was so stupid about it — nothing — I didn't do anything with it! I hide it behind a loose brick on the side of our apartment. 22 bricks across, three up from the bottom — I'll never forget. I kept all that stuff as trophies. It wasn't like I could walk around the apartment wearing bling or around my neighborhood — it would catch you a whoopin' and the bangers would snatch it."

"You didn't think to pawn it, huh?" Carter asked. "You could've bought a ton of Twinkies with the money."

"I didn't think at all back then. If I wanted a Twinkie, I took it."

"I see."

"One time, my school took me and my classmates on field trip to the burbs. You know how they always take poor, city kids out to the sticks to give them culture — to see things other than concrete and violence, and to see a world outside of shit? They took us to this little farm where we learned about animals and flowers and how to grow vegetables. There was a little red barn next to a big red barn, and inside the little red barn they had a lot of insects — aquarium after aquarium filled with creepy–crawly stuff. Most of the kids in my class screamed at the spiders they showed us, but not me. I thought they were so neat. I wanted to hold them. The guide taught us about tarantulas, brown recluses, the wolf spider and other furry critters. But you know what … this one spider really caught my attention."

Maria turned her wrist over on the table and Carter took notice.

"The Tegenaria ag — ag — ah shit. (Rubs her head) I'm still too tipsy to remember its science name*1 — but I used to know it. It's called (she inspects the tattoo) the funnel web spider or … the hobo spider."

"Why was it so fascinating?" Carter asked.

"Cause the hobo spider is a loner like me, Detective. It doesn't wait proudly on its web, showing off. The hobo spider hides at the bottom of their amazing webs — in cracks, or in tree hollows, or in bushes. They're so cool, you know? They're like beautiful art — their webs. Have you ever been to a mall and seen little kids rolling pennies down those big, plastic circles, where it takes the penny a long time to go around and around until it finally falls into the tiny hole at the bottom?"

"I know what you're talking about."

"That's like their webs," Maria said. "The hobo spider waits until a penny starts rolling around her web, and then she crawls out very fast, grabs her prey and drags it down the funnel before anyone notices anything went missing. It's amazing — the boost. When the tour continued on, I snuck back in the little red barn, stole a hobo spider and I brought it home for pet."

She slowly contoured her wrists from side to side so they both could inspect the tattoo further.

"Then, I built it a home and started studying the hobo spider. I copied it and if you left something near my nest, I took it. It was fucking mine! I took anything to feed my hunger. It was a new me. It gave me a sense of identity. Before, I was only the big sister of triplets. I might as well have been an only child. But then, I knew how to get things on my own. That way, my baby sisters could get more food and clothes and so mama didn't have to spend more on me. I got really good at pickpocketing, shoplifting — you name it I stole it. But then these things — cameras — start going up everywhere and I begin to get caught. My mother was devastated, because she finally knew it was me all along, and she kicked me out of the apartment. I lived on the streets, trying to survive, and people saw me as a piece of shit. It doesn't take long before all the stores see me coming a mile away — even if I put on a wig or makeup or fake mustaches and dress like a man — they knew it was me. I was blacklisted from most department stores on Michigan Avenue — the good places. I quit a couple of times — the stealing. To have the things I craved — those shiny things — I dated girls. That way, I could wear my girlfriend's necklaces and rings and bracelets. Not too many men buy nice jewelry for a girl my size. Girls would satisfy the urges for a little while, but I would always go back to boosting. Believe it or not, the stealing started making me sad. And when I got sad, I began to eat … a lot."

They shared silence.

"The hobo spider is me, as honest as I can be, Detective."

He studied her.

"I've told you some very private things. Things that I've kept in my heart — in my jewelry box. Things I never told anyone before, Detective. So, please, believe me when I say this … I don't know any of those peoples you asked about."

Before Carter could reply, Maria reached behind her right ear, retrieved his Montblanc Meisterstruck Solitaire pen (which she had swiped off the table without detection and had been hiding behind her flowing hair) and handed it to him.

"Ta-da!"

Carter was dumbfounded, for he hadn't even noticed it was missing.

"For my next trick, I will change a tiger's stripes."

SIDE 1. TRACK 12. LINER NOTE:

1. The genus name for the hobo spider is Tegenaria agrestis.

13. Peeling Pink Lotus Petals

At 2135 hours, Carter Woodbine was walking Maria Rivera out of the lobby doors at District 23 headquarters when Kaylee Fearn was walking in. The women exchanged a wait-a-second-I-know-you glance as they brushed past, but no words were exchanged. Carter mentally noted their acquaintance.

He greeted Kaylee with an extended hand.

"Kaylee?"

She handed him pulled taffy and nodded.

"I'm Detective Woodbine, Chicago homicide," he said, releasing his grip and showing her the door. "After you."

Kaylee, wearing a denim miniskirt, knee-high black designer boots and a black leather jacket, walked in front of Carter as they strolled through the lobby. They were buzzed through the door of the station by the CSO Mark Adams (who gave Carter an "ooh la la" face when he saw Kaylee), before they shuffled to the elevator. He pressed the up arrow and they waited.

"Thank you for coming down. I appreciate it."

"Not a problem."

"I know you gave a statement earlier today at the scene," Carter said. "But, I just have a few more questions for you, if that's OK?"

"Sure."

The elevator doors opened and he gestured for her to step in with a flopping open hand. As the doors shut, her perfume constricted the tight quarters and it instantaneously jogged his memory. It immediately left him with the cogitation she was a stripper.

"Say, do I know you from somewhere?" he said with a faux grin.

"I don't think so," she said in a convincing way.

"Man, I feel as though I've seen you before."

"I'm pretty sure I'd remember you," she said. "Since like, this is my first time I've ever been to a police station."

The elevator reached the third floor and opened. Carter encouraged Kaylee to step off first.

"You're probably right," Carter said, taking the lead and walking toward interview room No. 2. "Maybe you have a twin out there. They say we all do. I used to get that with Tom Selleck back when I was your age."

"Who?"

110

"Tom Selleck," he replied, letting a disbelieving, closed-mouth blast of air shoot through his nostrils. "You don't know who Tom Selleck is?"

"Sorry," Kaylee said with a shrug.

Carter nasally laughed again and almost shot a snot rocket out of his nose.

"You've confirmed it: I really am getting old."

They reached and entered interview room No. 2 and he encouraged her to take a seat opposite him as he plopped down behind the table.

As he bent over and reached into the evidence box, (which was still on the floor from the previous interview with Maria) he noticed her legs. He wanted to remain professional, but he couldn't contain himself. He tried sneaking a peek up her skirt while grabbing a manila folder, but she crossed her legs just in time. Sensing he'd been had, he quickly looked into the box and she pretended not to notice his kinkiness by looking up at the ceiling. He sat up, trying not to seem guilty, threw the folder on the table and retrieved the Montblanc pen from his pocket.

"OK, I hope you're going to be more of a help to me than Ms. Rivera was — you do remember Ms. Rivera, correct?"

"The woman downstairs?"

"Yes," he said.

"Yes," she said, twirling her big hair with a manicured finger.

"Say, what did she tell you about the incident? I know you talked to each other at the bar after it happened."

"She, like, pretty much didn't see anything," she said.

"Do you believe her?"

"Um, yeah, I mean, I don't even really remember seeing her at the accident," Kaylee said. "Only at the bar."

He scratched his head before rifling off another question, "Do you remember seeing her with a little audio recording device at any time?"

"A what?"

"Do you remember seeing a little silver — wait ..."

He cut himself off, reached into the evidence box — purposely avoiding looking anywhere near her legs, retrieved the audio recorder, which was wrapped in a clear plastic evidence bag.

"... Do you remember seeing this at all yesterday?"

"Um —— no," Kaylee said.

He tossed the recorder back into the box.

"So, let's go back to the incident, all right?"

"All right," Kaylee said.

"In situations like the one you were in this morning, 20 witnesses are going to recall 20 different things on what they think they saw. It's the way the brain stores information. It picks and chooses what it thinks is important and then, about 30 seconds later —— poof! —— it erases what it thinks isn't important. It has to. If it didn't, it would overwork itself. Can you imagine if the brain didn't have the ability to junk things? The brain is an amazing thing if you think about it. I mean, it even named itself. I think that's captivating. But, it has its flaws too —— especially when it sees something traumatic or unusual. 20 different witnesses are going to have inconsistencies to what they each saw. And there's going to be some embellishing too. The brain wants to be a big help, but it can jumble what it thinks it sees. But, the one thing each witness is going to share is a single thread of fact. It's my job to weave all of the facts together and create a strong rope. Since you had the best vantage point to witness this unfortunate situation, I'm counting on what you're about to tell me to be the thickest thread. The most important one. So, please, try your hardest to tell me everything that you can remember."

"OK," Kaylee said.

"Give yourself a minute if you need."

Kaylee fidgeted with her hair and was ready to go.

"I was walking on the sidewalk …"

"… Where were you going?"

"To get, like, a massage and maybe my nails done at Spacio," she said. "I had a gift card."

"Where's that place at?"

"It's, like, right there," she said. "Like, on the other side of the street."

"OK," he said. "So, then what happened?"

"I'm like, looking across the street, and I see the place is like, out of business, and I'm all oh poopy because I had like, $200 worth of gift cards on me."

"Got it," he said. "What happened next?"

"Like, I heard a car honk," said Kaylee. "I turn and I saw a man walking toward me with a hand in his vest pocket and then I saw like this big blue car going right for him. Then, I saw the guy had, like, a gun and less than a second later the car like, crushed him."

"You're positive you saw the man pull out the gun?" Carter said with a scowl.

112

"Yes," Kaylee unconvincingly said. "I'm pretty sure."

"Pretty sure or you're positive?"

"I'm, like, totally positive," she deadpanned.

"Did you know the man with the gun?"

"I've never seen him before in my life," Kaylee said.

"He wasn't, maybe, some guy who ..." Carter rethought the question he was about to ask and went down a different path instead. "... Has anything weird or strange or unusual happened to you recently that you're aware of?"

"Not that I can think of."

"You're a pretty girl — no new secret admirers or ..." he began to ask, but was cut off.

"... No," she interrupted firmly.

"OK," Carter replied, scratching his scalp yet again. "So, what do you think happened?"

"Like, I honestly don't know," Kaylee said. "Best guess, maybe those two guys had like a disagreement or something."

"What makes you think they had a beef?"

"I don't know," she said. "Maybe the old guy was after him for something. Why else would he have a gun if, like, he wasn't afraid of someone?"

"That's a good question," Carter said with an impressed look on his face. "That's what I've been asking myself too."

The room went silent. Kaylee, feeling the heat of being questioned, unstrapped her leather jacket to cool off and revealed her surgically enhanced breasts behind a tight white T-shirt. Carter had a difficult time making eye contact.

"Did the old guy say anything after it happened?"

"Not that I can remember," she said. "But, like, everything was so crazy — I don't really remember much afterwards. I didn't want to be around there anymore. Like, he died a couple of feet from me. It was the scariest thing I had ever seen before."

"I can imagine," Carter said empathetically for the sake of the interview, not because he actually cared.

They both drank in the quiet again before Carter jumped back in.

"Is there anything else you can think of that can help me figure out what the hell happened out there?"

"I'm sorry, like, I don't really think so," Kaylee said. "It all happened so fast."

She looked down, sadly. Carter looked her over, covered his mouth with his hand and swiped the remnants of crusted coffee off his lips. He looked up at the camera, gestured the symbol for slitting ones throat — insinuating Sgt. Mayfield cease recording the interview. Then he stood up.

"Well, Ms. Fearn," he said. "Thank you. You're free to go."

She stood up.

"Shall we?" Carter said with an open hand pointed toward the door.

She promptly walked toward the door, gained a fast three-foot lead on him, and just as she grabbed the handle, he held her up.

"Oh, Kaylee," he said. "I almost forgot. What was it that you said you did for a living?"

"I didn't," Kaylee said with her back to him.

"Huh. That's strange. Then how did I know you're a stripper?"

She shot him a nasty glower over her right shoulder.

"Just because I don't wear mom jeans and granny panties — probably like your wife does — it doesn't mean I'm a stripper, you fucking pervert. I saw you checking out my goods!"

"You don't leave much to the imagination, in here, or at the Admiral Theater, where you cocktease, now do you Champagne?"

Kaylee's mouth was left for the flies and her gum almost fell out.

"C'mon," he said. "You don't remember me? You don't remember this face?"

Kaylee stood silent with her hand squeezing the doorknob tightly.

"Ouch. We've practically bumped uglies, you and me. I haven't been dry-grinded like that since high school — I'm surprised my pants didn't start on fire from zipper sparks."

She hung her head, beaten. He let his words sink in for a few beats before his tone went from a sarcastic one to a grim one.

"Stop reverse cowgirling me, turn around and look me in the eyes."

She slowly spun and her focus never left the floor. Once they were square, she gave him the doughy part of her eyeballs.

"Are you 100 percent sure you didn't know the dead man?"

"I — I — I swear I never saw him before," she answered with a trembling voice.

"You're sure he wasn't some psychotic stalker regular of yours?"

"Yes!"

"So, if I go into the Admiral and start showing your co-dancers some pictures of the dead guy, you promise none of them are going to tell me they know him?"

"I totally promise!"

"What about the old man — the driver?"

"Like, what about him?"

"Is he one of your regulars? Did you and him have something worked out?"

"I've never seen him before either!"

"Why can't — why don't I ..." Carter intentionally trailed off his question when he thought about his cacology. He regrouped, clutched his pen*1, and chose a better set of words before continuing. "... Ms. Fearn, Kaylee, put yourself in my shoes for a second — pretend they're 12-inch fucking stilettos if you want to — I'm trying to solve a death investigation and the three people involved are two widowers and an untrustworthy stripper. And you're trying to tell me the whole thing is ... is one big coincidence?"

Kaylee was at a loss for words.

"Let me show you out," Carter said, rushing past her.

SIDE 1. TRACK 13. LINER NOTES:

1. After Carter's interview with Kaylee concluded, Carter raced to the "panic room" and had Mayfield replay the tape of him and Maria's interview. In particular, he was looking for the pen swipe.

Her sleight of hand was nothing short of astonishing. It took Mayfield several tries to slow the video footage's speed down enough for them to finally catch her — her left wrist snapping outward like a blackjack dealer, grasping the pen off the top of the desk in a blur and then stowing it behind her right ear in less than a third of a second, before calmly tucking a strand of hair behind her ear and showing him her wrist.

14. The Legend of Chetan "Hawk" Littlejohn: Cheating the Baseball Game of Life

At 2154 hours, Carter sat at his desk with his back turned to the computer monitor and faced the dry-erase board mounted to the wall. A timeline of events and the names of people of interest were scribbled on the glassy facade in black marker, like it was a movie storyboard only a director could piece together.

He just got off the phone with his boss, one Lieutenant Harrison Fenton. He insisted to Fenton he didn't need any assistance and advised his superior that he was close to solving the case and he would email him his preliminary report later in the evening.

Next to the dry-erase board was a corkboard. Pinned to the board were photos of each person of interest — retrieved from either their driver's licenses or a previous booking photo.

Under both boards was a wooden table, housing heaps of manila folders, scattered paperwork and evidence. On the table was:

● Three handguns retrieved from Bill Dodanno's safe*1 — each had been previously removed from the separate burlap sacks they were found in, dusted for fingerprints and sealed in their own individual clear-plastic evidence bags. Nine prints were lifted from the guns and ran through the fingerprint data system machine. Once entered, the system compared the retrieved prints to any prints previously entered and then stored in the main database. Officer Lapp would brief Carter if the system hit on any and or all matches.

● The Glock 34 GEN 4 9mm handgun found at the crime scene, confined to its own clear-plastic evidence bag.

● A manila folder with 67 pictures of the crime scene photographed by Lapp.

● A manila folder with the preliminary investigation report from Lapp.

● A manila folder with the preliminary investigation report from accident investigator, Detective Stuart Grimsen.

● A manila folder with the preliminary investigation report from Officer Matt Lyons.

● A manila folder with the supplementary report to Lyons's preliminary report, written and signed off by Sgt. Dennis Bowers.

● A manila folder with the preliminary investigation report from Chicago Fire Department Paramedic Vance Durham.

● There were also nine additional manila folders stacked in two piles. Each folder contained paperwork of any police contacts or information pertaining to everyone who was connected to the case. On the front cover of each, Carter gave each person of interest a moniker, labeled in black marker.

Pile No. 1
Bill Doddanno = DEAD GUY
Jackson S. Schmidt = SUSPECT

Alex Hedlund = GUITAR PLAYER
Desiree DeRosa-Hedlund = JUNKIE WIFE
Cody Grantland = THE MONGOOSE

Pile No. 2
Tommy Shannahan = DRUMMER BOY
Blue Trillium = CAT EYES
Maria Rivera = KLEPTO
Kaylee Fearn = STRIPPER

● Also on the table was the Sony digital audio recording device and Bill Dodanno's cellphone. Both items were secured in a clear-plastic evidence bags.

It was getting late. The midnight oil had become charbroiled sludge. Carter was closing in on burnout and looking forward to blacking out with drinks. He had already left three messages on Tommy's voicemail and he had a feeling Tommy was buying some time. Carter couldn't understand exactly why he was ducking him — although he had his suspicions.

While looking at the board and the cast of characters, Carter got up from his chair, walked a few feet over, picked up the audio recording device, removed it from the evidence bag and replayed Alex Hedlund's audio recording for the 11th time. He was trying to pick up on any small detail he may have missed. As the last seconds of Alex's recording wound down, Carter's cellphone rang. It was his wife again and he ignored answering her call for the eighth time since they last talked in Bill's office.

He had two options — sleep at the police department or take his work home with him. As much as he hated the thought of fighting with his distraught and cantankerous wife, he chose the latter, only because his drink-boner was still hard.

He called Sgt. Mayfield from the in-house telephone and advised him to collect the case evidence in his office and then secure it in the evidence vault. Upon hanging up with Mayfield, he loaded several of the manila folders and Alex Hedlund's audio recorder into a cardboard box. He situated his duty bag, notebook and some other odds and ends as Mayfield shuffled into the room pushing a metal cart.

Carter signed off on the evidence after Mayfield took inventory. He got a copy of the inventory receipt, threw on his peacoat, hoisted the duty bag strap around his shoulder, grabbed the box, told Mayfield he should tuck in his uniform shirt and rushed out of the door. It was 2209 hours.

At 2216 hours, Carter parked his unmarked squad in front a convenient store. He wouldn't put it past the wife to have already opened and dumped out every last beer in the house*2, so he purchased a 12-pack of Old Style, a bottle of Dr. McGuillicuddy's Intense Mentholmint and a pack of smokes. He wouldn't have the time tonight to drink all the beer he normally would and wished he could, but he hoped the McGuillicuddy's would help get him to sleep. Menthol schnapps was about the only hard stuff his paper-belly*3 could handle these days.

At 2219 hours, Carter cracked open his first beer and finished nearly half of the can in mere gulps. It was cold, fizzy, a bit tinny and sweet. He blasted the car horn and yelled, "That's what I'm talking about!"

At 2221 hours, he finished the beer and tossed it out the passenger-side window as he turned on to his street. Seconds later, he killed the headlights and swerved around his daughter's red 2001 Honda Civic. Navigating the narrow driveway was a pain in his ass ever since the day they bought their daughter the used jalopy. She could never park it to his satisfaction and it made him wonder how she passed her driver's test.

Each time this parking dilemma happened, he would curse himself for not cleaning out the crap in the garage that prevented them from parking two cars in there. Then he'd curse his daughter for having her mother's DNA when it had anything to do with automobiles.

After finally parking and turning the engine off, he realized he forgot to call his daughter like he told his wife he would. He justified his neglect by being extremely busy on the case. After seeing her car in the driveway, he was content with knowing she finally returned home. Having another thing to worry about was the last thing he needed to worry about.

He stuffed the beer and schnapps into his duty bag and flung the strap over his shoulder. He grabbed the cardboard box, hit the door lock button with his elbow, and hip-checked the door shut as quietly as possible, giving it just enough torque to get it to latch. He stood there looking at his dark, two-story brownstone, waiting for a light to turn on or a witch on a broom to fly out of one of the front windows. A minute vaporized with no sign of movement inside. He painstakingly wobbled everything he had up to the front door. While standing on the front steps, he prayed his wife wasn't on the other side of the door.

The door was miraculously unlocked. He gave it a quiet turn, slightly pushed it open and put his ear to the crack. He heard nothing and assumed Shelby had knocked herself out on meds. He continued to stealthily creep inside his own home like a cat burglar.

He took an immediate right, found the handrail to the basement steps and was about to tiptoe down when one of the cans of beer fell from his duty bag. It bounced and took a muffled tumble down the carpeted stairs. While he listened for footsteps, he paused at the threshold with an ear tilted to the ceiling and clutching the duty bag. Twenty seconds went by, and he heard nothing.

With the coast clear, he pranced down the steps, trying not to drop any more beer. Once he reached the carpet entering his White Sox memorabilia-laden man cave, he flipped on the light switch, thinking he was home free.

But there she was — sitting in his favorite recliner chair naked and reaching for anything to cover herself up with. She was breathing heavily, and her face was flushed red with embarrassment — no, no, it was red from physical activity — Carter quickly corrected his thinking. A sweet and sweaty, raw-skinned scent clung to the air and Carter instantaneously identified the stench of sex. A shriek shot out of his mouth, and then a clawing-climbing sound was heard scurrying off in the dark distance near the window well where salamanders went to die.

Carter's duty bag and jaw dropped at the exact time. Instincts kicked in and he reached for the gun on his hip. The cold barrel was unexpected and his index and middle fingers slightly jumped back. He looked at her in astonishment. He tried to speak, but nothing came out. More clawing and climbing was heard in the shadows, but before Carter could react, a window screeched free from its latches and a set of bare feet appeared to levitate into thin air and out the window well.

His eyes went back to her. There were tears. They were his, the eyes he was looking at —— glacier-blue, majestic and frigid. But the tears didn't fall from those he stared at. The glaciers melting were his own. His naked daughter, Chloe, shielded only by poor lighting and a pair of balled-up jeans, was now laughing at the sight of him. She had never seen him cry before and her chortling was not a derivative of nervousness, but merely retribution. He was taken aback by her snickering, as if though he was standing on a battlefield, but couldn't recall ever enlisting for war.

He turned to his left, raised his right hand to his right eye forming a curve like an easily spooked thoroughbred wears blinders and lowered his head toward the carpet.

"Get the fuck out of here, Chloe!"

She gathered up her clothes and swiftly brought them up to her torso.

"You don't want to talk about this, Dad?" she said in a baiting tone.

"I don't ever want to think about this again, much less talk about it!" he yelped, without giving her question a chance to register.

She slowly walked past him, whispered, "Goodnight, Daddy."

"Get the fuck out of here, Chloe!" he said through grinding teeth. "You make me sick."

She took her time going up the stairs and once she reached the top of the stairs, he set the cardboard box down, reached over to the duty bag, ripped a beer free from the box, cracked open the can and pounded down half of the Old Style in few giant gulps.

As he stood there, fighting to keep the beer down in his stomach, but pushing a burp up at the same time, he couldn't believe what just happened. He clawed at his itchy head and grimaced. His mind was tortured. He quickly recapped the worst things he had seen on this horrible day numerically from worst to less terrible.

1. Walking in on my teenaged daughter fucking some guy on my favorite chair in my man cave.

2. Talking to my wife.

3. Seeing the dead guy's brains seeping out on the sidewalk.

He chugged the rest of his beer and released a huge belch, deliberately filtering the gas through his nostrils until it burned his sinuses free the way a bite of wasabi on sushi felt painfully clean.

He reached down, grabbed the 12-pack, pulled another can free and walked the box to the refrigerator near the back of the room. He flicked on an overhead light and the room came to life. It was a Chicago White Sox fan's dream —— memorabilia, baseball cards secured in clear cases, posters of legendary players, mitts, autographed balls and bats, plastic helmets, bobblehead dolls, framed pictures of players and ballparks were everywhere and anywhere to be found. Carter even had a row of three conjoined green seats, Nos. 163, 162, 161 from left to right, that were part the old Comiskey Park before it was dismantled and torn down in 1990 to make way for the new park.

He made his way to the open window, where mere moments ago, some scumbag was having his way with his daughter. The thought of his little girl having sex flip-flopped his stomach. He leaned his head inside the window well and looked up. He hoped the little punk was still outside so he could grab a hold of him and wail on him, but the kid was long gone and Carter gave him credit for being smart enough not to stick around. He closed the window and battened back the latches.

He walked to the front of the room and paused at framed picture of himself as a 19-year-old kid wearing a Salt Lake City Trappers uniform. Even though the picture had been in the room for years, incredibly, he'd forgotten about it. The photo was an afterthought because it was camouflaged with dozens of framed pictures of ballplayers. In the picture, he was wearing catcher's gear with the mask crowning atop a helmet with its bill pointed backwards. A beaming smile projected from his face and two black smudges under his eyes appeared to block the happiness from blinding him. As he looked at himself, it felt like 10 lifetimes ago when he was a pro baseball prospect.

He walked over to the row of old Comiskey Park seats, sat down on the uncomfortable No. 163, lit a cigarette and looked at the cardboard box lying on the carpet.

He checked the time and it read 2229 hours. There was still a lot of work to be done, but that didn't bother his indefatigable mindset. He made a mental checklist of what was next on his agenda:

TONIGHT

1. Compare Jackson S. Schmidt's statements with Lapp's mathematical findings.

2. Compare Jackson S. Schmidt's statements with that of witness Fearn's statement.

TOMORROW

1. Attempt interviewing Tommy Shannahan and Alex Hedlund.

2. Re-contact the narcotics task force regarding Cody Grantland — find out when they are going to raid his house.

3. Email Department of Child and Family Services my summery per their request.

4. After approval from Lt. Fenton, email a press release to the media (remember to use good syntax, so I don't look like an idiot).

His thought process was interrupted by his conscious. His brain reverted back to walking in on his naked daughter. He looked at the schnapps protruding from his duty bag and wished he had bought something stronger.

"What the fuck happened to my life?" he asked aloud, closing his eyes, picturing his daughter the way he always had — still an innocent 9-year-old with her long hair in perfect pigtails and a snarky smile.

He got up and walked back to the picture of him playing baseball in the Pioneer League for the Salt Lake City Trappers. He removed it from the wall, walked back to seat No. 163 and flopped down. He stared at himself staring back at himself, and his mind moseyed down memory lane.

He had all the talent in the world. He was going to be a big league catcher back in the late '80s and early '90s. He was a major contributor of 1991 championship Trappers team that won the Pioneer League and he was also on the roster in 1990, when the team finished second.

Carter could hit for power and average. He ran the bases harder than a galloping thoroughbred and surprisingly, he had great speed for a catcher. He could field his position as good as anybody and he had a cannon for an arm. He also knew the game and how to play the game, which, in his opinion, and that of scouts as well, was a big difference.

He modeled his ethic after his favorite player, Hall of Famer and Chicago White Sox great Carlton Fisk. Hustle was his motto and he implied it to every second he was on the field. But his biggest strength was he could call a game better than any prospect. He had a niche for realizing what kind of stuff his pitchers had when they took the mound and he would exploit his opponent's weaknesses with the pitcher's strengths. He religiously studied scouting reports of the opposition's hitters and he even updated his own baseball journal between innings in spiral notebooks. Carter's data collecting was done before the aid of computers and the team had to make extra room on the team bus for all of his notebooks. But as statistically savvy as he was, it was his love for the game and intelligence that had scouts interested.

It was May 14, 1992, when it happened. He was behind home plate at Derks Field, drinking in the snow-capped Wasatch Mountain in the distance. He was grinning, because he felt he was ready to be called up to the majors at any moment. He knew who the scouts were there to see. He knew where they were sitting, for they had been in the same seats all week, watching his every move.

He was in the middle of his best hitting streak, batting .689 since it started nine games ago. It was though the ball was the size of a watermelon when the pitcher would fire it, and time stood still when he swung his bat. Each time he connected, he drove the ball with authority to an unoccupied pasture of green grass or over the fence. Even the few outs he made during the streak were bullets he hit right at the defense. They seemed to catch the balls to protect themselves. Opposing teams took note of his recent surge and started pitching around him — throwing balls out of the strike zone. They even intentionally walked him if Trappers' runners were on second or third base and first base was unoccupied.

By the 10th game of his streak, he was only seeing one or two pitches per game that were worth swinging at. He figured in order to impress the scouts, he'd have to make those few hittable pitches really count.

In the sixth inning, he stepped into the batter's box to face a lanky, left-handed sinker-baller for the Billings Mustangs named Pete Sanukus. Carter knew Sanukus better than the kid knew himself. Carter knew Sanukus didn't like to start hitters off with a fastball. He liked to offset the batter's timing with a slow, rolling sinker. Carter swung at Sanukus' first pitch, a sinker Carter guessed correctly, and he drove it deep into the right-center field gap. The two outfielders merged, but couldn't track the ball down before it trickled to the fence.

As Carter raced toward first base, he knew he had a chance to stretch a sure double into a triple once he saw the ball skip past the defenders. He wasn't showing off for the scouts when he dug his cleats hard into the Utah clay, rounding second base in an attempt to make his triple. As a matter of fact, he'd forgotten they were there during his adrenaline-laced strides.

121

While he was picking them up and putting them down, Carter heaved his shoulders forward and gave the run everything he had. The centerfielder threw a perfect strike to the second baseman who was standing in the middle of the outfield, ready to relay the throw to third.

Carter never looked back to see how close the play was going to be, because he heard the ball smack the second baseman's glove. He knew the outcome of the play would take place in just a few fleeting moments. If he had time to smile, he would have, for plays like these was why he loved the game of baseball more than anything in the world.

He was barreling toward the bag like a runaway locomotive when he heard the ball whip by his ear as he started his headfirst slide. He aimed between the third baseman's cleats as he was protectively straddled the bag, waiting for Carter. Carter touched down, skipping into the base like a jumbo jet skidding across a runway with malfunctioning landing gear. When the dust settled, Carter was wrapping his arms around the base like it was his favorite pillow.

"Safe!" the third base umpire yelled.

Carter stood up with an ear-to-ear grin and dusted himself off. He looked up toward the scouts and they were all writing away in their notebooks. It was the proudest moment of his career up to that point, because he knew he was headed to The Show.

As he stood there, breathing in the aether, there was no way of knowing it would be the last time he would ever stand on third base again.

The next inning, he was squatting behind home plate and still basking in his head-first-slide-triple glory. The Trappers had the game in check with an 11-2 lead. In the dugout, putting on his chest protector, Carter questioned why his manager was letting him take the field. The skipper explained to Carter that he wanted the scouts to see him hit one last time and maybe he'd get another good pitch with the game being so lopsided.

There were two outs in the top of the seventh inning when Carter put down two fingers, giving his pitcher, Larry Playfair, the sign he wanted a curveball. The Mustangs had a runner on second base — their oak tree of a first baseman, a Native American man named Chetan "Hawk" Littlejohn*4. Mustangs catcher Dave Manson stepped into the batter's box and popped the first pitch up and toward the grandstand along the third base line near the dugout. Carter tossed off his mask and raced for the ball, but he ran out of room. He stood in the shadow of the grandstand, watching an elderly lady overdramatize being in close proximity to danger, while she covered her face in her hands and as the ball bounced off the concrete steps several rows away from the woman.

He found his mask in the grass, dusted it off, walked back into the sunlight and squatted at his post behind the plate, adjusting his equipment. Carter put his two fingers down between his legs again, and as he was doing so, he felt a tickle in his nose. There was no time to call time out, because Playfair received Carter's sign and fired the pitch without hesitation. Manson roped the hanging curveball up the middle for a single.

Carter flung off his mask and watched Littlejohn taking a colossal angle heading for third, a sure indication the man had no intentions of stopping. Carter looked out into the bright sunlight, gauging where Trappers centerfielder Carlito Gomez would scoop up the ball in the outfield. When he did so, his tickling nose turned into a feeling of head-filled ecstasy. He tried to hang his lungs up with his breath the way a teacher snags running children in school hallways, but it was to no avail. He knew a violent sneeze coming on and even though he tried with everything he had in him to quash it, he couldn't prevent the monster sneeze from escaping.

In between fluttered blinking and his head flitching like he was being jabbed by an invisible fist, he could see motion in the distance. Gomez launched the ball toward home, but Carter was clueless as to where it was heading. His option at this point was to force the sneeze, instead of trying to deny it, and pray he had enough time to get it out of his system and locate the ball before it hit him in the face.

But the sneeze wasn't his only problem — Chetan "Hawk" Littlejohn was blazing down the third base line like his underwear was on fire and Carter was the cool pool he would be diving in.

The sneeze ripped through Carter's sinuses like a hurricane, spraying snot and spit in a majestic mist. When Carter collected himself, blinking his watery eyes rapidly and trying to regain balance, it was far too late. The sting of the ball hitting his right wrist was just a small fart in the diarrhea storm on the horizon.

The next thing Carter felt was Littlejohn's boulder of a shoulder driving into his jaw. The impact threw Carter into the air like a lawn jart. As he flew backward, he was turned upside-down and time slowed down long enough for him to brood over how surreal the ballpark and its fans looked from his convoluted line of vision. When he landed on his head, neck and shoulders, his legs flung behind his ears. The force of Carter's body crashing into the clay left a dent in the dirt. His cleats caught the ground behind his head, but there was so much momentum in his limp body, he somersaulted backward once more.

As Carter was about to be sprawled out in one final dusty heap, inertia continued propelling the head-long, human-projectile-missile Littlejohn, and he toppled onto the lifeless body of a now unconscious Carter. Littlejohn's billboard-sized forehead barreled into Carter's left knee and fibula, shattering his kneecap and tearing his anterior cruciate ligament. As he got up, Littlejohn buried his elbow deep into Carter's throat, and used it for leverage while he stood up in a distasteful act of gamesmanship.

When Carter first opened his eyes, he saw a hard-bodied woman tippy-toeing on a small chair while reaching for a drawstring that had become tangled at the top of a window curtain. He had an excellent vantage point to see her blue nursing scrubs contorting around a firm, apple-bottom while its circulation was being cut off by a tiny set of panties. His view would be the only good thing to happen to him for quite some time.

When the doctor relayed the damage, he recited the problems to Carter like he was a mechanic giving an estimate for a car that had been pulled from the wreckage in a demolition derby — a wired and broken jaw, three cracked teeth, two missing teeth, laceration to the left inside cheek, a punctured left lung, fractured left knee cap, torn left ACL, punctured left quadriceps, internal bleeding from stomach cavity, laceration on the left kidney, hairline fracture on the right wrist and several other small cuts and bruises. When it was all said and done, Carter was informed he was in and out of surgeries for nearly two days and had been put in a medically-induced coma for nearly a week while his body healed.

Carter was devastated. His professional baseball career was in dire jeopardy. After the initial self-wallowing subsided, he was bound and determined to one day return, hopefully better than ever.

The rehab process was a grueling one. Over the course of a year and half, Carter was headstrong and made astonishing progress, but sadly, in the end, it wasn't enough. His left leg was never the same. He tried to rejoin the Trappers (who moved to nearby Ogden and became the Raptors), but was quickly cut. Carter tried out with a couple more organizations, but they were disheartening endeavors. On June 11, 1994, Carter officially retired. He couldn't get over the fact that something as minor as a sneeze ruined a prosperous future. He spent the next several months having himself a pity party at various bars in his old stomping grounds and childhood neighborhoods of Edison Park, Chicago, before his father encouraged him to follow in his footsteps and become a cop*5.

It wasn't until many years later, and as a patrol officer, when his partner, Officer Everson Walls, asked him if he was allergic to the sun and added, "Do you ever notice how you sneeze every time you walk outside?" Carter couldn't reply. But when he truly thought about it, Carter realized Walls was correct, and it boggled his mind.

The invention of the Internet led to the invention of Google, which then led to Carter finding out he had a bizarre condition called photoptarmosis, or Photic Sneeze Reflex (aka "sun sneezing") in which 18 percent to 35 percent of the population probably did not know they had. Basically, PSR is a phenomenon of uncontrollable sneezing in response to numerous stimuli, such as looking at bright lights, but its exact mechanism of action is not well understood in medicinal science.

Since he learned of PSR*6, it was a kick in the junk every time he sneezed ⎯⎯ thinking of what his future could have been as a professional baseball player instead of becoming a functioning alcoholic homicide detective who combed through the blood and guts of mostly losers in an attempt to justify which loser ended the other loser's miserable life. Upon finding out about his condition, he never mentioned PSR to any of his co-workers. He couldn't afford to find out what the brass might do if they knew he sneezed every time he walked out of a dark room. Obviously, the longevity of his career could've been at risk, considering carrying a gun was an important aspect of the job.

SIDE 1. TRACK 14. LINER NOTES:

1. The uncracking of the safe turned out to be an anticlimactic endeavor. Sgt. Bowers made a phone call, summoning Officer Randall Rhode, who had experience with small devices and safes, and was on the force's bomb squad. Rhode ended up slamming a flathead screwdriver into a seam along the lid and simply popped it ajar with a single strike on the screwdriver's handle. Although they were pleased with recovering the weapons, Carter was hoping for much more. "This was worse than when Geraldo Rivera wasted two hours of my fucking time on live TV, knocking down a brick wall looking for Al Capone's loot. Boys, I was hoping we'd hit paydirt and go home splitting thousands. Now, I got more shit to stuff into the evidence cage. This is blue balls for a wet dream I tell ya, and I'm sorry I wasted your time."

2. On certain days after arguments between Carter and his wife, he would return home to find all of his beer missing. He always assumed it was just another way of her attempting to get under his skin, and sometimes it was. But unbeknownst to Carter, his daughter picked up on her mother's strategy and would steal a few cans here and there before Shelby dumped them all out, so she could sneak them.

3. Carter was a beer drinker these days. He had spent about a decade as a gin and tonic guy, but the gin had worn away at the lining of his stomach and esophagus, and it gave him terrible ulcers and

heartburn. The beer didn't leave the damaging effects on his stomach or generate prolonged hangovers. Also, the beer wasn't as detectable the next morning when he shared tight quarters with coworkers.

4. Chetan "Hawk" Littlejohn was born and raised in the Fort Peck Indian Reservation in northeast Montana. As a child, Littlejohn built his renowned power by chopping wood and stretching cowhide with his bare hands. As he grew, he quickly became the largest person in his tribe, but struggled with mental development. By the time he was 15, allegations arose that he was a perverted mongoloid and he was outcast from most communal functions. The legend of Littlejohn being a boogeyman grew as fast as his body (he stood 6-foot-6 and weighed 260 pounds). Around his 16th birthday, he was subsequently driven off the reservation and hadn't returned since. The decision, albeit not clear, voiced the tribe's beliefs and concerns that a hypersexual teen of enormous size, but little brains, posed a serious danger. The exact incident surrounding Littlejohn's exile wasn't exactly clear either. The most widespread yarn had something to do with him raping several women of the Assiniboine tribe, who shared common ground. Another tale suggested he murdered a fellow tribesman, who mysteriously went missing, with a hatchet. One thing was certain — every person who came to know Littlejohn, including his own mother, could attest he had more than one screw loose.

Over the years, he was taught baseball while working on a cattle ranch outside Billings. He was nicknamed "Hawk" by a fellow cowboy because of his beak-like, curvy nose, which segued nicely from the actual foundation of his Native American first name which, in fact, meant, "Hawk." Eventually, he was persuaded by fellow broncobusters to try out for the Billings Mustangs of the Pioneer League after legends arose that he was crushing baseballs more than 500 feet with a handmade pine bat he allegedly whittled with an old buck knife and then sanded down smooth with arrowheads (supposedly while channeling the spirits of his ancestors as he did so).

In 1988, he made the Mustangs and quickly built a tremendous fanbase after having an astonishing rookie season and leading the league in home runs (27). His face, the spitting image of famed Indian Sitting Bull was posted on every marketing tool the Mustangs' brass came up with. No one accurately knew his exact age, but it was later suggested he was in his 30s when he joined the team. As good as his rookie season was, most franchises weren't willing to take a chance on him because of his extremely strange demeanor and he struck a nervous chord with any and everyone who spent brief seconds in his company. His measly presence even made his own teammates jumpy and he was never included to anything outside of the baseball-related activities. By 1990, he wasn't even considered a blip on any Major League teams' radar after attrition left him feeble. He officially retired in 1993 — never even notifying management — and his whereabouts are currently unknown.

5. Carter's father, James "Jimmy" Woodbine, put in 30 superb years with the Chicago Police Department before retiring. Although he never climbed a rank higher than patrol officer, he was treasured by fellow officers and high-ranking administrators. He was always hopeful Carter would one day follow down the path and become a cop. After Carter's injury, Jimmy encouraged his son to test with the force and put in the good word*A to friends who in the hiring process.

The two never worked in the same district, but Jimmy took his son under his wing — often educating him the ins and outs over beers. Jimmy unexpectedly died six years ago and Carter never got the chance to say goodbye.

A) The "good word" Jimmy put in for his son was a case of The Glenlivet 12-year-old Single Malt Scotch, to several administrative personnel atop of the hiring process. He sent another case of Scotch to those same personnel, after Carter became an officer and while they were figuring out what district to place him in.

6. After learning about Photic Sneeze Reflex, it somewhat consumed Carter's mind. He could predict when he was going to sneeze, and for several months after his discovery, he even kept statistics on its frequency in a notebook.

On the odd chance he didn't sneeze within 25 seconds of stepping outside and into sunlight while feeling a sneeze brewing, but one that would not surface, it would drive him crazy. He would then look toward the sky or anything bright and try his hand at forcing the reflex to kick in with a series of short, intentional breaths and nose crinkles. Unperceived to Carter, the face he often made while struggling to achieve a sneezgasm was not the most flattering one and some of his coworkers would make an animated imitation of it behind his back when he was being discussed.

15. Pig Tales

Tonight, as Chloe Woodbine was in her bed, only minutes after her father caught her fornicating in his favorite place on the planet, her heart was still beating with adrenaline.

She was devastated with what her life had become. She put her mind on rewind, and thought about how she got here.

When she was 14, she would hear the front door of the house shut before she started her morning routine. She never relied on an alarm clock. Growing up, her alcoholic father would usually wake her with a nasty cheek-kiss before he left — the booze still heavy on his breath, reeking like juniper-scented hand sanitizer, as she laid there, pretending to be asleep as best she could. But at 14, and a couple of years outgrown from the parting kiss, he had conditioned her inner clock to an early rise. Once she heard his squad car start up and pull out of the driveway, she would begin another miserable day by doing the only thing she knew would feel good throughout it.

She had stolen and kept one of her mother's vibrators hidden behind her headboard. It was the safest place for concealment in Chloe's room, because it would require a move of the bed to reach it, and no meddling person would ever think anything was behind there. It was stowed carefully in a contraption she devised with two loops of masking tape — pinning the tape to the backside of the board, where only a skinny wrist and diminutive fingers would have enough access to reach under the curve of the wood to unsheathe it.

Chloe had to take all the precautions necessary when having a snoopy cop as a father. Sometimes he would search for contraband in her room when she wasn't home. She could always tell when he did, because something was always moved. Sometimes a pair of fluffy socks would be disturbed from their precise spot in her sock and underwear drawer*1. Or sometimes an ink smudge would appear on her journal*2 that she left on a closet shelf. Or sometimes she would see his size 13 footprint in her neatly vacuumed carpet, blotching up the perfect lines*3 she made.

Chloe was very sexually active for a 14-year-old. Neither of her parents knew this. To them, she appeared to be the perfect child. She earned good grades. She dressed proper and less risqué than 90 percent of the girls in her class. She was bright, friendly and polite, and every teacher she ever had said she was as pleasant as they come. Chloe was also a star on her freshman volleyball team and had a promising future.

But Chloe had a secret side to her and was quite good at pulling the wool over her parents' eyes. She had the "I'm-sleeping-over-at-a-friends-house-but-really-lying-to-your-face-and-going-to-an-underage-drinking-party-instead" routine down pat. Even with her father being an extremely good homicide detective, she never was caught, nor did they ever suspect her cunning ways.

Her first salacious encounter with the male gender*4 happened early in her freshman year at a "rainbow party" where she and two of her drunken girlfriends applied a heavy amount of colored lipstick before going down on six male classmates after the lights in the room were turned off. The premise of the "rainbow" part of the party was when the girls would each take turns swapping partners while performing fellatio, and after the lights were turned back on, the different colored lipstick left on the participating members' penises would showcase which girl did what and when.

Chloe thrived on the attention and the power. Her parents were in the middle stages of a brutal, decade-long war of words and bitterness. Her voice, needs and actions often went unnoticed when they fought and Chloe owned a mindset that craved notice.

She lost her virginity two weeks after the "rainbow party." It happened after another fake sleepover pledge went undetected. She ended up getting drunk off two beers and a senior named Hunter Blackburn deflowered her. He was aggressive and left her torn and sore for two weeks. But that didn't stop her from continuing her promiscuous ways. Two months later, she got with another boy, missed her period and had a pregnancy scare that ended in the good fortune of a miscarriage she didn't even know she had.

From her sophomore to senior year, she continued to be a model student and athlete. She grew six inches, was muscular and thick — standing at a whopping 6-foot-2. She even earned a full scholarship to Winona State University in Minnesota for volleyball. By the start of her senior year, Chloe did have a reputation of being a "slut" from the inner circle of classmates who knew her, but she either shrugged it off or told the boys who called her names such as "Chloe Woodbone ya" or "Chloe Woodgrind you" to "fuck off or fuck on" in a flirtatious challenge. And if any of her female peers confronted her about some of her dicey, sexual decision-making, she would tell them she was in a "self-discovery mode of liberation" or "it's not a big deal and I practiced safe sex" or "don't be jealous because no one wants you."

Her parents hadn't the foggiest idea she was considered a slut because Chloe had always gone above and beyond to hide her unchaste lifestyle from them. Second, her mother was usually too paranoid or too high on prescription medication to leave the house to hear about her lax and lubricious ways. Lastly, her father had never known her to have a boyfriend or any inkling she was even interested in men, and he attributed it to her busy schedule and the simple self-esteem issues most "big-boned" girls have when they enter the gaudy stages of puberty.

He also never found any evidence supporting her wild ways after all the times he snooped through her room looking for red flags or warning signs to any trouble she may have been in and may have been too embarrassed to talk to him or her mother about.

The boys who used her, always kept her on the backburner for moments of desperation or when their girlfriends wouldn't put out, so her sexual activity was never leaked to coaches or teachers who may have helped address the issue to her guidance counselor or parents. Plus, none of her concerned girlfriends*5 had the confidence in handling an interrogation from her intimidating cop father and knew they wouldn't be able to convey Chloe's actions through her stoned mother's head.

Aside from those lovely blue eyes she inherited from her father, Chloe knew she wasn't the most attractive girl and she was far from being beautiful. She also understood the cards that were dealt to her weren't what the popular and handsome boys in class were interested in, so she used the power of sex to get those boys and held no reservations about doing so.

But everything changed two weekends ago.

Chloe was at another party with some boys she didn't know from a rival high school. She and her friend, Annessa Weir, met the group in the parking lot after a basketball game and decided to go to a party the guys knew of in a foreclosed home. She remembered everything was going great at the party — everyone was laughing, dancing, drinking — doing what teenagers do without parental supervision. She remembered taking a mixed drink from one of the boys and soon after, not remembering anything at all.

The next morning, she found her clothes thrown about the bare room with her one functioning eye. The other was swelled shut. Her eyes weren't the only things that were swollen. She also remembered three boys bunking with her; however she couldn't remember who they were or wanting them there. She remembered only bits and pieces of the night before and had the immediate urge to get out of there.

As she sat on the worn-out carpet, hysterically putting on her clothes, she noticed the blood in the taupe shag. She wished she had her vacuum with her to erase the previous night with perfectly groomed lines, the way she did her own carpet, but it was far too late for any of that. She eventually stumbled out of the room, found the house to be in complete disarray and trashed, and searched for Annessa. Each room she entered was completely abandoned. She found her cellphone in the kitchen and found she had two awaiting messages, both from Annessa.

Text No. 1 at 11:23 p.m. from Annessa Weir read: Looks like you're getting it in! YOLO! U SLUT LOL! I had to go home so I wouldn't get busted by the parentals. Don't get preggers biotch LOL!!!

Text No. 2 at 11:25 p.m. from Annessa Weir read: PS. The sliding glass door will be unlocked. DON'T WAKE MY P'S WHEN YOUR WASTY ASS GETS HERE!

Chloe staggered out of the house and had no idea where she was until she wandered to the street corner of West Thorndale and North Newark. She flagged down a cab, went home, swallowed a "Plan B" pill, showered and never told a soul about what happened.

When Annessa called her later in the morning after recognizing Chloe wasn't at her house like the girls planned, Chloe never mentioned that she was raped, but told her she "hooked up with the cute one." Neither of the girls could recall what "the cute one's" name was nor did either girl get phone numbers or the last names of any of the boys at the party. Chloe and Annessa went about their lives as if it was just another typical Friday night. Chloe lied and told her father she got elbowed in the eye at volleyball practice after he actually noticed the black eye for the first time, three days later. Her mother was completely oblivious of the injury altogether.

Back in her bedroom, after Chloe was caught by her father in his favorite chair in the basement, her mind raced as she stared into the dark room looking for any signs of light. She couldn't believe him on what she perceived as yet another lack of concern on his part. It was her last cry for help and it seemed he didn't even care. If he didn't pick up on her warning signs as a detective, he never would.

Then, all of the sudden, with her heartbeat winding down like time she would never get back, everything become crystal clear to her in those misty moments. She came to grips with the fact that she had gone through most of her life hardly noticed, underappreciated, and lost — and she began conjuring up a plan to change it all.

SIDE 1. TRACK 15. LINER NOTES:

1. Carter wasn't a pervert by any stretch. In his daughter's early teen years, he may have been guilty of being an overly protective father, but not a pervert. During his tenure on the police force, he was conditioned to know where woman kept their private belongings.

It was often commonplace during a homicide and other varying investigations, to find dirty secrets in underwear drawers. The mental psyche often reflected the unusual association of keeping something private, like drugs or weapons or journals or naked pictures or sex toys, near something else that was personal to a woman, like their underwear.

Countless times while probing love-triangles or jealousy-related-homicides, Carter, more often than not, found helpful clues in a woman's underwear drawer. It was under that pretext, as to why he invaded Chloe's privacy, and his only focus was to be preemptive to any warning signs. He also had qualms she might steal her mother's unlimited supply of prescription medication, because it was omnipresent in the house.

Throughout his career he vowed never to be like some of the naïve parents he met along the way, ones who lost sight of their children. For the last two years, or as Chloe matured into what Carter thought was a responsible young lady, he ceased searching her room altogether.

2. Chloe, accustomed to her father's prying ways, kept two journals. One, which she would often leave intentionally exposed, consisted of fabricated accords of how wonderful her life was. She would make entries about how excited she was to get a full scholarship playing volleyball at Winona State University. She would lie, confessing how great her senior year was going and how amazing her friends were. The other diary she kept was filled with truths and raw emotions, the polar opposite of the one she intentionally left out to keep her dad off her trail of despondency. She kept it on a Word doc inside her password protected laptop and it'd never been tampered with.

3. Chloe was fanatical, in an Obsessive Compulsive Disorder way, when it came to vacuuming. She had developed a technique that made triangular shapes in the carpet. She would start vacuuming at the far back corner, working from right to left, with a straight-forward glide and then she would reverse the motion at a 45-degree angle until she reached a desired length, only to push it straight-forward again before angle-reversing in a faultless fashion. She would repeat the steps over and over, to create a select row. Then, she would follow suit, with a new row beneath the previous one, and so on and so forth, until she worked herself out of the room.

Once finished, the entire carpet looked like a diamond-patterned area rug. The OCD vacuuming began after she first noticed items in her room had been tinkered with, and then, as mistrust persisted, the compulsion became, albeit unusual, a pleasant leisure for Chloe.

4. Chloe's first sexual experience was when she was 12 while attending a three-day, summer volleyball camp hosted in Grand Rapids, Mich. A 15-year-old female named Bailey (her last name escaped Chloe), who was also attending the skills camp, engaged, peer-pressured and then seduced Chloe to partake experimental and titillating touching while they were left unsupervised in a woman's locker room. Bailey told Chloe the act was a part of a secret club — where only the cool and most athletic volleyball players became members. The "exploring" happened two more times during the camp, and even though she felt something wasn't right about the behavior, Chloe never tried to reject Bailey's advances.

It wasn't until a few years later when Chloe understood the acts were violating. In the incidents' aftermath, Chloe became disturbed by what transpired, because she was completely heterosexual in nature and any thoughts or reminders of lesbianism gave her anxiety. She took her anger out on her father, not with verbal altercations nor with any physically destructive manners, but with her promiscuity among the opposite sex. After all, Carter pressured her into attending the out-of-state camp, because he thought it would be a great opportunity to master her skills and showcase her talent in front of some important figureheads in the sport — some who often scouted potential stars.

She pleaded with him for half of the three-hour drive around Lake Michigan that she didn't want to go, but her wishes fell on deaf ears when he dropped her off and told her to "have fun and do good." As years progressed, in a game-like and in a warped cry for attention, Chloe left clues (the elephant in the room should've been the extreme vacuuming) she was protecting something — to see how far her father was willing to investigate her profligate ways and to see how much, if at all, he truly cared.

5. Chloe only had one friend who ever tried to alert Chloe's parents of her promiscuity. Her name was Haley Ackerman and she wrote Chloe's mother a note of her concerns. Haley tried to slip the note into Shelby's purse one day while hanging out at the Woodbine home, but Chloe saw it out of the corner of her eye while her back wasn't completely turned to Haley. Chloe pretended not to see Haley being mysterious around her mother's purse and after Haley left the residence later on in the evening, Chloe retrieved the note before Shelby knew of its existence. Chloe felt extremely betrayed and she cut Haley out of her life completely in an extremely devout vow of the silent treatment.

"Focus your audios."

SIDE 2 TRACK LISTING:

1. God Father Hipster

2. Hair of the Dog

3. Moonshine & Potato Guns

4. Even the Sun Shines on a Dog's Ass Every Once in a While

5. Skywalker: The Unintentional, Chicken & Waffle-Loathing Lunch Guest

6. "Sharpen Your Snags."

7. Victim Blaming

8. "I'm a cop. I love being a cop."

9. The 17-Year Cicada Bug

10. The Mookie Brownstone Blues

11. Fris·son (frē´sôN) n.: a moment of intense excitement; a shudder, thrill

1. God Father Hipster

The old man woke early after a night of troubled sleep. He walked downstairs to have his standard glass of orange juice and then walked back up to the bedroom. He threw on his typical non-Sunday-garb — black-framed glasses, an ugly purple sweater over a red plaid shirt, a vintage pair of Levis with inseams that seemingly grew as his geriatric body shrunk and a brown trilby he'd owned for decades. The jeans needed a good cuffing at the hems and he did so after he laced up a pair of brown leather boots. He retrieved his epoch, 1970's sleek, snug-fitting medium brown sheepskin jacket with a wide-collar and side slit pockets. And then he tied a pink checkered bowtie around his neck. He gave himself a glance in the mirror — an unintentional hipster. He had been dressing the same for decades, a patriarch of said fashion, but it was way before you ever seen anyone do so.

At the foot of the bed, he realized he threw his Sunday suit coat atop the comforter. As he went to hang it up, he noticed something protruding from the pocket. He stuffed his hand in the coat and retrieved a white business card. It read:

Detective Carter Woodbine
Chicago Police Department
Homicide Division Office: (312) 555-5676
Cell: (312) 555-4144

Jackson S. Schmidt looked the card over — he was completely baffled. He wondered how the card ended up in his pocket. Maybe he found it on the ground? Was he supposed to call the detective? Did he have information?

He jogged his memory and could only remember it was a Sunday and Father Paul talked about looking for signs from God in his sermon. Was Father Paul playing a joke on him? Father Paul was the only person Jackson remembered talking to. After speculating for several minutes, he became so frustrated, he decided to give the detective a call.

He dialed Carter's cell number and after eight rings, he reached the detective's voicemail. Jackson was always worried whether he left voicemails correctly, so he hung up.

He decided to pay Father Paul a visit. Maybe he could help him out, or at least fess up to the prank, if it even was one. He began looking for his car keys, and when he couldn't find them, he became perplexed again. He tore apart his home searching for the keys — drawers were dumped out, cabinets were left wide open and articles of clothing were tossed about. He even checked his suit coat four times and tore the stitching on the right pocket. After a half-hour, he ended the probing when he flopped down on the floor like a toddler and had a temper tantrum. He couldn't understand how he lost them. Then it dawned on him — did he drop the keys on the garage floor? Or, maybe they were still in the ignition? Getting to his feet was no easy task, but when he walked out to the garage and noticed his Lincoln wasn't there, its absence dropped him back down to the ground.

He eventually returned inside to retrieve the jacket he flung off his steaming body during the fevered hunt. As he was about to leave to visit Father Paul on foot, his phone rang.

"Hello!" he shot into the receiver.

"This is Detective Woodbine," said the weary voice from a man on the other end. "I'm sorry I missed your call — it's a little early for me. Is there something I can help you with this morning?"

"Well," Jackson said. "I'm not sure. Do we know one another?"

"I'm sorry," Carter said. "Come again?"

"How do you know who I am? Have we met?"

"I don't know," Carter said. "It depends on who I am talking to."

"This is Jackson S. Schmidt."

"Are you fencing me, Mr. Schmidt?"

"I don't understand."

"What don't you understand?"

"How you know me?"

"Mr. Schmidt," Carter said. "I interviewed you yesterday. This should be clear as a bell."

"Interviewed me?"

"Mr. Schmidt," Carter began, "Are you OK?"

"Yes, I'm fine. But I want to know what you want from me."

"You called me," Carter said. "When you left the station yesterday, I informed you that you could call me if you thought of anything else about the accident. Do you have anything else to share?"

"About … what?"

There was a long pause.

"Mr. Schmidt," Carter began. "Do you remember what happened yesterday?"

Jackson shuffled his irksome bones along the backstreets of his neighborhood, mostly with his head scraping the sidewalk, during dawn's early light. Twenty minutes had elapsed since Carter had informed him he ended a man's life the day before and Jackson couldn't believe it. He knew someone would be at Saint Rita of the Angels and hopefully he could get Father Paul out of his quarters.

"Bless me Father for I have sinned," Jackson S. Schmidt said behind a partition in confessional.

"Go ahead, my son," the affable Priest said.

"Father, I have done a terrible thing," Jackson said in a trembling voice.

"Go on, my son."

"A terrible, terrible thing, Father."

"What could be so bad, my son?" the Priest almost cackled*1. "You're a fine man and a great believer in God."

"I killed a man, Father."

"Can you say that again, my son?"

"I killed a man," Jackson said. "I didn't mean to do it. There was an accident."

"Jackson, are you feeling well?"

"Yes, Father Paul."

"Have you been taking your medicine?"

"Yes, Father. I haven't skipped once."

"What makes you think you killed someone?"

"I talked to a detective," Jackson said. "He said I ran a man over with my Lincoln yesterday. How would he know I drove a Lincoln if it wasn't true?"

"How did this happen?! What did the detective say?"

"He said I ran a man over with my car," Jackson said, sobbing. "He said the man had a gun."

"Do you remember doing this?"

"No."

"Where — where did this happen at?"

"By the flower shop."

"What's this detective's name?"

"Wood ... Wood something," Jackson said. "I have his name and number on this card."

"Give me the card, my son."

Carter slid the business card through a small opening in the partition.

"This is a horrible mess I'm in. I'm going to Hell."

"I'm going to help you, my son," Father Paul said. "I will help clean it. For, Jesus washed the feet of peasants for his sins, surely we can wash your hands as well."

SIDE 2. TRACK 1. LINER NOTE:

1. Father Paul had known Jackson S. Schmidt since the day he was accepted into the church. He found Jackson to be the most honest and trustworthy person he had ever met. Even out of all his fellow brethren, Father Paul found not one of them was as genuine as Jackson. That is to say, until the dementia grabbed a hold of his wits like hair near an electrically charged balloon.

2. Hair of the Dog

Tommy Shannahan awoke on his parents' living room couch to the sound of their Irish setter, Reagan, licking his balls in fevered laps. Befuddled with slumber, he rubbed his eyes.

"Where am I? What time is it?" he thought.

The dog hopped up on the couch and curled up next to Tommy in the middle of the night. After he'd fallen asleep, his mother covered him with a green blanket she crocheted decades ago. He sat up, looked at the dog and cursed him off the couch. With the dog out of the way, Tommy flopped back down on the couch, stretched out his arms, and blearily checked his phone for the time. Upon doing so, he noticed he had missed five calls from 312-555-5676, which was not a number saved in his phone's contacts, but knew belonged to someone from the Chicago Police Department. Yesterday's events began to dance in his mind, just like Reagan's hair and dander were twirling in a sunbeam after he gave himself a collar-rattling, coat-shake.

He continued searching his missed call log, where there were three from Blue, one from Michael Jr., one from Cal and, astoundingly, none from Alex. He quickly dialed Alex. There was no answer.

He scribbled, "Thank you for the meatloaf" and "See you at Christmas" to his mother on an empty margin of a crossword puzzle she was working on at the coffee table. As he finished writing the notes, he completed a word in the puzzle that she must've been stuck on. Then he stuffed six $100 bills into the inner hinge of the book, put on his boots, folded the blanket and snuck out of the house.

Once inside his van, he called Blue. She groggily answered while he was driving away. Within a minute of listening to her, he spun the van around in a screechy-tired U-turn and was en route to Alex's apartment.

On the 26th knock, Alex answered the door wearing only his boxer briefs and brandishing a butcher knife. His typical, wild rock 'n' roll hair was unusually flat and it was matted to the left side of his head like it had been steamrolled by construction equipment.

"What the fuck, man?" Alex said.

"I should say the same to you!" Tommy said.

He let Tommy in.

"Where's your wife and ..." Tommy started to ask, but trailed off when he noticed the disorder.

Alex flopped down on couch and Tommy stood over him.

"I've been trying to get ahold of you since yesterday," Tommy said. "Don't you check your phone?"

"I've been sleeping since the last time I saw you, man." Alex said.

"Well, wake up! Things are fucky — we're in some shit!"

"What are you talking about?" Alex asked, rubbing sandman out of his eyes.

"You know the thing you wanted me to get for you yesterday?" Tommy said. "Well, the guy who was bringing it to me was fucking murdered or some shit — a block away from the bar! And here's the real smoking gun of it all — your dumb ass dropped a tape recorder, basically explaining us doing some illegal bullshit and guess who the fuck has it?"

"Oh, shit!" Alex said, hanging his head. "Who?"

"The fuckin' cops do!"

"What? How do the cops have it — I was nowhere near a murder?" Alex said.

"I just got off the phone with Blue — one of our bartenders," Tommy started. "Some crazy lady gave it to her at the bar. Blue listened to it, must've mistook you for my hot dog guy and served it up to a detective on a silver fucking platter. Probably put mustard on the fucker too. We're fucked, buddy boy!"

"Holy shit." Alex said.

"What did you say on that tape?" Tommy said.

"Fuck if I know," Alex said. "I was going on two days without sleep."

"Where's your wife?" Tommy posed while looking around. "You need to tell me what's going on. I got this cop calling me every 10 minutes. He's a pit bull and he's not gonna just go away. I gotta know what to say to him."

Alex rubbed his face and quietly spun his wheels.

"Desiree left me and took the kids," he began. "She's shacked up with her meth dealer outside fucking Rockford, man. Someplace called Byron. I need to get my kids out of there. I wanted to leave my kids a message if anything bad happened to me. That's why I made the recording."

"What did you say on it — about me, specifically?"

"I may have mentioned you — again, I was so out of it." Alex said.

"But, what about me?" Tommy pleaded once again.

"I may have said I was going to get a gun from you." Alex said.

"Jesus-Mary-Motherfucker!"

"Tom, I'm sorry, man," Alex said, hanging his head in his hands. "I was just trying to get my kids back."

"I get it. I'm sorry." Tommy said. "Where was the last time you had the thing?"

"Not sure," Alex responded. "I thought it was in my car."

"Wait ..." Tommy pinched the bridge of his nose. "Now I remember. You had it in the bar. I remember seeing it in your pocket. I thought you were going to play me some riffs."

"I bet it happened when the drink splashed in my face, man." Alex replied. "I knew I was forgetting something when I left."

"That big, Hispanic woman must've found it and turned it in," Tommy said. "Blue was trying to do me a favor — trying to figure out why my friend was dead. It all makes sense now."

Moments passed with both men nervously thinking about the severity of the situation. Alex found his phone wedged in between couch cushions and gave it a look. He discovered he missed several calls from Tommy and a half-dozen from a number he didn't recognize. He showed Tommy the strange number and Tommy confirmed it was the same number he was getting calls from.

"What are we going to do, Tommy?" Alex pleaded.

"We gotta get out of here," Tommy stated. "We have to go somewhere and figure this shit out before he tracks us down. Get dressed."

3. Moonshine & Potato Guns

At 0802 hours, Carter Woodbine walked up the steps to the entrance of Saint Rita of the Angels church and paused. The air smelled earthy and clean, like petrichor, but he didn't recall seeing any rain on the drive over. He entered through the wooden doors, pausing once again. He wanted to see if the holy water would start boiling at his presence. Over the years, the horrific sights associated with being a homicide detective were the catalyst for his belief in atheism. But today, as he hovered over the stoup, and as blasphemous as the idea was, he entertained the notion that if even one bubble surfaced, he would reconsider God's existence.

Father Paul, who'd been waiting for him, emerged from behind the shadows and greeted Carter with a wet sock.

"Detective Woodbine?" the priest said, while he shook his hand.

Carter scanned the priest over and was surprised to find him to be a man in his 30s.

"Father Paul?"

"Yes."

"You're not the Father Paul I pictured when I spoke to you on the phone," Carter said. "Are you guys dunking people in the fountain of youth over here? What's in the holy water?"

"We all have to start somewhere, Detective Woodbine." Father Paul said.

"I never thought about it that way," Carter said. "But, if you crack open a bottle of blood, I might have to check your ID."

"Would you like to follow me, Detective Woodbine?" Father Paul asked with an open-palm hand pointing toward a hallway. "He's waiting in the cathedral."

The suit-clad Carter tracked behind the younger man to the grand entrance of the massive cathedral. Carter couldn't help but be spellbound by the pulchritudinous interior. The six massive archways lining the rowed pews were handcrafted of the finest wood and were utterly breathtaking.

As he continued, he recognized Jackson S. Schmidt sitting on a pew near the altar. Carter tried to focus on Jackson's demeanor, but the light-pink painted color scheme on the semicircle dome, accompanied by the architecture and colossal windows, lifted Carter's gaze with an invisible string.

While taking in the view, he felt a sneeze come on and he let out a loud blast which echoed in the massive room. Jackson, slightly rattled, turned to the sound and seemed to want to say something, but didn't once he saw Carter.

"Jack, this is Detective Woodbine." Father Paul said.

An acataleptic Jackson stood up.

"Did you find out who stole my money?" Jackson eagerly asked.

141

A second sneeze knocked on Carter's door. He looked back up and wretched out a discharging spray. Again Jackson appeared to want to say something, but held off.

"God bless you," Father Paul said to Carter before turning to Jackson. "Jack, your money isn't missing. Don't you remember? You changed banks. It's all there."

"It is?" Jackson said.

"Yes, Jack," Father Paul said. "I swear on our good Lord."

"Whew."

"Jack, Detective Woodbine is here to talk to you about a few things that happened yesterday. Do you remember what happened yesterday? What you told me in confessional this morning?"

Jackson looked Carter over, paused at the badge around his neck and brooded things over.

"He's here for Joey Gillespie isn't he?" Jackson said to Father Paul.

"Who's Joey Gillespie, Jack?" Father Paul said.

"Every cop worth a darn knows Joey Gillespie," Jackson said and then looked at Carter. "He's been shooting his potato gun in the alley again, hasn't he?"

"No, Jack," Father Paul said. "Detective Woodbine isn't here for Joey Gillespie."

"You should be," Jackson said while looking at Carter. "He and his buddies get drunk on Tennessee moonshine and fire potatoes at sweet old ladies walking down the sidewalk. He dang near took Mrs. Donelson's leg off with one of those spud guns. I think Joey's friend Butch … Butch Baines — he sneaks the hooch up in mason jars. You should run a check on him."

"Thank you. I'll look into it," Carter said. "But right now I've got more important things to talk to you about other than Joey … Gillespie was it?"

"That's him," Jackson said. "Always firing them potatoes at sweet old ladies while hopped up on the shine. Butchy boy bootlegs that white-lightning-poison up from the South and he carries them in the saddle bags on his Harley."

"I'll get a guy on it, Mr. Schmidt." Carter said.

"Good." Jackson said.

"Do you remember talking to me yesterday?"

"I talked to you yesterday?"

"Yes," Carter said. "Do you remember calling me this morning?"

"How could I have called you? I don't even have your number."

142

Carter messaged his temples and Jackson sprung up to his feet.

"What time is it — you're going to make me late. I have to buff the west wing floors before Mass."

Father Paul gave Jackson a stop sign.

"Jack, you already finished the floors."

"I did?"

"Yes," Father Paul said. "You finished them two days ago."

"Oh," Jackson said and slumped back down on the pew.

"Shall we ..." Father Paul asked Carter while motioning with his head for the two men to take a walk away from Jackson.

"Sure," Carter said.

"Jack, Detective Woodbine and I are going to have a meeting in my office," Father Paul said. "And while we're gone, I want you to stay right here and say your prayers. OK?"

"Yes, Father," Jackson said, closing his eyes and bowing his head.

Father Paul and Carter walked away from Jack's earshot.

"It pains me to see him like this," Father Paul said.

He led Carter through a maze of corridors before finally reaching a wooden office door. He opened it with a minuscule gold key and allowed Carter to enter first. Once seated, Father Paul took his seat behind the desk and faced the detective.

"I brought you here to shed some light on this unfortunate set of circumstances," Father Paul said. "I feel somewhat responsible for all of this."

"Why's that?"

"I planted the seed in his mind to go get those flowers," Father Paul said. "He's dropped off poinsettias on Cheyenne's grave — on his wife's grave, every Christmas for many, many years now. I didn't want him to forget. I was hoping maybe it would trigger some old memories of her."

"You weren't driving the car," Carter said. "You can't beat yourself up for trying to help a guy out. These things happen."

"But," the priest began, "I should've never let it get this far. I should've been more proactive."

"What do you mean?"

"We've been making arrangements to get him into an assisted-living facility," Father Paul said. "I kind of dragged my feet — that's my fault. I thought he had more time. I thought he was doing well enough on his own — he lives so close. He's always here. I'm always here. We had the paperwork and the facility finalized, but there were hiccups. He doesn't have any children or next of kin and his insurance — well, he doesn't have any insurance. He's living on his social security. The red tape was ... we just didn't have the scissors to cut it."

"So is it Alzheimer's or ..."

"Late-stage dementia," Father Paul said. "He's had it for a while now, but it has come on real strong of late. It used to be simple lapses here and there. But about a month or so ago, he no longer could remember his wife, and she was his everything. That's when I knew it was taking over."

"That's a shame." Carter replied, somewhat compassionately.

"It is," Father Paul said. "He's lived a great life. He's a wonderful man. He was a wonderful husband. His faith in our Lord is insurmountable. He's a shoo-in for Heaven, I can promise you that. That's what's so disconcerting about this — to see a man, an unblemished soul, to see him live to this ripe old age and only to have the tail end of it become tarnished — and by taking another man's life — and, not even knowing he did it — it's really, really sad."

"The flipside to that coin," Carter began, "is ... I have to question it. I have to go around twisting and tugging until someone finally screams "uncle." And when they do, well isn't it interesting? But when someone screams "Father," it doesn't have the same ring to it and it makes me wonder what I'm pulling on. And to be damn honest, it makes me wonder if someone's jerking my chain ... if someone is pulling my leg."

"Are you suggesting I'm lying for him?"

Both men searched for answers in their respective eyes.

"Even if he did remember something — anything," Carter began, "and even if he told you everything ... there isn't much you could tell me about it because he told you in a confessional, right?"

"Yes, it's true I'm protected by the Code of Canon Law to not to repeat anything disclosed in confessional," Father Paul said. "It's my moral obligation to uphold the oaths I have taken in the Seal of the Sacrament. But, I can assure you, there was nothing revealed in there. My concern is for the remainder of this good man's life. He doesn't remember a thing. I'm here to aid you in any way I can. To help you. To help him and do it as an honest man under the vision of God."

"What's his memory's shelf life — how much time does he have until he forgets everything?"

"It varies," Father Paul said. "Some days, it's maybe an hour. Other days, he'll remember things from the previous day. Sometimes, he'll mix up the days and events and things of that nature. Another time, he'll remember everything and can retain it for weeks. You never know what you're going to get or when you'll get it, if at all."

"What you're telling me is it would be wasting my time following him around all day on a hunch that stuff will fall out of his head?"

144

"If it ever falls out. If it was ever stored there in the first place."

"Can you unlock him? Is there any tricks?"

"What do you mean?"

"I dunno, I guess I'm wondering if you know how to get him to remember things. Is there anything you can do or say or coach him on, you know, to get him to come out of … out of the blankness?"

"I'm afraid there isn't a key for this," Father Paul said. "It doesn't work that way."

"What if I showed him the video of our interview? Do you think he might remember it then?"

"I suppose anything is possible," Father Paul said. "But, if you already have his testimony, what more do you need from him?"

"I'm looking for consistency in his story," Carter said. "What if the guilt got to him — what if he wanted to confess, supposing he did it intentionally? Who's to say he doesn't know what he's doing or remember what he did? Who's to say he could be using this condition to his benefit? I have to entertain every notion, even if it's justly squandered by dementia. And if it is legit, I won't apologize for being brazen. Unlike in your profession, kindness doesn't get me very far. People confess to you on their own free will. I have to pry a confession out of people and if my attitude is the crowbar, so be it. Up until Mr. Schmidt's morning phone call, I was about 99 percent sure I knew where this case was going. But this revelation, it potentially changes everything. I'm going to need medical reports, his doctor's prognosis … I'm going to need documentation. This job isn't about black and white. There's a gray area I have to toe-walk along. There's gray matter, Father, and I'm not just talking about what's in the man's brain either."

"I can assure you his condition is true," Father Paul said. "There's no con. The man … he's sick. It's an illness. Let me tell you a few things about Jackson S. Schmidt before you go around following him and upsetting him any more. He's been a father figure to me ever since I joined this parish. After he lost his job, he became our maintenance man. He's come in here every single day of his life, aside from a few sick calls, or a vacation, or those kinds of things. I know Jackson S. Schmidt like I know the bible. And I read it a lot, sir. Then, one day, not too long ago, I hear him pacing the cathedral floors, mumbling and singing. I get closer and I hear him repeating, over and over, 'John Jacob Jackson S. Schmidt. His name is my name too. Whenever I go out, the people always shout, there goes John Jacob Jackson S. Schmidt.' So, naturally, I'm a bit concerned. I ask him if he feels all right and he says, 'Yes.' I ask him why he's singing his name over and over to the tune of 'John Jacob Jingleheimer Schmidt,' and he comes clean. He says, 'Something is wrong in my noggin.' I asked him what he meant and he went on to tell me he was having trouble remembering his name. He said it took him half the day to remember it and when he finally did remember it, he began to sing the song so he wouldn't forget. He said the kids in grade school used to tease him with that when he grew up, but it turned out being a Godsend because in the long run, they ended up helping him out. For me, that's probably what you boys in blue would call a 'clue' and I knew something wasn't right with him.

"So, I started monitoring him and things increasingly become stranger. I started to see some very peculiar and very sad things coming from him."

"Like what?" Carter asked.

"Soon thereafter, after I found him singing his name — he races in here one day and says someone stole all of his money from his bank account. I do some research and come to find out, there's no money missing at all. He switched banks, for whatever the reason. He didn't remember doing it, but he did. It all checked out with his old bank and his new one too. It took me until 3 o'clock to convince him everything is fine and his money is all intact. Great. It's all right. He gets it. He's relieved. The very next day, he races in here again, hemming and hawing about all of his money being missing. 'Am I watching a rerun?' I think to myself. I research it again, just to make sure, and again, no money is missing. See, what he was doing was waking up and checking his old account — he remembered how to do that. He could even rifle off the account number and password like old hat, but for the life of him, he couldn't remember switching banks or me even helping him out at all the day before. It's a vicious cycle. This went on for two weeks straight, detective. And as you saw just a few minutes ago, it's still going on.

"I've learned through trial and error, whenever he isn't confident in my reassurance, all I have to say is, 'I swear to our God' and he believes and it saves me a lot of time and explanations. But it isn't just the bank account. Every day it's something new with him. Last week, I found him running in and hiding his billfold next to literature and chorus hymns on the back shelving of a pew. I confront him on what he's doing and he tells me there's a motorcycle gang outside who is trying to steal it from him. I look out at the parking lot and there's only one motorcycle out there. Its owner isn't even near it.

"Oh, I almost forgot, just the other day he sits me down. He's holding a notepad. He asks me to help him write some things down. Things like what his wife's name was. And what was she like. And what did she look like. He asks me to tell him what he did for a living. What some of his favorite things are. And ... and I'm starting to think, 'Whoa. He's getting it. He understands that he's forgetting things. He doesn't want to let go of the things that are dear to his heart. He's making a checklist of importance so he can turn to it when he's lost.' He had all these little notes that I couldn't make heads or tails of.

"So, we spend a good deal of time covering his life. Mostly things I remembered him telling me, but I have to say, his thoughts were a flowing river that day and I wrote everything down for him. The next day he comes to church and he says he wants to show me something — he's really frantic. He unbuttons his shirt. And there it is. It's this tattoo. Or a series of tattoos — with all these words, and they're inked into his flesh purposely backwards. The words are all these messages or reminders. Things like, 'cupboard next to sink' and 'drawer next to the bed.' About halfway down his chest, the words stop in mid-message — I can only assume Jack came to of sorts and wondered what in the world he was doing sitting in a tattoo parlor*1. So, I ask him what they mean and he doesn't know. He's a nervous wreck about it because, one, it's a sin — self-mutilation. He remembers that from the Bible.

"And two, he thinks some kids in the neighborhood must've held him down and gave it to him. He's in tears because he thinks it's a satanic message when he looks down at his chest and can't read it. And he also thinks they gave him AIDS after sticking him with a dirty needle — major damage control time for yours truly. I eventually talk him off the ledge. I go get a mirror and we try to work the puzzles out. It becomes clear to me after reading the ink that these notes were intended to help him find things. We walk to his house and I go to the cupboard next to the sink and sure enough, there's his medication. I go to the nightstand next to his bed and there's the notepad that we wrote everything down on. He wanted to be able to find these things when he looked at himself in the mirror. It's those types of things, Detective Woodbine."

Carter considered the priest's words. He stood up and walked over to the room's lone window. He glanced out into the winter's morning. His eyes started to sting and his nose started to itch. He breathed jerky and had a booming sneeze.

"God bless you," Father Paul said.

Carter nodded in gratitude. Then he tilted his head like a parrot listening to a car alarm for the first time.

"Per our phone conversation this morning, he told you he didn't remember a thing about yesterday, right?"

"Yes," Father Paul said. "He couldn't recall anything at all when he first spoke with me."

"I understand that the mind deteriorates and illness happens when people get old," Carter said. "But what if I told you I'm not buying any of this dog and pony show?"

"As a man of God, I promise you his condition is real."

"Father Paul," Carter said. "If a homicide detective took the word of every murderer or their accomplice who promised to be a man of God, who swore to Him, there wouldn't be a problem with overcrowding in our state penitentiaries, and I'd most likely be out of a job. I know for a fact, the victims' families would still be stuck grieving in a purgatory of Hell if I took those animals words for it. 'But he swore to God' is an answer I could give them, while the monster is free and allowed to roam the streets. I believe in science. I believe in statistics. I believe in documentation. I believe in facts. You're giving me your accounts. And I appreciate your help, if it's valid and agenda free."

"How could I make this up?" Father Paul said. "What am I to gain from this?"

"Maybe, he's propositioned you. He got himself into a big jam and he comes to you and you bail him out — hiding him under your religion, under your love of God, under this big church. You guys don't do that, though. Right? You guys don't turn a cheek when it comes to hiding truths. Nah. That's unheard of in the Catholic religion — unless, you were a molested altar boy. Right? I've worked those cases. I know what's been swept under the cloth — the rug. Or, now hear me out, maybe if you help him out of this conundrum, he writes you into his will? Or, let's say this condition is true, like you say it is, maybe you've written yourself into his will? How would I know? 'Here, sign this, Jackie boy. It means you get into Heaven,' you might say. Or, maybe, if this condition is true, while you're helping him recover his banking information, maybe you're helping yourself. How would I know where a man spends his money, if he doesn't even remember spending it? Motive, Father. Everyone has some."

"He's not a wealthy man, Detective. There's barely enough for him to get by."

"Maybe that's because he's given it all to you. Or, because you've taken it. How would I know?"

"Bank records. You can check his bank records."

"The same ones you manage?"

"You don't have to believe me. If you have an ounce of intelligence, you'll see he's sick. You'll see what a wretched affliction his dementia is."

"Are you asking me to sign a sympathy card?"

"That's impossible. You're a man who hasn't anything left in the well to give. Your jobs probably dried you up. Jesus has a way of replenishing it, though. It's never too late to turn to him."

Carter acquiesced with an astute smile.

"What would Jesus do if he were trying to solve this case?"

"He would have faith. Not all of His people are liars. Not all of His people harbor sin. He might even go take a look at his tattoos I was telling you about."

"I might just do that," Carter said. "I might have a nice gander at them when I'm taking his booking photos."

"Pardon me for saying this, Detective," Father Paul said, "but you're very obtuse. And arrogant. And miserable. And you're barking up the wrong tree. And — forgive me, Father — and you're an asshole!"

"What did you say his doctor's name was again?"

"I didn't."

"Oh, that's right." Carter said sardonically.

SIDE 2. TRACK 3. LINER NOTE:

1. Jackson did have an epiphany while sitting in the chair of a tattoo parlor. He became extremely confused and irate. The message the artist was inscribing into his skin backwards with black ink was "Ja…" It stopped there when Jackson had his meltdown. Despite of his rage, Jackson willingly paid $70 for the tattoos.

4. Even the Sun Shines on a Dog's Ass Every Once in a While

Carter was stopped at a traffic light thinking about Jackson S. Schmidt's odd behavior. He nonchalantly looked to his right, through the passenger seat window, and recognized a man who was walking out of a coffee shop named Joe Mamma's.

"How do I know that motherfucker?" he said to himself.

The man's wild hair stuck to the tip of Carter's tongue. But as the seconds ticked away, he couldn't spit it out.

The light turned green and Carter lifted his foot off the brake pedal. He was willing to let the speculating dissipate, where it would most likely resurface at a later time — usually when he was about six beers into his night. But as he was about to give his unmarked squad some gas, he made the connection and was surprised with his serendipity. He elatedly pounced on brakes, causing the car to forcefully rock.

"I think that's Alex Fucking Hedlund," Carter muttered.

The man standing before him was in fact Alex. Carter recognized him from the printout of Alex's driver's license he had in a folder on the passenger seat and had studied last night.

Carter began retrieving the photo to double-check. But he didn't need to search for very long, because when Tommy Shannahan walked out of the coffee shop, Carter finally put the situation together. He recognized Tommy's face from the picture of him in TheSkinny.

Carter retrieved his phone, punched a couple of buttons, rolled down the passenger-side window and waited.

Within seconds, Alex felt for his pocket, retrieved his phone, looked at the caller ID and gave Tommy a confound look. Tommy laughed and pointed at the phone in an I-told-you-so way.

"Alex!" Carter shouted through the open window, his phone still sewed to his ear.

Alex instantly turned to Carter's voice. Tommy followed suit.

"Answer your phone!"

Tommy and Alex briefly looked at each other in bamboozlement. Alex, in a state of shock, took the call.

"Hello," Alex softly answered.

"Get over here!" Carter said. "And bring your jagbag friend with you."

Carter flashed the badge around his neck as Alex and Tommy crept toward the car.

"Detective Carter Woodbine, Chicago Homicide," he said, unlocking the doors and pointing to the back seat. "Get in."

Alex opened the door and slid across the seat, leaving Tommy to sit directly behind the passenger seat.

"You're both musicians, focus your audios," Carter said. "Does either of you want to tell me why you're sitting in the back seat of a squad car?"

Neither man answered as they were still shocked at what was happening.

"Boys," Carter fulminated, "If you want to play hardball, I can get the paddy wagon over here right now and have you cuffed and stuffed in a matter of seconds! We can do this in here or at Cook County. Don't make me ask the same question twice."

"Yes," Alex said. Then Tommy copied Alex.

"Good," Carter said while alternating eye-contact with both men through the rearview mirror. "Next question: Do either one of you have any weapons on you?"

Simultaneously, Alex and Tommy replied, "No."

"Are you sure neither one of you is armed with a gun?"

Once again both men denied with a unanimous, "Yes."

"Let me ask you something, Alex," Carter continued. "Do you think that would be an important question to ask — assuming you were sitting where I am in this car?"

"It holds validly," Alex said.

"It sure as fuck does. And why do you think it does?"

"Because you just let two strangers off the street into your car?"

"You're cute," Carter said, piercing his eyes into Alex's. "If I was half as smart as you are stupid, I'd have a much better life. I'd be a genius — probably cure cancer instead of wasting my time tracking down losers like you. Want to give it another shot, smartass?"

"You probably heard my recording," Alex said.

"Oh, yes," Carter said. "Your recording."

Carter shifted his attention to Tommy.

"And you, drummer boy," Carter glared. "You're Tommy, right?"

"I am," Tommy responded.

"I know all about you — even read your write-up in TheSkinny. Good stuff actually. Have you heard Mr. Hedlund's recording? He mentions you in it."

"No, I haven't," Tommy replied.

"Well, there's some stuff he says in there, if made public, it probably wouldn't bode so well for your family's business or even your rock-star career."

The car grew heavy with silence while Carter studied the men with a vindictive glare. Alex felt compelled to come to the aid of his friend.

"What if I told you it was just fake ideas for a song we're going to record?" Alex said.

"I would make you out to be a liar while you make me out to be a moron," Carter said. "Let's quit cupping each other's balls, guys! Did it ever occur to you two chuckleheads, the reason most cops are fucking assholes, is because fucking assholes lie to us all the time? You go to work five days a week and listen to lie after lie, day after day, and year after year, and then you tell me how cool you would be."

Once again the car went silent. Carter lit a Red Apple cigarette and as he did, Tommy thought:

- I need a cigarette, but there's no fucking way I'm asking if I can have one.
- We're so screwed — this guy's not playing games.

"Look, gang," Carter said, in an attempt to reset the game, "We all know why we're all here. And I don't want to be a fucking asshole — let's not all be a bunch of fucking assholes. OK? How 'bout that? Does that sound fair?"

Alex and Tommy nodded.

"Tommy, gun trafficking isn't something the guys in my profession are too keen on. You're kind of seductively dancing with the RICO Act there, buddy," Carter said.

Carter let his testimonial sink in.

"And Alex, here's the thing, since you didn't actually obtain the gun, I can't really guillotine you on trafficking charges like I could your friend Tommy here, but plotting a murder — even if the person you want to put holes in is the biggest hunk of shit in the septic tank — and making a recorded message about it and then leaving it around for a homicide detective to hear, probably wasn't the smartest move of your life, I imagine."

Alex hung his head.

"Look," Carter said, "this case has been a very, very interesting one. There are some extremely bizarre set of circumstances surrounding it. I've never worked an investigation this complex before. Usually, I'm dealing with a dead gangbanger and it doesn't take very long until a confidential informant narcs out the killer. Usually these scumbags run their big, fat mouths in boast. So, the reason I've been trying to get ahold of you two guys like an overly-attached girlfriend is — it's because I need your help, boys. Alex, if you help me out, when I finish my report, I'll persuade the District Attorney's office to look past the conspiracy to commit a murder charge. I could tell them you made that recording in the heat of passion and before you did anything stupid and before you cooperated with authorities and promised to testify against 'The Mongoose' — which you're going to have to do.

"And Tommy, I'll also encourage the D.A. to oversee your involvement in gun racketeering — and I'll even do you one better — I won't spread the word to my friends in blue about the shenanigans going on behind closed doors at The Cow or open the floodgates with … ah … dropping a dime to Rolling Stone magazine — if your band makes it to the big time."

The air in the backseat got lighter.

"Does that sound good?"

Both Alex and Tommy nodded and agreed it was a great fairness.

"Fantastic," Carter said. "So, here's what I need you to do. I want you guys to help fill in any blanks I might have missed. Deal?"

Alex and Tommy agreed, "Yes," in unison.

Carter pulled out his voice recorder from his duty bag.

"Do either one of you object to me recording our conversation?"

Both men shook their heads and Carter pressed the record button.

"Alex, can you state your full name for me?"

"Alex Louis Hedlund."

"Thank you. Alex, after hearing your story — after you came to us, the Chicago Police Department, volunteering information, is it safe to say you were willing to do whatever it took to get your kids back. Is this correct?"

"Yes," Alex said.

"And per our previous conversation, you wanted to inform us that a man named Cody Grantland, AKA The Mongoose, is producing, manufacturing and selling the illegal narcotic often referred to as 'crystal meth' or 'ice' or methamphetamine?

"Yes," Alex said.

"So, you solicited the help of your friend Tommy Shannahan sitting beside you in the back of my squad car, correct?"

"Yes."

"Tommy," Carter said, "Can you state your full name for me?"

"Thomas Ian Shannahan."

"Thank you," Carter said. "Alex, you assumed Tommy's a man who knows a wide variety of people — because he bartends at Mrs. O'Leary's Cow — and he could help you out. Would you say

152

that's accurate?"

"Yes."

"So you solicited the help of your good friend, Mr. Thomas Shannahan, and he made a few phone calls for you, and he knew of a guy who can get you a gun. And that guy was Bill Dodanno ... is this correct?"

"Yes," Alex said.

"So Tommy, you call Bill Dodanno, because he's a man that's known to sell guns. Is this correct?"

"Yep," Tommy said.

"Did you and Bill do a lot of business together in the past?"

"No," Tommy said. "In all honesty, that was the first time I ever called him for that."

"How did you know to call him then? How did you know he sold guns?"

"He's a regular," Tommy said. "Well, he was a regular. One day we got to talking — he was drunk. He had a lot of financial problems since his wife died. He told me that he had some guns to unload — hopefully to help keep the lights on at his house and the hot dog joint. He said he was just a collector. Guns were his hobby. He wasn't a criminal, just broke."

"So, you thought, 'Hey, this sounds like a good idea to make some money,' and jotted his number down, right?" Carter asked.

"Not exactly," Tommy said. "We don't sell any food at The Cow, so we had his food catered for a couple music shows we hosted. That's how I got his number."

"I see. Did Bill ever talk about owing money to anyone?"

"You mean ... like a loan shark?"

"Yes."

"No," Tommy said. "I don't think so. I think he mentioned bill collectors were after him one time, but not one person specifically or anything like that."

"Did Bill ever say he had any enemies?"

"Not that I'm aware of," Tommy said.

"How often would he frequent the bar?"

"He'd walk over a couple times a week," Tommy said. "Sometimes, it would be a couple times a day. He was really going through a rough patch."

"So, you knew him pretty well?"

"Not really," Tommy said. "He only started coming in within the last six months or so. He mostly sat by himself and kept to himself. A couple times here and there, he'd get shitfaced and tell me about his sick wife — and then after she died, of course — he'd talk about that. I'd buy him a couple beers to try to help him through it. He did tell me about how some customer tried ruining his business after he claimed there was a bloody napkin in his hot dog or something. Maybe he was an enemy? But other than that, he pretty much kept to himself."

"Aside from his wife, did he ever talk about his family?" Carter asked.

"Nope," Tommy said. "He never said a word. I don't know if he even has kids."

"When you talked to Bill last, did he sound irritated or panicked or ... How did he sound when you made arrangements for the weapon. The handgun?"

"Fine," Tommy said. "He sounded normal, I suppose."

"Can you talk me through your phone call with him?"

"Sure," Tommy said. "Alex came in ... said he needed some help — something he never does — so I knew something was up. Then he told me what he needed. I remembered the hot dog guy — Bill — saying he had guns for sale. I never thought I'd ever need to call him about that. So I asked him about getting a gun and he said he still had something to sell and he'd be there soon. And ... and that was about it. When he didn't show up when he said he would, I called him again and ... and he never answered. Then I heard the sirens and ... and well, here we are."

"Alex," Carter said while changed his focus, "have you ever met Bill?"

"No, Sir," Alex said.

Carter was at a stalemate. He tossed his cigarette butt out the window.

"Do either one of you know a man named Jackson S. Schmidt?"

Tommy and Alex both shook their heads as Carter looked at them.

"Tommy, is there anything else you can think of?" Carter asked with a grasping-at-straws tone in his voice. "Anything at all that you think would help me out?"

"I wish there was."

"OK ... I was hoping you'd both have more news for me — not your fault. Sometimes you're the bug and sometimes you're the windshield. I'm trying to be the latter."

"I swear I wish I had more for you," Tommy said. "I feel terrible, sir. I didn't think I'd ever be in this kind of situation."

"I understand."

154

The three men sat in silence. Carter's cellphone's ringing broke the silence.

"Detective Woodbine," he said into the phone.

A garbled voice could be heard in the backseat of the squad. Minutes passed with Carter mostly listening to the caller or acknowledging with an "uh-huh."

"Thank you for the heads up," Carter replied, and ended the call.

"Alex," Carter said, "As we've been sitting here, a drug task force has raided the home of Cody 'The Mongoose' Grantland. Your children were not harmed. They appear to be in fine health. Cody and your wife on the other hand, well, they're in custody."

"Are you serious?" Alex asked.

"As serious as a grabber," Carter said while clutching his chest and making an awful, gasping-for-breath noise. "I took the liberty to check into some of the things you mentioned in your recording and sure as shit, my friends in the task force have had their eye on him for quite some time. After hearing what I had to say, they decided to obtain a search warrant and knock the doors down. Now that I've gotten the chance to finally tell you what's going on, you're going to get in your car and go to the Byron police station where they are waiting for you. You will help them out the best way possible ——— cooperate, answer all their questions. Hopefully, if all goes well there, you'll leave there with your kids."

"Thank you, Sir!" Alex said, patting Carter on the shoulder.

"Don't get too excited, kid," Carter said. "You aren't out of the thick of it yet. The Department of Child and Family Services is involved. Your boys are currently in their custody. When the drug task force is done talking to you, I imagine a member of DCFS will have a new set of questions for you. They're probably going to ask you things like, 'Why didn't you report this to the police weeks ago?' and stuff like that. I can't say for certain if they will relinquish the kids to you or not. I have made a suggestion that you have tried everything in your power — aside from calling the authorities, to find them. So maybe that will help you out. I don't know, though. I'm not a soothsayer (Carter covers the recorder with his hand in an attempt to muffle his voice) and those bleeding heart liberals can be a really big pain in your ass."

"Detective Woodbine, thank you so much. I ..."

"... Hold up a second, Alex ... I'm not finished. You must not forget there are people out there who aren't too crazy about rats. Like I said before, retaliation is a big part of why I collect a paycheck every two weeks. If they find out about all this shit — if they find out about your involvement, there's a good chance you'll have more than just a finger pointed at you. No one likes snitches. And that's what you'll be to them."

Alex slouched in his seat.

"So, with that being said, be careful. I don't want to solve your murder too."

"Thank you," Alex said.

"Well, guys," Carter said while stopping the recorder. "I have a shit ton of shit to do today. For now, you're free to go."

Tommy opened the door and both men got out.

"Thank you," Tommy said, getting ready to shut the door.

"And, guys," Carter yelled before the door was shut. "Next time I call — and I will be calling — answer the fucking phone."

5. Skywalker: The Unintentional, Chicken & Waffle-Loathing Lunch Guest

Chloe Woodbine tried leaving her house about an hour after her father did. When she got to the front door, her mother caught up with her.

"Where are you going?" Shelby Woodbine asked desperately.

"Out," Chloe replied.

"You can't leave me!" Shelby said with fright.

"Mom ..." Chloe tried to rationalize.

"Your father didn't come home again!"

"Yes he did. I saw him, Mom."

"No he didn't!" the panicking mother said. "He was out at the bars again and he has a mistress, doesn't he? I know he does! I smell his shirts. Sometimes I can smell her perfume. Sometimes there's glitter on them."

"Mom, I promise, he was here last night."

"So you're lying for him too now? Just like the bartender's do at The Green Mill or Mother's or Andy's Jazz Club when I call looking for him and they say he isn't there. What's that whore's name, Chloe? Please tell me her name!"

"Mother, you need to relax."

"What you need to do is stop him!" Shelby demanded. "He's ruining our family! He'll listen to you."

Chloe stood in the archway, giving her mother a blank stare. A moment passed before she turned around. Her mother rushed to her, dropped on her knees and latched on to her daughter's jeans.

"Please! Please don't leave me! Who will feed me if you go? You know I can't stick myself. You know I need my medicine!" she shouted.

"Get up, Mother! You have to stop doing this!"

Shelby wrapped her arms around Chloe's right leg like a sulking weanling and clung to it as she was dragged out to the porch. As Chloe lugged her mother further, Shelby's long, stringy hair gusted in the wind, weaving and wrapping itself around her daughter's trunk. When the pair reached the steps, and when Chloe reached her boiling point, she brushed her mother off with a bulky forearm and stood over her like a domineering giant.

"Well, where will you be then?" Shelby screeched.

"Don't know," Chloe said. "Downtown. I'm going downtown. I got Christmas shopping to do."

"No! You mustn't! It's not safe. Those buildings could fall on you! Don't go! I beg of you, Chloe. Don't go. Please don't go."

Chloe didn't turn around to see her weepy mother and she casually walked to the driveway.

"Twenty-seven hours of drug-free labor and this is how you repay your mother?" Shelby screamed.

Chloe got in her car, started it up and backed out of the driveway. She had nowhere to be, but anywhere from home.

With the car idling, she thought about how her life had turned to this. She used to hate seeing the state her mother's mind was in. But after all the medicine, all the therapy, all the overdosing, all the fear and panic, all the suicide attempts and all the cries for help, Chloe became callous and didn't care anymore. She was tired of making excuses.

She dreaded the thought of bringing her volleyball teammates over on a night where her mother was hiding under furniture and whimpering like a dog on the fourth of July. She envisioned losing it if she brought a boy she liked home and the second they get out of the car, he'd see her mother on the roof of her home with her binoculars pressed to her eyes, searching the sky for hijacked airplanes. Within the last week, Chloe had come to the conclusion that her mother was a lost cause. It saddened her greatly that after a decade of medicine, she was far worse off now. In her sorrow for her mother, there was sorrow for her father too. He was just a shell of the man he once was. He pissed his insides down the drain and the only way to stuff him full again was to get rid of what was draining him. But for whatever the reason, he was too stubborn to leave, and it irritated Chloe to no end.

She parked on a side street a couple blocks from the Magnificent Mile. She checked her phone — 19 calls, all from her mother. She put her phone back into her purse and made her way to the tallest skyscraper she saw.

She paid the $27.50 admission and an elevator swiftly took her to the John Hancock Observatory. Even though she lived in the city, she'd only been to the top of the famous skyscraper once.

She took a few steps off the elevator, steadying a slight queasiness from the super-fast, 20 mph ride up the 94 stories. She walked toward a section of huge floor to ceiling windows. She paused in front of a view that overlooked the monstrosity that is Lake Michigan and breathed it in. She stood there for several minutes, watching tiny boats inching along the lake's vast waters.

She turned and walked to the north-facing section of glass. Below, she could see dots for people walking along a section of paved beach. It was a tremendous view and made Chloe feel like a microspec in the grand scheme of life. She was one of those ant-sized, marching souls.

She was lachrymose as she walked to a western-facing section of windows, but no tears fell from her eyes. The lambent city drawn out before her was becoming too vast. She overheard two male tourists in their 30s, discussing how Chris Farley died in the building's 60th floor.

Their conversation about Farley continued and they made plans to eat at one of his favorite restaurants, Heaven on Seven, for lunch. Chloe had only seen a small amount of Farley's work. Most of the little she had seen was on the Internet — mostly Internet memes of him dancing in the famous Saturday Night Live "Chippendales" skit — but she knew enough to know he was tremendously loved. The notion of these two grown men, taking a tour of the last spots Farley was seen alive, struck her. She didn't understand why it would be so important, decades later, to eat where a sad, lonely man used to wolf down his food. But she did realize one thing — if a drug-and-alcohol addicted, prostitute-using, funny fat man, who died a miserable death alone, was being remembered 20 years later, she could be too.

She leaned her forehead to the glass and looked down. Busy Christmas shoppers littered the Magnificent Mile, surely buying wonderful gifts for their loved ones. She stood that way for several minutes and when she pulled her head back, she could see a red circular mark in the middle of her forehead from the reflection in the window.

She strolled out onto the Skywalk, an open-air walkway that faces to the city's south. She put her hands on the large screen which prevented anyone from falling off the building, looked at the enormously tall building off in the gloomy distance that will always be called the Sears Tower, and mulled over life. It was there on the Skywalk, where the cold wind blew away any warmth that was left in her heart, she finalized the last details of her future plan.

She left the John Hancock Observatory and decided to window shop the storefronts along Michigan Avenue. She looked up at the John Hancock building to get the opposite view of what she had just seen from atop, but the windows' glare prevented her from seeing anyone. When she thought about the perception, of her being unseen from below and like a tiny spec from above, she became down.

She checked her phone again — seven more missed calls from her mother. She put the phone back in her purse and continued to shuffle her feet along the busy sidewalk. She didn't understand what was so great about Christmas shopping despite the happy looks on the faces of passersby with enormous bags. She would not be buying anyone a gift today, nor did she have any intentions to do so.

She walked south, passing Water Tower Place. As a child, she would've taken note of how lovely the gothic, white-ash colored bricks of Holy Name Cathedral were. She would've slowly strolled in wonderment at how smart the people of Chicago were for preserving it. Today, she didn't find the Cathedral anything but eerie and it fit her mood. A car honked, snapping her out of the daydream and fueling her lament. She used the crosswalk at East Superior and continued down Michigan Avenue, peeking in the fogged windows of Saks Fifth Ave. There was something dazzling behind the window in the showroom and she went in to investigate it.

She walked out of Saks with a bag*1 and continued past the four levels of giant, beveled windows at Crate & Barrel, eventually ending up in front of the Eddie Bauer store at West Ohio. The warm-up in Saks was a teaser and she became extremely cold. She wanted out from beneath shadows of the large buildings and into sunlight like a lizard could find a hot rock. She found sunshine fighting through clouds and went west on West Ohio. She froze at the crosswalk at North Rush, not knowing what her next move was. She thought about going home, but she was having difficulty deciding how she was going to find her car.

For someone who grew up in the city, far north of the hustle and bustle of downtown, she made a mental note of how naïve she was at knowing her way around. It wasn't often she drifted away from her childhood neighborhood and when she did, she rarely was alone. She looked around at her surroundings and was beginning to get worried. She did a 180-degree turn and then, lo and behold, smack-dab above her line of vision, was the sprawled-out red Heaven on Seven sign.

She took the sign as, well, a sign, and she was compelled to go in. She wanted to see what Chris Farley had for his last meal and the walking had built up her appetite. She took the short escalator ride up to the second story, watching the people on the sidewalk getting smaller through the large windows. Once at the top, she stood in front of the restaurant's entrance and locked eyes with a hostess who acted like she would rather be somewhere else.

"How many are in your party?"

"Just me."

She followed the hostess to a small table around the corner of the main dining area. Aside from a few customers, Heaven on Seven was nearly vacant and she didn't mind one bit. Chloe took her seat and the hostess handed over a menu.

"Your waiter will be with you soon," the hostess said and then stomped off.

Chloe looked around, taking notice of the purple, green and gold tinsel hanging from various spots. There was a fake alligator mounted high on a wall near signs which read "restrooms" and "phone booths." She realized Heaven on Seven was a Cajun-themed restaurant and, being the meat and potatoes girl with a bland palate, she suddenly wasn't too happy about where Chris Farley liked to eat. She skimmed through the menu, trying to pronounce words she didn't comprehend, looking for anything basic. She saw chicken and waffles was the daily special and she elected to go with it, if the waiter ever surfaced. She felt her phone buzzing in her purse yet again. It was her mother. She had only called three times since the last time Chloe checked it. She looked at the picture of a picture of her mother's face on the display of her smartphone while it rang. She found the picture in an old album. The original was snapped back in a time when her mother was normal and loving and motherly, and when her hair was kept mange-free and falling out and long, and when the skin on her face hadn't been vacuum-sealed from all the drugs — the way Chloe wished she could always remember her.

She set the phone down and the waiter finally arrived.

"What was Chris Farley's last meal here?" Chloe asked.

The waiter had no clue. He said he could ask around if she wanted, but Chloe told him it wasn't necessary and settled on the chicken and waffles.

After he walked away, she was left to eavesdrop on the conversation of two foodies at a nearby table. They were both men in their early 30s, who were both serious about pogontrophy — their unique beards and moustaches were manscaped to perfection in sharp lines and precise shapes. Both men wore thick, black-framed glasses and were dressed dapper in suits and ties, their sleeves rolled up high on their forearms as if to desperately show off a new fashion of rose-colored, gold wristwatches.

Chloe inaudibly snickered at the watches. "Who needed a watch unless you didn't have a phone?" she thought. If her Daddy was sitting there with her, he would've told her they were begging to be robbed.

The man with his back to Chloe listened to his corpulent foodophile acquaintance talking about some wonderful transplant Chicago chef named Grant Achatz, and his amazing restaurant, Next. In between the sounds of chewing and poppysmicing, the fat man was explaining how lucky he was to get tickets to eat the "Paris 1906" menu, which was no easy task because the restaurant used a lottery system for its dinners. Chloe pretended to be texting when the man went on and on — describing every detail of the restaurant to his friend. It was all blah-blah, mumbo-jumbo to Chloe, but she listened anyway because she had no choice. Chloe grimaced listening to each item on the menu being explained.

As she thought about what a waste of money dining at a place like Next probably was, the man riffled off more courses as if he had a photographic memory, Chloe turned his voice off. She'd heard enough. She was blessed with knowing she could grab a hot dog or an Italian beef any time she wanted.

Once her chicken and waffles were dropped in front of her, she already felt full. She cut off a piece of the waffle, put it into her mouth and immediately wanted to spit it out. It wasn't that the waffle was disgusting, it was she had just realized she was eating alone — she had so much on her mental plate and there was no one to share the feast with. She swallowed the bite and didn't return for another. As she sat there, thinking about the future, she stabbed a fork into how she was going to make her plan work.

The restaurateur with the big mouth had moved on from the Paris 1906 experience and to telling his friend how he drunkenly sprawled into another famed Chicago chef, Rick Bayless, on the sidewalk of North Clark last Saturday night — his irritating voice finally breached her ear canals. He discussed how he was loaded on Hotel California Jamaica Margaritas and trying to tell Bayless how he had just eaten at his restaurant, Topolobampo. He wanted to thank him for being his "food God," but the chef kept backpedalling in petrification at the overly-excited, bumbling and stumbling approaching gastronome.

She listened while continuously poking at the chicken. She didn't know who Bayless was, so the story was as tasteless as her food, which had been dissecting into something that looked like an eighth-grade science frog. Then her phone rang. She looked at it in anticipation of it being her mother, but it wasn't. Her eyes sparkled when she realized it was her father.

SIDE 2. TRACK 5. LINER NOTE:

1. Chloe left Saks Fifth Avenue after buying herself two Christmas presents. The first was a snow globe of Santa and his reindeer flying across the Chicago skyline. The second was a green Hatley Girls Classic Raincoat, size 12.

6. "Sharpen Your Snags."

The portable house phone was delivered to Seamus Shannahan by his wife as he sat on a chair in the garage listening to The Beatles' White album on a record player. She told him it was Tommy and leaned in and softly kissed his cheek. He patted her fanny hiding underneath the aqua medical scrubs she was wearing and she walked out of the garage to go to work.

"Hello."

Tommy spoke for about a minute and then went silent. Seamus reflected for several moments.

"Son," he said, "I would love to see your show tonight. I appreciate the offer. I appreciate you trying to extend an olive branch. I really do. I know, you're right, 'tis the holidays. The holidays are about forgiveness. And someday, I might be ready to forgive. But, I'm sorry, I won't be able to make it tonight. Even if you were playing at a different venue and your shithead Uncle wasn't there, I still wouldn't be able to make it. I have begun a project. It's a Christmas gift actually and I'm knee deep in it over here. I hope you have a great show. Maybe someone will film it and you can show me on your computer tomorrow. One of these days, I'll see you kids live*1. I promise as much. Don't stay up too late tonight — you don't want to miss dinner by sleeping in all day. Your Mother says it'll be early this year. She's baking a ham, so sharpen your snags, you might be chewing leather — God bless her sweet heart. And I know … I know what you're thinking Son, and yes, one day, things will be all right. I'll see you tomorrow."

On the other end of the phone, Tommy Shannahan heard his father fumbling with the phone and thought:

- He's drinking whiskey again.
- He's up to trouble.
- He'll never reconcile with Uncle Junior.

Seamus finally ended the call after a series of misconnecting button pushes. He stood up, walked to the side door, opened it, and had a glimpse outside. His wife's car was gone and long down the road.

He went back to his chair, opened up his suitcase and retrieved a bottle of Paddy Old Irish Whiskey. He unscrewed the cap. He had a whiff. He had a smile. He had a stretched, guzzling pull and then rested the bottle in his lap. He sat there, forward-facing, masochistically waiting for the alcohol to wash through him. He looked at the life-sized fiberglass cow in front of him while the whiskey pleasure burned his stomach and opened his sinuses. A nippy tingle raced down his spine. He shook it off and felt his nipples come erect — the same way Irish whiskey always made them contract.

On the floor next to the base of the cow there was a Dewalt 120 volt cordless sawzall. A square, 3x2 section (above the utter, along the plate, between the fore flank and hind flank of the cow) of fiberglass was cut out and lying next to the sawzall. Next to it was a neatly packaged contraption of wires, wicks, fuses, black electrical tape and hundreds of configured fireworks. He had another whiff. He had another long sip. He had another smile. His nipples got hard.

SIDE TWO. TRACK 6. LINER NOTES:

1. Seamus had never seen Tommy and his band play live before. The reason was twofold. First, Michael Sr., Seamus' father, never attended any of Seamus' Golden Glove boxing matches when he was younger or any other activities. It seemed as though the learned behavior was a progressed character flaw passed along from one father to the next. The defect stemmed from the truth that Michael Sr. played favorites, something (to a lesser degree) Seamus did with his own kids as they grew up. After Michael Jr. was born a child with piercing blue eyes, a doughy pale face and dark, fine hair, and he began to resent the brown-eyed, freckly and colicky and coarsely redheaded Seamus when he came along less than a year later — literally "Irish Twins."

Although he never told her, Michael Sr. had a difficult time believing his wife, Nellie, didn't step out on him during Seamus' conception. At the time, he was spending many hours away from home while running his business and he had his suspicions Nellie was two-timing him with a redheaded fella in the neighborhood named Frankie McShane. However, his allegations were false. Seamus inherited similar genes and traits from that of his great, great grandfather, Lenny O'Leary's pedigree (a great bloodline of gingers).

As he developed, Seamus continued to not look anything like his parents and his roughhousing and blockheaded behavior didn't reflect either one of their calm and methodical natures either. Seamus spent a great deal of his childhood being yelled at or physically punished for his rambunctious ways. Michael Sr. often misread Seamus' intentions of fondness, assuming Seamus was an out of control bastard child with anger issues. He was quick to correct Seamus with the back of his hand and even swifter to console Michael after the siblings spat with one another — often giving into Michael with hugs and rewards of candy after kicking Seamus out of the house. While Seamus would pout outside, often tinkering around in the garage, Michael Jr. would regularly taunt his younger brother by showing him the candy through windows and while Senior could be heard in the background laughing.

As the boys grew into teens, Seamus became even more star for his father's affection — often choosing to fight for his love with athleticism. He would get into scuffles at school, tell his father tales of scoring touchdowns in sandlot games, frequent the boxing gym or knock Michael Jr.'s lights out when they disagreed about nearly anything.

When his physical toughness didn't win his father over, Seamus would fiddle with tools and machinery in the garage in an attempt to make his father gratified. For example, at the age of 13, he took apart a lawnmower and replaced its engine with a more powerful one. Seamus' hubris dragged his father outside to show off its newfound muscle and in the process of doing so, Seamus lost control of the machine, and it destroyed an oak tree yearling and a majority of his mother's favorite flower garden. Seamus took a good walloping for it. By his senior year, Seamus dropped out of school and began to take on odd mechanic jobs before getting his CDL and driving trucks for the Jewel-Osco company.

Even well after he was hired by Jewel-Osco, had bought his first and current home, and was adequately providing for his own family, Seamus continued attempting to gain his father's adoration, but the old man never budged. It was made heart-wrenchingly obvious he never succeeded when he left Seamus out of his will and out of the bar business. Michael Jr. followed in his father's footsteps and chose schooling as opposed to a blue-collar career, where he graduated from Northwestern University with a master's degree in finance.

As his own children grew in his household, Seamus favored Kevin over Tommy because he shared more of his physical characteristics and rogue adolescent behavior which contrasted against

Tommy's more articulate and artistic one. The second reason as to why Seamus never watched Tommy and his band play live was chiefly because of Michael Jr. having financed some of the band's equipment and needs, to go along with housing them at The Cow, and Seamus had a difficult time being around another family-oriented-thing his brother had his hands in.

7. Victim Blaming

Carter stormed through the entrance of Heaven on Seven. He brushed by the hostess, scanning the restaurant. He cut off her helpfulness with an open hand once he found Chloe behind a wall where hundreds of miniscule hot sauce bottles from throughout the country were on display. He marched toward his daughter and when she saw him approach, her eyes lit up.

"Daddy!"

"Don't Daddy me," he said. "Chloe, what the fuck's going on? Where's your car? What are you doing here? Your mother is worried sick about you and I'm in the middle of a huge case. I might even earn my stripes if I don't fuck it up. Do you know how long I've been trying to make sergeant?"

"I'm sorry," she said. Her eyes returned to glass.

He noticed her slump in the chair and it prompted a collection of his emotions.

"No, I'm sorry," he said. "I guess I'm not the only one here who's in the middle of important stuff."

She lifted her eyes and she was still his little girl. He looked at her plate on the table.

"What did you get?"

"Chicken and waffles," she said. "Supposedly this was Chris Farley's favorite restaurant. I don't know if this was his favorite meal, though. Do you know who Chris Farley was?"

"Do I know who Chris Farley was? I'd do his 'fat guy in little coat' bit right here and right now, if I knew it wouldn't embarrass you. Farley was the best. He died before his time. It's a shame. One of the guys I'm buddies with on the force worked his death investigation. It's sad how a person, who was so loved by so many, died all alone."

"It is sad."

"How's the food — any good?" he asked, grabbing a quarter of the waffle and having a bite.

"I don't know. I couldn't taste it."

Carter's face indicated the waffle was indeed good. After he swallowed, he wiped the sticky syrup off his fingers and onto a napkin. He licked his lips and gave her a stern glare. She tried to debunk his seriousness with a smile, but it didn't work.

"You know," he said, his face becoming red, "I think we've done enough bullshitting. I never thought I'd say this — I've never had to say this before — but Chloe, I have to say, I'm very disappointed in you. I never thought I would be the one giving you the birds and the bees talk. I always thought your mother would be better suited to talk with you about these kinds of things, but we both know she isn't suited for much of anything. But what happened last night, goddamn it Chloe ..."

"... Dad, I don't need the birds and the bees talk. I know all about the birds and the bees," she interjected hastily.

"Well excuse me — you're absolutely right! You do know all about it. How could I forget walking in on you and your little fuck buddy knocking boots in my recliner? A real, proud father moment let me tell you."

"Dad!" Chloe said, blushing. She gave her father an intentional eye-point to the adjacent gourmets who began to listen in on their conversation after Carter raised his voice.

Carter turned to the gentleman and gave them a despicable scowl.

"I think it's time for you guys to get a to-go box," Carter said while flashing his badge.

The men pushed away from the table and shuffled to the bar, Carter never taking his eyes off them until they were out of earshot. He then returned his focus on Chloe.

"Do you know how disrespectful that was?" he said.

"Good! Why do you think I did it?"

"Because you're a teenaged girl and your hormones are all out of whack and you kids these days hump like rabbits — I just hope he wore a condom. You can ruin your volleyball scholarship — your whole life, if you get knocked up! Goddamn it, Chloe! C'mon, use your head. You're better than that."

There was a long pause. Carter hung his head and rubbed his temples. Chloe shot lasers at him with her eyes.

"Dad," she said, her voice a foundation of moving cracks, "I was raped."

Carter lifted his head. He let her words sink in for a brief moment.

"The guy from last night!? He was raping you? Why didn't you tell me when I walked in? I would've shot him right then and there! What's his name!? Tell me right now — I'll fucking kill him! He got away once, but it won't happen twice!"

"No," she said, hanging her head. "Not him. He … that … it was … last night was con … consensual. I was raped a few weeks ago."

"Are you OK?"

"Physically … I've healed. Emotionally? No. I'm not OK."

"Who was it, Chloe? Was it a boy from school — did it happen on the street — did someone drag you in an alley? Where did …"

"I … I … I don't know who they were."

"They?"

166

"I think there were three of them ... maybe more."

"What? What the hell happened? Tell me everything!"

"I went to a party with my friend. We met some guys from a different school. The party was at an abandoned house. I can't even remember what street it was on. I got drunk. Someone slipped something into my drink — they had to put something in my drink. The next thing I remember ... I was waking up ... In the middle of it. They took turns. There was a couple of them ... they bit me. They hit me. They were rough. They tore me. They raped me, Daddy!"

Chloe burst into tears. Carter bawled his fists and bit on a knuckle. His blood boiled.

"Did you go to the hospital? Did they do a rape kit?"

She shook her head and wiped a single globule from an eyelash.

"You didn't go to the hospital?"

She shook her head again.

"Did you call us — the PD — of course you didn't, or we would be talking about three dead scumbags right now instead of three soon-to-be-dead scumbags."

Carter spent a minute trying to come to grips with what had happened. Chloe's hysteria slowly lessened to whimpers as he mused.

"What school do they go to? We can find them in a yearbook."

"What you're asking me to do ... every boy in that school would become a suspect."

Frustration turned to anger.

"You should've known better than to put yourself in that situation, Chloe!"

She lifted her head and was astonished with his lack of compassion. She tried to advise him as such, but the words wouldn't come out.

"How many times have I told you to be careful? How many times have I told you to use your best judgment? How many times have I told you about this type of shit? I see it all the time, Chloe. I find girls like you dead all the time because they don't think! They didn't listen. You're smarter than this, Chloe! Haven't you learned one damn thing that I've taught you?"

Again, she tried to speak, but nothing would come out but gasps of breath.

"Why didn't you tell me right away?"

"I tried."

"When?"

"I'm always trying to tell you things. You just never listen, or you're never home, or you're arguing with Mom, or you're too drunk."

"Oh, get off it, Chloe. When's the last time you saw me drunk?"

"A couple weeks ago — when you dropped the chicken pot pie on my arm*1."

"That was an accident and I wasn't drunk … I was slightly toasted."

"Just like my arm."

Carter scratched the caterpillar above his lip and thought about her words.

"Are you pregnant?"

"No."

"Are you sure? I can run out and buy a stick right now …"

"… I already did that. I'm not pregnant."

"Thank fucking God."

He kept playing with his moustache while searching the hot sauce bottles on the wall for answers. He nearly harangued her on responsibility, but his phone rang before he could. He briefly looked at the caller ID before answering.

"Homicide, Detective Woodbine speaking."

He listened to the caller keenly.

"Whoa, whoa, whoa," he said into the phone. "Slow it down, man. Relax."

He stood up, pointed to the phone while giving Chloe an I-have-more-important-stuff-going-on-right-now-and-I'm-really-sorry-but-I-have-to-go expression. He reached over the table, rubbed her head like she was a mischievous puppy before walking away from the table, telling the caller, "I'll be there in 10 minutes."

Chloe turned off the faucet of waterworks and an icy blood shot through her veins. It was the first time in her life she viewed her father as a man she hated.

SIDE 2. TRACK 7. LINER NOTE:

1. Carter did accidentally drop a freshly baked chicken pot pie on his daughter's arm. And he was intoxicated when he did so. The instance befell when Carter and Chloe's paths actually crossed for more than mere minutes inside their residence. Carter was smashed after touring some of his regular watering holes and Chloe was up studying when her father came home. They genuinely carried on a lengthy, memorable conversation while the frozen pot pies cooked. After the kitchen timer went off,

Carter retrieved one of the two pies, and tried to deliver it to his daughter with his bare hands. He was carrying it with the thumbs and index fingers of both hands, when the pot pie became too hot for him to handle. He was hastily bringing it to the table, but as he did so, he snagged the knob of Chloe's chair back and the pot pie toppled over and flew in the air before landing all over Chloe's arm and the table. Carter immediately blamed Chloe for his mistake, by saying, "Your big ass should've been scooting your chair in when you saw that my hands were on fucking fire!" But, Chloe's back was turned to him at the time. Chloe stormed off to her bedroom and Carter ate his pot pie in silence, repeatedly burning his tongue as he did so. Carter had completely forgotten the incident took place until Chloe brought it up.

8. The 17-Year Cicada Bug

Carter drove directly to Millennium Park from Saint Rita of the Angels church and parked. Thirty minutes before, he was explaining to a corybantic Jackson S. Schmidt, yet again, why the goldenager was holding his business card and why a reporter had knocked on his door inquiring about an accident he knew nothing about.

Carter explained to Jackson he was conducting a death investigation where Jackson was driving his Lincoln when he struck and killed a man, and that the reporter went to his house after a press release was sent out. Upon hearing the news, Jackson became confused and worried and distraught. Carter monitored his reaction penetratingly, and this time around, he 100 percent believed Jackson's dementia to be a factual illness. But, he didn't let it be known to Father Paul, who stood by and bulwarked the elucidation as it unfolded.

Carter stormed out of the church and lit a smoke. The affirmation to what he thought had transpired in the middle of the intersection, a pronouncement he was on the nib of submitting to his boss, and one he had previously seen so clearly, had now become clouded. He was back to square one and in his mind's eye, the sergeant stripes he had been dreaming of wearing proudly on his sleeves, were beginning to unravel.

At 1339 hours, Carter strolled through the park and to The Bean, or Cloud Gate, the bean-shaped and futuristic-looking sculpture comprised of 168 stainless steel plates welded together and polished smooth without any detectible seams. He dropped a Red Apple cigarette butt on the cold concrete next to his shoe and the sound reminded him of a minor moment from last summer.

It was a humid night and he was sitting in a deck chair on his back porch, when a 17-year cicada flew past his head and crashed into the sliding glass door. For whatever the reason, the dense and crunchy noise reverberated within him. And now, several months later, the familiar sound of the cigarette crashing to the algid stone next to his feet triggered introspects into the life of an insect that burrowed itself deep into the Earth for 17 years — the same amount of time his daughter was surfaced. If the Bill Dodanno case looming over his head wasn't gloomy enough, the informative luncheon he had earlier with his daughter was the lightning bolt striking his antenna.

He walked under The Bean and looked up at his reflection. It was distorted and grotesque, and it gave him an oracle — his reflection was exactly how his daughter perceived him as, and justly so. The conception made him cross.

"How could I have buried the poor child under my problems like a bug?" he thought. "It shouldn't have taken a priest calling me an asshole to apprehend what I am and have been. All I had to do was look into my little girl's eyes a long time ago. How much damage has been done? How can I correct this? Can I correct this? Will she ever forgive me? Damn it, Chloe ... I'm so sorry."

He walked away from The Bean trying not to cry and dialed her number. She didn't answer. He tried to leave her a message, to say he was sorry, but his voice was broken and nothing came out. He hung up.

He walked through the park and sat on a concrete partition where "WRIGLEY SQUARE" is engraved in the facade. The Y lined up directly in between his legs and when he looked down, he found the letter emblematic. He said, "Why?" aloud and looked at the spectacular view of the city for answers. The old Chicago Public Library building stood directly before him and he gazed up at its stunning marble pillars. Then he sneezed. And then he sneezed once more. After the brief PSR fit, he swiveled his head 180 degrees from left to right, taking in all of Michigan Avenue. The buildings were the only thing he found beautiful anymore.

At 1406 hours, his stomach rumbled and it interrupted his visual meditation. He tried to recall the last thing he ate. Then he harked back to the hot dogs from yesterday. He would kill someone for another one of those dogs. He looked around the park and only found shivering tourists. A cartoon light flickered on above his head. He flipped through his notepad, found a number and dialed it.

"Dee?" he said into the phone. "This is Detective Woodbine. Say, I think I've got an idea for you. Do you ever go to Millennium Park to think?"

(DeVon "Dee" Whitaker's voice, inaudible)

"Well," Carter said, "I do some of my best thinking here and sometimes I work up a big appetite while I'm doing it. And you know what I never see over here?"

(Whitaker's voice, inaudible)

"Exactly," Carter said. "You're a good kid, Dee. You deserve to know what I'm about to tell you. Your old boss, ol' Billy boy, well, he rented that space you're standing in and the bad news is, the owner is going to be closing the doors to Doggy Style Hot Dogs on Wednesday after he gets back from Christmas vacation. I dunno how all of that stuff works — there's a lot of red tape and legalities and shit that isn't my specialty, but you might want to do what you gotta do before he returns. Maybe I'll see you around ... if you know what I mean."

Carter hung up the phone and traipsed toward his parked squad. Along the way, he passed a large wreath hanging around a light pole. A gust carried the scent of juniper into his nares. He went from hungry to thirsty and hungry for something else. He felt he had put in enough hours on what should've been his day off and maybe the answers would flow if he poured himself an attitude adjustment or two ... or 10. As he reached his unmarked squad, his phone began to ring.

"Homicide, Detective Woodbine speaking," he barked into the receiver.

As the voice on the other end of the call ceased talking, he bobbed his head.

"I'll meet you at Mrs. O'Leary's Cow in 20 minutes."

9. "I'm a cop. I love being a cop."

At 1419 hours, Carter arrived at The Cow and approached Officer Matt Lyons. The rookie was in plain clothes and was working on his first beer when Carter entered the nearly deserted pub. The pupil shot off the stool to greet his senior.

"Thanks for meeting me — great pick, by the way!" Lyons said with an over-excited handshake. "I like this place — nice view (eyeing the bartender)."

"I wanted to see the crime scene one more time," Carter said, slithering his hand from Lyons' meaty grip and taking a seat.

Lyons thought about Carter's words and then Nodded. He then tried to get the bartender's attention with an erratic wave, and when it didn't work, he obnoxiously whistled. The act backed supercilious glares from Blue Trillium, who was at the end of the bar talking to two customers — the only other people in the bar. Once she saw Carter sitting next to the whistler, her face softened. She sauntered to them only way she knew how — making lecherous an affinity.

"Get this man anything he wants and put it on my tab," Lyons swanked.

"Hello, Detective," Blue said, bypassing Lyons and engaging Carter.

Impressed the beautiful girl knew who he was, Lyons patted Carter's back.

"Hello, Blue," Carter said in an empowering tone.

"Tonic and … two limes, was it?" she inquired.

"Very good memory. But I'm off the clock, honey. This time hit it with some poison. Bombay Sapphire — and drown the ice cubes, if you wouldn't mind."

Blue turned around and started making Carter's drink. As she did so, Carter faced Lyons.

"Pro tip: Don't whistle at a bartender," Carter said. "You whistle at a dog or a crack head, but not a bartender. They're servers, not servants."

"Got it," Lyons said.

"This girl here," Carter said while pointing at Blue, "she's sweeter than just her looks."

Lyons looked Blue over as she made Carter's drink and slowly nodded.

"So," Carter began, "what brings me down here?"

Lyons twisted his attention from Blue's long legs to Carter's long face.

"I wanted to thank you," Lyons said.

"For what?" Carter asked.

"For letting me watch you work. I learned a lot of things from you out there on the scene and when you interviewed the old guy. One day, I hope I can be as badass as you."

"Lyons, you don't want to be anything like me. But thanks for the compliment. Now that all the brown-nosing is out of the way, what do you really want to talk about?"

Blue delivered Carter his drink and froze their conversation.

"There you go," she said, setting the drink on a bar napkin.

"Thank you," Carter said.

She leaned forward, rested her arms on the bar and gazed into Carter's eyes.

"We don't like to be called 'honey' either, Detective," she said.

"Don't call them 'honey' either," Carter told Lyons.

"If you're looking for Tommy, he isn't here," Blue said.

"I'm not," Carter said.

"Then tell me, Detective," she said, "what did I forget to give you yesterday that you're here to pick up today?"

"Just your smile, honey," he said.

As much as she didn't want it to happen, a slight smile slowly emerged. Before it got too big, she clamped her teeth and abruptly righted herself.

"For some reason, I don't believe you," she said.

"That's unfortunate," Carter said. "I'm only here to have a drink with my friend (points to Lyons) here."

"Out of all the bars in Chicago, you chose this one? I don't know if I feel flattered or worried. I wish it was flattered, but I don't think it is."

"You have nothing to worry about."

"I'm not worried about me," she said, walking to the end of the bar.

Lyons smiled in awe of Carter's authoritative presence, but Carter didn't notice because his eyes followed her callipygous rump as she strolled away.

He had a quenching sip. Upon completion, he double-banged the glass on the bar top and whispered, "That's what I'm talking about" before returning focus to Lyons.

"So, Lyons, you were saying?" Carter asked.

173

"I wasn't brown-nosing," Lyons said. "I don't want to be a uniform my entire career. I'd love to be a detective one day. Don't get me wrong, I love being a beat cop, but I've always wanted to be a detective. My thank you is sincere. I really appreciated you letting me watch you interview that guy. Part of why I wanted to meet with you is — I guess I'm kind of curious where the case is headed. For me, it's like renting a movie, and right when things are getting good, the DVD freezes. So that is one reason why I called you."

"What's the other?" Carter said, his words muffled by the glass pressed against his lips.

"If you don't mind, I have a few questions about this case," Lyons said.

"I don't mind," Carter said.

"Well, here's the thing," Lyons said and continued, "I didn't want to step on any toes yesterday, but there's one thing that I found strange when I first got on scene and that you didn't ask the old man about."

"What's that?" Carter said scrunching his brows.

Before Lyons could answer, Blue returned to check on the boys' drinks.

"So, Detective, have you figured out why that guy got murdered out there?" she asked.

"We haven't officially ruled that case a homicide," Carter replied.

"Are you going to?" Blue asked.

"Maybe," Carter said.

"If I buy you a drink, will you tell me if Tommy's in any trouble?" she said.

"You can buy me a drink if you want to buy me a drink, not because it's collateral for information. But, I will say this … I wouldn't worry about Tommy if I were you."

Blue smiled at Carter and then moseyed away to go text Tommy. She intentionally stayed within earshot in an attempt gather any information.

"Who's this Tommy guy you keep talking about?" Lyons asked.

"Tommy's a bartender here," Carter said, observing Blue and looking around the bar for privacy. "But why don't we take this conversation over there."

Each man grabbed their beverage, turned and walked to the front of the pub. Blue, with her plans to eavesdrop foiled, gave herself a facepalm.

"Tommy was the middle man for the gun-trafficking dead guy," Carter explained. "He's the reason we're here today."

"I see," Lyons said.

They reached the stools and sat down. Carter gazed directly across North Halstead and ogled the red doors on the fire station that Engine No. 55 called home.

"Fucking firefighters," Carter said. "Now that's the life, kid. You're always a hero. Everyone loves a fireman. I checked the wrong box, back in the day. It's not too late for you to jump ship and go hang with the good guys. I wouldn't blame you one bit."

"Fuck that shit," Lyons said. "I'm a cop. I love being a cop."

A wry smile crept across Carter's face.

"So, what were we talking about?"

"When the old guy runs the dead guy over with the Lincoln, how come he didn't back up?"

"That's a good question," Carter replied.

"If I ran a guy over, I'd probably get out, check on him, jump back in the car and then throw it in reverse. But the old guy, he just walked to the front and stood there."

Carter agreed with a nod.

"And when you were interviewing him, he said he was trying to protect the girl, but from what I gathered, he was already aiming for him before the dead guy pulls a gun."

Carter raised his glass, looked at its contents, put it to his lips, and had a tall sip.

"What about the directions we found in his bible. That didn't make sense either."

Carter shot Lyons a peculiar look.

"You opened the bible right?" Lyons asked.

"What do you say we have about a dozen more of these and we solve this case?" Carter said.

Lyons clanked Carter's G&T with his pint glass.

10. The Mookie Brownstone Blues

Mookie Brownstone stood in front of the splintered mirror in his cramped bathroom and adjusted a skinny, black tie around his skinny black neck. He could barely notice the contrast of black on black. A droplet of water collected at the faucet head of the grimy sink and trickled a single drop. Exactly three seconds after it fell, another followed suit. It was the only way to measure time in his minuscule, rundown second floor studio apartment.

Mookie flung his right arm through the sleeve of his black suit coat like he was leaning over a pier, trying to catch a fish with his bare hand. He then pitched the remainder of the coat over his narrow shoulders and hurled his left arm through the airborne left sleeve in a fluid motion. His shoulders were snuggly surrounded by the coat before the next suspended drip of water fell in the sink. He inspected the coat. His neck and the coat were the only things he could see. His face was perched far too high above the mirror to see anything else. He fastened the middle button and ironed the front panel with his freakishly long fingers. He took three strides back to see his entire reflection, which put him in the middle of the apartment's only other room. He buried eight fingertips into his perfectly round afro and repeatedly flicked at various points like he was fluffing rice with a fork. He ran both index fingers atop a thin beard which started at his ears and followed down past his cheeks where it ended as a chinstrap for his hair helmet.

There was bickering outside the liquor store a story below. Someone owed someone money — it was the same song Mookie always heard. Tonight, the chorus wasn't loud enough for him to high jump over the bar and flop into the bathtub. If it were a steamy summer night, he would've laid in the tub, waiting for the gunshots and then the sirens, before venturing out to leave. His neighborhood was always a valid excuse for tardiness, amongst other things. But tonight, the weather was cold. Even though he hated the way the winter wind licked his skin, it was far less painful than the violence that typically attached itself to a summer breeze blowing in the streets.

He stared momentarily into his brown bug eyes. They had seen a lot of terrible things in their 37 years. But tonight, they were looking back at a happy man. He retrieved his black leather fedora off the mattress on the floor. The bed didn't have a frame and took up 75 percent of the floor space in the studio — tattered and blanketed with stains. But compared to the places he's rested his head in the past, the mattress might as well have belonged to a king. He set the hat atop his Nerf hair and the lighting from the bathroom cast a shadow on the wall that was redolent to a three-scooped ice cream cone. He reached down and unlatched the black guitar case sleeping in it. A beautiful maple acoustic was lying in a casket of gray velvet. There was a secret compartment built into in the bottom of the case reminiscent of a jewelry box. Mookie lifted the lid. In it, a shiny silver .22-caliber Champion pistol with a wooden handle. A box of bullets rested nearby. He stuffed the gun into the right flap pocket of his suit coat. Next to the bullets was a set of handcuffs. The cuffs had six inches worth of metal links connected to the swivel of each cuff. He retrieved them, shut and latched the guitar case, and then fastened one of the cuffs around his left wrist and the other to the handle of the case.

He didn't have a car, so he didn't grab any car keys. He had keys to lock the door, but a clumsy toddler could knock the cheap thing down with an errant trip, so there was never a point to doing so. He gave the room a final look, walked out and was about to go down the flight of stairs when he remembered something.

He returned, walked to the small kitchenette three feet from the mattress and two feet away from the radiator. Above the single burner and what might as well have been an Easy-Bake Oven, there was a small shelving unit. He reached up next to a trifling stack of plates and a coffee cup containing silverware and found an old fishbowl. It once was home to the only pet he had ever had — a Siamese fighting fish named Buddy. The fish had recently died*1 for reasons murky to Mookie.

In the bowl was a guitar pick — his lucky guitar pick. It was given to him by Buddy Guy, his mentor, when he was a teen playing for change outside of Comiskey Park*2. He thought about the memory as he fished out the pick and then stashed it in his right trouser pocket, where it joined his money clip, keys and a stack of Magnum condoms.

The motherfuckers were outside banging when he walked down the 14 steps. He unlocked the metal door, stepped outside and then relocked it. The door was more of a deterrent against gusted garbage collecting at the bottom of the staircase and against any motherfucker who had plans on using the landing as a urinal, than it was a method of protecting his apartment. The motherfuckers were always in front of One Stop Food and Liquors at the corner of West 35th Street and South Western Avenue — drinking malt liquor, smoking blunts and selling crack. The motherfuckers had all the time in the world to motherfuck him when he tried to walk by or wait for a bus.

"Yo motherfucker, what's in the case?" they'd ask in bewilderment that anything other than a guitar would be in it. "Hey motherfucker, you bringing in cheese playing them songs?"

Mookie would attempt to move on with his life, but sometimes doing so was easier said than done. "I know you making ends, you big dumb mute. I know you can talk motherfucker. I can make you talk if I want." Or a motherfucker would say, "You think wearing your suit makes you better than me, motherfucker? Gimmie some of what you got mute, or I'll give you some of what I got." Mookie would flash his ivory at them. Sometimes the smile worked, other times he was less fortunate. "You like to play music, motherfucker?! I can make your motherfucking head sing!" a motherfucker said one time, while he and his motherfucking friends kicked Mookie's motherfucking face in, and eventually robbed him of his motherfucking guitar*3 and his motherfucking money.

Mookie wasn't mute, but there were only few people who knew it — his family, the U.S. Army, his landlord, some fellow street musicians and anyone he was forced to talk to for practical and survival purposes. The reason why Mookie rarely conversed wasn't because he was introverted or retarded, either. The reason was he had possibly the worst stutter in the history of the world. Sometimes, a sentence as basic as "May I please have some milk?" could take Mookie 30 seconds. Since he first began to talk, the speech disorder plagued him. His grandfather, Tyrrell Tussell, found a soft spot for Mookie after his stammering was first acknowledged. He taught Mookie how to play the guitar at an early age. Tussell spent his weekdays as a mailman with a penchant for impregnating women on his routes and his weekends as a guitar player in his Baptist Church's band. Sensing the frustration in the youngster, he wanted to give Mookie an outlet for communication and felt the guitar was his best way to do so. "Let your fingers do the talkin', Mook," he'd encourage. It was unknown who Mookie's biological father was, and his grandpa became his father figure until the day he died.

This evening, Christmas Eve, the motherfuckers let Mookie wait for the Chicago Transit Authority's 35/35th bus without resistance, but he kept his hand in his right flap pocket just in case. The bus took him eastbound 11 stops to 35th and South Normal Avenue where he elected to get out and grab two dogs naked at 35th Street Red Hots. After scarfing down the food, he continued east, walking underneath the bridge that carried train tracks to an old stockyard — a place where, as a teen, he played his guitar uninterrupted and escaped the heat, his Mother's drug addiction, and all the brothers and sisters she endlessly kept filling the house with.

Before the city rehabbed the area, there were a series of broken-down and abandoned boxcars along the tracks near West 37th and South Canal streets. Mookie took refuge in a rusted-out, mint green car, the paint was chipped off and faded away and where white lettering spelled a barely legible "Wabash."

During the summer of his 15th revolution around the sun, he holed himself up in the car and started calling it home. He lasted until mid-November, until it became far too cold.

When he first moved in, he would sit on a wooden chair with the guitar his grandpa gave him, listening to three albums on an old record player his grandfather also gave him. The albums were Son House's "Father of the Delta Blues: Complete 1965 Session," Memphis Minnie's "I Ain't No Bad Gal" and Buddy Guy's "Alone and Acoustic." He ran juice to the boxcar via 27 linked extensions cords, that he boosted from stores or open garages, from a neighboring apartment project. He hid the last cord under a trench he dug with an old coffee can while the motherfuckers were sleeping, or not at their traditional post on the porch. He buried the wires so any snooping motherfucker wouldn't see it plugged into the power supply outside the complex and then trail it back to his humble abode.

He would play a Son House song, learn the notes by ear, and play them verbatim before needing to repeat the song for a third time. Then he would move on to the next song and do the same. He devoured the entire "Father of the Delta Blues: Complete 1965 Session" within a day. He then moved on to Memphis Minnie and then to Buddy Guy until there was nothing left.

Sometimes, the power would go out and he was forced to listen and play along to the music in his head. Other times, a chew-happy rat would shred an extension cord. But on the nights he had electricity, he'd play alongside Memphis Minnie and pretend the cheering from the crowd inside Comiskey Park were applauding for the concert he and Minnie were putting on. He'd finish up practicing when he would see fans starting to dissipate from the ballpark or hear fireworks shoot off from the exploding scoreboard (signaling a White Sox victory) and then he'd walk over to the stadium with his trusty acoustic guitar in hand. He'd set up his stage in a parking lot. Some nights, he'd bring home $40 in change — that was if the motherfuckers didn't take their cut, or all of it.

On Mookie's 15th birthday, Tussell died of pneumonia. The loss was devastating for Mookie, and not because of their shared fondness of the guitar and the blues. It was because Tussell was the only person he genuinely loved and trusted. Mookie became recluse soon after, spending all of his time mastering the guitar in the boxcar. The more he consumed music, the more it consumed him. When the three albums his grandfather left him weren't enough anymore, he hankered for more. There was a record shop about 20 blocks away he and his grandpa frequented.

After the weight of Tussell's death began to lighten on Mookie's fragile psyche, he started spending hours in the store every day listening to free music. A couple of weeks went by and the shop owner, an obese man who always smelled like barbecue ribs, grew tired of him not purchasing anything. He warned Mookie that he needed to buy something if he wanted to stay, but Mookie didn't adhere. The owner even offered taking $3 per day and Mookie would be welcomed to listen to any album he wanted to, but Mookie couldn't afford it. He was eventually banned from the store, and he couldn't understand why — he merely stood around with headphones on, never conversing with anyone.

Bored with the three albums his grandfather left him, Mookie devised a plan to steal what he was no longer welcome to. While formulating his plan, he tore a legging from a pair of pantyhose he found in the boxcar and used it to cover his face, distorting his identity good enough to use.

His plan wasn't rocket science. He hid in an alleyway across from the record shop and monitored foot traffic going in. He had the legging ready to deploy atop his cornrowed hair as he waited for a handful of shoppers to enter the music shop. Mookie charged through the doors with the makeshift mask covering his face, and took as many albums as he could before the shop owner had time to comprehend he was being burglarized or even had the time to get his fat ass out from behind the register to stop him. By the time he exited the building unscathed, Mookie had boosted six albums: Little Walter's "Hate To See You Go" 1969 Chicago record 1st press, Muddy Waters' "They Call Me," Junior Wells' "Hoodoo Man Blues," Sonny Boy Williamson's "More Real Folk Blues," Johnny Winter's "The Progressive Blues Experiment," and Howlin' Wolf's self-titled album. It took less than a week to finish memorizing all the notes. He hastily became disbursed with his newfound talent for stealing, and he returned to the record shop every time he needed a withdrawal.

Some days, he'd return to the boxcar with the entire loot of six or seven. But other days, the motherfuckers would shake him down and he'd return with nothing but a black eye or a bloody lip. The day he raced into a music store and stole his first brand-spanking-new electric guitar — a black with maple neck 1988 Fender Stratocaster MIJ he'd been eyeing for weeks outside the storefront windows of The Piano Bench at West 47th and South Damen, the motherfuckers didn't get him. The guitar became Mookie's first girlfriend and he named her "Honeydripper" after his favorite Buddy Guy song.

Mookie got away with lifting 37 albums before he was finally caught. He was running out when someone happened to be walking in and there was a massive collision in the doorway — sending the cardboard album covers crashing like a house of cards. But he wasn't arrested. The store owner belly flopped on him while he was trying to get up, and beat a punishment into Mookie instead of calling the cops. He suffered a broken nose and his eyes were swelled shut for nearly three days. But that was as nice as the injuries got. While the store owner was in his fevered fury, he mentioned something about how the Saudi Arabians penalize thieves — by cutting off fingers. But while Mookie laid there incapacitated, the store owner couldn't find anything sharp enough to do any cutting, so chose to do the next best thing to inflict as much damage to Mookie's hands as he could — he stomped and stomped and stomped on both of his hands with his size 9 ½ EE width wingtip shoes. Mookie was dragged out of the store, where he eventually walked to medical assistance — his arms raised up to his chest like a begging trick dog.

After seeking treatment at an emergency room, he departed with seven broken fingers, a dislocated right thumb, a broken right wrist and a broken left radius. To add insult to injury, he returned back to his mint-green boxcar and found his guitars had been stolen. After the walloping, Mookie never returned to the store, never returned to stealing and almost never returned to playing the guitar.

Two years later, Mookie enlisted in the U.S. Army and was eventually stationed at Fort Leonard Wood in Missouri shortly after his 18th birthday. He was discharged in less than a year because of intestinal problems*4 but stayed in the South*5 more than a decade, and even picked the guitar back up before returning to Chicago.

Once home, he lived in homeless shelters and continued trying to earn money as a street musician. He recorded some music and would leave his cassette tapes in public places, hoping one day to be discovered by someone in the music industry. He would also leave self-illustrated flyers*6 downtown in hopes of finding a girlfriend.

Tonight, he reached the Sox-35th CTA's L station and took the Red Line train north. No one on board thought twice about giving the 6-foot-9 well-dressed black man handcuffed to a guitar case any bit of trouble. They were too busy being trannies or hookers or were too high on crack to notice. He took his right hand out of his right flap pocket and sat down. In about a half hour, he would be in a different world, seeing a lot of different people — people who would take much notice in him.

He exited the train at the Fullerton stop near DePaul University. He walked a few blocks, and at about 9 p.m., he reached the tail end of the long line of fans waiting to pay the $10 cover charge to see The Farrow Moans. He was immediately recognized by two slightly bundled-up 22-year-old white girls*7.

"Mookie!" the pink-haired rocker yelled as he approached. He put a shush-finger to his lips, not wanting to gain any more attention. He outstretched his free arm and the giddy girl took it. His hand, swallowing hers, slightly pulled her closer to him. He bent forward and whispered something into her ear. She nodded in response, turned to her friend and said, "I'll be right back" to which her friend encouraged her to go with a double hand wave and a smile coated in jealousy. Mookie led the girl south on the sidewalk. Few words, if any at all, were spoken as they strolled along in the brisk night, his free arm draped around her tiny waist. They reached West Schubert, took a left, and ducked out of vision.

When they reached the darkness of an alleyway, he reached into his pocket, removed the key to the handcuffs, freed himself and set the guitar case down. Before he could rub his wrist free of any discomfort of the shackle, the girl had taken off her jacket, exposing her The Farrow Moans T-shirt, laid the jacket on the rocky ground and dropped to her knees. She unzipped his trousers, pulled out his kick start, and began to fire up his engine. He played with her punk-teased, pink hair and smiled like he won the lottery. As she was doing her thing, he thought about how he got to this point in his life …

One Friday, in June, Mookie attended the Chicago Blues Festival at Grant Park. He found the balmy night perfect for such an occasion because it reminded him of the nights when he lived in the South — where he would listen to the dirty blues coming from the old-timers who played the dives. On the Front Porch stage at Grant Park, a voice that sounded like a hell hound on its trail filled the air. It belonged to the fabulous Tail Dragger, whom the legend Chester Burnett gave him the moniker.

Both bluesmen were favorites of Mookie and he wished he could've joined Tail Dragger on stage. But, no one had ever heard of Mookie Brownstone, because he was a no one. As Tail Dragger, accompanied with Billy Flynn and Jimmy Dawkins on guitars, finished out their epic set with beloveds, "Treat Her Right" and "Tend to Your Business," Mookie was filled with jubilation. Why hadn't he ever started or joined a band? What was he afraid of? For, he was just as good if not better at the guitar than the old fogies jamming with Tail Dragger. When they waved the crowd goodbye, Mookie wandered away from the side stage and went hunting for another act. Upon doing so, he noticed a flyer taped to light pole near a sea of port 'o potties. The flyer had a unique picture on it. It was the band's logo — several piglets surrounding a nymph. And there was something about the nymph that mesmerized Mookie. Below the symbol a message stated: GUITARIST WANTED. There was a telephone number listed to set up an audition. Mookie didn't set up an audition*8, but he did some prying and eventually found out who The Farrow Moans were. A couple of weeks had gone by when Mookie walked into Mrs. O'Leary's Cow and watched the band gauchely play a set in the glowing "the emerald isle." He found the lead singer to have a tremendous voice and stage presence, and when he closed his eyes during some of their bluesy numbers, he never would've guessed the guy belting out the lyrics was a white boy. He also took note that the drummer was extremely talented as well. The bass player, well Mookie found him average, which wasn't shocking, because bass players are bass players and bass players are average. And the guitar player? Mookie couldn't believe the kid had the nerves to walk on stage. He found him to be horrendous and even covered his ears during the kid's solos.

After the band's first set, the members left the stage to chat with their small volume of fans, and Mookie snuck on stage. Nobody noticed when he picked up a guitar and strapped it around his torso either. But everyone noticed him when he started playing the last tune the band played. Cal quickly turned to the stage and was shocked at what he was hearing. The song, "Banana Seat and Sissy Bars," was a freshly-cut original, and it was the first time the band had ever played it outside of practice. Tommy and Cal looked at one another astonished. The crowd cheered Mookie on and he continued to play without anyone stopping him. He dazzled the chords for 20 minutes — zigzagging various styles and rhythms and carving out sections of famous songs here and there until the crowd became frenzied. The members of The Moans took the stage to join him — with the exception of their newly acquired guitar player, AJ Arient — and the group had an impromptu jam session with the tall stranger.

Mookie stayed on stage, picking up instructions and musical directions from Cal on the fly, and he managed to play Moans songs he never heard before like he had been with the band since its beginning. When they finished the show, Cal dropped to his knees and gave Mookie a "we're-not-worthy" gesture. Even though Mookie was a complete stranger, and considerably older than the kids in the band, Cal offered him to join the group, to which Mookie accepted. When Cal asked him what his name was, he handed him a white business card*9 with only the word "Mookie" engraved on it. Cal read the card said, "Nice to meet you, Mookie! Our next show is tomorrow night at Metro. Can you be there at 7?" to which Mookie nodded again, shook Cal, Steve and Tommy's hands, and walked out of The Cow to a roaring applause. AJ Arient, who was watching the proposal, grabbed his guitar and stormed off the stage.

It only took Mookie two shows and three practices to master every song in The Farrow Moans repertoire. He even shared songs he had previously written and the band welcomed them with open arms. Soon thereafter, the band went back to the studio and rerecorded the entire "Once We Got to the Edge ..." album with Mookie as their lead guitarist.

Right around the six-week mark of being a member of the band, a membership that had quickly gained them virtuous notoriety in Chicago, they found out he wasn't mute and heard his unfortunate stuttering. It happened after a show at Lincoln Hall, when the band was shaking hands and talking with fans, and when Mookie interrupted some small talk and said to a young female admirer, "Ca-ca-ca-ca-ca-can I-I-I-I u-u-u-u-use yo-yo-yo-yo-yo-your pa-pa-pa-pa-pa-pussy a-a-a-a-a-as ma-ma-ma-ma-ma-my ha-ha-ha-ha-ha-hump ta-ta-ta-ta-toy?"

The band couldn't decide what was more shocking — that the man they thought was mute could talk? Or that he had such a horrible stutter? Or that the young, beautiful girl actually walked out the door with Mookie right then and there? They were all completely blown away and discussed it for hours*10.

Tonight, while the pink-haired vixen was giving him a knobber, he thought about how fun the pending tour was going to be. He thought about how bountiful the money was going to be. He looked down at the top of the girl's head and he thought there was going to be a lot more moments like the one he was currently enjoying. He grinned, guided her up to her feet, and sank his long fingers down her jeans. He played her strings and it quickly became her favorite song — her breath sweet and warm and billowing up to him as she rested her head on her own shoulders, aiming her closed eyes to the sky. He pulled her jeans down, turned her around and neither one of them had any shame at all as she held on to the side of the dumpster and bucked back, fretting his fiddle with the scent of burnt garlic wafting out of the garbage receptor.

When he finished, he walked her back to her awaiting friend. She was purposely out of line and when she saw them returning, she was giddily proud for her friend like it was a star-struck moment. The two girls briefly hugged and then he gently put his arms around both of their shoulders, chauffeured them past the masses, and straight through the front doors of The Cow — saving them $10 each in cover charges and a flashing of ID. Once inside, he was welcomed by excited fans. He coolly received their excitement, but continued toward "the emerald isle." As he reached the threshold, he whispered something into the ladies ears and left them there. As he headed for the stage, the girls hopped up and down and then hugged one another tightly before excitedly chatting away like schoolgirls.

SIDE 2. TRACK 10. LINER NOTES:

1. Buddy the betta died after Mookie inadvertently placed the fishbowl in front of the bathroom sink mirror after changing the water and heading out. Bettas have historically been the objects of gambling and are often bred for fighting, and it isn't uncommon for one to try to attack itself when placed in front of a mirror. But Mookie was unaware the species of fish reacted this way. He only purchased the fish because it was colorful and he was lonely.

2. On July 5, 1988, at Comiskey Park, the Chicago White Sox beat the Baltimore Orioles, 4-1, upping their record to 38-44. A then 15-year-old Mookie was plugged in to a small amp outside the ballpark playing his Fender Stratocaster for tips, when legendary bluesman Buddy Guy was exiting the confines. Buddy heard a familiar tune off in the distance, his own "First Time I met the Blues," and he was taken aback in delight with Mookie's rendition. Buddy dug into his pockets, retrieved a single guitar pick out of dozens he had to give to fans. He wrapped a $100 bill around the pick, crumpled the bill into a ball, and tossed it into Mookie's opened guitar case. Mookie, with his eyes shut and consumed in electric ecstasy, never noticed his mentor splash the bucket and it wasn't until later on in the evening, when he was counting his money in the boxcar, where he understood Buddy had heard him play and rewarded him so generously. It was his proudest moment of his life.

3. Mookie had three guitars stolen from him in his lifetime. Two of them, "Honeydripper," the 1988 Fender Stratocaster he boosted at the age of 15, and the maple acoustic his grandfather had given him (a guitar so old and handed down the brand name was no longer decipherable), were both taken from the boxcar the day he caught a beaten for stealing at the record store.

Mookie believed in karma, and believed he deserved it, and he also believed that would've been the end of it. But, it wasn't the case. The last time he had a guitar swiped from him, a Gibson Robert Johnson L1 Acoustic Sunburst, was when a group of five or more street thugs jumped him outside of his apartment in broad daylight. Mookie was crushed. He spent months playing downtown Chicago to save the $2,400 he paid for the Gibson and he knew the ruffians would pawn it for peanuts. After hearing the news of Mookie's mugging, the boys in The Farrow Moans all chipped in and bought him a new acoustic (the slim-necked Xtone AC-30EQM maple) and accompanying guitar case. Mookie built the hidden compartment inside the case and then he bought handcuffs and a hot pistol. He was never going to allow another guitar to be taken from him again. He kept his polka dot Stratocaster with the band for practical traveling reasons, but he could never be a few feet away from an acoustic.

4. Mookie's medical discharge transcripts from the U.S. Army listed Trichuris trichiura or whipworm, as to the reasoning behind his release. But, it wasn't true. He enlisted in 1991 after the Gulf War broke out and after giving up on the dream of being a famed guitar player. He barely made it through two weeks of boot camp before the Army decided to pull the plug on him. His dreadful stuttering was to blame. It drove drill sergeants crazy any time he tried to speak or respond to a question. One night in the barracks, where a nasty stomach virus had been swirling, it became Mookie's turn to fall ill. The Army brass decided it was the perfect time to have him committed to the infirmary where they could "document" his "acute and enduring" stomach worm and abdominal distress issues.

5. After being booted from the Army, Mookie stayed near Fort Leonard Wood. He found work as a janitor at a library in neighboring Lebanon, Mo. At night, while making his rounds pushing a broom, he would read books about the blues. He became so enthralled with the history of the blues, he created an itinerary of places to one day visit and even mapped out a route for a potential spiritual pilgrimage to retrace the blues' roots. He spent the next seven years working at the library, saving as much money as he could. He also bought his first guitar in Lebanon and began to play again. Finally, in 1998, he socked away enough money to follow his dream — in an attempt to gather as much quiddity and blues essence as he could. He started his travels to the Mississippi Delta from Memphis, Tenn., via the famous Route 61 — a road known as "Blues Trail" which follows the Mississippi River, starting in Tunica and then through Lula and then down to the renowned Clarksdale along the shadowy river. He didn't have a set timeframe for any stop he made along the way. Sometimes, like when he visited Shaw, Miss., he stayed for three months and his head slept where it crashed.

His most notable moment in Mississippi was visiting the fields outside of Tutwiler — where the blues are rumored to have originated. The indigo plant grew on plantations, which was used to dye cotton blue and then was woven into clothing worn by the people of West African cultures for mourning ceremonies. Those people, decorated in blue, would sing and chant in the fields about their suffering as slaves — hence the "blues." He found a patch of True Indigo shrubs, ripped the violet flowers from their branches and rubbed them in between his hands. He rolled the petals into a ball evocative of a tobacco chaw and popped it into his mouth. He swashed it around and it tasted sweet, floral and peculiarly like home. Throughout his transcendent peregrinating xenization across the Delta, he transformed into what the local mossbacks thought was an apparitional, Presque vu bluesman from the past. He took countless bus rides, he hitch-hiked, and he walked hundreds and hundreds of miles over five years to complete his wanderlust resurrection. His last stop was back to where it started — in Memphis — and he ended up staying there for almost a year as a street musician, studying the fusion of the dirty, Delta blues and the more rapid, rock 'n' roll style which eventually made its way north and morphed into what he grew up with — the Chicago blues. When he finally returned home to Chicago, he had been spiritually cleansed.

6. Because of his speech disorder, Mookie was no good at getting to know women. As much as he longed to find a mate, his fear of talking to the opposite sex was paralyzing. He tried to counteract his stuttering by writing a small synopsis about what he was all about, alongside a hand-drawn self-portrait of him wearing a suit and playing the guitar. He taped the flyers to light poles and storefront windows downtown Chicago, hoping to find a companion. His message read: "Hello, Ladies: my name is Mookie Brownstone. I'm a marvelous man. I'm self-employed and rich with freedom. I pay my rent on time. I lodge alone, but I'm hoping you'll change that. I'm not a movie star or anything close to what resembles a stud muffin. I'm not ostentatious either. And yes, I do know what the word means. I know a lot of other words too and I can write them down for you if you'd fancy it. Or, I can play you a song if you come visit me at Millennium Park. I'm always there. I like grits, train rides, morning time,

and black coffee. I'm 6ft 9in and 200 pounds. Come find me playing my guitar at Millennium Park if you're a nice, pretty lady. Do it! Mookie Brownstone … out."

7. The two 22-year-old girls were not 22. They were both 19-year-old groupies with fake IDs hoping to get through the door at the 21 and over show. Mookie knew the girls were under 21, but didn't care. The man had spent 99 percent of his lifetime being repulsed by women and he was going to milk his local stardom for all it was worth.

8. Mookie didn't call the number provided on The Farrow Moans' flyer to set up an audition, because he didn't want to ruin any chances of getting the job with his stuttering. He asked a favor of his landlord, Harold Lawson, and the man put in a call to ascertain information about the band per Mookie's request. Lawson posed to be interested and quizzed Cal Slankard about the band while Mookie listened to the conversation via the speaker function on Harold's phone. After hearing Cal talk about the styles and genres of music the band gravitated toward, Mookie wrote a note to Lawson to ask Cal if the band was practicing anytime soon, to which Cal advised they play at Mrs. O'Leary's Cow regularly. Mookie wasn't engrossed and signaled Lawson to hang up.

Lawson, a slumlord who was always spying the rent money, set up a fabricated audition under the name "Cliff Roberts" in the event Mookie changed his mind. In the ensuing weeks after the call was placed, the band's logo — the nymph in particular — strangely kept teasing Mookie. He started taking the red line to Lincoln Park almost nightly in hopes to catch The Farrow Moans. He eventually caught the band practicing on a Monday night when the bar was deserted. He found them promising, but yet again, the anxiety in connotation to his stuttering prevented any befriending or harmonious sharing. It wasn't until he heard Cal's voice and saw his stage presence that he decided to follow through.

9. Mookie's speech impediment was so demoralizing, he had business cards printed with only his name. He purposely would grab his throat as he handed them out, gesturing like he had laryngitis or he was mute. He would often carry a pen and notepad as well, writing responses to questions he was asked or writing questions he wanted answered. He communicated with bandmates with pen and notepad for several weeks before spilling the beans the night he was poon hounding.

10. The night the band learned of Mookie's stutter, they did spend several hours discussing the enigma that was Mookie Brownstone. They deliberated him over beers at (a closed) Mrs. O'Leary's Cow*A while they listened to old blues records*B on a turntable that filtered the music through the speakers of "the emerald isle." Aside from him being a savant with the guitar that lived on the south side of the city and loved young white women and didn't stick around after shows, they knew nothing about the man.

They never saw him carrying a phone, nor did he ever provide them with a number of where he could be reached — which wasn't originally questioned because, well, they collectively assumed a phone wouldn't serve of much purpose to a mute. Things with Mookie were simple — they would tell him a time and a location of where their next meeting would take place and Mookie would show up ready to go, and on time. They assumed he wasn't a wealthy man, but none of them were sure of that because he had some of the most expensive suits they had ever seen. For all they knew, the "deprived black man" bit could've been a ruse and he was really using "Mookie Brownstone" as a pseudonym for a megastar on a secretly-recorded reality TV show. The theories became more and more pathetic the more and more they drank. At one point, deep into the early hours, they became sold on the fact Mookie was a legendary guitarist who had been experiencing writer's block and he was using the band to recharge his batteries. While they sipped beers and formed more suppositions of who they thought he was, they all admitted to personally Googling his name at some point since he joined the group, but none of them found any valid results. As the night neared ending, Cal was swayed to believe he was a man on the run from the law, possibly from the South, because of the way he played the dirty, Mississippi blues and that Mookie Brownstone was an alias.

Tommy didn't buy into Cal's theory. Tommy thought Mookie was hermit without friends and a man who was never taken seriously because of his stuttering, and who only played the guitar as a necessity for communication. And neither Cal nor Tommy cared what Steve Wiley thought, because he was the bass player. But the Mookie-deliberating beer session didn't end without some resolve. The band all celebrated that Mookie and his guitar was their meal ticket and they made a pact to provide money, rides, a place for Mookie to sleep and anything else they could do to keep him from wandering away — including other gestures of grandeur, like when Cal would promise young groupies who wanted to have sexual relations with him to, "show my friend Mookie a good time and I'll show you one in return."

A) Tommy often took exception to possessing keys to Mrs. O'Leary's Cow, and he would occasionally sneak friends or bandmates into The Cow after the allotted timeframe of the establishment's liquor license. His uncle Junior was aware he would sometimes host the illegal and private parties and he didn't have a problem with it as long as it was done sparingly and consisted of no more than 10 or less people, and that the party was restricted to "the emerald isle" with the front lights off and the window blinds drawn down, and only if they abided to his rule that they only draft beer was to be consumed and the heavy stuff was off limits.

B) After Mookie joined the band, and after he was mugged for his guitar, he showed up one night at The Cow with a mammoth wooden chest. In it contained his extensive blues album collection, a record player, several dapper suits and other items of sentimental value. He explained to Tommy that his apartment was no longer safe to keep his possessions from becoming stolen and Tommy had no problem keeping the chest in the back room for him — he even bought Mookie a padlock for it and kept an extra key behind the bar in the event Mookie lost his. The nights Mookie wasn't around, Tommy would unlock the chest, and the band routinely sat in "the emerald isle" listening to his rare albums on his turntable.

11. Fris·son (frē´sôN) n.: a moment of intense excitement; a shudder, thrill

Tommy parked his van in the alley behind Mrs. O'Leary's Cow and used the back door to unload equipment. Wearing his drumming garb — a red Chicago Blackhawks T-shirt and khaki cargo shorts — he shivered each time he went outside. Blue saw him and shuffled from behind the bar to greet him. She flanked him while his back was turned and while he was wheeling a large amplifier to the stage. She bear hugged him from behind.

"I'm so sorry," she said, squeezing him tightly.

He patted her arms.

"No worries. Like I told you earlier, it's not your fault. Don't beat yourself up over it. I got myself into this mess, no one else."

She released her clutch and he rotated to face her.

"I don't like that detective."

"Me neither. But don't sweat it. He doesn't have shit on me."

"I got him wasted tonight, but every time I tried to hear what he was saying to the other cop, he'd button his lip."

"It's OK."

"I want you to know, I was just trying to help you. I never met Alex. I never met the hot dog guy."

"I know."

She leaned into him and gave him another hug.

"I'm so sorry, Tommy," she whispered.

"I am too. Don't sweat it, though."

She released him again and glanced at the bar.

"People are probably getting thirsty."

"You should go," he said.

"Yeah," Blue said and gave him a dreamy gaze. "You're going to have a great show. I can tell. I can see it in your eyes."

She turned and walked away before he could reply. He watched her saunter. He didn't stop staring until The Farrow Moans bassist Steve Wiley snuck in through the propped open back door and shouted, "Tommy!"

186

"Steve-O!"

They bumped fists.

"Are you ready, buddy? This is going to be a helluva night!" Steve said.

"Yessir!"

"Let me give you hand with that," Steve said, pointing to the amp.

After they unpacked the van and set up the equipment, Steve adjusted his bass and Tommy meandered to the bar. The Cow was going to be busy and electricity began to fill the air. Along the way, Tommy shook hands and chatted with fans, friends and patrons who recognized him. When he got closer to the bar, he noticed Raymond McMahon holding court at his emblematic seat. He was bending the ear of a younger man reading a small packet of papers. Tommy wondered why Raymond was still up — it was well past his bedtime. He circumscribed behind Raymond while he was in mid-conversation and interrupted Raymond's rambling by wedging himself between Raymond and the young man he was talking to. He gave the man a sympathetic smile and then put a hand on Raymond's shoulder.

"What are you doing here so late? Won't your wife kill you?"

"I got a hall pass because tomorrow's Christmas. I remember you mentioned your band was going to be playing tonight."

"You're actually here to see us? Wow," Tommy said.

"Don't get too excited, kid. I'm only here to drop off some literature and then I'll probably have to get going. Tomorrow morning, I dress up as Santa Claus and go deliver my wife's sticky buns and presents to my nephew's kids. It's an old tradition of mine."

"Sticky buns?"

"They're like Cinnabons, only more sinful, and before they turned into franchise whores and ruined the good thing they had going."

"What kind of literature?"

"I hope you don't mind — I didn't think you would, if I hand out my manifesto to some of your fans."

"Manifesto?"

"Well, sure. I'm retired. I have the time. I'm tired of talking about all the problems with this city — with the country, with the world, and the people. It's time to fix things. Talk the talk, walk the walk, type of thing. I have a plan for saving our streets. That's what it is: An S.O.S. That's what I'm calling it. It's geared for the kids your age. There isn't much an old fart like me can do to change things anymore physically. But, I can with my noddle. I hope you don't mind if ..."

Raymond reaches down under his barstool and retrieves a leather briefcase.

"… if I pass out some of these packets."

He opens up the briefcase and hands Tommy a copy.

"I was just telling that young man a little smidgeon of what it's all about."

Tommy skims a few sentences.

"Sure. I don't mind … on one condition," Tommy said.

"What's that?"

"You have to stay and hear at least one of our songs."

"Will do*1. But I can't stay late. Those little shits get up damn early for Santa."

"One song. And make sure you're close to the stage."

"All right." Raymond said.

Tommy looked behind the bar and found Blue looking at him. He winked and then motioned with his head for him to meet him in the middle of the bar.

"Hey," Tommy said, "do me a favor."

"Are you sure? The last time I thought I was doing that, I giftwrapped you like a Christmas present and played Santa to the police."

"It's in the past," he said, covering what would've been a warm smile with a hand. "I want to buy that old dinosaur down there his next round."

"Why do you do that?"

"Buy grumpy old men beers?"

"No," she said. "That dumb thing you do when you smile. You block it. I bet you have a great smile, but I would never know, because you never show it."

"I do?" he said while looking down at his hand.

"Yeah."

"Huh," he said, "I didn't realize I did."

"I think you shouldn't do it anymore."

"You do?"

"I do."

"I'll try to remember that."

"You should."

"I will."

He began to give her the type of smile she requested, but then he remembered something else. He removed a neon green lanyard attached with laminated paper from around his neck.

"Oh, I almost forgot. There's going to be a reporter here to give us a review ..."

He handed the backstage pass to Blue.

"... Can you make sure she gets this?"

"Crystal Loch?" Blue said.

"Yeah, how did you know?"

"She's great — you haven't read the article she did with you yet?"

"No. Is it any good?"

"It is."

"Cool. I'll have to read it later. I'm running out of time."

"Go have a great show. Bang the tar out of those drums. I'll be watching you."

Blue smiled, spun around and went to pour Raymond his next beer.

Tommy returned to the stage after bumping into more fans and friends. When he ran up the stairs and looked to the dimly lit rear of the stage, he noticed Cal and Mookie hadn't showed up yet, and he began to worry.

"Two bucks says Cal won't show up until 10," Tommy said to Steve.

"That's a bad bet," Steve said matter-of-factly.

"How do you figure? He's never on time."

"It's a bad bet because if he's late, you'll be more aggravated than you already are and if you're wrong, then you're out two bucks. It's a bad bet. He'll be here, Tommy."

"I know he will. After 10. We promised a 9 o'clock kick-off."

Tommy left Steve, and the electronics he was in the middle of setting up, to tighten the cymbal on a hi-hat. With the unsettledness around his last 24 hours, no one caught on that he was in such a moral and legal dilemma, because he went about waltzing through the bar and setting up his equipment in a pang-wangle manner. It had been hours since he was in the back of Woodbine's squad car, but he couldn't shake the nerves. The recklessness he put himself in wasn't what was stirring the panicky pot either. He was coming to grips with the fact Bill Dodanno died, not directly, but somewhat arbitrarily, on account of him. He was thinking about how short life was, for everyone, and how if he hadn't called Bill to help out a friend, the man wouldn't have died. He wondered if it would haunt his life for the rest of its interval and if so, for how long would that be? He lugubriously dwelled as he pumped the kick drum:

- How does God flip a switch and turn you off — how does he decide when he wants you?
- Why is he picking on me? Right when things are going great. All I did was make a phone call.
- Why didn't I listen to Raymond McMahon? His gun story was a sign and I didn't hear it.
- How will I die?

As Tommy was bent over, tinkering with his kit, the long-legged, suit-clad Mookie Brownstone climbed up the six stairs to the stage in two strides.

"Ah-ah-ah-ah-ah-ah-are ya-ya-ya-ya-ya-you ca-ca-ca-ca-ca-cats ra-ra-ra-ra-ra-ready ta-ta-ta-ta-ta-to ja-ja-ja-ja-ja-jam?" Mookie said just shy of 25 seconds.

"Oh, hell yes, son!" Tommy said, erecting himself.

They gave each other a brief side-hug-back-pat.

"Mook, I brought your polka dots," Steve said and pointed to a Stratocaster guitar case resting on the stage.

Mookie smiled, set his acoustic case on the ground and walked over to the Stratocaster. He undid the latches and reared his head back and slanted it like he was anticipating a jack-in-the-box to pop out. He removed the black-and-white polka-dot electric guitar and his mouth was full with grin. He raised the guitar above his head while he squatted and looked up at her like it was a sword that saved a kingdom. He brought it down to his lips and gently kissed it.

"I ne-ne-ne-ne-ne-need ma-ma-ma-ma-me sa-sa-sa-sa-some ja-ja-ja-ja-juice," Mookie said.

Steve plugged a cord into the guitar before Mookie could finish his sentence.

Mookie followed Steve and the cable to a small amp. Steve handed him a pair of headphones. Mookie put them on and sat down with his back leaned against the amp. Steve plugged the headphone jack into a red plug and powered on the amplifier. Mookie situated the guitar on his lap and softly strummed the chords. He made a few adjustments and looked up at Steve, who was on standby for anything Mookie requested, and gave Steve an approving nod. Steve returned the nod and went back about his business. Mookie rested his head on the top of the amplifier, closed his eyes, lifted two fingers to his nose, and then breathed her in deeply. Then he tossed off his hat, clapped his hands and began to shred the strings with his elongated fingers. Tommy and Steve both took glances at him and then to one another, smiling in unison with a he's-on-his-game look.

Cal Slankard entered the room, and the groundswell proved Tommy wrong. Excited girls with shrieking voices and men's thunderous clapping gave him away. When curiosity got the best of Tommy, he looked toward the gathering crowd and noticed Cal's head was on a swivel, seeming to be searching for someone.

"The stage is up here, dummy," Tommy said aloud, but nobody heard him.

Cal, wearing a fake smile, plunged past eager fans who wanted a moment of his time, giving quick high-fives. He took the stage donning a red shirt and jeans and he was clutching a laptop. He approached the band with a blank expression on his face.

"Where's the sticker dude?" Cal asked.

"Who?" Steve said.

"Hey, Mook," Cal said while giving Mookie a head nod and then he turned back to Steve. "My sticker guy. Franklin ... Franklin something. Bearded dude who's always smiling?"

"I have no clue what you're talking about," Steve said, tinkering with some equipment. "Gimme your computer."

Cal handed the laptop over to Steve.

"The guy was supposed to be here by now," Cal said. "I had Blue draw up a decal just for tonight's show. Franklin ... the sticker dude — he promised me he'd have them ready before a line formed. This place is already filling up and he isn't here yet. He's got all of our stuff."

"This is all news to me," Steve said, programming the computer. "Come here. This is what we're going with, right?"

Cal leaned over Steve's shoulder and looked at the monitor.

"Yeah, that's it," Cal said. "You can sync the set list with the lights, right?"

"Not a problem," Steve said. "Is your voice ready?"

"Yeah, I sang along with Muddy Waters the whole drive here," Cal said. "That Franklin ... that dude better show up here and hand deliver every sticker to every fan. They might be a collector's item one day. I want this show to be a send-off for all these good people who've followed us around and paid their good, hard-earned money on us — even when we sucked. The sticker was for them to put on their bumpers. To let them know, when they ride with us, we ride with them."

Tommy, sensing he was being ostracized, joined the two at the table positioned at the back of the stage where the computer and other equipment were situated.

"What's the problem?" Tommy asked Cal.

"The sticker dude hasn't shown up yet," Steve said before Cal could open his mouth.

"What sticker dude?" Tommy asked Cal.

191

"The bearded-sticker-dude," Steve interjected, again setting a calm tempo before the two men started bumping heads.

"I don't know anything about it," Tommy said. "Where are our T-shirts and CDs? Where's all our stuff, Cal?"

"The sticker dude's got it," Steve interposed.

"Tom," Cal said. "I've got it all handled. Relax."

"Really? You got it all handled, huh? It doesn't look like it."

"He'll be here."

"I hope so or it's on you. Let's go over the set list," Tommy said as he had a look at the computer.

"It's already taken care of," Cal said.

"Without my approval?" Tommy said while shooting Cal a virulent look. "I don't think so."

"Tommy, it's just like we talked about," Cal reached into his breast pocket, "I printed you and Mook a copy. Let Steve-O do his thing."

Cal handed Tommy two pieces of paper. Tommy read the set list over, crinkled his nose at a couple of Cal's choices and placements, and then consulted with his inner monologue:

- "Slumpbuster" should go before "Mint Car."
- I suck at "Group Flogging." Is it 4/6 4/6 4/6?
- "City by the Lake" is a good way to close. Good call.
- His list is all right. I liked mine better, but let the big baby have his way. I don't want his codpiece bunching up.

Tommy gave Cal a "not bad" smirk and left the programming to Steve and Cal. He handed Mookie the second set list and then he saw Junior walking toward the stage with a troubled look on his face. Tommy met him at the bottom of the stairs.

"What's up?" he said.

"There's a line out the door that goes down the block. You guys have outgrown this place. Don't get me wrong, I'm like a proud father watching his boy turn into a man. This is excellent, but I've never had this problem before. We don't have the staffing for this. Bianca just got here and she's helping Blue behind the bar and I called a couple cocktail servers — those Jameson promo girls we used before — they're on their way. I even had to borrow two bouncers from the Hidden Shamrock to help me with security. We're probably going to run out of everything. You have to make an announcement and tell these people to please be patient. We can only move so fast."

"No problem, Uncle June," Tommy said, climbing back on stage.

"Hey, and Tommy ..."

Tommy turned to his uncle.

"Rock this fucking place down to the ground!"

Tommy smiled before running up the last of the stairs.

Junior dredged through the growing crowd and to the bar to observe how business was functioning. He stopped next to an attractive and lanky blonde, who was wearing a The Farrow Moans T-shirt ——— which was 100 times too small and cut-off just below the bottom of her braless breasts. The ensemble was accompanied by a blood-flow-restricting pair of tight blue jeans and a pair of blood-red, 5-inch stilettos. She was sitting alone, drinking a Cosmopolitan martini and sending a text message. Her name was Carmen Swisher.

When Junior was satisfied with how smoothly everything was going, he walked to the front door.

A few minutes went by before Cal Slankard snappishly appeared in front of Carmen. He had a rancorous look on his face.

"Hello, Slanky panky," she said, seductively.

Her attempt at beguiling was blocked by his glare. He leaned into the drape of her neck and whispered, "I'll take a ball-peen hammer to my own cock if the thought of fucking you ever crosses my mind again. I'm going to walk away and when I do, you're going to sip your drink, act like a lady, and by the time I turn around, you're going to be fucking out of here."

Carmen's jaw dropped and Cal speedily walked away. With him gone, she sloshed down her martini and walked away. As her seat became vacant, a husky female wearing a black shirt, camouflage jacket, a black skirt with black stockings, and black military boots sat down. She placed a notebook and pen down on the bar top. Within moments, Blue walked over to her and laid a backstage pass over her head like she just got off a plane in Hawaii.

"You're Crystal Loch, right?" Blue said.

"How did you know?"

"I read your stuff all the time. You load awesome pictures on the website. I recognize you. Tommy told me you would be here. Your presence is requested backstage."

"Very cool," she said, looking the pass over.

"Before you go, what can I get you to drink? It's on me."

"I have to retry the Guinness."

As Blue poured Crystal a draught, Cal returned to the dais and approached Steve.

"I have a stage-5 clinger and you need to dump her from all social media."

"Who?" Steve said.

"Carmen Swisher."

Tommy, who overheard Cal and Steve's conversation, walked over and butted himself in.

"I thought you two were a thing?"

"A thing? No-fucking-way. Get your head out of your ass. She was just a sleepover, Tom. And she's crazier than a three-peckered Billy goat."

"What happened?" Tommy said with an intrusive scowl.

"The other night, I took her back to my place and I'm getting ready to plow her fields and she stops me. I mean, I'm a centimeter away from her hatchet wound. She says she wants to use a condom she's brought — some new thing, with tingly lube or some shit. I'm thinking, 'OK. Fine. Whatever. Let's do this thing — Paul Bunyan's*2 ready to go.' So she walks into the bathroom to retrieve it from her purse. A couple minutes go by and I'm wondering what the fuck is taking so long. I go to investigate. I peek through the crack of the door and this kooky girl is jamming the sharp point of her earring into the fuselage of the condom. This crazy bitch is trying to poke a whole into it! I say, 'Whoa! What the fuck are doing?' And she backpedals and says, 'I couldn't get the wrapper open, so I'm trying to use this earring.' I say, 'Bullshit. I saw what you're doing. Are you insane!?' I tell her to scram. I'm not about to be no daddy. She pleads with me and I push her toward the door. She says she's sorry and she's in love with me. She admits she wanted to get pregnant and told me our child would be 'The Next Coming of Christ' because she can 'feel it.' I kicked her out and tell her to lose my number. Coo-coo. Coo-coo. The cheese has definitely slid off this chick's cracker. Ten minutes ago, she sends me a text. I thought maybe it was Franklin … the sticker dude. Nope. It's Carmen. She says she's here. She found out about the show on our webpage. Steve-O, you have to block her."

Cal's phone buzzed in his pocket. He terminated the rest of the story and retrieved the phone. It was text message from Franklin, the sticker dude.

"See, nothing to worry about," Cal said to Tommy, showing him the text. "The sticker dude is at the back door."

Cal jumped off the stage and went to the service door to let Franklin in and Steve followed. An amusing nous of schadenfreude immersed Tommy when he realized Mr. Casanova — Mr. Codpiece — was capable of having lady troubles. After briefly ruminating Cal's misfortune, Tommy went to help his mates erect a merchandise table near the corner of the stage.

While setting up a T-shirt display, Crystal Loch approached Tommy and they had a long hug followed by a brief conversation. Then, she left a stack of the newspapers on the table, and wandered about the crowd.

The group ironed out last-minute merchandise details before returning to the stage. A round of stouts that Junior sent over awaited them. Cal, two pints in hand, tapped Mookie on the shoulder, and then handed him a beer. He took off his headphones, unplugged the polka-dot guitar, and then met with the rest of the band. They huddle together in a circle.

"All right guys," Cal said, pausing his vision on each member's face. "This is it. This is going to be our big thank-you show. Let's give our friends something they'll never forget. They've earned it."

They clanked their glasses together, said cheers and then each had a universal swig. Tommy took to his kit. Steve grabbed his bass. Mookie plugged in his polka-dot Stratocaster into the main amplifier. And Cal waited in the shadows of the back stage area. He started a program on the laptop and the lights dimmed. Tommy yelled, "One. Two. One, two, three, four ..."

... And as Tommy hit the drums, he didn't think about his involvement in a death investigation. He didn't think about his father missing another of his gigs. He didn't think about Crystal Loch reviewing the show. He didn't lust for Carmen Swisher anymore, because after Cal's story, those feelings were now washed away. When he hit those drums and heard the crowd cheer, the little hairs on his neck stood up, and the only thing he thought about was the music.

SIDE 2. TRACK 11. LINER NOTES:

1. After Raymond McMahon promised Tommy he would stick around and watch at least one song in order to pass out his literature, he bilked. After handing out the last of his manifesto*A he scooted out the front door of The Cow.

A) About 90 percent of the leaflets Raymond handed out either ended up on the floor or in garbage cans.

2. Cal, who often talked about his promiscuity unabashed, habitually referred to his penis as "Paul Bunyan" an innuendo to the giant, fabled lumberjack.

Bonus Tracks.
Tuesday, Dec. 25. Christmas.

"… and the 911 calls lit up the dispatch centers' phone lines like a Christmas tree."

BONUS TRACKS

1. "Operation: Four Walls and a Carpet"

2. Naked, New and Never Again

3. Suicide by Cop

4. Mrs. Claus' Sticky Buns

1. "Operation: Four Walls and a Carpet"

Tommy stood behind the bar, sipping a draught. The neon shamrock sign behind him hummed as the green light cloaked Blue's face while she sat on a barstool opposite him. They were alone. The glow made her teeth appear even whiter than before. Tommy couldn't believe it was possible. Robert Johnson's "King of the Delta Blues Singers Volume II" quietly played from the stage speakers.

Aside from Tommy and Cal nearly throwing fisticuffs*1 in the back lot after the show, The Farrow Moans' gig was a success. Tommy stayed to help Blue clean and usher out patrons. He even signed his first autograph.

"We're really going to play truth or dare?" she asked, swirling the Chopin Potato Vodka and tonic in her hand.

"Yes! Is it sophomoric? Yes. But c'mon, it'll be fun."

"Sophomoric? I haven't played it since grade school," Blue said.

"Then you haven't been living."

"I might be a little too fuzzy to be any good. I did way too many shots behind the bar tonight."

"You're fine! Come on, I'll go first," Tommy said.

"OK, fine. Truth or dare?"

"Dare."

"I dare you take a shot of that stuff," she said, pointing at a bottle on the shelf.

"Malört — oh hell no!" he said.

"Hey, this is your game, buster. You started it. It's a dare. Is Mr. Rock 'n' Roll's gonna chicken out? Mr. Autograph isn't going to live up to the hype?"

"No chicken here. Dammit, that's a good dare. I never welch. I'll do it."

He grabbed the bottle with the yellow label and what-had-to-be cautionary red lettering that spelled: Jeppson's Malört Liqueur. He filled a shot glass.

The key ingredient in Malört is wormwood, and when he smelled the potent odor coming from the glass, his saliva glands secreted a watery drool the way they usually do before vomiting.

Tommy spun the bottle in his hand and read from the back label, "It is not possible to forget our two-fisted liquor. The taste just lingers and lasts — seemingly forever. The first shot is hard to swallow! PERSERVERE! Make it past two 'shock-glasses' and with the third you could be ours ... forever."

Blue laughed at Tommy shaking his head.

"This is going to be terrible," he said while pinching his nose. "Believe it or not, I've never tried it."

"At least now you won't be a hypocrite. You're always force feeding that crap to anyone who's just turned 21 or tricking people into it when they're really blotto. Something about payback being a …"

Tommy took a deep breath, gave Blue a here-goes-nothing look and slammed it. Immediately his face gave way to a look of pure terror. His eyelids clenched their respective balls — rearing back into his frontal lobe. His mouth puckered so tightly, wrinkles were left on his upper lip like an elderly lady who smoked for 50 years. He tried shaking off the taste, but his eyes watered and he held his tongue from his mouth like a panting dog.

Blue chuckled hard, and slowly drooped down —— finding herself in a balled-up fetal position on the floor.

"OMG," she said in bursts of laughter. "I'm going to pee a teaspoon. Your face … it … was … classic. I wish I took a picture of it."

Tommy didn't share her enthusiasm and he was concentrating on not puking.

"What's it taste like?" she yelled.

"It tastes like … hate … rage … formaldehyde. It tastes like when you fall down and bang your tailbone."

Blue rolled over on the floor and slapped it.

"It … it keeps on burning," he said, spitting in a garbage can. "This taste … it's not going away. In fact, it's getting stronger."

His last statement encouraged more laughter from Blue. After a few beats, they both collected themselves. Blue climbed back up on her barstool and her face was tired from laughing. And Tommy's was left aching as well —— but from squishing his inner cheeks to pool saliva for spitting. Blue wiped joyous tears from her eyes as he wiped tears of agony away from his.

"That was horrible," he said. "But now, now I'll get my revenge. Truth or dare?"

"After watching you, there's no way I can say dare. You'll just make me do a shot of it in retaliation. I'm going with truth."

"Weak sauce," he said. "But, I don't blame you because that's exactly what I would've made you do."

He rinsed his mouth with a swallow of beer.

"Ok … hmmm … tell me something I don't know about you?"

"I can handle that," she said. "Let's see … OK, here we go … After my high school graduation,

I packed up my crap and I drove to Chicago's west-most suburb, Arizona …"

"… Uh, Blue, I know this already …"

"… Hold your horses, puke face. So, shortly after I moved to Tempe, I started dating this guy, Brad … Brad — blah blah — and I eventually moved in with him because … because I was a dumb-dumb and that's what 19-year-old boy-crazy girls do. Anyways, he had this cat named Cornbread and he loved the dang thing. I don't know why anybody would, because Cornbread was the meanest and nastiest cat you had ever seen and he was inbred to all holy heck — all cross-eyed and he looked like a hyena. Another thing about this evil cat was — he had the hugest set of balls you had ever seen on a cat — I swear, those balls gave Brad a self-esteem complex — they were that big. Like that (points behind the bar) bottle of Crown in the purple velvet bag."

"Dude," Tommy said, laughing.

"I swear. Huge. The story goes, Brad found him eating out of a dumpster in an alley off Bourbon Street in New Orleans, when he was living there and before he moved to Arizona. I can't quite remember if he was eating throwaway cornbread or if he was named Cornbread after his fur color — it doesn't matter. Anyways, I was waitressing at this place off campus, on University Drive called — believe it or not — Stray Cat Bar & Grill. I would get home real late and I would walk through the front door, arming myself with my purse, or sometimes I would take off a shoe, because Cornbread loved to ambush me — he loved to ambush anyone who walked in our apartment. Brad worked early in the morning, so usually when I would come home, the place was pitch-black and I was always ready for that ninja cat. But no matter how prepared I would be, he'd still get me. I mean, Cornbread used to hide in various spots — under the couch, on top of the bookshelf, on a dining room chair — but shielded under the table, he always mixed it up, and he would attack when you least expected it. Sometimes, minutes would go by without him surfacing and I would think I was in the clear. 'Maybe he snuck outside?' or 'Is he finally bored of the attacking?' and then — ROAR! — he'd latch onto flesh. I hated wearing shorts or a skirt because he always aimed for your thighs. If he got a hold of one, forget about it, it was toast. He would claw my calves and bite my inner thigh at the same time and he wouldn't stop until you punched him off. He broke blood — countless times — and my legs ended up looking like they were hacked by a butcher's cleaver.

"One time, after a really vicious chomping, I chucked one of Brad's Doc Martin boots at his head as hard as I could and it hit him right in the face. Get this, the cat licked his paw and then rubbed his head where I hit him with an, 'I'm going to shank you in your sleep, lady' look on his face. I used to plead with Brad to get rid of him or at least get him declawed and neutered, but I swear he loved Cornbread more than me. He'd laugh and tell me it was just Cornbread's way of showing affection. Pretty sadistic, right?

"Anyways, one night, I couldn't take it anymore. Brad was playing spades with some buddies and I decided it was time to end the shenanigans. I cautiously walked up to him and got all sweetsy-sounding. "Hi kitty-kitty. How are you?" and then I threw a bed sheet on him — wrangling him up in the thing and then I tied a belt at the top and that little savage still managed to claw the heck out of my hand when I did it. But I did it. I caught him and I marched him down the three flights of stairs — two neighbors gave me baffled looks when they heard some wild creature hissing and saw the satchel shaking, but I just played it off with a smile. I tossed the sack on the passenger seat of my car and I drove him down Highway 60, all the way out to Apache Junction and onto 88, and out by the Superstition Mountains — the entire time he hissed and dug tunnels in high thread-count cotton. I pulled off on this old dirt road near a novelty Wild West town, where they have rattlesnakes in glass cages and fake gun fights, and you can pan for gold — you know, one of those places. I remember thinking, 'What a perfect spot,' because if I knew that cat like I thought I did, he'd have no problems mooching off one of those carneys or he could live off of dumpster garbage from tourists. I mean, I do have a heart. I'm not an evil or deranged. I'm a lady. But Brad left me no choice.

"Anyhow, it was a beautiful night — the sun was setting, just gorgeous behind the mountains when I pulled over. I opened the door and I threw him down on that desert dirt and I undid that belt and I opened up the bag and I jumped back in my car real fast before he could get me ... and he climbed out of that satchel so pee'd off and then he gave me a good, long stare down. Then, I could see the sadness in his crooked eyes and it was like he knew what was happening. I felt remorseful for about one second ... and then I gave that little jerk the bird, honked the horn, peeled out and rode off into the sunset. When I was driving home, I kept looking in the rearview mirror; expecting to see him hanging on with his big lion claws — like something you'd read in a Stephen King novel. I was all nervous and jittery about it. But, he didn't hitch a ride and for the first time ever, I walked in the apartment without fear and I plopped down on the couch and put my arms behind my head and I let out a big sigh. What a feeling. What a relief.

"A couple days went by and Brad kept asking, 'Have you seen Cornbread?' 'No, no ... I haven't seen him,' I would say.

"See, in the past, it wasn't uncommon for Cornbread to sneak out the door when we were coming or going, but he'd always return a day or two later ... sometimes with dead birds. He loved doves. Loved 'em. By the end of the first week he 'went missing,' Brad taped fliers to everything in our neighborhood. 'Maybe a coyote got him?' I would offer. 'No way, he's tough as nails. I saw him take down a raccoon one time. Epic battle. Nawlins' street fight,' the B.F. would answer. About a week or two later, Brad had given up hope. I convinced him Cornbread must've met his match with a diamondback — nosing around like he shouldn't have been, but always did.

"So this one night, about a month after I drove Cornbread out to the desert, Brad's out with his buddies and I'm lying on the couch and I got the windows open and there's this really beautiful and gentle breeze coming in — a rarity — and I hear this meowing. At first I didn't think anything of it. And then it keeps getting closer and louder and I'm all, 'No way that's Cornbread. It's a cat that sounds just like him, but no way it's him.' Twenty minutes goes by and this cat won't stop. Finally, I go out onto the deck to investigate and I couldn't believe it ... there was this cat that looked an awful lot like Cornbread bellowing up at me from three stories down. Again I thought, 'No way. This cat is much thinner than Cornbread. It can't be him. Cornbread's baking in the desert. He's scorpion food by now.' But when he saw me, he let out this heart wrenching roar, and I knew it was him. He sprinted up the three stories and I opened up the door and he just about knocked me over when he brushed up against my leg. He was so excited to see me. So, I bent down and had a look at him ... those familiar crossed-eyes looked back at me: One aimed at my right ear, the other on my left cheek. He smelled like he had been in someone's house — like fresh laundry. And he had lost about 10 pounds, but it was most definitely him. He found his way home by a feeling. I patted his head — a truce — and he never attacked me again. Truth."

Tommy raised his glass. "That's incredible! Did you ever tell Brad the truth?"

"No way! He would've killed me if he knew what really happened. You don't understand how much he loved Cornbread."

"I can't believe it found its way home," Tommy said.

"Right? It had to be at least 20 miles away. It actually felt good getting that story off my chest. I've never told it to anyone before and I probably wouldn't have told you if Cornbread didn't return. In hindsight, it was pretty cruel what I did. But, if you saw this one scar on my thigh from that psychoholic, you would've done the same thing. Missed my … my kitty kat by … not by much."

"I dare you to show me," Tommy said quasi flippantly.

"Ah-ha, it's not my turn," she said, wagging her finger.

"Just tricking on you — I had to take a shot."

The air suddenly got warm. The evening had turned into an unbeknownst tryst. It was the first time either one of them could remember stepping out of the friend-zone and orally being coquettish.

"I guess I'll take dare," he said, trying to nip any latent ungainliness in the bud.

"Speaking of taking a shot, how about this … you can either do two shots of any kind of booze you like or you have to do one more shot of Malört?"

"Are you trying to get me drunk?"

"Maybe."

"The plot thickens," he said. "I'll do Rumpleminz."

"Mouth wash? You're losing street cred, rock star."

"I have to do something to get the taste of bad out of my mouth," he said. "As a matter of fact, I'm done torturing people with this shit. Let's put this baby to bed."

Tommy tossed the open bottle of Malört into the garbage and grabbed the Rumpleminz from a cooler. He looked her over while he lined up two shots of the minty schnapps. She was slightly wavering, delicately biting her lower lip and noticeably becoming more flirtatious. He stalled before slamming the shots and contemplated:

- Is she really flirting with me or is she just drunk?
- Am I drunk? What's the proof of Jeppson …

"… Swig it already, buck-O," Blue interrupted.

He snapped out of his musing and guzzled the shots down one after another like pistons firing.

"Nicely done," she said, adding an impressed smile.

He fogged an invisible breath and slightly bowed to her.

"Would you like to keep playing?"

"Oh, heck yes! I never remembered this game being so much fun," she said. "Plus, I'm getting fudged up, so things could get interesting."

"I told you it would be good times. But new rule: No more shots for me. Deal?"

"Deal. My turn right?"

"Yep."

"Then the truth shall set me free."

"I loved that story," Tommy said. "Tell me another one — tell me something else I don't know about you."

She hesitated, lowered her head and then gave him a shy smile.

"I'm crushing on you ... hard."

"Could you say that again? I'm kind of deaf from the show."

"No you're not. You heard me just fine — you've got bartender ear. Your hearing is better than anyone I know. You heard me all right, but I don't mind repeating myself. I've had the biggest crush on you for the longest time."

"Are you messing with me?"

"Nope. How do you feel about it?"

He prepared to toss her a verbal bouquet of flowers, hoping she'd take a whiff.

"I feel like it feels after hearing the crowd cheering for us at a show — goose bumps and tingles down your spine — but only times it by infinity more. I wish there was a word for it. Since the day we hired you, I've had a thing for you too — but I always thought you were way out of my league ... like I had no chance."

She bit her lower lip and gave him big, puppy eyes. Things stirred within him. He was now a carcass filled with butterflies.

"I feel nervously good right now — I need a cigarette," he said.

He pulled a Kool from its package and lit up.

"You can't smoke in here," she said.

"The bar's closed. The lights are out. I'm the owner's nephew. You just dropped some serious knowledge on me. I need a smoke."

"Then give me one too," she said. "That was a big confession."

He handed her a square with a trembling hand. After she put it up to her lips, he lit it for her. She thanked him with sultry eyes. He reached under the bar and slid a stashed ashtray to her. They coolly smoked and shared silence for several moments. As they did, Tommy daydreamed:

- Don't fuck this up, buddy! She actually likes you!
- Do I move in for a kiss? What do I do? Why am I so nervous?
- Why is she telling me this now? She's way out of my league. Is it because we got signed to a label?
- Nah, that's crap. Blue's the nicest girl I have ever met. She doesn't even swear, for fuck's sake! Maybe she really does like me. Wait — she does like me! It all makes sense now: The smiles, the "I'll work for you any time you need me to," the insinuations, the little flirts, the coming to our shows. It wasn't the T-shirt sales. It was me the entire time! This is awesome!

She fired a smoke ring at him and it popped his ponder bubble. They locked eyes.

"Why didn't you ever tell me this before?" Tommy asked.

As she tapped the cigarette over the ashtray, her face changed.

"It would be cliché if I said it was because of the old school rule: You shouldn't blank where you eat. But that's not true. The truth is: We would never work out."

He leaned across the bar in an attempt to become eye level with her.

"What do you mean? Why do you say that? Why couldn't we?"

She took a deliberately slow sip from her V&T and ruminated. She had a long drag from the cigarette, her arm extended outward and her eyes were shut as if the smoke would blind her. The cherry near the butt was dangerously close to burning her fingers. A look of nauseated exasperation jumbled her face. She spewed a sideways blast of smoke from the corner of her mouth with an expression that said, "How'd this get here?" or "Who is making me do this?" Once the smoke drifted away, she snatched another cigarette from the pack lying on the bar, brought it to her lips, monkey fucked the new one with the previously lit one and snuffed the old one out in the tray.

"Operation: Four Walls and a Carpet. That's why," she finally said, ejecting another exhale.

"Operation what?"

"Let me tell you another story from when I was living in Arizona," she said. "When I was with Brad, everything was perfect at first. You know, the first-six-months-of-bliss, puppy-dog-love thing was in full effect. A couple of months after that stage — around nine months into our relationship, things started to change. He became … distant. Absent would actually be a better word to describe him. And I started to become wary when he would dish out the token red flag bull crud like, 'I had to work overtime' or 'I was playing cards with the boys — the game ran late,' type of crap. As the excuses started piling up, I started having my suspicions. I mean c'mon, you don't go from having sex all the time to having no interest in me at all, if something else isn't going on. And it wasn't like I was holding out on him either. I wasn't rationing sex. It was the opposite, actually. I'm sorry if this is TMI."

"No, no. You're fine. You know me," he said, while smothering his smoke.

204

"All right — cool. Anyways, I threw myself at him several times thinking he'd get out of his rut and he would give me the old, 'Sorry, babe. I'm too tired' bit. Don't give me that junk. That's our line. That's what girls say when we're not in the mood. Or we don't like someone anymore. I've never heard of a guy saying he's too tired, especially when the only thing a girl is wearing is thigh-high socks and her own dewy musk and trying to jump his bones. Even if the big brain was exhausted, the little brain never is. I know how it works."

"Uh, what an idiot," Tommy said.

"Thank you. So, one day, I followed him in my car. I was doing good, staying a couple car lengths behind him — I was like a spy. I was proud of myself. I didn't want to be 'that girl' but he didn't really leave me an option. 'That girl' is not this girl, and I promise you I'm not a stalker, but it was something I had to do. Anyway, I'm following him and at one point the traffic merged near a construction zone and some cars turned off and I got stuck directly behind him at a light. Luckily, the dummy didn't see me — talking on his phone while I slumped down in my seat and pretended to be looking for something on the floor. We drive on and he ended up pulling into an apartment complex. I did a drive-by or two before finally parking way in the back and faced the building. At first I thought, 'Maybe he's just buying a bag of weed. Maybe he's hiding it from me.' But that didn't make any sense, because I didn't care when he smoked pot. I mean, who would? It's pot — big whoop. Then I was like, 'Maybe he's in to something harder. Maybe it's coke?' But that didn't make sense either. He never had the tell-tale signs of being a druggie. No bad skin. No scratching. He didn't show signs of any erratic behavior either — aside from him not coming home when he typically used to. So, I was going through all these scenarios and an hour goes by and he walks out with some chick I'd never seen before and then they got in her car: A little souped-up "too fast, too furious" thing. Even then I didn't think he was stepping out on me — it didn't register. She didn't seem like his type. He wasn't even a car guy. I tailed him again and they eventually pulled into a mall. I watched them walk hand-in-hand and ... and then ... they kissed right there in the lot like it was no big deal — like they had been a couple for years. I was so devastated. I could feel my heart break, which was something I never felt before. Literally, I felt it hurt inside of me. I mean, I loved this guy. I really did. The tears turned to anger as the minutes passed sitting in my car. I started thinking about how I was going to confront them. Maybe I would make a big huge scene in the mall and let everyone know what a piece of crap he was? But, I couldn't do it. It's not me. That's not my style. I chose the next best thing I could think of: I started letting all the air out of her tires. Genius, right? What a way to get revenge. God was I so stupid and naïve back then. But it was the only thing I could think of while I was seeing red. I ended up getting three out of the four tires down to pancakes and then, wouldn't you know it — guess who comes walking up as I'm squatting down and halfway finished with the last tire? Them."

"No way!" Tommy said. "What did you do? Did you run out of there — I would've booked down the road so fast."

"It was really awkward — SO AWKWARD!" she said. "I kind of froze up and said, 'What are you doing here?' with a silly kid-caught-with-a-hand-in-the-cookie-jar stupid face. And they both looked at me like I was some sort of nut. The girl, a real revolting-looking B, she starts threatening me — she even wove her car keys in between her fingers and made a fist with them in there like she was going to punch-stab me. She's screaming and carrying on and Brad has to hold her back. She finally calms down and tells me she's going to call the cops if I didn't put the air back in the tires of her 'baby' and making me feel like the bad guy."

"Are you kidding me?" Tommy asked.

205

"I wish," she said while ashing the cigarette.

"Did she think you were just a stranger being a weirdo or do you think she knew about you and what's-his-nuts?"

"That's a good question," she said. "One I don't have an answer for."

"Wow. Sorry. Sorry to interrupt. Please, go on!"

"No worries," she began, "There I was, all embarrassed and nervous, and you know what I did? I start apologizing and begging for her not to make that call. I didn't want to get in trouble. Little miss goody two shoes. The girl says she's giving me 30 minutes and if it's not done when she comes back, she's calling the 5-0. And then they walked back into the mall — his arm around her shoulder, frickin' consoling her as they go. He didn't say a word to me out there and I, like I said, I was completely frozen so I couldn't say anything to him. I ended up driving to a hardware store and lucky for me, they had a portable air compressor and I buy it and it costs me like $40 and I go and I fill all her tires back up. Then I leave. Who does that? This idiot does. Man, I wish I had Cornbread's huevos back then. I would've clawed Brad's eyes out and carved something like 'SPLOOGE RECEPTOR' or 'I'M A FUCKING SLUT' into her paint job!"

"Atta girl, Blue!" he said. "I think that's the first time I ever heard you cuss."

"Well, I deserve to after that," she said. "I felt like a piece of garbage. It was right then and there when I decided that was it for Mr. Brad. I mean, what was I to do? I wasn't going to fight for him. What was the point? He made his feelings known when he walked back into the mall with that skank. So, I couch surfed at my friend Alley's place and solicited the help of a couple guys I worked with — two big bouncers and one of our bartenders. The next morning, I rented a moving truck and we waited for Brad to leave. We parked across the street at various spots in a couple different cars and were calling each other on our phones while we waited, 'Do you see him?' and 'Is that him?' type of covert stuff. We felt like we were on a secret mission and somewhere in the conversations, somebody started calling it 'Operation: Four Walls and a Carpet' — I think it was Alley who coined it — because when asked what I was planning on taking, I said, 'Everything but the walls and the carpet.' And we were all cracking up. Anyways, he finally came down the stairs, got in his car and took off. It took a heck of a lot of restraint keeping the meathead, roid-rage-bouncers from driving over there, boxing him in and punching his lights out. I was their darling, you know. Those guys love to play the hero role and would take a bullet for me. The second he was gone, we raced over to the apartment and started taking all my stuff out of there. And I do mean all of 'my' stuff: Our couch, our bed, our furniture, our TVs, our stereos, the dishes, silverware, books, DVDs — if it wasn't bolted down, you name it, I took it. Hey, at least that would provoke a call from him and I could get some sort of resolution. When we were done, there were literally four walls and a carpet left. OK, we left his clothes, the ceiling and Cornbread, too, but that was about it.

"Good for you," Tommy said.

"Now check this out. The jerk, he never even called me afterward. Not after the day I caught him with her, nor after we cleaned him out. A couple of days went by and I was waiting and waiting and nope, he never called. Can you believe this guy? As time went on, I remember thinking this entire thing was a blessing in disguise. Imagine eventually marrying him or heaven forbid, having kids with him. Yuck! I was just about to put the entire thing to bed, and then I remembered I forgot to grab something very sentimental and important to me during the move. It was this little yellow book my late Grandmother, Billie, gave me. It's like a family heirloom to me. It was a book called 'Epaminondas and His Auntie' by Sara Cone Bryant. I forgot I removed it from our bookshelf and hid it atop a linen closet a couple weeks before 'Operation: Four Walls and a Carpet' after inviting one of my friends over for drinks — she's black and I didn't want to her to think I was racist if she came across it looking at my books."

"What? What the hell kind of book is it?" Tommy asked.

"Have you ever heard of Little Black Sambo?" she asked while extinguishing the cigarette.

"No, I don't think so."

"Well, they're these old folktales about these little black boys from the South. They're kind of viewed as taboo or having racial overtones — kind of like how the Blackface stereotype can be seen as bigoted — if you know anything about that."

"When white people painted their face black for plays and movies, way back in the day?"

"Exactly," Blue said. "In the case of Epaminondas, he and his 'Mammy' were misconstrued as being brunt-of-the-joke-unintelligent — possibly and purposely written as a negative depiction of all the blacks from the south — but more realistically, it is because the story is funny and that's how people used to talk back then. Because of the cartoonlike drawings of Epaminondas, you could see how people would lean toward using the race card. I mean, if a teacher read this story to kids at a school in today's PC world, and a multiculturally sensitive parent caught wind of it, the teach would probably be canned and then chastised in the news for it. Anyways, my Grandma Billie, she was the closest thing to a saint you could find on this planet. Truth. And she was the furthest thing from a racist. Also truth. She loved everyone and was metaphorically colorblind. She grew up on a farm outside of Wichita, Kansas, and the story was passed along to her from her grandma. On nights I slept over at her house, she would tuck me into bed and recite the whole story to me in her Wichita drawl — and I can still hear her voice when I close my eyes."

Blue's eyes watered and Tommy picked up on her sentiments toward her grandmother. He walked his beer around the bar and took a seat on a stool right next to her.

"Do you remember how it goes?' Tommy asked.

"Verbatim," she said.

"Tell it to me, just like she did," he said.

"I'm too buzzed …"

"… I don't care, I want to hear it," he said gleefully.

"You're sweet — you just got some major brownie points. But I'll lose track of my point if I tell you it now. Maybe later?"

"Fair enough," he said.

"After my Grandmother died, she left me a copy of her original book and wrote a beautiful inscription in it for me — I didn't even know 'Epaminondas and His Auntie' was a book. I always thought she made the story up, so you could imagine my delight to be able to hold the story in my hands. As the days went on, I was going through my storage unit and it hit me — I'm missing the book. I had to have it back. Sure, maybe Epaminondas wouldn't be a big deal to 99.9 percent of the population, but to me, it was my childhood. I had to have it. I had to be able to read my Grandma's words whenever I needed them. And under the circumstances, at that time in my life, I could've really used her words and a good laugh. So, what do you think I do?"

"You went back to get it, didn't you?" Tommy said.

"Darn straight!" Blue said. "I went back to the apartment, saw his car there and I waited for Brad to leave — this time his little Trixie is with him and when they're good and gone, I climb up the stairs and beeline right for the apartment. I go to unlock the door and home boy already changed the locks! Not even a week had passed. Can you believe it? So, I decide I'm going to, you know, put a little oomph into it with my shoulder, thinking maybe it'll pop open. But, that doesn't work. I'm standing in the hot Arizona sun, crying and trying anything I can think of to open the door. Then, out of frustration, I kick the thing and it blasts open. I couldn't believe it. 'Shoot! This isn't good,' you know? I walk in, because, well, I might as well go through with it and you won't believe this — he had already moved the new hussy in — all of her stuff was there — clothes, paintings, dishes, knickknacks. To this day, I'm still dumbfounded by that. Makes me wonder how long he was seeing her. Anyways, I grab my Grandma's book and get the heck out of there. A couple hours later, I get a phone call from some cop and he asks me to come down to the station. I'm all, 'what for?' And he's all, 'you know what for.' I didn't say 'go get yourself a warrant, pal,' or anything cool like that. Instead, I volunteer to go down there. This cop takes one look at the shoes I was wearing and matches it right up to a picture of a dusty footprint I left on the door and they charge me with criminal damage to property and trespass. First and only time I was ever arrested. Brad even went as far as to get an Order of Protection against me, saying I was a threat to him. Me. All 117 pound me. Can you believe it?"

"I can picture it all so vividly — this is one of the greatest stories I have ever heard," he said trying to hold in a laugh. "I'm not laughing at you, I'm trying to make light of it all."

"I know," she said, chortling herself. "It's funny in retrospect."

They tenderly looked into each other's eyes. They wanted to lock lips, but neither one of them could find the key, so they searched for it in their respective drinks. After a swallow, Tommy's mind became fuzzy from a blend of alcohol, flirtation and the perfectness that was circulating in the air. He gave himself a mental pep talk:

• This could be one of the best moments of my life. Do not forget how everything feels right now and please don't ruin this for me, Tommy.
• She is so beautiful.

"Why'd you stop with the story?" Tommy asked while betraying the silence. "I was digging it. And how have you kept this legend a secret?"

"It's not easy to tell people that someone you were in love with, was someone who thought you sucked at life so much, they traded you in without you knowing it. Even an old, sick dog knows his master's been looking at a new doggie in the window."

"You and I both know what he lost," he said and put a sympathetic, yet I'm-trying-to-be-seducing hand on her thigh.

She gave his grope an analytical gaze.

"That's when I decided to get the funk out of dodge and come back home. So, the point of all of this — why it wouldn't work with us …"

She purposefully looked at Tommy's hand on her leg once more. Her eyes turned sharp and went to his eyes.

"… here it is," she said, "The point is, I do really stupid things when I've been cheated on. And my heart gets torn apart. It takes a long time to suture it up and I feel it every time the needle goes in threading. I don't want you to rip my heart apart. I don't want to worry about your faith for me when you're out on tour and groupies are throwing themselves at you. You're a man. I get it. It's gotta be very difficult to turn the feeling of being wanted down. It's probably impossible. All that hot pussy, right there for you. Yeah, I'm not stupid. Yeah, I said it. P-U-S-S-Y. Vagina is the regime dictating a man's decision-making. Vagina … regime … the 'vagime.' The vagime has a way of making the one you're with become out of sight and out of mind — and its powerful stuff. The vagime is why we were all born. Think about it. It would be your fault if you cheated, but it's really not your fault. Young men are manimals. Ladies are human. Bat-crap crazy sometimes, but human. Young, band-crazy groupies are wild, freshly bloomed flowers ready to be plucked. Deflowering is the rock 'n' roll lifestyle. I am exactly the reason I would be worried about you out on tour — I have a thing for drummers — just like hundreds of other girls do. And if another me came along and was half as crazy about you as I am, how could you turn it down? The scene never gets old. So, my redline is this … I don't want to do another 'Operation: Four Walls and a Carpet' mission if we got together and you stop beating my heart and start drumming someone else's. I won't be shared. I don't want to keep making mistakes. And you and I both know that's what would happen."

He removed his hand from her thigh and took her hand in his. He squeezed. She didn't turn to him, however she looked at him through the mirror behind the bar. Then she looked at herself. And then she viewed their reflections as a pair.

"And besides, you're shorter than me," she said with a sarcastic smirk.

"Not if you're barefoot and I'm wearing boots."

He noticed her smiling in the mirror and then he leaned the side of his head into the side of hers and rested it there, being careful not to coconut-crash into her brain bucket while he did so. She didn't recoil. He couldn't help but to notice how pristine and aromatic the skin along her neckline was — wafting daffodils, hyacinth, crocuses, jonquils, green shoots, wet dirt and a bit of moss. He wanted to kiss her so badly — waves of torment raced inside of him like a young child whose swelling trick or treat bag was swiped by a wicked teenager. He briefly machinated how he was going to get his candy back.

"I can hear you thinking," he said. "I can hear your thoughts right now. They're like music to me. You know how I feel about music and you said I had the best hearing that you know of, so I promise you, I can hear your thoughts. What you just told me — I understand. About the cheating, I get it. The worry, the jealousy, the 4 a.m. insomnia kicks in and your brain says, 'I wonder what he's doing right now in Austin or Denver or wherever the hell he is' and when I don't answer my phone —— because I'm actually sleeping, alone, your mind becomes flooded with dread. I get those concerns. But that's not your foremost fear. You're not afraid of me cheating on you at this very moment, because you're not afraid of something that doesn't have the potential to become a real worry —— a something that can't happen without there being a relationship first. There's nothing worth worrying about if it never existed to begin with. What you're afraid of is … you're afraid that if I don't give you a valid reason for you to believe in me, right now, that you won't even have the opportunity to worry about it down the road — nor will I have the opportunity to prove to you that I would never become an infidel. You're afraid that I won't promise you that I would never do that, which is a way for you to see if the way I feel about you is reflective to the way you feel about me. You're also worried that I might respond to your apprehensions and anxieties by saying something arbitrary or unintentionally hurtful like, 'You're probably right' or 'The girls on tour are crazy. Maybe we could try dating when the tour is over,' but, I'm not gonna say that and I won't, and the only way I can prove your pre-fears wrong, is to hop on the train and go for a ride with you and let's see where this thing rolls to. I'm willing to give it a try. I can be faithful. I know I can, because I've been cheated on in the past and it hurts so fucking bad — I would never do that to someone that I care about — to someone I might potentially fall in love with one day. The pattern of unfaithfulness stops with me. It's learned behavior and something that doesn't have to be passed along. It's not a gene. I can promise you, it won't happen — I can shout it from the rooftops. I can paint it on a billboard. I can say it on a Jumbotron at a ballgame in front of thousands of strangers. But until you allow me to try, doing any of those things wouldn't matter."

She pulled her head away from his and turned her face to his. He followed suit.

"It's truth or dare, Blue," Tommy said. "And I dare you to give us a chance."

"Then I dare you to be truthful," Blue said.

She leaned into him with her puffy and puckered lips and he caught them with his own maw mitt. There literally was a static electric shock when their lips met and they both reacted with a slight flinch and then with bewildered cackles. They tried the kiss again and there was another spark, this time metaphorically. Tommy found her mouth to taste peculiarly like cotton candy and the flavor was sweeter than he ever remembered. It was sweeter than anything he'd ever tasted. They osculated lasciviously for several minutes, but time was irrelevant.

When they concluded, they held each other tightly — their lips busted and ecstatically pulsating. Tears of elation formed in Blue's eyes, but she kept them from dropping, not wanting to ruin the moment. It was the greatest kiss of Tommy's life.

"I'm so happy right now," she said. "I want to dance! Do you want to dance with me?"

They held hands, vied to "the emerald isle" and clambered up on stage. Tommy cranked the volume up on "Sweet Home Chicago" and the song couldn't have been more perfectly timed. They danced the night away, only taking breaks to kiss or refill their drinks or to change old blues albums on the turntable.

In the wee hours of Christmas morning, Tommy delicately unwrapped his present. Her shirt and bra: Ribbons. Her pants: A bow. Her silky, turquoise thong: Softly opening the box. It was a moment he dreamed of since the day he met her, but never imagined would come true. She had been naked before him before plenty of times when he rehearsed apodyopsis, but her body was even more stunning live amd not trapped in his imagination. He gracefully brought her down to the floor and scanned her spindly body over. He marveled at how leggy she was. 'Runways leading to heaven,' he thought.

"Your legs are so long," he whispered, softly kissing her inner thigh just above the knee.

"I'm taller than you, remember?" she said with a snicker while seductively spreading her legs.

"I've always wanted to go up on a girl."

The jest was a remedy to any trepidation either party had. He worked his way toward her center, peppering her leg with more kisses. She fanned them out further for him. He inhaled deeply through his nostrils like a truffle-hungry-pig — savoring the entire experience. Tommy tried to remain cool and calm, but wanting to explode with delight. He thought:

- Pheromones. I can smell her pheromones right now. This is amazing. I'm getting hard. Science, man! Pheromones. The Farrow Moans. Pheromones.
- I can't believe I'm actually doing this! She is so beautiful. She is so cool. She is so awesome! I love my life!
- Oh my god — she tastes so good. Like honey—ambrosia — nectar of the Gods.
- Find her spot. Make her feel good. Take your time. Don't ruin it. Slow. Soft. Sweetly.
- Is this her spot? This is her spot — I got it! Don't lose it. Soft. Swirl. Soft. Lick. Lick. Lick. Swirl. Make a song out of it. A cadence. Lick. Swirl. Lick, lick, lick, swirl.
- Find her other spot too. You're a drummer, use your hands. Find her rhythm. Find that textured spot. Slightly bend your fingers up. There it is. Yes! Slow, slow, slow… steady, steady, steady. Don't forget your mouth too. Use your tongue. Use your fingers. Splash her cymbals.
- Its working! Yes! Her legs are quivering like a tuning fork! Don't lose the beat. Hold on!

Blue arched her back, yowled in ecstasy, came and then shot up — kissing his mouth tenderly.

"That was so fucking hot," she whimper-whispered. "And I'm not just saying that because it's something you say after something like this happens. No one's ever done that to me. You're amazing."

He pulled off his shirt while she stripped him of his cargo shorts and boxer shorts. Then she laid back, resting her elbows and forearms on the stage.

"Are you sure you're Irish?" she asked while looking at his hang low.

"100 percent — Gramp's Gramp was off the boat. He came through Ellis Island."

"Then everything everyone's ever told me about Irish boys isn't true."

She grabbed a hold of his drumstick and eagerly pulled him down on top of her.

"I'm going to Kegel on you so hard," she said with a giggle.

As they were on the cusp of fusion, he could feel rising heat from her erogenous honeycomb. He intentionally stalled in the threshold of her sweltering and tacky empyrean to look into her eyes. He ran the Cupid's bow of his upper lip along the entirety of her scar, giving small kisses every few millimeters. Upon completion, she sucked his lower lip and pulled his shoulder blades toward her

211

bosom. She stamped his passport and he entered her country. It was the greatest moments of his life.

After the coda, they held each other for forever and a day under the green glow of "the emerald isle." Tommy eventually got Blue to tell the story of "Epaminondas and his Auntie" in a southern twang. She couldn't decide if she was more delighted with his request or with his candid laughter upon her completion of telling it. Too dizzy to walk or drive, the new couple decided to build a bed on stage rather than go home.

Tommy raided a supply closet inside the office. He took a stack of clean bar rags and an old blanket Junior brought back from Ireland and kept there for the drafty, winter nights he did paperwork. When he returned to the stage, he found Blue fading into a sleepy trance. He stood over her as she mumbled something and used the last of her stamina on a lighthearted laugh before trailing off. As he watched her fall sound asleep, it felt like he was watching a seraph float to the sky. He rolled up a bar rag and then another over the first one, creating a small pillow. He propped Blue's head up and tucked it under. He tossed the blanket in the air over her naked body and it delicately parachuted down on top of her. He stood over her and was transfixed on her breaths lifting the blanket and then tenderly easing it back down.

Stupefied, he thought, 'She's my Baader-Meinhof.'

Now punch-drunk and drunk, he wanted one last celebration beer and cigarette. He flipped side 2 of Sonny Boy Williamson II's "King Biscuit Time" album over on the turntable, dropped the needle, pushed the repeat button, turned the volume low, grabbed his glass and was en route to the bar. He sat bare-arsed on a stool in the middle of the bar sipping a freshly poured Guinness, puffing his Kool, listening to the music and looking out the front window. The only thing alive outside on the dark street was the wind, which was howling, and if Blue wasn't sleeping, he would've howled along with it too. He wondered if he was the only man to ever to get lucky in Mrs. O'Leary's Cow. He also wondered if he was the only man that's ever sat nude at the bar and enjoyed a pint. For the first time, he actually felt like a rock star, and if God struck him dead right then and there, he could justly say he lived his greatest day of his short life.

He yawned and looked at the clock on the wall. He was too drunk to read it, but he knew it was last call, and he gulped the remainder of stout. He puffed one last drag and looked at his reflection in the mirror. He smiled and did a spontaneous air-drum-solo —— crashing invisible cymbals and then he quietly laughed upon completion. He wished his reflection a Merry Christmas and then he kissed the pint glass before setting it down. He snuffed the cigarette out in the ashtray, the cherry dismembering from any un-charred tobacco incased in white paper.

He got off the stool, walked behind the bar and dumped the tray into the garbage can before stowing it back into its original hiding place. A walking brownout, he stumbled back to Blue, but he was too chocolate-wasted to grasp that the ember of his cigarette wasn't fully extinguished or there was smoldering smoke faintly wafting from the trash can that housed the open and spilled bottle of Jeppson's Malört Liqueur.

BONUS TRACK 1. A-SIDE. LINER NOTES:

1. After their show concluded and after The Cow closed its doors, Tommy and Cal tussled in the parking lot. The wrestling match started as the band members were loading their equipment into Tommy's van and when Tommy revisited a previous argument with Cal pertaining to the song,

"Louisville Lovers."

Tommy was heated with Cal for two reasons. Cal hadn't included the song "Louisville Lovers" on the set list he provided before the show and he thought Cal's explanation ("I'm sorry, Tom. We were in a groove and needed to go with it right then") was a blatant lie. And, Tommy was even more furious they played the song without him on drums (during a two-song, acoustic encore set), because Tommy wrote the music and the lyrics.

Tommy felt disrespected and he was pissed. He had suspicions Cal was trying to take ownership of the song by putting his distinctive falsettos on the chorus and adjusting the lyrics. Tommy asked Cal why he changed some of the words and Cal's response was, "I forgot how it went," once again Tommy believed he was fibbing.

Cal got the worse of the business — a large mouse under his eye from one of Tommy's shoulders and a broken smartphone. He dusted himself off, checked his eye in a side mirror of the van, before scampering off into the night. Tommy's body was left unscathed and aside from the collar of his Chicago Blackhawks T-shirt becoming stretched and torn, no one would've ever guessed he had been involved in a fight.

2. Naked, New and Never Again

Jackson S. Schmidt, chapped lips and broken teeth, got out of bed. He had big plans for the future, big plans indeed. Staring at his reflection, he couldn't help but smile. This raggedy fellow before him — vintage clothes, thick glasses, sunken eyes and hollowed cheeks — would soon be gone. His replacement was already alive, living enthusiastically inside his active imagination — not quite ready to reveal himself, but excited nonetheless.

He turned from the mirror to the bedroom. The mattress, the blanket and the pile of clothes were his only frills. He wouldn't miss them. He took one last breath, tried to pull the whole room through his nostrils — careful to store every stale speck somewhere in his memory — to remind him later what he had been, what he still was and what he would be until the moment he left.

It was yesterday, in the dark and dank crawlspace of his old home, where he made the remarkable discovery that would transform his future. Almost forgotten, camouflaged and hidden with the rest of the memories and heirlooms that a couple accumulates after decades of marriage, rested a dusty wooden crate. While carrying the crate upstairs, he couldn't see where to step to avoid the raised nail-heads that would sneakily snag his socks.

For two flights, he cradled the last of the 1982 Chateau Lafite Rothschild Bordeaux Blend*1 like it was a priceless watercolor in a rainstorm. The shrilled shriek from the third to last stair was always an anticipated sound for his nagging bones. That he did remember. Almost everything else though, was locked somewhere in the blank vault. He finally managed his way to the top of the staircase, panting and hoping he could brace himself without taking a groggy, tumble back down. He set the crate down on ledge beneath the windowsill in the bedroom and took a moment to slow his pulse. But that was easier said than done, because carved out in front of him was his grotto — dresses and sweaters and blouses and coats were hung and stored just how she last left them. He inhaled deeply and each nostril flared. Her perfume was still attached to the clothes and it gave him the strange feeling she was standing in the room.

He uncorked another bottle. Pop. He poured a third of the ruby liquid into a mason jar, had a whiff, and then had a gulp — swirling the flavors of jammy cherry, sun-warmed mulberries, pencil-shavings and the subtle hint of smoked ham hock in his mouth before swashing it down his throat. It reminded him of the perfect breakfast, and he was suddenly transported to the driver's seat of a gunboat Lincoln. He was grinning while clutching the steering wheel on his 16th birthday, when a curvy brunette appeared at his window and poked her head into the car. By the time he finished the bottle, he relived their wedding day, their honeymoon and the purchase of the very home he stood in.

He preserved the last bottle of Bordeaux, leaving it in the wooden box. He decided to lay in bed with his eyes closed — keeping his wife alive and active until the alcohol subsided and burned all the remembrances off like morning fog in deep-fried sunlight.

Earlier, after he woke, he'd forgotten everything from the night before. He sat up confused and wondered who left the bottles of wine, because he couldn't remember having any guests. As he searched the bottles for answers, he found a note he wrote to himself. He read it twice.

He uncorked the last of the wine and took a pull right from the bottle. He sat down on the bed and re-read his letter, sipping from the bottle. As the Bordeaux became dearth, he was holding his dead wife in his arms minutes after she died at the Clybourn train stop.

He returned to the mirror. He was serene and found himself handsome, even if his face was shadowed by his broken life. He pulled his shirt over his head, pulled down his pants, chucked off his underwear and looked at his reflection again — naked, new and never again. He opened the door and walked out of his life.

The Christmas morning air clobbered his skin, but he didn't feel it, nor did he know it was Christmas. He was flooded with the calmness you only feel when you lose everything, but never knew it was gone. All he would do was walk and to where was anyone's guess. At one point, he found himself in a vacant alley, bending over to pick up a lit, half-smoked cigarette. The smoke disappeared from his breath with the grace of a man who was lost. The last time he had this much pep in his step, his hair hadn't yet seen a ghost. He marched down sidewalks without a care in the world while his nude body was still blanketed from the darkest moments of the morning.

He reached the maroon metal bridge on West Cortland and looked at the sign. He could barely see it in the dark, but it read, "1997 North River Industrial Corridor. Richard M. Daley, Mayor." He then walked to the barrier, designed to keep anything from falling off the bridge, and looked across the way at the city's skyline twinkling in front of him.

He loved the skyline. He loved this city. He looked over the railing and down to the crisp, Chicago River below him. He climbed the rail before swinging his legs over the top bar and having a sit. He looked at the muddy water below. He didn't even give a countdown before he shoved off.

He didn't feel the curglaff people normally would after plunging into frigid water. As it submerged him, astoundingly, he felt thermal. As he sunk, he closed his eyes, exhaled the last of his breath and envisioned his wife's green eyes. Time passed. Death was just around the corner. Jackson could see the light. He could feel his soul resting on his wife's bosom. Then, out of nowhere, he was ripped away from the blessedness by a cop who was resting Jackson's limp body on his beer belly for buoyancy.

"The fuck you doing, you dumb old drunk?" the cop shouted into Jackson's boozy face.

It didn't take police long to track the old man down. Naked, wandering old-timers didn't go unnoticed in a city of more than two million people and the 911 calls lit up the dispatch centers' phone lines like a Christmas tree. Even though it was still pitch-black in the wee hours of the morning, people saw Jackson flipping-and-a-flopping at West Cortland and North Elston while he walked under a red "River West" sign mounted to a brick building.

Two officers were running and shouting at Jackson before he jumped, but the old man never heard them. He never knew they were there. When he hit the icy water, the westerly current dragged him under the bridge and the cops radioed to other patrol units to the direction his lifeless body was floating. Officers fished him out with a tree branch and an arm-to-arm buddy system along the shoreline and near a factory off West Armitage. They wrapped him in their coats until an ambulance arrived with blankets. After he came to, they repeatedly asked him what his name was, and Jackson couldn't recall it. They studied his tattoos, one cop even used the mirror on a squad car in an attempt to decode the inscriptions, but he couldn't decipher their meanings.

After the denouement, Jackson was transported to a hospital for evaluation. After being cleared of any health issues by the medical staff, he was taken to a psychiatric hospital and given the name "John Doe" until someone claimed him.

BONUS TRACK 2. B-SIDES. LINER NOTES:

1. Even if he had a spotless mind, Jackson would've never known that the extremely sparse 1982 Chateau Lafite Rothschild Bordeaux Blend he had would bring in nearly $20,000 a bottle at auctions. The circumstances of how he happened to come into ownership of the tremendously sought-after wine was as rare of a strike of luck as that of its contents. The wine had been in a basement storage facility below Saint Rita of the Angels for decades.

It should be worth noting, Jackson S. Schmidt consumed around $100,000 worth of the choice wine in less than 9 hours.

3. Suicide by Cop

When Chloe Woodbine awoke, she was the only thing under the family Christmas tree in the living room. She yawned, but the air escaping her lungs was more of a sigh of relief than it was anything else. She got to her feet and walked to the kitchen. She looked at the telephone on the wall and had a seat at the table. She looked at the clock on the microwave. It read 5:41 a.m. She walked to the phone. She started to cry. Then, she stopped herself. She started to cry once more — elevating the hysteria in her voice. The second cry was as brief as the first. She began to hop up and down while shouting at the top of her lungs. She stopped and shook out her legs like she was warming up for a race. She wailed again — screeching a sound reminiscent to a rabbit caught in the jowls of a fox. She intentionally panted. After two minutes, she stopped. She cleared her throat. Then she picked up the receiver and dialed three numbers.

"Oh my God! Oh my God! Both my parents are dead! I heard a gunshot! Help me! Help me! Hurry! You have to hurry! Oh my God! Oh my God! He must've killed her! They're both dead!"

Chloe sobbed as the person on the other end begged for answers to questions Chloe wasn't answering.

The first officer on the scene was a gun-drawn beat cop with a carved chin. Chloe tossed herself face down and thrashed in hysterics at the front door before he entered. He briefly skimmed her over as she frantically led him downstairs to the man cave with rapid finger points. When the officer reached the basement, he found Carter Woodbine's slumped-over body in the recliner. There was an open box, the handgun and one spent bullet casing on the floor. Carter appeared to have a self-inflicted gunshot wound to his right temple — the blood had flowed down, saturating the contents in the open box that contained the paperwork pertaining to the Bill Dodanno death investigation. On the coffee table in front of him rested a near-empty bottle of gin, a half used bottle of tonic, an empty glass and a small bag of melted ice. There also was his opened laptop.

When the officer returned to the middle level of the home, he shouted for the whereabouts of her mother. Chloe ignored his inquires and uncontrollably sobbed. He scooped her up and tried putting her out on the front porch. But, she was far too heavy for him and carrying her turned into a struggle where her T-shirt was pulled over her head, exposing most of her body. The officer cautiously re-entered the home, saw the staircase leading upstairs and took them — ready to fire the gun at the first sign of movement.

When he cleared Chloe's empty room, he went into the next bedroom, where he found Shelby Woodbine dead in her bed. She had an apparent gunshot wound to her forehead and was covered in down feathers. Next to Shelby was a large assortment of prescription medication, a belt and a soiled syringe.

When backup arrived, they secured home, took Chloe away and found out who's deaths they would now be investigating. It was blue day for the boys in blue. Chloe was taken to a hospital. They wanted her vitals checked out, sedated and kept for observation. As she rode in the ambulance, a female paramedic stroked her hair. Chloe purposely transfixed her vision on the ceiling as if she was comatose and in shock. She methodically retraced her steps, hoping she hadn't left any incriminating evidence. She recalled the night before:

3 a.m. Remember everything he's taught me*1. Put on latex gloves. Grabbed the needle, the

spoon, the cotton ball, the drugs and the lighter. Went to the sink. Added water to the spoon. Added the drugs. Cooked. Drew. Tapped the needle. Let it cool. Woke mother. Persuaded her to take more medicine because she was screaming in her sleep again. She bought it. Tied the belt around her arm. Administered the medication. Untied the belt around her arm. Left it next to her. Put the needle on the nightstand. Tucked her back into bed. Waited until it kicked in. Placed the spoon on the nightstand next to the drugs. Returned to my room. Wrapped the present. Left open the top flaps of the box. Signed the tag, "to: Chloe, from: Aunt Joanna." Put the bow on the box. Threw the sticky piece of the tag in the box. Grabbed the snow globe. Shook it. Watched the snow float around Santa and the skyline.

     3:34 a.m. Took off my pajama top. Took off my bra. Put on my "How About Them Apples" T-shirt. Pulled my pajama bottoms off. Took off my panties. Chucked them on the floor next to my pajamas and bra. Ruffled my sheets. Punched the pillow. Got in the bed. Covered up in the covers. Frantically tossed the duvet cover. Fluffed the pillow. Folded pillow around my head. Found Mom's vibrator behind the headboard. Grabbed it. Got out of bed. The pillow looked used. The bed looked slept in. Tossed the vibrator on the bed. "This isn't a girl who just killed her parents. This is a girl who masturbated herself to sleep," is what the detectives will say. Put on the shower cap. Put on my rain coat — price tags still on it. Tucked the tags inside the hood. Hoodie up. Tiptoed down the stairs. Peeked in at him. He was passed out in front of his laptop and still wearing his work clothes. He almost drank a whole damn bottle too. Perfect! Lifted his hand. No response. Remember thinking, "if a bomb went off right now, he wouldn't have heard it." Tiptoe to the green stadium seats. Retrieved his gun from his belt and holster in his duty bag from chair No. 163. Unbuttoned the holster. Removed the gun. Took it off of safety. Placed the gun in his hand and held it there. Anticipated him to wake up. He didn't. Put my index finger on the trigger. He didn't flinch. Got on my knees — staying low enough so my body wouldn't block any blood spatter. Looked at the computer. Got the suicide note idea. Back to task at hand. Wrapped the gun around his hand and held it together. Raised his arm with the gun in our hands. It was heavier than I thought it would be. Held steady. His breathing never changed. He didn't move a muscle. His breath stunk like he ate a Christmas tree. Put the gun close to his temple. There was no turning back. Remember thinking, "It's his fault. How does it feel to be the victim, Daddy? I loved you so much. Why? Do it, Chloe! Don't quit now! Don't cry! Hold it together! Things will never change if you don't. It'll only be worse. Goodbye, Daddy." Squeezed trigger. It was so loud! "Is he dead? He's dead! Did it wake her? If she stumbles downstairs, I'll tell her I just found him like this." Waited. Didn't hear her. "Did it wake the neighbors? Hurry." Sprinted up the stairs. Looked out the window of the front door. Listened. No barking dogs. No lights turning on. "Make sure she's not awake." Ran up the second floor stairs. Slowed things down. Took a breath. All I heard was my heartbeat. Stopped. Listened. Peeked in. "Is she still sleeping?" She never stirred. She never heard a peep. Whew. Moved slowly. Didn't wake her. Climbed on the bed. Straddled her. Slowly lifted a pillow. Jammed the gun into the pillow. Held the pillow and gun up to her face. Aimed for her breath. Lined it up. Steadied the flimsy pillow. Remembered thinking, "Crimes of passion are up close and personal." Told myself, "Do what he could never do. Put her out of her misery. You used to be so good, Mother. What happened to you? I love you. This is for you. No more medicine. No more paranoia. No more pain. No more needles. One. Two. Three. Goodbye, Mother." Squeezed. Done. "I'll see you in Heaven one day." Back into stealth-mode. "Do you hear any dogs barking? No. Hurry." Ran back downstairs. There's blood everywhere. Didn't want to look. Couldn't help but look. Held the gun up to where his head would have been if he was sitting up. Dropped the gun on the floor next to the recliner. Made sure the gun didn't look staged. Ran back upstairs. Ran to my room. Took off the gloves. Took off the shower cap. Took off the coat. Put the gloves into the inside left pocket of the raincoat. Zipped the left inside pocket closed. Put the shower cap into the right inside pocket. Zipped it closed. Zipped the jacket up. Pulled out the price tags. Folded the raincoat nice and properly. Smoothed it. Put the raincoat in the box. Taped the box shut. Put the present in my closet. Grabbed the scissors. Put them in in my underwear drawer. Buried the scissors under the underwear. Grabbed the tape and wrapping paper. Ran to the bathroom. Checked for any blood on my face. Not a spec. Checked for any blood on my legs. There was none. Checked for feathers. There was none. Went to the window. Didn't hear any dogs. Didn't see any lights turn on. Ran downstairs. Worried about tripping. Didn't trip. Ran to the garage door. Opened the door. Turned on the light. Put the wrapping paper and tape inside the cardboard box with the Christmas decorations. Shut the flaps. Tucked them in. Grabbed the box and climbed it up to top of the storage shelf. Put the camping gear on top of it. Carefully climbed down the shelving unit. Listened. Heard nothing. Turned off the light. Opened the door. Ran to the phone in the kitchen. Waited for any sirens or knocks or the doorbell. Caught my breath. Then re-corrected my thinking, "You're startled, remember? You just heard your Dad shoot your mother and then turned the gun on himself. You're making the 911 call before they get to the door." Breathed really hard just in case they were coming.

4:04 a.m. No sirens. No knocks. "I did it! They're gone! I pulled it off! They're in Heaven now! Merry Christmas, Chloe. Welcome to your new life. Now what? Throw up. Are you going to throw up? Hold it in. Relax. Slow your breathing down. Final step. Go down stairs. "You can do it. Find the courage." Walked down. "Don't look at his face. Grab the pen out of his breast pocket. Tunnel vision. Don't look at him. Tap the mouse*2. Think. Think. Think. Tap the keys with the pen. Don't turn around. He's dead. That noise is Mother Nature." Typed*3. "He's drunk, 'member?" Made it messy. Finished. "Take the pen with you — don't leave any prints." Ran to the stairs. Ran to the Christmas tree. "Find the baby Jesus ornament*4. Pray for forgiveness." Found the ornament. Cried ... hard. Don't remember falling asleep.

The driver of the ambulance screeched a siren, snapping Chloe out of her trance. She began to think of her future:

Aunt Joanna will become my guardian until I turn 18. I'll get his pension. The bank will sell the house — maybe I'll get some of the money — I don't really care. I'll graduate. I'll get a big round of applause at the ceremony when they call my name. When I receive my diploma, I'll be remembered as the girl who overcame tremendous adversity. I'll start a new life in college. I'll play volleyball, because I love the sport and not because he forced it on me. I'll graduate with a degree in psychology. I'll learn to forgive everyone, including myself. I'll move far away from this dreadful city. I'll council children. I'll listen to my kids. I'll change lives. I'll be remembered. I'll remember them. And then, one day, I might even get married.

BONUS TRACK 3. DOUBLE A-SIDES. LINER NOTES:

1. Along with Chloe's parents' arguments and her father's cigarette smoke traveling up the vent from the basement and into her room, so did countless hours of him talking to Lt. Fenton and other colleagues on the phone about numerous homicide cases. She notoriously eavesdropped*A on his conversations and snooped through his field notes whenever he wasn't around or passed out. She recalled and retained information to things detectives have to do in their everyday work.

A)   Carter's predilection for gumshoeing was passed to him from his father the same way he passed the inquisitive curiosity to Chloe. Chloe regularly found Carter's discussions and insights to the cases he worked to be captivating. She would take breaks from studying, watching TV or talking on the phone to listen to his tales shoot up through the vent the way people used to listen to radio detective programs from the 1940s.

219

Listening to her dad talk shop was a double-edged sword for her. On one hand, she would hear his cleverness, work ethic, expertise, great sense of humor and charm piping into her room and she thought he was the greatest man on the planet. On the other hand, she couldn't believe the same man was also a sad drunk who didn't have a clue of what was going on in his daughter's life. She found the paradox perplexing and disheartening, and no matter how much investigating into the enigma she did, she couldn't solve the mystery.

2. After Chloe tapped the mouse with a pen to get the monitor to power on, she started typing on the space below her father's final summery report he was submitting to Lt. Fenton via an email about his concluding assumption to the Bill Dodanno death investigation. It appeared Carter passed out mid-sentence —— too intoxicated from the gin and tonics to finish typing. Here was the sentence: "In summary, based on all eyewitness statements and accords, based on the physical, mathematical, and recorded evidence, based on my interviewing and interrogating findings, and based on the toxicology reports, it has been determined by me, Detective Carter Woodbine, badge #41 of the Chicago Police Department, that Jackson S. Schmidt …"

3. This is the suicide note*A Chloe created in the email her father was in the process of sending:

To: Lieutenant Harrison Fenton,

It is a great disappointment to me that my actions will disappoint you, but I no longer have a choice. Harry, you're a great leader and I was proud to call you my best friend. You held the reins tight and have steered all of us to the clear time after time after time again. Down the hall doesn't know how good they have it with you running the show. You will make one helluva superintendent one day, mark my words. And outside of work, you were a helluva friend too. I called you almost every night and you've always kept me from coming unglued. I've never forgotten that time you dumped your beer all over that little old lady while trying to grab a foul ball at that Sox game! I don't think I ever laughed so hard in all my life. I never forgot what kind of a man you were, right then and there, when you instantly took your shirt off and started to dry her off. I'm sorry to do this to you.

To: the Dicks*B assigned to this case,

I was better at your job than you ever could be. But, I'm sympathetic and I'm sorry you had to find my head hopefully blown apart and not waiting for me to wake up from a coma. Any money you find in my wallet, take for yourself and buy all the drinks you can. That's on me. While you're reading this, probably thinking about the shit you saw oozing out of my dome, let me give you a little advice: Don't read too deep into this investigation. You have two sick, miserable people who both needed to get out of the way of our kid's future. It's cut and dry. Look at her medicine cabinet and my recycle bin if you don't believe me. We're very ill. Put this thing to bed in a few sentences. Husband shoots wife. Husband kills himself. Done.

To: my brothers and sisters on the force,

This job was never really for me. I should've been a ballplayer. As in every homicide I've ever investigated, it only takes a few seconds to change the course of someone's life. It only takes a brief, sometimes chance, encounter to be forever linked to someone. A big, dumb Injun ruined that for me many moons ago when he took my career. I never recovered, and I'm not talking about the physical injuries either, although they did weigh me down. What he changed, that Indian, was me into a monster. I've been a monster to myself, to my wife and to my precious daughter. We turned that sweet, innocent kid into our pawn and it sickens me. Don't do what I did. If you're in a rut, use the counselors the PD provides us with. I want you to know, I always had your back and I'd take a bullet for every one of you.

To: my friends (if I have any at all) and to my favorite bartenders and fellow drunks,

I could no longer take it. I could no longer take the crazy, drug-addicted woman I share my home with. She's too much. All the medicine in the world can't fix the clinically insane. If you're a single guy out there, do yourself a favor: Don't stick your dick in crazy. It's bad news. You'll have to take her out of her misery, don't you see? She asked me to do it thousands of times and I finally listened. It wasn't hard to do. I will be right behind her and we'll live on together somewhere else, hopefully, like it was in the beginning. Don't judge us. You didn't live a real-life nightmare.

To: the Chicago White Sox,

It was a shame you couldn't win me another championship. 2005 was the best fall of my life.

To: my beautiful, intelligent and talented daughter,

Chloe, I loved you more than anything. Even baseball. I'm sorry. I'm sorry. I'm sorry. It's not your fault. None of this is. But, this is the greatest Christmas gift I could ever give you. You might not see it now, or tomorrow, or even in a couple of years, but trust me, you one day will. I'll be watching over you and one day, we'll see each other again in a paradise. Until then, you've been on your own for so long, you'll continue to be fine. Every time you spike a volleyball, I'll be cheering for you. I love you,

Dad

A)	Throughout the original suicide e-note, Chloe deliberately misspelled words, used poor grammar and made sentences illegible in an attempt to make Carter appear to increasingly become intoxicated as his writing progressed. The above letter is a legible transcript of what Chloe wanted her father's words to messily convey.

B)	Chloe often overheard her father refer to himself or a fellow detective as a "Dick."

4. A week ago, Chloe went out to the garage, found the family Christmas tree on a shelf, and erected the enormous plastic monstrosity in the living room all by her lonesome. Since then, neither parent had acknowledged it was even on display or put any presents under it. A family tradition in the Woodbine home was a game Shelby devised years ago, where she would hide a small ornament (the clear glass decoration with a plastic figurine of baby Jesus sleeping in the manger inside of it) somewhere in the tree. The rule was that before Chloe could open any of her presents on Christmas morning, Shelby would advise that she needed to "find Jesus" first. As the years went by and as Chloe got older, Carter would tell his wife the game was dumb, which usually provoked a slight argument, but Chloe always enjoyed it and frolicked about until she located the ornament.

This Christmas, while she was decorating the tree by herself, she found the ornament in a box, turned her back to the tree, closed her eyes and blindly tossed it somewhere into the needles. It miraculously stayed in the tree on her first throw and remained out of eyesight while she put the last of the decorations up.

4. Mrs. Claus' Sticky Buns

At 6:44 a.m. Christmas morning, white glistening pinwheels fell softly from a black sky and began to stick to the ground like cotton in the South. At exactly the same moment, these people were doing these things across Chicago:

Tommy Shannahan was the big spoon and Jenna "Blue" Trillium was the little spoon as they slept naked on stage in "the emerald isle" of Mrs. O'Leary's Cow. Sonny Boy Williamson II's "Sonny Boy's Christmas Blues" was tenderly playing. A roaring fire was fleetingly being contained inside the garbage can behind the bar. Smoke was billowing from the front bar area and toward them, in the back, but neither incapacitated person arose.

♫ Sonny Boy Williamson II: Got me some mighty sad news and I ain't got nothin' to say ♫

When the smell of smoke entered his nostrils, a dreaming Tommy thought:

● This deep-dish pizza is burnt. Once I get the waitress' attention, I'm going to send it back. I hate to do it, but this tastes terrible.
● Lou Malnati's pizza is better than Gino's East. They never burn a pie at Lou's.
● Zzzzzzzzzzzzzzzzzzzzzzzzzzzzzzzzzzzzzzzzzzzzzzzzzzzzzzzzz.

♫ Sonny Boy Williamson II: I heard some mighty sad news and I ain't got nothin' to say ♫

Alex Hedlund, with tears streaming down his cheeks, sat proudly on his couch while his boys opened presents from Santa.

♫ Sonny Boy Williamson II: My baby left me, started me drinkin' on Christmas Day ♫

Former kleptomaniac Maria Rivera reported to the Englewood Corps Red Shelter center at 945 W. 69th as a volunteer. She stood in the cold, handing out Christmas gifts to more than 300 underprivileged families. Sometimes, she would hand a less privileged person a gift from her personal inventory.

♫ Sonny Boy Williamson II: Lord, I tried to fetch religion but the devil would not let me pray ♫

Exotic dancer and skyline porno actress Kaylee Fearn posted a picture of her new Louis Vuitton Tivoli PM designer handbag accompanied with a protruding bottle of Louis Roederer Cristal (2008) champagne on her social media newsfeed. She captioned the photo, "Guess who has a secret admirer? Merry Christmas to me!"

♫ Sonny Boy Williamson II: Lord, I tried to fetch religion boys, but the devil would not let me pray ♫

DeVon "Dee" Whitaker was loading Bill Dodanno's original hot dog cart onto a trailer attached to a pickup truck in front of Doggy Style Hot Dogs stand.

♫ Sonny Boy Williamson II: Ooh, on a Christmas Day, you know that's one day I hate to have the blues / you know when she walked out and left me / she give 'em to me, so I have to drink 'em all away ♫

Mookie Brownstone was sprawled out, butt-necked in a posh, king-sized bed on the 11th floor of the historic Drake Hotel. He rented a King Drake Executive Lakeview Room with the money he earned at last night's show. Staying at The Drake was something he always dreamt of doing, especially after standing hundreds of hours under its shadow playing the guitar for tips.

He briefly opened his eyes and scoured his surroundings. He observed the indulgent, ivory duvet covering his elongated limbs and torso, and then the bodies of two young white girls wearing only their birthday suits. He smelled two fingers on his right hand. He wasn't dreaming. He grinned and whispered, "Ga-ga-ga-ga-ga-ga-Goddamn ri-ri-ri-ri-right!"

♫ Sonny Boy Williamson II: I don't even have a Christmas tree in my house unless she comes home / but if she do happen to come home, I will enjoy this Christmas ♫

The Farrow Moans bassist Steve Wiley was … well, he's a bass player and no one cared where he was.

♫ Sonny Boy Williamson II: Yes run here baby and let me tell you what I got to say ♫

Cal Slankard was sleeping alone in his bed with a bag of frozen peas resting on his shiner.

♫ Sonny Boy Williamson II: Please, please run here darlin' and let daddy tell you what he got to say ♫

Father Paul was reviewing his handwritten homily and getting ready for Christmas Mass. He looked out the window, watched the dancing snowflakes and was curious why Jackson S. Schmidt wasn't at church yet, salting the sidewalks like he always would.

♫ Sonny Boy Williamson II: Unless'n you come back to me, I'll be drunk all day Christmas day ♫

As he promised atop his barstool the night before, Raymond McMahon walked south on North Halstead dressed as Santa Claus, carrying a satchel. He was following a route to his nephew's house in the neighborhood, delivering his wife's homemade "Sticky Buns." As he walked north near Diversey, he looked south and witnessed the strangest of things: There was a pickup parked zigzagged and taking up both lanes. In the bed liner was a life-sized fiberglass cow. The truck then reversed onto the sidewalk in front of Mrs. O'Leary's Cow, inching across in a precise manner. When it came to a stop, a man got out and scurried to the back of the truck. It was far too dark for Raymond to identify the man. But he did witness the man drop the tailgate, climb aboard and lower a skid from the bed to the sidewalk. The man then climbed back up on the bed and shuffled the cow down the ramp. He pulled the cow in front of the pub and positioned it precisely to his liking. He retrieved a tire jack and raised the front cement base high enough to kick out a wheel dolly. The front of the cow landed on the sidewalk before kicking the second dolly out behind the rear of the cow in the process.

223

The man bent down, tinkered with something under the barrel of the heifer and cleaned everything up and drove off to the adjacent strip mall with the tailgate still down. He did a two-point reversal and backed into a parking spot near Dunkin' Donuts. Now parked, the driver had an impeccable view of the fiberglass cow.

Raymond thought about going to inspect the item, but he assumed it was just a Christmas gift being dropped off from a member of the Shannahan family. Besides, right before he left, he received a phone call from a nephew saying his kids were up — ready for a cameo visit from Santa — and The Cow wasn't on the route to the house. He went west on Diversey and decided he'd inquire about the gift the next time it was beer-thirty.

But, had Raymond continued on and inspected the large fiberglass cow, he would've noticed a message written in permanent marker just above the green shamrock and on a white section of the cow's hindquarters that read: TO: MICHAEL JR. FROM: SANTA, MERRY CHRISTMAS! and also PUSH ME with an arrow pointing to a handcrafted ignition button.

And had Raymond continued to The Cow, he may even have smelled the smoke.

♫ RECORD SKIPPING ♫ RECORD SKIPPING ♫ RECORD SKIPPING ♫